EAST GREENBUSH COMMUNITY LIBRARY

W9-ASD-034

The
Invasion Year

Also by Dewey Lambdin

The King's Coat

The French Admiral

The King's Commission

The King's Privateer

The Gun Ketch

H.M.S. Cockerel

A King's Commander

Jester's Fortune

King's Captain

Sea of Grey

Havoc's Sword

The Captain's Vengeance

A King's Trade

Troubled Waters

The Baltic Gambit

King, Ship, and Sword

The
Invasion Year

An Alan Lewrie Naval Adventure

Dewey Lambdin

THOMAS DUNNE BOOKS
ST. MARTIN'S PRESS
NEW YORK

This is a work of fiction. All of the characters, organizations, and events portrayed in this novel are either products of the author's imagination or are used fictitiously.

THOMAS DUNNE BOOKS.

An imprint of St. Martin's Press.

THE INVASION YEAR. Copyright © 2010 by Dewey Lambdin. All rights reserved. Printed in the United States of America. For information, address St. Martin's Press, 175 Fifth Avenue, New York, N.Y. 10010.

www.thomasdunnebooks.com

www.stmartins.com

Maps copyright © 2010 by Carolyn Chu

LIBRARY OF CONGRESS CATALOGING-IN-PUBLICATION DATA

Lambdin, Dewey.

The invasion year : an Alan Lewrie naval adventure / Dewey Lambdin. — 1st ed.

p. cm.

ISBN 978-0-312-55185-8

1. Lewrie, Alan (Fictitious character)—Fiction.   2. Ship captains—Fiction.   3. Great Britain—History, Naval— 18th century—Fiction.   4. France—History, Naval—18th century—Fiction.   5. Naval battles—History—18th century—Fiction.   I. Title.

PS3562.A435I58 2011

813'.54—dc22

2010039056

First Edition: January 2011

10   9   8   7   6   5   4   3   2   1

This one is dedicated to Forrest

"Nathan Bedford," my "little general," and his "bubba" Mosby's groomer, fellow prankster, and "hot water bottle" on cool nights. Forrest was white-furred, with a grey tail, ears and nose, and the brightest, widest jade green eyes. He was an ambusher, a talker who'd hold long conversations with me, or any message left on the phone, and could purr louder than any other cat I can remember. He was only 9½ when he left this life on July 2nd, 2010, and Mosby and I miss him very much, and wish he could have stayed with us many years more—if only to help Mosby open every under-counter cabinet door in the house, or lay side by side to "paddle" all the sliding closet doors open so they could get inside and prowl.

Forrest was my shadow, and my foot-warmer under the desk whenever I wrote even a short letter, much less a chapter of the books, and I miss that very much, too.

Forrest, I give you the Sunday wardroom toast,
"Absent Friends."

Full-Rigged Ship: Starboard (right) side view

1. Mizen Topgallant
2. Mizen Topsail
3. Spanker
4. Main Royal
5. Main Topgallant
6. Mizen T'gallant Staysail
7. Main Topsail
8. Main Course
9. Main T'gallant Staysail
10. Middle Staysail
11. Main Topmast Staysail
12. Fore Royal
13. Fore Topgallant
14. Fore Topsail
15. Fore Course
16. Fore Topmast Staysail
17. Inner Jib
18. Outer Flying Jib
19. Spritsail

A. Taffrail & Lanterns
B. Stern & Quarter-galleries
C. Poop Deck/Great Cabins Under
D. Rudder & Transom Post
E. Quarterdeck
F. Mizen Chains & Stays
G. Main Chains & Stays
H. Boarding Battens/Entry Port
I. Cargo Loading Skids
J. Shrouds & Ratlines
K. Fore Chains & Stays
L. Waist
M. Gripe & Cutwater
N. Figurehead & Beakhead Rails
O. Bow Sprit
P. Jib Boom
Q. Foc's'le & Anchor Cat-heads
R. Cro'jack Yard (no sail fitted)
S. Top Platforms
T. Cross-Trees
U. Spanker Gaff

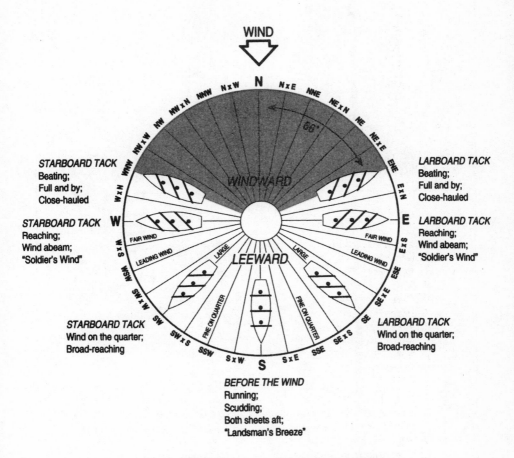

POINTS OF SAIL AND 32-POINT WIND-ROSE

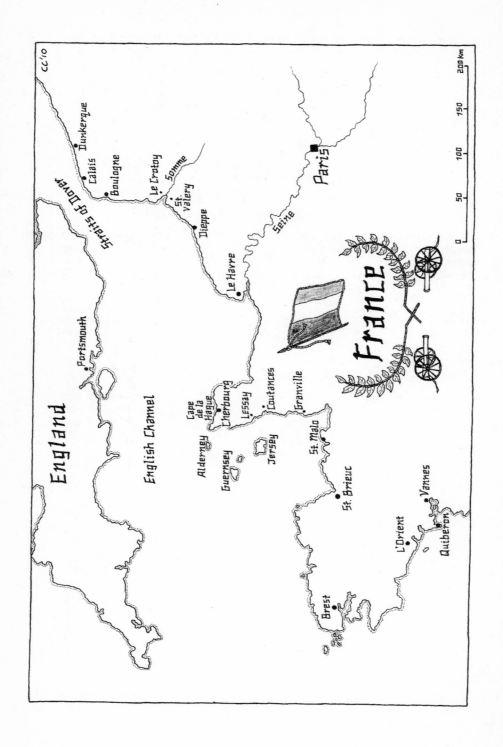

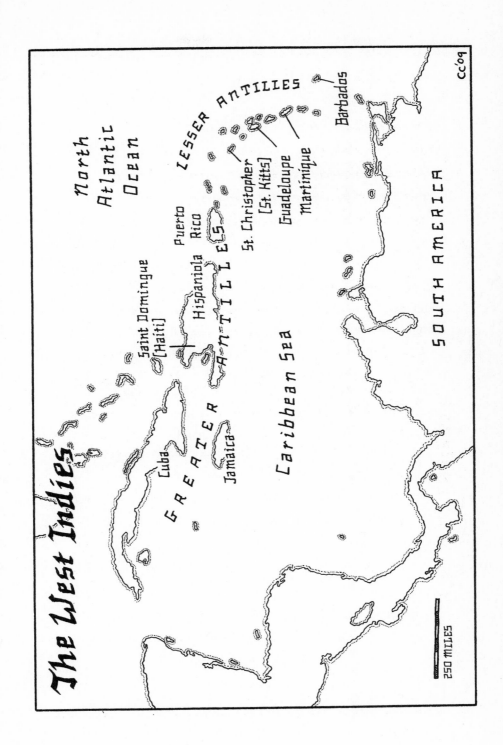

The West Indies

North
Atlantic
Ocean

LESSER ANTILLES

Barbados

St. Christopher
[St. Kitts]
Guadeloupe
Martinique

Puerto
Rico

Saint Domingue
[Haiti]

Hispaniola

GREATER ANTILLES

Cuba

Jamaica

Caribbean Sea

SOUTH AMERICA

250 MILES

CC'09

*Pateant montes silvacque lacusque
cunctaque claustra maris; spes et metus omnibus esto
arbiter. Ipse locos terrenaque summa movendo
experiar, quaenum populis longissima cunctis
regna valim linquamque datas ubi certus habenas.*

Let mountains, forests, lakes
and all the barriers of ocean open out before them;
hope and fear shall decide the day for all alike.
I myself by shifting the seat of empire upon earth
shall make trial which kingdom I shall elect to let
rule longest over all peoples, and in whose hands I
can without fear leave the reins of power once bestowed.

—*ARGONAUTICA*, BOOK I 556-560
GAIUS VALERIUS FLACCUS

PROLOGUE

Vae victis.

Woe to the vanquished.
-*HISTORY*, BOOK X
TITUS LIVIUS (LIVY)
59 B.C.-17 A.D.

CHAPTER ONE

*D*amme, but I do despise the bloody French!"

"Understandably, sir," the First Lieutenant softly agreed.

"Their bloody general, Rochambeau," Captain Alan Lewrie, RN, further gravelled, "he'd surrender t'that murderous General Dessalines and his Black rebel army, but he's too damned proud t'strike to *us?*"

"Well, Dessalines *did* give them ten days' truce to make an orderly exit, sir," Lt. Westcott pointed out. "Else, it would have been a massacre. Another, really."

"If they don't come out and surrender to us, soon, it'll be all 'Frogs Legs *Flambé*,' and Dessalines' truce be-damned," Captain Lewrie said with a mirthless laugh as he extended his telescope to its full length for another peek into the harbour of Cap François . . . and at the ships anchored inside, on which the French now huddled, driven from the last fingernail grasp of their West Indies colony.

Evidently, the Black victors of the long, savage insurrection were getting anxious over when the French would depart, too, for those solid stone forts which had guarded the port from sea assault showed thin skeins of smoke, rising not from cook-fires but from forges where iron shot could be heated red-hot, amber-hot, to set afire those ships and all the beaten French survivors aboard them—soldiers, civilians, sailors, women, and children.

Root and branch, damn their eyes, Lewrie thought; *burn 'em all, root and branch!*

He lowered his glass and grimaced as he turned to face his First Officer, Lt. Geoffrey Westcott. "Is it askin' too much, d'ye imagine, sir, that the Frogs could face facts? Which is the greater failure or shame . . . admittin' the rebel slaves beat 'em like a rug, and surrenderin' t'them . . . or strikin' to a civilised foe, like us? They've *done* the first, so . . . what matters the second?"

"Perhaps it's the matter of Commodore Loring's terms, sir," Lt. Westcott supplied, inclining his head towards their senior officer's flagship, idling under reduced sail further out to seaward. "He will not let them disarm and sail for France on their parole."

"Be a fool if he did," Lewrie said with a dismissive snort, "and Admiralty'd never forgive him for it if he did. We'd, escort them to Jamaica, intern their civilians . . . make the women and kiddies comfortable . . . Rochambeau and all his officers'd be offered parole, quarters, and funds 'til they're exchanged. . . ."

"Of course, we'd sling all their sailors and soldiers into the prisoner hulks," Lt. Westcott added with a touch of whimsy, then, in a tongue-in-cheek manner, said, "And surely some of those French *jeunes filles,* or fetching young widows . . . surely some of them *are,* sir . . . might find themselves in need of a British officer's 'protection'?"

"Hmm, well . . . ," Capt. Lewrie allowed, rocking on the balls of his feet, making his Hessian boots creak; they were new from a cobbler at Kingston, still in need of breaking in. "I expect *you'd* be one to make such an offer, Mister Westcott? I warrant you're a *generous* soul," he said with a leer. Since their first acquaintance fitting-out their new frigate at the renewal of the war with France a little after Easter, Lewrie had discovered that Geoffrey Westcott was a Buck-of-The-First-Head when it came to putting the leg over biddable young ladies . . . almost himself to the Tee, in his younger, frivolous days.

"Well . . . I *hope* to be, sir," Lt. Westcott replied, shrugging in false modesty, or piety (it was hard to tell which), and flashing a brief, teeth-baring grin before turning sober and "salty" once more.

"Wish ye joy of it," Lewrie said, turning to probe the harbour with his telescope once more.

Cap François, casually known as "Le Cap" in better days, had at one time been the richest *entrepôt* on the French colony of Saint Domingue, rivalling Jacmel, Mole St. Nicholas, or Port-Au-Prince itself. Nigh a thousand ships had put in there each year with all the luxuries of Europe and the Orient, and had cleared laden deep with sugar, rice, molasses, and rum, making Saint Domingue the richest prize of all the Sugar Islands, richer than all the British possessions put together.

Cap François and Mole St. Nicholas further west out towards the extreme Nor'western cape of Saint Domingue were well placed for trade—on the North side of the colony, accessible to the passages out into the broad Atlantic, which made for shorter voyages to American or European markets.

Give the Frogs a little *credit,* Lewrie thought; *at least they made something of their half of Hispaniola.*

The eastern half of Hispaniola was held by the Spanish, but San Domingo had never produced a pittance of wealth compared to the French half; cattle herding, sheep and pigs, subsistence farming . . . along with the *boucaniers* who dressed in hides, and had become the dreaded *buccaneers* of pirate lore.

Now, though . . . it was all lost, to both France and any other nation which might try to possess it; as Great Britain had in those early days of the French Revolution, when they'd landed an army ashore, and had been fought back to the beaches and piers by the rebel slaves . . . when they weren't fighting their former *grands blancs* masters, or the *petits blancs* and half-bloods, or each other, for dominance.

That brute General Dessalines had once been an aide to the former house slave Toussaint L'Ouverture, who'd turned out to be a much more brilliant general than any that the French had sent to fight and die here. Over thirty generals, Lewrie had heard tell, and over fourty thousand French soldiers had perished, including Napoleon's brother-in-law, General LeClerc. Oh, LeClerc had managed to lure L'Ouverture to a parley and had enchained him, then shipped him to die in an alpine prison in France—dead of cold, hunger, and heart-break that Napoleon Bonaparte would betray him, the "Napoleon of The West," and break all the promises of the French Revolution, of *Liberté, Fraternité,* and *Egalité,* of the heady vows of abolishing slavery anywhere in every French colony, in hopes that without L'Ouverture, the rebellion would end.

It wasn't even Saint Domingue anymore, either. Now, the rebel slaves had begun to call it Haiti, or Hayti, which—so far as Lewrie could tell from the many battles-to-the-death, the ambushes of whole battalions at a whack, the massacres of masters, mistresses, and overseers, and pretty-much anyone else of the former ruling castes, and the betrayals that had taken place here—translated from Creole *patois* as "Hell On Earth."

The last desperate refuges for the surviving French of Saint Domingue were the ships in harbour, anchored as far out as they could from the shore guns, but still be in the port proper; to venture out further would put them at risk of being raided and boarded at night by the blockading British squadron.

"One'd hope that Rochambeau had wits enough t'spike his coast artillery, before he abandoned the forts, Mister Westcott," Captain Lewrie said to his waiting First Lieutenant.

"Well . . . he *is* French, sir, so there's no telling."

Their frigate, HMS *Reliant*, along with the rest of the squadron that had sailed from Portsmouth in May on an independent mission, lay three miles to seaward of the coast, right at the edge of what had come to be accepted as the limits of a nation's, or island's, sovereignty, the Three Mile Limit. Three miles because that was the Range-To-Random Shot of the largest fortress gun then in use, the 42-pounder. *Had* the French ever had 42-pounders emplaced on Saint Domingue? Lewrie didn't know, but, just to err on the side of caution, that was how far out Commodore Loring had decided they would come to anchor.

"He couldn't be *that* huge a fool as t'leave 'em in place, then anchor right under 'em," Lewrie commented.

"As I said, sir . . . he is French, after all," Westcott said.

"Most-like, the rebels have only field guns . . . regimental guns of six-, eight-, or twelve-pound shot," Lewrie speculated.

"Twelve-pounders firing heated shot would more than suffice, at that range from the shore to the anchored French, sir," Lt. Westcott opined as he briefly doffed his hat to swab his forehead with a faded handkerchief; almost the last day of November in the Year of Our Lord 1803 or not, it was a bright, sunny, and almost windless day.

"Mmm-hmm," Lewrie agreed, intent again on the ships yonder.

There appeared to be at least two large *Compagnie des Indies* three-masted ships, as big as East Indiamen, perhaps another brace of similarly-sized French National ships of the line that seemed to be crammed from bilges to poop decks with humanity.

En flute, or completely dis-armed, Lewrie judged them. *Else, they'd be* completely *elbows t'arseholes if they're still armed, and of a mind t'resist us,* he told himself with a wry grin. *With no place t'put the women and children if they tried.*

There were a couple of frigates, one of them a very handsome and big one of at least 38 guns or better. There were some lighter, smaller two-masted brigs, even some locally-built schooners. Did the French see the sense of it and strike to Loring's squadron, there'd be a nice pot of prize-money due . . . even if it had to be shared by every British warship then "in sight" at the moment of their striking their colours.

Don't half mind the French *perishin' in flames, but . . . we all could use some "tin,"* Lewrie thought; *be a shame t'lose those ships.*

Beyond the ships, ashore . . . Lewrie had seen Cap François back in 1783, at the tail-end of the American Revolution when he had had his brief, acting-command of the *Shrike* brig for a few weeks. It had looked prosperous then. He had trailed his colours before it in the 1790s in HMS *Proteus*, his first frigate, during his first Post-Captaincy, when the slave rebellion had burst aflame, and Cap François had even then seemed safe, secure, and ordered, as if the French had kept the uprising and slaughter at bay, deep inland, and well away from the port.

Now . . . it was dowdy, charred, and filthy, the looted mansions and goods warehouses broken and gaping, and the harbourside streets and piers teeming with taunting, jeering ex-slaves. What possessions the French had abandoned in their haste to flee made a colourful sea of silks and satins being haggled or fought over by the victors, and draped the native women. There was street dancing, some very faint snatches of music, making Lewrie think that he was watching some feral Carnivale. And, when the gentle sea-breeze faltered, he could almost make out the dread, rhythmic thud of *voudoun* drumming, the sort that had made him prickle with fear his one night ashore long ago at Port-Au-Prince, the drumming that had presaged the evacuation of the British Army to cut their losses to battle, poisonings, small-party ambushes, and the ever-present Malaria and Yellow Jack.

If there were any French left ashore for lack of room aboard the anchored ships, then God help them; they'd have been hunted down, torn from even the deepest hidings, then butchered, raped, and tortured, or burned alive or beheaded—perhaps guillotined in proper French fashion?—as the last to atone for centuries of slavery and all of the cruelties that came with it.

Or, he imagined, for the vindictive, victorious *fun* of it!

One more day, and, upon the 30th of November, the French would sail and surrender, or burn in Hell, and Haiti (or Hayti) would become an independent Black republic, the only one of its kind in the world, born in a decade or more of blood-rain monsoons.

"Signal from the flag!" Midshipman Entwhistle piped up from the taffrails aft of Lewrie and the First Lieutenant. "Our number, sir . . . 'Captain Repair On Board,' sir!"

"What the Devil?" Lewrie wondered aloud.

"I'll pass word for your Cox'n and boat crew, sir," Lt. Westcott said in a crisper tone, with a doff of his hat.

"Aye, but . . . whatever *for*?" Lewrie muttered to himself.

CHAPTER TWO

*W*hen one was summoned by a senior officer, it was a given that it would be "With All Despatch," with no time frittered in shaving, sponging off, or primping. Pettus had come up from his great-cabins with Lewrie's everyday sword belt and hanger, and a clean uniform coat to replace a cotton one long ago gone bad, a sorry experiment in tropical clothing that had faded and bled dark-blue dye to the point that it had gone a spotty sky blue, the gilt lace trim verdisgris green and sick-making.

But, it *was* comfortable, was so bleached it could ruin no more shirts, waist-coats, or breeches, and it was *cool*, unlike the requisite broadcloth wool coat.

Liam Desmond, his Coxswain, stroke-oar Patrick Furfy, Desmond's long-time mate, and the rest of the boat crew had been ready below the entry-port by the time Lewrie had taken *Reliant*'s ritualist departure honours, and within minutes, they were off for a long mile row out to the two-decker flagship.

Plenty of time for Lewrie to fret, that. On the one hand, he and the other officers of their wee four-ship squadron had won fame and a pot of prize-money back in September when they had succeeded in chasing down a French squadron that had sailed from French-occupied Holland for Saint Domingue, then New Orleans. They had met them off the Chandeleur Islands, east of the Passes into the Mississippi, and had fought a spirited hour's action resulting in the capture of one two-decker 74, a frigate and two *corvettes,* and an East Indiaman that had been reputed to carry a battalion of troops and government officials for the ceremonial handover of New Orleans and all the Louisiana Territory to the United States, after recovering them by treaty from Spain.

That fame had come with a tinge of scandal for Lewrie, for he had run down the Indiaman alone, then decided to let the French civilians—refugees from Saint Domingue for the most part—be put ashore from Lake Borgne to make the fifteen-mile trek to New Orleans and freedom. Some newspaper accounts thought it an honourable gesture of Christian magnanimity, the act of a proper British hero . . . fellow officers in the West Indies had deemed it daft, and soft-hearted—dash it all, but hadn't Napoleon Bonaparte ordered Lewrie's death over some insult during the Peace of Amiens, and the Ogre's men *had* killed his wife with a cowardly shot in the back at the very moment they had almost made a clean escape by boat? Damme if the French hadn't! So, why would a chap like Lewrie show a whit of mercy to the Frogs? Had they been in his boots, *they'd* have not, by God!

Raised from the cradle to hate the French like the very Devil, as all good Englishmen should, with anger and grief over Caroline's murder to stoke his hatred white-hot, still . . . Lewrie could not make war on helpless civilians, on women or children. He'd had a moment, admittedly, when ordering a broadside had been *so* tempting, but he had not. He could have taken them all back to Jamaica with the navy crews of the other prizes, but . . . had they not suffered enough? *They* were innocent of Caroline's death, and New Orleans had been so close by.

Which camp's Loring in, I wonder? Lewrie thought as the oarsmen set a powerful stroke seaward; *Am I saint or sinner, to him?*

"Ah, Captain Lewrie, welcome, sir," Commodore Loring said, with all evident delight as Lewrie entered the great-cabins. "A glass, will you, sir?"

"Aye, that'd be fine, sir," Lewrie replied, looking about at the gathering of officers. A steward came with a glass of cool Rhenish for him, and Lewrie took a tentative sip.

"Captain John Bligh, of *Theseus,*" Loring went on, doing the introductions, "Captain Barré . . . Captain Lewrie of *Reliant.* Pardons, for my brevity, but, French pride, and their touchy sense of honour, force me to be brief. I am sending a delegation to General Rochambeau once more, his last warning. Does he not sail out and strike his colours, I will leave him to the doubtful mercies of the rebel Blacks. At the same time, I am despatching another delegation ashore to speak with this so-called General Dessalines, and his cohorts. Bligh and Barré are to speak for me, Lewrie, but, given your long experience with the colony of Saint Domingue, I thought it useful to send you along with them, Lewrie . . . to supply these gentlemen with your insights."

What? Lewrie thought, gawping. His mouth dropped agape at the idea, his eyes went wide. What *bloody experience?* What *insights?*

"Beg pardon, sir?" Lewrie said, once he'd got his breath back. "In a previous commission, I came t'know the *coasts* main-well, but as for what passes ashore . . ."

"Did you not enter Mole Saint Nicholas?" Loring snapped, peering at him owlishly. "Spend some time ashore at Port-Au-Prince, when our army was here?"

One night . . . in a whore-house, Lewrie recalled.

"We were *close ashore* at Mole Saint Nicholas, sir, providing indirect fire for our troops," Lewrie explained. "I *did* go ashore for a day, to visit a friend at his regiment, and *dined* ashore that night, in Port-Au-Prince . . . the night the city was invested by L'Ouverture and his army, and we began the evacuation, sir."

Those damned drums! He remembered how they'd thudded like bloody beating hearts, ripped from the chests of the massacred. *They scared the piss outta me, for certain, and put my "high-yellow" girl into pluperfect shits, t'boot. Don't see how that's useful.*

"No fluency in their Creole lingo?" Captain Barré asked, a brow up in doubt. "No background information?"

"I doubt anyone speaks their private *patois*, sir," Lewrie told him, "but, they deal with the outside world in French, don't they? As for background information, well . . . I did pick up on who-hates-who and how much, the various massacres and betrayals, but . . ."

"Know much of Dessalines, do you?" Captain Barré pressed, now with a faint sneer of disappointment. "Christophe, Petion, and Clairveaux?"

"All four of 'em have been betrayed, betrayed each other, even turned on L'Ouverture, more times than I've had hot suppers, Captain Barré," Lewrie replied. He had no wish to go ashore and deal with the rebel generals, no wish to put himself at *that* much risk, but the way Barré spoke to him rankled. "None of 'em have a *shred* o' trust for any Europeans, at this point," he added, after a sip of his cool-ish wine.

"And with good reason," Commodore Loring interjected. "After what the late, un-lamented, General LeClerc, and this chap Rochambeau, did to them. They came with a plan for complete extermination of any Blacks living on the island, and thought to re-populate it with fresh slaves, unaffected by thoughts of independence, or liberty. That is the only way that Saint Domingue could be returned to profitability," Loring said with a shrug. "Their principal exports *depend* upon slave labour. Rochambeau deliberately rounded up Blacks and Mulattoes, and drowned them by the umpteen-thousands, right here in Le Cap Bay, not a year past."

"They'll burn the ships, and the survivors, to Hell," Captain John Bligh said with a sigh. "With very good cause. Unless we arrange for the French departure."

"I will offer Rochambeau and his naval officers rescue from that fate," Loring told them. "But, only if they sail out by the deadline he has agreed to with Dessalines, tomorrow. I will allow them to fire broadsides, as honourable *tokens*, before striking their colours. But, that is *all* I will allow. For the sake of humanity, I wish the rebel generals to accede to that arrangement. You gentlemen will deliver to Dessalines the full meaning of my terms to Rochambeau, and extract from him an agreement that he will not fire upon the French ships,"

"*If* they obey you, sir, and leave harbour," Lewrie pointed out. "If Rochambeau does not? Fort Picolet's forges are *already* kindled."

"Then, let us pray that General Rochambeau has seen that, too, and will be convinced that departing Cap François is in his best interests, hmm?" Commodore Loring replied.

"*All* of us, sir?" Captain Barré, ever a skeptic, enquired with a cutty-eyed glance at Lewrie.

"Aye . . . all of you," Loring told the man with a shrug, cocking his head to one side as if thinking that three was more impressive than two; or, that, seeing as how they were already up and *dressed* . . . ?

"Well, then . . . let's be about it, hey?" Lewrie said, tossing off his wine and plastering a confident smile on his phyz, no matter the gurgly qualms in his nether regions that threatened to make themselves known to one and all.

Aye, I'll go, he told himself; *if only to rankle Barré!*

CHAPTER THREE

*T*hey landed at the quays in Commodore Loring's barge, a rather more impressive conveyance than any of their captains' gigs, with her oarsmen tricked out in snowy white slop-trousers, shirts and stockings, flat tarred hats with fluttering long ribbons painted with the name of Loring's flag-ship, in fresh-blacked shoes with silver-plated buckles, and dark-blue short jackets with polished brass buttons.

And, just in case, with cutlasses, muskets, and pistols stowed out of sight under water-proof tarred tarpaulins in the boat's sole!

They, and their white flag of truce, were met by a guard of honour, and a fellow who introduced himself as a Colonel who spoke fluent, almost Parisian, French, and heavily accented English. The soldiers of the guard, warm though it was, were accoutred as well as any soldiers that Lewrie had seen in Paris during the Peace of Amiens, from their brass-trimmed shakoes to their trousers, with dark blue tail-coats and white waist-coats, white-leather crossbelts with brass plates shining. None wore stockings or shoes, though.

The Colonel, by name of Mirabois, wore a fore-and-aft bicorne hat with an egret plume and lots of gold lace, a snug double-breasted uniform coat with lavish gilt acanthus leaves embroidered on pocket flaps, his sleeve cuffs, and the stiff standing collars of the coat.

Sweat himself t'death, in all that wool, Lewrie thought.

"*Bonjour, messieurs! Vous* 'ave come to surrender to us, *oui?*

"Er, ehm . . . what?" Captain Bligh gawped, taken by surprise.

"Ze *tout petite plaisanterie,* ha ha? Ze wee jest?"

"Oh. Ha ha. I see, ehm," Bligh flummoxed. "Commodore Loring, ehm . . . our Commodore in command of His Britannic Majesty's squadron now lying off Cap François, has directed us to deliver a proposal to your General Dessalines, and a request to speak with him, should that be possible," Bligh explained in halting schoolboy French.

As nigh-illiterate as me, Lewrie thought, noting how Captain Barré, their resident critic, pursed his lips and almost grimaced to hear it. Bligh was surely senior to him, else Barré would have been the one to conduct the negotiations. And was certain that he would've been more effective at it. He was frowning like an irate tutor at his student's lack of fluency!

Bligh introduced them all, then waited, his document held out in expectation that it would be accepted, and whisked off to Dessalines, instanter. In the short period of their landing and introductions, a substantial crowd of the curious had gathered; poor field slaves still in the cheap nankeen short trousers and loose smocks of slavery, their women in shapeless longer smocks, and the children in barely any garments at all. Many of them had cane-cutter knives or *machetes* shoved into rough rope belts . . . or in their hands. Ominously, some of the better-garbed looters in incongruous finery, and better-armed with captured muskets or pistols, joined them, muttering and scowling.

French, English . . . bloody Russians, Lewrie thought with a bit of rising dread; *We're White . . . their blood enemies. This could get* very *ugly!*

"*Messieurs,* I leave ze guard *pour vôtre* boat, *oui? Et,* I will escort *vous au Le Tigre,* 'is own face," Colonel Mirabois offered, then turned and barked orders to his men. A round dozen of his soldiers formed a protective line to protect the barge, its wide-eyed Midshipman, Coxswain, and oarsmen, at the head of the quay, and another dozen formed to either side of their party.

Like prisoners, off t'the guillotine or firin' squad, Lewrie imagined, with (it must be admitted) a bit of a chill shudder.

A Black sergeant gleefully called a fast "heep-heep" pace as they were marched off to see "Le Tigre," Dessalines, face-to-face.

"Think they'd've laid on some horses," Captain Bligh whispered from the side of his mouth, panting a bit at the pace.

"Already ate 'em, most-like," Lewrie whispered back, unable to quell his sense of humour, no matter the risk they faced. "And, how come there's still so many Whites ashore, I wonder?" he pointed out.

It was uncanny; it was downright eerie, that long march through the littered streets. Now they were under official escort, the Blacks and lighter Mulattoes stood and scowled at the strange officers, with no sound; no jeering or hooting as they'd heard at the quays. Around the edges of the crowds stood White French colonists, men, women, and children; Lewrie could pick out the ones he imagined had been wealthy planters and slave owners, rich traders and exporters, by the finery of their clothing. The *grands blancs*, Lewrie recalled their being called. The others, though . . . the ones in humbler suits or working-men's garb, with their women in simpler, drabber gowns, and the children in the same sort of hand-me-down "shabby" one could see in poorer neighbourhoods in England, were the artificers, the shopkeepers, the greengrocers, fruiterers, and skilled labourers, the *petits blancs* who might never have been able to aspire to owning slaves.

What had Jemmy Peel told him, when in the West Indies on Foreign Office Secret Branch doings in the '90s and sniffing about how to undermine the French, the slave rebellion, or both?

Saint Domingue, or Hayti, was a bubbling cauldron of rebellion; poor Whites versus their betters; Mulattoes versus darker, illiterate field hands; house servants siding with masters in some cases, murdering them in others. *Petits blancs* then siding with Mulattoes like General Rigaud down south round Jacmel to fight L'Ouverture, Dessalines, and the others . . . and all wrenched from time to time by siding with the French if they'd seemed to have the upper hand, with the British when their own army had landed, even looking for shelter and security by allying themselves with the Spanish in the other half of Hispaniola, if that looked better!

"Uhm . . . Colonel Mirabois," Lewrie asked, at last, his curiosity aroused, "I note a fair number of . . . *blancs* still in the city. Were they not able to find space aboard the ships?"

"*Mais oui, M'sieur Capitaine . . . Le . . . pardon, seulement, vôtre* name I cannot say, ees *très difficile, n'est-ce pas?*" Mirabois laughed rather drolly as he explained. "Zey *refuse* place in ze ships, *m'sieur!* 'Ave been *born* here . . . 'ave property *et* business interests, *comprend?* Hayti ees open to ze trade, so zey make . . . *accommodation*. Wis ze ozzer *blancs* 'oo go away, Hayti 'ave need of zem, so . . . ," he said, shrugging in very Gallic fashion.

"Incredible," was all that Lewrie could think to say.

"Ze *blancs* 'oo stay, zey *know* z'ings we *pauvre Noirs* do not," Mirabois said further. "'Ave ze education, ze dealing wis ze outside world," he admitted, with another of those pearly-white smiles, then sobered quickly to look almost feral. "Until *we* learn zese z'ings, z'en . . .'oo knows. *Moi,* I desire *blanc* servants. Ha ha ha! I make *ʒe pauvre plaisanterie,* again, *n'est-ce pas?* Aw ha ha ha!"

Their escorts led them from the looted, charred shabbiness of the harbour front to wide streets leading inland to a mansion district of substantial houses, what Lewrie took for banks, and perhaps government buildings, all smoothly stuccoed and painted, once, in white and gay tropical pastels; all with even more substantial double doors and impressive sets of iron bars on the tall windows.

Most were shut tight against the victorious slave armies, their window shutters double-barred. Some had been nailed shut perhaps years before as their prosperous owners fled the colony. Some of those were now in the process of being torn open with crow-levers, or smashed open with heavy mauls, though it seemed an orderly process, not a looting by a jeering mob; the deeds were done by work-gangs or companies of Black troops, supervised by their officers.

Their escort halted in front of a pale yellow–painted government office building with blue doors and shutters, and Spanish-looking roof tiles. Soldiers in neat, clean uniforms stood guard over the entrance, though they made no moves to stop the stream of officers, runners, and idling gawkers, both military and civilian, who wandered in with pipes or *cigaros* fuming, chatting and pointing at their former masters' splendours as gay as magpies.

Colonel Mirabois left them for a long time, standing in direct sunlight and steamy heat, before returning and gesturing them inside; across the high and spacious lobby, and up a long, curving flight of stairs to the upper floor, then into a receiving room large enough to accommodate a good-sized hunt ball of two hundred or more very energetic couples at a *contre-dance.*

"*Messieurs, mon Générals* . . . ," Colonel Mirabois loftily began as he introduced the British delegation, then made introductions for the splendidly uniformed men who stood behind a massive oak-and-marble desk.

"General Dessalines . . . !" Mirabois said as that worthy glared at them, a big, tough, brutal-looking man.

"Illiterate, I heard," Lewrie whispered to Bligh and Barré.

"General Christophe . . . !"

"Once a British slave, brought here. Hotel waiter here in Cap François," Lewrie further whispered. "Speaks English." Christophe was not as big as the rest, and didn't look quite as threatening.

"General Clairveaux . . . !" Mirabois said of a solid Mulatto man.

"Betrayal's his meat an' drink," Lewrie related. "Play any side 'gainst the other."

Captain Barré turned his head slightly to look at Lewrie, with an eyebrow up; the sort of look one gave to a talking dog.

Damme! Lewrie thought; *I must've picked up more than I thought I had, from the last time I was here. Useful insights . . . gossip!*

After that, Lewrie stood aside, having no role to play as Bligh presented his formal written proposal from Commodore Loring. Colonel Mirabois took it and handed it to General Dessalines, which was fruitless, since he *was* illiterate, a former field slave. Grudgingly, that worthy had to pass it to either Christophe or the better-educated General Clairveaux, glowering even darker and fiercer, first at the British delegation which had put him in that embarrassment, then at his two "compatriots," who, mostlikely, were scheming to become the supreme leader of their new nation.

"Clairveaux's a schemer?" Barré muttered from the corner of his mouth, barely moving his lips.

"Supposedly loyal to France and Sonthonax when *he* was here, then Rigaud and his Mulattoes down south, then L'Ouverture, and the Spanish? Slippery as an eel," Lewrie whispered back. "Might've backed LeClerc, 'fore he died of Yellow Jack."

"You puny, lying White bastards!" General Christophe barked angrily after he'd read the letter and heard Bligh out. "Go back to Europe, the rest of the Indies, and *slaughter* each other! But do not dare to dabble in Hayti's affairs any longer. Damn *all* you British, but if not for your presence, the French would *already* be gone!"

That was shouted in English; Christophe turned to his compatriots, Dessalines and Clairveaux, and repeated himself in rapid, slurred French, wind-milling his arms and going so far as to spit on the floor, and pound a fist on the marble table top so hard that he made it jump, massive and heavy as it was; about the size of a jolly-boat, to Lewrie's lights.

General Dessalines rumbled out an equal flood of bile in a deep *basso*, glaring at the trio of British officers and gripping the hilt of his elegant sword so hard that his dark fingers changed colour. Clairveaux, not to be outdone, barked out his own flood of threats.

Not exactly Nelson's "band o' brothers," are they? Lewrie told himself. He found it amusing . . . until the roars for "slaughter" and "blood bath" reached the ears of the many revolutionaries beyond those double doors, and Lewrie heard a blood-chilling chant he hadn't heard in years.

Eh! Eh! Bomba! Heu! Heu!
Canga bafio té! Canga mouné de lé!
Canga do ki la! Canga li!

"Sound in good spirits," Captain Barré commented, turning about to cock an ear, with a confident smile (false, most-like given their hosts' attitude).

"It means 'We swear to destroy all the Whites and all that they possess; let us die rather than fail to keep this vow,'" Lewrie nervously translated in a low mutter. "This is gettin' serious, sir."

"*Mon Général,* Dessalines, 'e say, *messieurs,* z'at you British are ze *so* despicable, ze grasping beasts, as bad as ze French!" Mirabois translated, looking a tad nervous himself. "You kill-ed z'ousands of *nôtre pauvre* soldiers, came to Saint Domingue to conquer and enslave! E' say 'e *despise* all of you, and v'ish *every* White devil to die . . . *seulement* . . .'e also say if Rochambeau surrender to you and leave ze harbour tomorrow, 'e will not fire on z'eir ships. Z'ey stay *une* hour longer, 'e *will* fire upon z'em, and burn z'em all to Hades. 'E agree wiz *vôtre* Commodore Loring in z'iz. You 'ave 'ees word of *honnour*. 'E say *vôtre* Commodore mus' be satisfy-ed vis z'at, not ze correspondent letter. *Maintenant,* you go! I see you to ze port in safety, or pay v'is my life. *Vite, vite!* Go!"

Captain Bligh opened his mouth as if to say something further, but clapped it shut as Colonel Mirabois began urgent shoving-herding motions, backing them ignominiously towards the doors, and looking back over his shoulder to see if any of the bile the British had engendered from the victorious generals would stick to *him* for bringing them.

In a trice, they were down the stairs, across the grand lobby, and out into the sunshine, with their escorting soldiers guarding them even closer with bayonet-mounted muskets held out to fence off and deter the chanting, fist-shaking, *weapon*-shaking mob. Picking up on their officers' nervousness, and the hostile mood in the building they left behind, those soldiers set a wicked pace back to the quays and their waiting barge, forcing Bligh, Barré, and Lewrie to trot double-time.

Once the barge was shoved off and under oars, with a wee Union Jack in the bows, and a *large* white flag of truce stood up by the Midshipman in the stern-sheets, they finally got their breaths back, and broke out a small barrico of stale water from beneath the seat for the barge's Coxswain. They took turns gulping from a battered pewter mug and swabbing their reddened faces; ruddy from being un-used to so much exertion after the restrictions of shipboard life, and the embarrassing manner of their departure. They had almost been *shoved* aboard the boat!

"Bit iffy there, for a moment," Bligh commented.

"Be back in ten years," Captain Barré breezily opined, now that he was in calmer takings. "Can you gentlemen imagine that those three jackanapes, or their other generals, Petion and Moise, can *really* run a country?" he scoffed. "More-like, it will be a decade of civil war between them, before the country is so devastated, and de-populated, that it will be ripe for the plucking."

"We had hopes that the Americans'd beg t'be back in the fold, too, when we left in 1783," Lewrie pointed out.

"Barbaric as are our American cousins, sir," Captain Barré rejoined, "they don't hold a candle to *those* savages back yonder. And, the Yankee Doodles are *White*, and civilised, after all."

"Different kettle of fish," Captain Bligh stuck in with a mirthless laugh. "I say . . . let us take a slant to starboard, and look over our future prizes . . . assuming General Rochambeau has a lick of sense."

"Aye, sir," their Midshipman in charge of the barge agreed, and the tiller was put over to angle their boat closer to the French ships.

"Indiamen, there, a brace of 'em. Don't see any guns in their ports," Lewrie pointed out. "That'un, though, she's a two-decker, a Third Rate seventy-four. And, *still* armed."

All the gun-ports on each beam of the 74 were hinged open for desperately needed ventilation, any wisp of a breeze that could sweep through both her over-crowded gun-decks to relieve the panting of the hundreds of pale faces pressed close to the openings. Those people had no other place to go, for the weather decks, gangways, poops and forecastles, and quarterdecks of all the French vessels were already teeming with refugees, almost arseholes-to-elbows.

"*Lovely* pair of frigates, there," Captain Bligh said with an avid note in his voice as they passed the two-decker. "*Chlorinde* . . . and *Surv* . . . *Surveillante*," he read off their name-boards on the transoms. "As big as our frigates of the Fifth Rate . . . thirty-eights or better."

The frigate closest to them had her single row of gun-ports open, too, with children and teenagers sitting on the barrels of her guns to be close to the fresher air, and haloes of faces round every edge.

"Might be nigh a thousand people aboard this'un, alone, sirs," Lewrie said with a grim shake of his head. *Were I a Frog, I'd be on-board one of 'em, too,* Lewrie thought; *Beats bein' murdered all hollow!*

"Be a shame, does Dessalines set them ablaze," Captain Bligh told them, sounding sad. "Yon brace of frigates would fetch us fifteen or twenty thousand pounds each, perhaps thirty thousand for that Third Rate, and about the same for the Indiamen, each."

"Head and Gun Money for all the sailors and soldiers captured, to boot," Captain Barré pointed out.

"Well, perhaps but half that much, sir," Lewrie told Bligh. "I think our Prize Courts would most-like steal half for themselves."

"Oh, tosh!" Barré said with a chuckle. "They ain't cut up from a drub-bin', and won't need serious refits, like most French warships we've made prize. Even so . . . aye, it *would* be a pity, do those apes ashore burn them up."

"Dessalines might just do it for spite," Bligh suggested. "To show us how little he cares for us, or the French, or any Whites."

"Beg pardon, sirs, but there's a breeze coming up," their Midshipman hesitantly interjected, pointing an arm to the wind-rippled patch of water off their barge's larboard bows. "Are your observations done, sirs, I'd care to steer for it, and hoist the lugs'l."

"Might be enough wind to carry us beyond the harbour mole, and out to a decent sea-breeze, aye," Captain Bligh, senior-most of their party, agreed. "Spare your oarsmen three or four miles of rowing, hey?"

"You left your gig at the flagship, Captain Lewrie?" Captain Barré casually enquired.

"Sent her back to *Reliant,* not knowing how long we'd be away, sir," Lewrie told him.

"She's closer inshore than the flag? Well, now our duty has been done, there's no reason to detain you any longer," Barré said as the barge crossed the mill-pond flat water for that disturbed patch, now as big as a lake and growing larger as the breeze picked up. Two of their oarsmen stowed away their oars and began to fetch up the lug-sail which, with its simple running, rigging, was wrapped about its upper gaff boom.

"Make for the *Reliant* frigate, once under sail," Captain Barré directed the Midshipman. "We'll spare Captain Lewrie, here, the long time it'd take him to send for his gig, twiddle his thumbs aboard the flag, and another hour or two to return to his ship."

"That's most kind of ye, sir, thankee," Lewrie told Barré as he pulled out his pocket-watch to note the time. It was already almost a quarter to one P.M.; aboard *Reliant* they'd soon be sounding Two Bells of the Day Watch, and her Commission Officers, Sailing Master, Lieutenant of Marines, and Surgeon would be sitting down to take their mid-day dinner, now that the ship's people had had their own mess. If Barré had not made the offer, even with a decent wind, it would have been at least 2 P.M. before they would have fetched the flagship, and perhaps two *more* hours before he could expect to sit down to a meal of his own; there *might* have been some leftovers from Commodore Loring's table, if he begged properly, but . . . even this quick return to his ship would result in whatever cold collation that his personal cook, Yeovill, had at-hand. The ship's cook would be just beginning to boil up victuals for the crew's supper, with nothing to offer him.

It'll be wormy cheese and ship's bisquit, Lewrie bemoaned; *some jam, or a slice'r two off last night's roast. The cats' sausages?*

And, Lewrie was feeling *most* peckish, by then!

CHAPTER FOUR

*T*he appointed morning dawned cooler than the day before, though the sea-breezes that had blown light but steadily throughout the night began to fade and clock round the compass by the start of the Forenoon Watch at 8 A.M. If anything, it was replaced by a faint land-breeze as the island of Hispaniola was heated by the risen sun. The waters about HMS *Reliant* dropped to a slight two-foot chop, and long, rolling wave sets that slatted the remaining wind from her fore-and-aft sails and spanker, and fluttered her square sails, to the accompaniment of slapping rigging and the loose squeal of blocks, to the *basso* of the hull as it rocked, heaved, and scended, her timbers groaning.

"The tide ebbs from the harbour . . . when, Mister Caldwell?" her captain enquired a tad impatiently, pacing about the freshly cleaned quarter-deck, from the starboard bulwarks facing Cap François to the binnacle cabinet and double-wheel helm, and back.

"By my ephemeris, sir, it should have turned half an hour ago," *Reliant*'s Sailing Master informed him, after another quick peek at his book of tide tables, and a sidelong glance at the gathered officers.

"Mean they *ain't* coming out?" Marine Lt. Simcock complained.

"The land-breeze *seems* to be strengthening . . . a bit," Lieutenant Spendlove, the Second Officer, noted. "That, and the ebbing tide, should carry them out nicely. If they're of a mind."

The *Reliant*'s people, from her captain to her Commission Sea Officers to her Midshipmen, Warrants, petty officers, Able and Ordinary Seamen, her Landsmen, "Idlers and Waisters," her Marines and ship's boys and servants, were all on deck, Half were on watch, of course, but the rest were there to satisfy their curiosity . . . and to see if their prize-money would actually sail out and surrender; or if they did not, their burning would be a "raree." Wagers slyly made during the night rode on the results.

Even Lewrie's cats, Toulon, the older, stockier black-and-white, and Chalky, the grey-splotched white'un, were on deck this morning, and when not perched atop the canvas coverings of the quarterdeck hammock nettings, were scampering about in pursuit of a champagne cork with a length of ribbon tied round it, footballing it from one end of the quarterdeck to the other, hopping up on their hind legs in mock battle to play tail-chase when the champagne cork toy palled.

"Ye'd think someone slipped 'em some fresh catnip last night," Lewrie grumbled, forced to halt his pacing as Chalky chased Toulon aft right through his booted legs. "Damn my eyes, ye little . . . !"

"They do seem *very* spry, today, sir," Lt. Westcott, the First Officer, agreed, watching them go, flashing his teeth in a brief grin as Toulon fluffed up, turned sideways, and hopped in warning at his playmate, one paw lifted and his bottled-up tail lashing.

"Deck, there!" Midshipman Rossyngton called down from his wee seat on the main mast cross-trees. "The French . . . are . . . making . . . *sail*!" the youngster pealed out, each word distinct.

"Come on, yer beauties!" a sailor on the starboard gangway was heard to hoot. "Come out an' fetch us yer guineas!" which raised a great cheer and laughter.

Lewrie went to the binnacle cabinet to fetch his telescope . . . just in time for Chalky to be the pursued, and take bottled-up refuge atop the cabinet. Toulon, always the less-agile since he was a kitten, could only stand on his hind legs with his front paws on the woodwork and make moaning sounds, whilst Chalky hissed back and spat.

"Ever'body's celebratin', seems like," Quartermaster Hook, at the helm, chuckled.

"Many a slip, 'twixt the crouch and the leap, though," Lewrie said with a grin. "Keep yer fingers crossed," he cautioned as he went to the bulwarks for a better view.

"Yes, by God!" Lewrie crowed, once he'd had a look-see. Faded, patched, and sun-worn parchment-tan canvas *was* sprouting aboard every remaining vessel in harbour. Closer to shore, several British barges or cutters were loafing with idled oars or furled lug-sails, waiting with small boarding parties from various ships to go aboard them once their "honourable" broadsides were fired, and their colours struck, to oversee their disarming. Lewrie lowered his telescope a trifle, just in time to see one of the boats hold up a single signal flag from the new Popham Code . . . "To Weigh"!

"Excuse me, sir, but, should we Beat to Quarters?" Lt. Westcott asked, close by Lewrie's side, with a telescope of his own.

"In case they mean t'make a fight of it?" Lewrie asked back with a grin. "Ye didn't see how many people they've taken aboard, Mister Westcott. They're *beyond* over-crowded, without enough room to swing a cat, much less serve their guns."

Dear as I'd desire it, Lewrie told himself; *if it was just us and their sailors and such . . . without the civilians, I'd* love *to lay into them, the murderin' bastards!*

"Deck, there!" Midshipman Rossyngton called down, again. "The French . . . are . . . under *way*! A seventy-four . . . is . . . leading!"

"Took their own sweet time," Lewrie said with a snort, now he was satisfied that they would come out.

"The tide will help fetch them out, but they *have* waited a bit too late, sir . . . the land-breeze won't last long," Westcott said.

"With just the tide, aye . . . they'll be boxin' the compass in an hour," Lewrie agreed. "Un-manageable."

"Perhaps the smaller of them could employ sweeps?" Lt. Westcott posed, tongue-in-cheek.

"Were it me, I'd paddle a log with my hands, to get out of port," their Third Officer, Lt. George Merriman, added with a guffaw.

The leading ship, the two-decker, came on as ponderously, and as slowly, as treacle poured on porridge on a winter's day. Even under all her course sails and tops'ls, and with her jibs and staysails loosely sheeted and bellied out, she barely was making steerage way. A vessel so heavy and deep-draughted found it hard to overcome her own inertia, even on a good day, with a following or beam wind. Lewrie pulled out his pocket-watch, stuck an upright thumb against her to measure with, and growled under his breath as he realised that the two-decker was not making much more than two or three knots, and was *still* no larger than his thumb-nail, after a full half-hour under sail! It would take her *another* half-hour just to pass the breakwater to the open sea . . . with her potentially swifter and lighter consorts bunched up astern of her, and their own sails trapping and stealing the wind of the land-breeze . . . which was slowly fading.

Should've let the wee'uns sail, first, Lewrie thought; *but, hey, they're French, and they* will *do it orderly, t'look proud.*

"At long, bloody last!" Lt. Westcott muttered as the flagship of the French squadron passed through the breakwater and reached open waters . . . as a weak gust of wind arose, and soughed cross their frigate's decks. The Nor'east Trades were coming back to life, and over yonder, the French two-decker's sails shivered and rustled in gross disorder for a moment before being sheeted home and braced round to adapt to it, *slowly* bearing up roughly West-Nor'west, presenting her larboard side to *Reliant* and *finally* showing a tiny mustachio of foam under her forefoot as she put on another knot or two.

And, when she was about a mile offshore, still two miles short of *Reliant*, her guns began to roar down her larboard side; first the spewing of gunpowder smoke, then seconds later the flat thuds of the explosions.

"A full broadside, I say!" Lt. Clarence Spendlove, the Second Officer, exclaimed. "Her pair of bow chase guns would have sufficed."

"Showy," Marine Lt. Simcock commented.

"And to Hell with you perfidious Britons," Lt. Westcott added with a laugh. "Ve show *vous* 'ow to surrender vis *panache*!"

And, once the last after guns of her upper and lower batteries had shot their bolts, and the immense pall of spent powder smoke was drifting leeward enough to see the two-decker again, the blue-white-red Tricolour of France was hauled down to drape over her taffrails and transom. A lug-sailed cutter flying a British Jack quickly made its way alongside her to take possession.

Next came the Indiamen, large merchant ships or former ships of the line employed as troop transports; they mounted many fewer guns than the warship that had preceded them, so they fired off only a half-dozen for their "honourable broadsides," perhaps only bow-chasers and some light quarterdeck pieces, before striking their colours, as well. One of those impressively big frigates passed through the breakwater, after, and found her wind, rapidly gathering an impressive turn of speed before firing her final broadside, and striking her colours . . . followed by a gaggle of brigs, snows, or locally-built schooners, all overloaded and clumsy on the ebbing tide and the scant wind, but making decent progress to freedom and safety. The second frigate, however . . .

"Damn my eyes, but, has she taken the ground, yonder?" Lieutenant Spendlove declared, a telescope to his eye. "She doesn't seem to be moving. There, sir!"

"Yawing all over Creation before that, aye, Clarence," Lieutenant Merriman was quick to agree with him. "Good God, it appears that she *has* . . . just past the breakwater!"

"The land-breeze failed her before she got much way upon her, it appears, sir," Lt. Westcott said, turning to Lewrie. "She looks aground on the eastern breakwater . . . must have been crowded onto the shallows."

"Or, carried there by the tide, with no steerage way," Lewrie supposed aloud. "Mister Caldwell?"

"Uhm, there's a rocky shoal, upon which they built the breakwater, sir," the Sailing Master quickly supplied, with no need to refer to his harbour chart. "And a wide field of spoil rock and sand either side of it, and, if not dredged properly, has encroached on the entrance channel. Do the Trades turn brisk, she'll pound herself open. Poor devils."

A British rowing boat, one waiting to take possession of a prize, was wheeling about and stroking hard towards the French frigate, now to render what assistance she could. Another, the flagship's barge that had borne Lewrie and the others to the Cap François quays the day before, was approaching her, too, now displaying a long signal flag held up by her Midshipman; "Assistance."

"Now, *he's* come prepared for anything," Lewrie japed.

"Is there any aid we might give them, sir?" Lt. Spendlove, ever a generous soul, asked.

"Hmm," was Lewrie's reply as he mulled the matter.

The Frogs could row their anchors out, and warp themselves off, he reckoned in his head; *Or, we could rig tow-lines of the stern anchor cables, but . . . that'd put us on a lee shore, in those rocks.*

"Mister Caldwell, how close could we anchor to her?" Lewrie asked the Sailing Master. "Near enough to pass her towin' cables?"

"Sadly, no, sir," Caldwell told him. "None of our cables are as long as would be needed . . . less the warps taken round the mizen mast or capstan."

One hundred twenty fathoms was the length of the fleet and the bower anchor cables; 720 feet, and *Reliant* would put herself in that French frigate's predicament did they try to get that close.

Lewrie took another long look with his telescope, pondering and mea-suring. "She might need a *lateral* haulin' off, in addition to what forward haul they might get with their own anchors. We enter the harbour, tack round, then come to anchor *abreast* of her . . . ," he schemed aloud. "No," he decided, lowering his glass. Did he sail *Reliant* in, it was good odds that Dessalines and Christophe would mis-interpret it as a bloody *raid*, and fire all that waiting heated shot at *them*. Even if they could dash in, swing wide, and tack round, to try and anchor in the entrance channel by the second, starboard, bower, would leave their stern swinging Sou'west, driven by the Nor'east Trade Wind, and no good for the French would result from that.

"Signal from the flag, sir!" Midshipman Grainger called from the taff-rails, right aft. "Our number, sir, and it's 'Render Assistance.'"

Oh, fuck me! Lewrie groaned; *We would be nearest! Loring won't give up better than fifteen thousand pounds o' prize-money that easily!*

"Very well, Mister Grainger," Lewrie replied with a false air of enthu-siasm. "Hoist a positive reply. Mister Westcott, Mister Caldwell . . . haul our wind and shape a course for the main channel. I wish to come to an-chor a *safe* distance from the frigate, but within decent rowing distance. Mister Spendlove, ready the second bower for dropping, once we've come about. Mister Merriman, see that all our ship's boats are brought up from towin' astern, and ready t'be manned."

"Aye, sir."

"Bosun Sprague!" Lt. Westcott called out. "I'll see two hands on the fore channel platforms, with sounding leads!"

Why couldn't Commodore Loring call on somebody "tarry-handed," 'stead o' me? Lewrie gloomed; *I've never done this in me life!*

CHAPTER FIVE

*H*MS *Reliant* obeyed the flagship's order, but cautiously, feeling her way shoreward under reduced sail, with Lewrie fretting over a chart pinned to the traverse hoard by the compass binnacle cabinet, a ruler and a pair of brass dividers handy.

"Do we come about here, Mister Caldwell," Lewrie posed, "about two cables off the breakwater, in the middle of the channel . . . then, clew ev'rything up quick in Spanish reefs . . ."

"Uhm-hmm, sir," Caldwell replied, already sounding dubious.

". . . we'd glide forrud for a bit, perhaps half a cable more, as the sails are taken in, still in six fathoms o' water," Lewrie went on. "Let go the second bower and lay out but a four-to-one scope, we'd be . . . about *here?*" he said, tapping a tiny circled X in the middle of the entrance channel, just outside the breakwaters.

"In my professional opinion, Captain, I'd not risk it," Caldwell said with a quick shake of his head. "Does the anchor not get purchase at once, we'll drag astern God knows how far. And, *does* it get a firm grip, it would be the *departure* just as bad . . . streaming bows onto the Trades, our stern a'slant the channel without a kedge anchor laid out to keep her head Due North or Nor'west, sir? Soon as we broke the bower loose, we'd drift aground on the *western* breakwater shallows. I'd not recommend it, sir. Strongly."

"Then there's not much we can do to aid them, is there, Mister Caldwell?" Lewrie gravelled, standing fully erect and looking forward over the dipping jib-boom and bow-sprit at the stranded frigate, that was now only a mile off. "Come about and fetch-to, in *ten* fathoms of water, a mile off, and launch our boats, is all."

"Sadly, that would be best, sir," Caldwell grimly allowed.

"Very well, then. Relate that to Mister Westcott, and advise him to when you wish us to put the helm over," Lewrie directed.

Damme, if the Frogs can't get themselves warped off, do I *end up with all her people crowded aboard* my *ship?* Lewrie thought. If all else failed, the French refugees *had* to be saved, even if the valuable frigate was lost to the rebel slaves . . . and what the Commodore would make of that didn't bear thinking about!

I'm deep enough in the "quag" already, over refugees, Lewrie lamented to himself; *French refugees, in particular.*

"Almost there, Mister Caldwell?" Westcott enquired, rocking on the balls of his feet, and his eyes dashing to take in everything that could affect their ship at once.

"Uhmm . . . about half a minute more, sir," Caldwell told him.

"Once we're fetched-to, Mister Westcott, you will have the ship 'til I return," Lewrie announced of a sudden, just after the idea came to his mind. "I'll take my gig over t'see what needs doin'."

"Ah . . . aye aye, sir!"

"Ahem!" from Caldwell.

"Ready about!" from Lt. Westcott in a quarterdeck bellow, with the aid of a speaking-trumpet.

"I'll save you a *jeune fille*," Lewrie told Westcott with a smirk.

"Ready all? Ready all? Helm's *alee!*"

And round *Reliant* swept, even under reduced sail, rapidly going about. "*Rise,* tacks and sheets!" And she kept on swinging, cross the eyes of the Trade Wind, sails rustling and slatting like musket fire, her jibs and stays and spanker whooshing over to larboard, and quickly hauled taut to keep forward drive on her on the starboard tack, whilst the square sails were wheeled about, pivotting on their rope-and-ball parrels about the masts, most clewed up into untidy bag shapes, "Spanish reefed," and the fore-course and fore tops'l braced flat a'back to keep her from driving forward under the jibs' pressure. She ghosted on for a bit, slowing, slowing, then . . .

"Do the Trades pipe up, Mister Westcott, use the second bower, if you think it truly necessary, and we'll use our boats to haul her bows off-wind enough to get way back on her," Lewrie said, readying himself to debark. "If we can't get that Frog frigate off, then . . . well, we may end up with a horde o' guests aboard, 'til we parcel 'em out to the rest of the squadron."

"Aye aye, sir," Lt. Westcott said, nodding in surprise, teeth bared in a "news to me" grin.

"That way, you can choose your *own* young lady, without trustin' *my* taste," Lewrie said, leaning close to mutter.

Lewrie took all four of *Reliant*'s boats, his gig, the cutter, the launch, and the jolly-boat, each with a Midshipman aboard: Mister Houghton, his competent but dull twenty-one-year-old; Mister Entwhistle, "the honourable" nineteen-year-old; Mister Warburton, their cheeky sixteen-year-old; and lastly, Mister Munsell, only thirteen, but shaping main-well as a tarry-handed tarpaulin lad, all his most experienced.

The French frigate, *Chlorinde*, Lewrie noted from her name-board, *seemed* to be in decent shape . . . so far. She sat fully upright on an even keel, and did not seem to have taken the ground so jarringly that her masts had sprung; her upper masts and yards still stood, her lower mast trunks were picture-perfect vertical. She just wasn't *going* anywhere, and, though she was solidly aground and seemingly at rest, her hull gave off alarming groans of timbers and thumping, strained scantling planking as her outer hull rose and thudded on the rocky bottom.

"Hoy, the ship!" Lewrie called as his gig came alongside of her larboard entry-port. Irritatingly, no one paid him any mind. Instead, he could hear rhythmic chanting of French "pulley-hauley," then noted that *Chlorinde*'s main course yard was being used as a crane. Slowly, a 12-pounder or 18-pounder gun was hoisted clear above her starboard bulwarks, even more slowly swung clear of the hull, and lowered. They were lightening ship by jettisoning all her artillery overside, to the shallow side.

There were more *basso* grunts as more of her crew laboured on the capstan. Her best bower anchor had been rowed out towards the channel depths, and the cable was now bar-taut, in an effort to drag her bows free. No matter how strongly her people breasted to the capstan bars, though, dug their shoes or bare toes into the deck and pressed forward with all their strength, that didn't seem to be of any avail so far.

"Bugger their side-party," Lewrie muttered. His bow man had a good grip with a gaff on the frigate's main chain platform, and his gig was close alongside. Lewrie stood and made his way through his oarsmen, stepped onto the boat's gunn'l, and hopped onto the platform. "With me, Desmond, Furfy."

"Aye, sor!" his Irish Cox'n replied.

The battens were not sanded, and the man-ropes strung loose on either hand of the battens were old and grey, but they held. Lewrie made his way upwards, step at a time, thinking that stringing the man-ropes through the battens to make taut hand-rails, as his own Navy did, made a lot more sense.

"Anybody home?" Lewrie asked once he'd gained the larboard gangway. "Anybody bloody *care*?" As he'd judged the day before, there *were* at least a thousand people aboard the *Chlorinde,* sailors, soldiers of Infantrie de Marine, survivors of infantry regiments from shore, and civilians everywhere, all intent on heaving things overside on the far side of the ship.

"*Qui vive, m'sieur?*" a French Midshipman asked him, eyes wide in surprise. "Uhm, *M'sieur le Capitaine?*"

"Lewrie . . . Royal Navy . . . here to . . . *pourvoir assistance?* Or, *secours?*" he answered, pointing out towards his fetched-to frigate.

"Ah, *mais oui*! Lieutenant Veeloughby? *M'sieur?*" the Midshipman said with a relieved smile, then turned to bellow.

"What the bloody . . . ! Aha!" a Royal Navy officer, his hat off and his waist-coat undone, barked, crossing the quarterdeck through a throng of furiously labouring people to Lewrie. "Josiah Willoughby, sir, of the *Hercule,* seventy-four."

"Alan Lewrie, the *Reliant* frigate," Lewrie replied. "Sorry we can't get her close aboard you, but . . . we'd end up in the same predicament. I've four boat crews and some spare hands with me, so . . . what needs doing, first, Mister Willoughby?"

"Just about everything, sir!" Lt. Willoughby quickly replied with a disarming grin. "Cast her guns and carriages overboard, and may the rebels have joy of them . . . all her roundshot. We've started her water butts, gotten a bower out. No joy there, yet, but we're trying, and the French sailors are doing their best."

"My cutter could take her kedge out to mid-channel, to wrench her stern free, if there's something that could serve as a capstan, or a purchase," Lewrie offered.

"That'd be grand, sir . . . though, she's already beat off her rudder, so, do we manage to get her off before the rebels open fire on her, there's no telling of how she'll handle."

"We'll get right to it. Desmond, summon all our boats under her transom, and tell Mister Houghton to be ready to take aboard a kedge."

"Right away, sor!"

A chorus of axes rang out as a gun carriage, too heavy to bear up in one piece, was being hacked to bits below on her gun-deck, with the resulting chunks heaved out open gun-ports.

"I've cut away her second bower, sir, and jettisoned its cable, and was just *about* to jettison the kedge and *its* cable, before your arrival," Willoughby related, taking a second to mop his streaming face with a handkerchief and allow himself a rueful grin. "Don't *quite* know if we can get her afloat before the forts set us all afire."

For a fellow in his straits, Lt. Willoughby was in a damnably good mood, as if danger and difficulties were his meat and drink.

"If you can't, I s'pose we could ferry her people out to my ship," Lewrie offered. "Women and children first, though I don't know how the rest would feel about standin' passive and takin' heated shot as we do so."

"It's a wonder the rebels haven't already, sir," Willoughby said with another of those beaming grins. "The deadline's long past."

"Well, you keep on doin' what you're doin', Mister Willoughby, and I'll see to her kedge," Lewrie told him, tapping the brim of his hat as Lt. Willoughby knuckled his own brow in shared salutes.

Once back in his gig, Lewrie had himself rowed aft to the tuck-under of *Chlorinde*'s squared-off stern, where Midshipman Houghton and his cutter were waiting. A leather hawse-buckler was torn free, then a kedge cable was passed through the hawse-hole, then taken back onto the deck to be seized to the upper ring of the so-far-unseen anchor.

Long minutes later, and the kedge appeared, suspended from its cable, with handling lines bound to its upper cross-arms to ease the thing down. Midshipman Houghton, an excellent boat-handler, chivvied the cutter forward a foot or so, aft a foot or so, then starboard for a few feet 'til the kedge—nowhere as monstrous-heavy as a bower, but still a weight to be reckoned with—could be lowered into the midships of his boat.

"No after capstan, sorry, Captain Lewrie, but, they've a fair-heavy windlass, for purchase!" Lt. Willoughby called down, sticking his head and shoulders over the taffrails for a second; now coat-less, to boot.

"Pass me two more lighter lines, Mister Willoughby, and we'll see what we can do towards haulin' her stern off," Lewrie said back.

"Done, and done, sir!" Willoughby right-cheerfully shouted.

Ye'd think he relishes this! Lewrie sarcastically thought, as two more four-inch lines were heaved over, through after gun-ports as if by magic.

"One for you, Mister Entwhistle, and one for you, Mister Warburton," Lewrie ordered. "Lash down, and haul away!"

Eight oarsmen in the launch, only six oarsmen in the smaller jolly-boat, could not generate much effort with those lighter lines; once extended to their full length, the boats remained in one place, no matter how hard *Reliant*'s people strained. It was the kedge cable that bore the bulk of the draw, once Midshipman Houghton let it go over the side at mid-channel, at right-angles to *Chlorinde*'s hull. The cable went bar-taut, rising from the water, dripping water, then spraying droplets and groaning as it was wrung like a wash-rag by the strain put on it by the lower-deck windlass aboard the French frigate.

"I could take one of those light lines, sir," Houghton offered once he'd returned from deploying the anchor. "I've more hands aboard than the jolly-boat."

"Aye, go close aboard her, and call for Lieutenant Will . . . ," Lewrie began to say, before he spotted what he took for an abandoned admiral's barge being rowed out to them from shore by a crew of shirtless, dark brown oarsmen. "Willoughby!" he bellowed aloft, instead. "*Trouble* coming!"

"I've seen them, sir!" Willoughby shouted down to him. "What should we do? Begin evacuation?"

"I'll try to stall them," Lewrie replied, wondering just how he'd pull *that* off. "Hold on a bit . . . I *know* that bugger!"

In the stern-sheets of that gaudy barge was Colonel Mirabois, their interpreter of the day before.

"Row us out to the barge, Desmond, meet her as far from the Frog ship as you can," Lewrie urged, standing up in his own stern-sheets, a hand on Midshipman Munsell's shoulder. He waved his hat and dug a white handkerchief from his breeches' pocket to wave, too, in *lieu* of a proper flag of truce.

"Hallo, Colonel Mirabois! *Comment allez-vous, ce après-midi?*"

"Ah, *bonjour, Capitaine Le . . . Capitaine!*" Colonel Mirabois said back as his barge slowed. The barge was commanded by a young fellow in the uniform of an *Aspirant* of the French Navy, its Cox'n a *cigaro*-chomping brute in a sleeveless shirt, two bandoliers for cartridge boxes, and a cutlass, his phyz as a'squint as a pissed-off pirate.

"Let us talk, Colonel," Lewrie offered with a false grin on his face, once he'd determined that they could confer at least an hundred yards short of the frigate. "Easy all on yer oars, hey?"

"*Capitaine Le . . .* Luray . . . *pardon, soulement,* z'ere ees *une difficile, n'est-ce pas?*" Mirabois said, seated amidships of his padded thwart, booted feet planted primly together, and his hands gripping the edge of the thwart in a death-grip. Even his dark complexion looked ashen, as if he was terrified to be out in a boat on the water.

"A difficulty, Colonel?" Lewrie genially asked as the oarsmen of the barge, and his gig, tossed their oars so the two boats could come gunn'l-to-gunn'l. "What sort?"

"Z'is ship ees still in ze 'arbour, *Capitaine, et* eet ees long pas' ze deadline for departure," Colonel Mirabois said, his smile the sort of rictus seen on a corpse who'd died terrified. "*Mon* generals, Dessalines, Christophe, Petion, z'ey send me to deman' eet's surrender, *et* ze surrender of all *Blancs* in 'er. If z'ey do *not* ze surrender, ze forts are prepar-ed w'iz ze 'eated shot, *comprendre?* If z'ey do not ze surrender *immédiatement,* I weel signal for such to be done. *Z'at* ees ze *difficile, M'sieur Capitaine.*"

"She's aground, Colonel . . . we're tryin' t' warp her free," Lewrie told him. "It's not *their* fault they haven't left harbour."

"Z'at ees of no matter, *Capitaine,*" Mirabois told him, somewhat firmer than before.

"There are British sailors aboard her, rendering assistance," Lewrie rejoined, stiffening his back and turning grimmer, himself. "I must protest. *Royal Navy* sailors of His Britannic Majesty aboard her, *comprendre,* Colonel? His Majesty, King George the Third, would deem such an action on your part as an act of war against Great Britain. We've been here, before, Colonel . . . do you want *another* ten years of foreigners in Hayti?"

"*Vous* v'ould perish as ze French 'ave perish-ed!" Mirabois shot back, getting his own back up.

"We get her warped off and under way, this little *emmerdement* is solved, Colonel," Lewrie suggested. "Give us 'til sundown. If we can't save the ship, then we are determined to rescue the Frenchmen aboard her."

"*Défendu!*" Colonel Mirabois barked of a sudden; it was a word that Lewrie had never encountered. "Z'at ees . . . forbidden! Ve mus' 'ave z'em all, eef z'ey weel not sail away! *Non, non!*"

Got the stew-pots lit, already, have ye? Lewrie sourly told himself, sure that everyone ashore was looking forward to one, last hearty massacre of White people.

"For the moment, Colonel Mirabois, I intend to return aboard her, and see what progress is being made," Lewrie temporised. "Now, if you wish to open fire upon her whilst *I'm* there, well . . . one might consider the consequences of any rash action. Once I've ascertained our progress, I'll come back to speak with you, if you'll wait here?"

Killing British sailors, killing gentlemen-officers, and one of them a Post-Captain, evidently seemed to check Mirabois's ardour for blood; there most-like *could* be a very long war with Great Britain if he waved his signal; a war his masters surely would wish to avoid. He agreed to the delay, ill-mannered and as petulant as any Frenchman.

"Hoy, Mister Willoughby!" Lewrie shouted up to the *Chlorinde's* quarterdeck once his gig was back alongside. "What-ho?"

"She's coming, sir, inch by inch, but she's coming free!" that energetic worthy called back down, still sporting that joyous, beamish grin of his. "Might I enquire what the rebels said to you, sir?"

"Surrender her and all her people for massacre, perhaps as the *entrée* for the celebration supper, instanter, or they'll fire heated shot into her, sir! I've warned him that there are *British* sailors aboard, and that he'd best give it a *long* think, if he don't wish a new war with *us!*" Lewrie called back, grinning in spite of things, himself. "Let us work her off, cut their losses, call it a bad—"

"That gives me a *marvellous* idea, sir, if you will indulge me for a moment?" Lt. Willoughby interrupted. "Be back in a trice!"

He'll inflate the hot-air balloons the women've made from their silk gowns, and he's ready t'fly her off? Lewrie thought.

Several hundred voices, male and female, began to sing, of all the daft things! It was the French national anthem, that boisterous, blood-thirsty, martial tune. There came the sharp, crack of a swivel-gun, a light 2-pounder, then the Tricolour was fluttering down from the after staff, and cut free to drape the entire stern.

Up went a British Union Jack in its place.

Willoughby came back to the bulwarks, with a French officer in a fore-and-aft bicorne hat and gilt epaulets.

"Captain Lewrie, sir! Instead of waiting 'til she's made her offing to strike her colours, her captain, here, has agreed to strike now . . . making *Chlorinde* a British prize, and, un-officially, a ship now to be reckoned a warship in the Royal Navy!" Lt. Willoughby cried down to Lewrie. "Do they open on her, it surely *will* be a war!"

"Oh, *very* good, Lieutenant Willoughby! Mine arse on a *band-box*, but that's good!" Lewrie congratulated him. "I will relate the news to Colonel Mirabois . . . and hope he chokes on it!"

. . .

It was late afternoon before *Chlorinde*, many tons lighter, finally hauled her hull off the rocks. Despite the loss of her rudder and some stove-in underwater planking, resulting in several leaks that could be patched with fothering and spare canvas, she floated; she'd not sink!

"Once you've made your offing, signal me if you need towing," Lewrie offered, ready to depart for *Reliant*, and a celebratory glass of something cool and alcoholic. "One *hellish-fine* piece of work ye did, Mister Willoughby. Should your captain need a seconding to your report of the day, he's but to ask."

"Thank you for saying so, Captain Lewrie, and I expect we *will* need a tow," Lt. Willoughby replied, looking exhausted but immensely pleased with an arduous job well done.

"Ehm . . . I wonder if we're related or not, Mister Willoughby," Lewrie hesitantly asked, making the younger officer cock his head in expectation of a pleasing coincidence. "My father is Sir Hugo Saint George Willoughby. His family's estate *was* in Kent . . . was once with the Fourth Regiment of Foot, 'The King's Own' . . . then with the 'John Company' army in India, commanding the Nineteenth Native Infantry?"

"Uhm," Lt. Willoughby replied, looking as if he fought a grimace, or a beetle had just pinched his testicles. "Sir Hugo, you say? And . . . might *his* father have been one *Stanhope* Willoughby, who once resided near Linton?"

Heard *of us!* Lewrie sadly realised.

"I believe he is, though he didn't talk of him, much," Lewrie told him. *And, with damned good reason,* he told himself; *Father can't hold a candle t'that old scoundrel's sins! The both of us are pikers, in comparison . . . eligible t'take Holy Orders!*

"Oh, that would be the, ehm . . . that *would* make us kin, sir. Of a *sort*, though . . . ," Lt. Willoughby hemmed and hawed, nigh to blushing.

"Well, I won't mention the connexion, if you won't. No sense lettin' on you're related t'that old rogue . . . or us. Bein' the son and grand-son to 'em is bad enough."

"Quite understood, sir, thank you," Willoughby said with a very relieved smile. "The French wish to give you departing honours, sir. After the assistance you rendered them, and me, they appear grateful . . . for Frenchmen. An admiral's side-party . . . minus the muskets."

"And I'll accept, gladly," Lewrie said, grinning.

CHAPTER SIX

*C*ommodore Loring took his prizes, his prisoners, and his waif-like refugees back to Kingston, Jamaica, as quick as he could quit the coast, escorting, or guarding, the French and their vessels with his entire squadron. Well, almost all of his squadron.

The much smaller four-ship squadron, of which HMS *Reliant* was a part, which had been despatched under "Independent Orders" to pursue the French ships that had sailed from Holland back in May, had never been Loring's favourites, from the time they had entered the Gulf of Mexico and Loring's bailiwick, his "patch," without the usual courtesy call at Kingston to announce their presence. It hadn't helped to form good relations with the senior officer on the Jamaica Station that they had hunted down their quarry off the Chandeleur Islands of Louisiana and had brought them to action and beaten them, taking four prizes in honourable battle, either; the Royal Navy in the West Indies had been successful at taking *islands,* but that sort of knock-down-drag-out sea fight had so far eluded them . . . most pointedly, Commodore Loring.

Their assigned duty done, Captain Stephen Blanding's four ships—the 64-gun *Modeste, Reliant,* and a brace of older 32-gun frigates, *Cockerel* and *Pylades*—had been sent to loiter off the other harbours of Hispaniola, both the bloody Saint Domingue and the Spanish Santo Domingo (even though the Spanish showed no signs of becoming belligerents and French allies, again); the almost total elimination of their over-seas trade and hundreds of merchant ships, the drubbing they had gotten at the Battle of Cape St. Vincent in 1797, and the general ineffectiveness of their Navy in European waters might have made the Dons leery of taking another shot at war.

And so it was, again. Commodore Loring's last orders, before he danced over the horizon with a fine following wind, was for Blanding's little clutch of ships to make a final reconnoiter of Saint Domingue's, or Hayti's, lesser seaports, and report back to Kingston . . . *after* the welcomes and celebration balls!

"Ah well, such is Navy politics," Captain Blanding told them all with a dramatic heave of his broad shoulders, punctuating those words with so loud and trailing a sigh that he sounded much like a "Montague" skewered by a "Capulet" sword in *Romeo and Juliet,* and "eating all the scenery" as he over-dramatically "expired."

Lewrie hid his smirk at Captain Blanding's antics; the man was one of the most eccentric officers ever he'd met in his whole naval career. It was uncanny how boisterous, loud, and excitable Blanding could be.

"A glass with you all, gentlemen," Blanding proposed, as both of his cabin stewards bustled about to top up their wine. There were only six of them dining this evening as the squadron stood "off and on" the coast, out into deeper, open water, then back. Captain Blanding liked to dine his captains in, quite often, and, over the months since they'd first gotten orders to serve together, had, for the most part, formed a "chummy" association.

In addition to Lewrie there was Captain Parham, a younger fellow with a single gilt epaulet on his right shoulder, denoting that he was a Post-Captain of less than three years' seniority. Parham had served in HMS *Jester,* Lewrie's first major command, as a Midshipman, and now had HMS *Pylades.* Parham was a very likable and pleasant fellow. HMS *Cockerel*'s captain, Stroud, was also new to his "Post" rank, once the First Officer of *Myrmidon,* a Sloop of War that Lewrie's *Jester* had been teamed with in the Mediterranean and Adriatic in 1796. Stroud was the odd-man-out; he was workman-like, immensely competent, but immensely dull in social situations. Yet, at the same time, if he *wasn't* included in off-duty things, he took it as a slight, and was ever pressing for his *Cockerel* to be given the lead, to prove what he, and she, could accomplish. They all walked small, round Stroud!

And, with their host came Captain Blanding's First Lieutenant, James Gilbraith, "Jemmy the One," as Blanding sometimes teasingly called him.

In point of fact, he and Blanding were both much alike: big, bluff, hearty, and stout, extremely fond of their "tucker," and it did not do to get between them and the sideboard or dining table. Jemmy Gilbraith was also one of those poor fellows whose hide did not agree with harsh tropic sunlight; he was forever red and peeling.

Lastly, there was Blanding's Chaplain, and a rarity aboard most Royal Navy ships, the Reverend Stanley Brundish, for the very good reason that most "padres" *willing* to ship aboard were the equivalent of the Church of England's ne'er-do-wells, its drunks and failures with so few of the vitally necessary connexions and "interest" that could not land a rectory or curacy even in the poorest London "stew."

Brundish, however, was from Captain Blanding's own parish, and was a distant "cater-cousin," an erudite and well-read fellow in his mid-thirties who could actually put together a sensible, logical homily, instead of droning through bought sheafs of sermons written by others, and could cite *correct* chapter and verse off the top of his head, quite unlike the "Mar-Text" reverends Lewrie had come across. Brundish also had a voice like a Bosun's that could reach the beak-heads from the quarterdeck nettings, could stir up a crew with the enthusiasm of leaping Methodists, tailored his homilies with nautical references, and encouraged all with loud, lustily-sung hymns of the muscular sort. Chaplain Brundish was a constant presence by Captain Blanding's side . . . if only to keep him from cursing and blaspheming.

"I give you a duty most honourably done, at long last!" their senior officer intoned, seconded by a hearty, "Hear him!" from Lieutenant Gilbraith, and they all emulated Captain Blanding by tossing back goodly gulps; though they skipped licking their lips and smacking, as he did.

"Well, sirs . . . supper is laid, and a toothsome repast I assure you it will be," Blanding promised. "Let us take seats, what?"

A fine meal it was, too, and a most jovial one. When close on the Haitian shore the day before, one of *Modeste*'s Midshipmen had come across a sea turtle, and it made for a thick and meaty soup. "I saved some turtle meat for your blasted cats, Captain Lewrie, haw haw!" the squadron commander joshed.

Both Blanding and Brundish fancied themselves talented anglers, and, whilst *Modeste* had sat fetched-to off Cap François, or cruised at bare steerageway, they had hauled in a large red snapper and a small grouper. Captain Blanding's personal cook had turned the grouper into breaded tarts, using dust from the bottom of the bread bags and flour, a puree of "portable" pea soup, paprika, and fresh lemon juice. Those tarts came as a second appetiser on a large platter for all to share, whilst the red snapper made their first *entrée*.

Following those dishes came a roast quail for each guest. Captain Blanding insisted on quail and squabs, along with ducklings and chicks, to be stocked in *Modeste*'s forecastle manger, along with the usual piglets and goat kids, since they are so little and matured so quickly. Captain Blanding was right high on rabbits, too, for like reasons. Their removes were boiled potatoes, somewhat fresh from the chandleries at Kingston, and mixed beans in sweet oil and vinegar, with fine-diced onion. Captain Blanding was *very* fond of beans of all sorts!

Next came a pork roast with cracklings; a *bordeaux* replaced the *sauvignon blanc* to accompany it. Last, before the nuts, cheese, and port bottle, came an approximation of an apple pie split six ways; the apples were from England, shrivelled and old, but stretched out with soaked ship's bisquit, with extra sugar and goat's milk's sweetness to disguise the lack of actual fruit.

Through the meal there had been a great deal of relieved japing and chit-chat, now the French had surrendered and struck their flags without casualties, with Lewrie's tale of going ashore to beard those devils, Dessalines, Christophe, and Clairveaux, in their own den one of the highpoints, then the rescue of *Chlorinde* for yet another source of amusement.

"I must say, Captain Lewrie, you have developed quite a talent for rescuing French people in their most desperate moments," Brundish said, leaning forward on the table with a glint of glee in his eyes; a tad canted by drink, and the glint might have been a bit un-focussed.

"Confusion to the French!" Parham proposed, which prompted all to up-end their glasses and wait for refills.

"Man of many parts, is Captain Lewrie," Gilbraith said loudly.

"Just as the Good Lord has bestowed upon you, sir, the talent for making war," Brundish went on, "perhaps He also blessed you with an innate skill which only now emerges. War, implacable, then mercy in war's aftermath, perhaps? As befits a Christian gentleman."

"An *English* gentleman!" young Parham stuck in. "Hear, hear!"

"I'd rather not make a habit of it, though, Reverend," Lewrie replied, trying to shrug a serious moment off with humour. "God also gifted mankind with the joy of music, an ear for its enjoyment, and a talent for makin' it, but . . . look what I've made o' *that'un*!"

His tootling on his humble penny-whistle was legendarily *bad*.

"Saving the dashed French from the results of the folly they get into is one thing, Brundish," Captain Blanding told him. "Saving the French from overweening pride . . . Popery, or that heretical Napoleon Bonaparte and his global ambitions, is quite another."

"Successful war cures *some* of those problems, sir," Lieutenant Gilbraith pointed out. "Pride . . . ambitions. We can handle that."

"And *you* may convert them from Popery, sir," Lewrie suggested to Chaplain Brundish. "Or, *are* they outright atheists, *lead* them to salvation."

"Now, *that'd* be as hard as making them *humble,* haw!" Captain Blanding hooted.

"Just so, sir! Well said!" Lt. Gilbraith seconded.

Toady! Lewrie thought him. Still, it worked for Gilbraith, and for Blanding, too, who laid back his head and bellowed laughter to the overhead. A glass later, and the tablecloth was whisked away, and the cheese, nuts, sweet bisquits, and the port, with fresh glasses, were laid for them. As the bottle circulated larboardly round the table, Captain Blanding got a speculative look on his phyz.

"I wonder, gentlemen, do we discuss our orders for a moment in . . . well, I cannot term it *sobriety,* haw haw! But, could any of you tell me the value of making yet another circumnavigation of the island of Hispaniola, and peeking into every little dam . . . blasted harbour?"

That thought didn't sober them up, but it did shut them up, for a bit; 'til Captain Stroud, who'd been mostly quiet during supper, silently appreciating the camaraderie, hesitantly spoke up.

"Well, sir, I expect we could forgo Port-Au-Prince. The French lost it long ago," he said.

"Anything in the Gulf of Gonaïves," Parham seconded, looking a tad squiffy, himself; pie-eyed in point of fact, and sure to need the bosun's sling to get back aboard his own ship, later. Perhaps into his gig from *Modeste!*

"Gonaïves, Saint Marc, Leogane," Lewrie recalled off the top of his head. "The Isle Gonâve, too? I b'lieve we can safely determine the rebels hold all those. After we peek into Port de Paix and Mole Saint Nicholas tomorrow, the last place a French detachment could yet be holding out would be at Jérémie, on the Sou'west peninsula's tip, and that would just about do it, as far as the French half of Hispaniola goes."

"We *know* Jacmel, on the Southern coast, is rebel-held," Lieutenant Gilbraith supplied.

"Explore the Spanish half?" Blanding asked, gesturing impatiently for the port bottle.

"Well, sir," Stroud cautiously replied, looking suspiciously sober in comparison to his supper-mates. "There's General Kerverseau and his . . . regiment? . . . taken over Santo Domingo from the Spanish, and that General Ferrand at Santiago, with the few troops *he* was able to evacuate, but . . . Commodore Loring already had us look into their situation before we rejoined him, here off Cap François, and I can't see anything changing in the last week."

"Don't know whether those two blasted scoundrels are setting up their own little empires, or have interned themselves with the Dons," Captain Blanding grumbled. He took a sip of port, smacked his lips, and added, "And, it's not as if there will be any other deuced French ships coming to rescue them, any time soon, hey? Did they not flee in local luggers, and such?"

Deuced . . . he's found another substitute for "bloody," Lewrie thought, with a grin; *Or "damned"!*

"We saw no sea-going vessels in either port, sir," Lt. Gilbraith reminded him. "They're surely stuck 'til next Epiphany."

"Couldn't have gotten away with much in the way of victuals, so, when they run short, they will have to start . . . requisitioning from the local Spanish," Parham supposed aloud.

"Best not have landed short of ammunition, then!" Lewrie stuck in with a snicker. "Once they start in stealin', hmm?"

"Or, mess with the Spanish women!" Lt. Gilbraith hooted.

"Don't quite *know* if our superiors ordered those ports watched," Captain Blanding grumbled on, sounding querulous. "But, I think we may consider our orders fulfilled by looking into Port de Paix, Mole Saint Nicholas, then Jérémie, before sailing for Jamaica to rejoin the Commodore. Captain Stroud?"

"Aye, sir?" Stroud perked up, eager for any duty to show what he was made of, and make a name, after so many years in the background.

"I'd admire did you and *Cockerel* look into Port de Paix in the morning," Blanding instructed. "And, though it's good odds that those rebel slaves have invested the old buccaneer haunt, the Isle of Tortuga cross the strait from Port de Paix, you might go in as close inshore as you may, for a look-see, as well."

"Of course, sir . . . delighted," Stroud replied, trying to hide a grin and maintain his serious façade.

"I'll place *Modeste* off the coast, halfway 'twixt Port de Paix and Mole Saint Nicholas," Blanding went on. "Within signalling range of all ships.

Fetch to . . . stand off-and-on under tops'ls . . . get some more fishing in, hey, Reverend, haw haw?"

"Oh, haul in a *large* grouper, this time, aye, sir!" the Reverend enthused. "Nigh as toothsome as lobster flesh, ha ha!"

"Lewrie . . . you and Captain Parham's *Pylades* are to sail into the Mole Saint Nicholas . . . close enough to determine if that bast—"

"Ahem, sir," Chaplain Brundish gently chid him.

". . . If that *worthy* General Noailles still holds the port, and determine how many, and what sort, of vessels he still possesses," their squadron commander grumpily amended. "Make a show of force, for whomsoever still is there . . . seagulls, crabs, the French, or the Blacks. If Noailles *is* there, make him the same offer Commodore Loring made General Rochambeau . . . I'm in no mood to fart-arse about . . . shilly-shally, rather, *ahem*! Sail out, fire off a gun for his honour, then strike to us."

"And, if he's made a similar accommodation with whichever Black general's in charge of the siege . . . ," Lewrie replied with a touch of worry. "Damme, that means I'll have t'go ashore and deal with one o' those devils, too."

"Ahem," Chaplain Brundish admonished *his* "damme," too!

Oh, buggery! Lewrie thought; *If a sailor can't curse, what's the bloody world comin' to, I ask ye! It'll be no* drinkin', *next! Hmm* . . .

He drummed his fingers on the dining table, considering that once a fellow was made "Post," it was understood that the only way his lieutenants, juniors, and favoured *protégés* could advance their own careers would be for *them* to go off and perform something neck-or-nothing dangerous, to get favourable notice in reports at Admiralty, be "Gazetted" in a London paper which would be read *everywhere*, and have the reports from their captains re-printed in *The Novel Chronicle* . . . whilst said Post-Captains sat back and fretted in relative comfort and a lot more safety!

I could send Westcott, his French is bags *better than mine*, he silently speculated; *He* seems *hellish-eager t'stand out.*

"Yet another opportunity to exercise your new-found talent for rescuing Frenchmen, Captain Lewrie," Chaplain Brundish told him.

"Or, palaver with the Saint Domingues," Parham added. "Twice in two days."

"Well, I was just there for show, mostly," Lewrie had to admit. "It was Captain John Bligh Number Two, and Captain Barré, who did the most of the negotiations. Their French was better. I just stood by, and got cussed at."

"Yet, if the Black generals round Mole Saint Nicholas have much the same skill with proper French, sir, 'stead of Creole *patois,* then you'd be on a part with them!" Parham teased.

"Or, perhaps I should delegate, and send *you,* Parham!" Lewrie said in mock-warning, with a leering grin directed down-table.

"And here I always thought you *liked* me, sir!" Parham exclaimed, laughing uproariously, in which all joined in; Lewrie, too, just to show that he really didn't *mean* it . . . much.

"Just so long as none of my officers end up on a platter, with an apple in his mouth, sizzlin' on a bed of rice, by . . . Jove!" Captain Blanding bellowed, slamming a meaty fist on the dining table, and laughing so hard that he had to lay hold of his middle to prevent his shaking to pieces.

"Sirs . . . if I may?" Captain Stroud asked in his ponderous and sober way, once that amusement had petered out, wiggling his glass in suggestion. "A toast to the morrow?"

"Aye, Stroud! Charge your glasses, sirs!" Blanding agreed.

"Gentlemen, I give you 'confusion . . . and cowardice! . . . to the French!'" Stroud grimly intoned, and they tipped their heads and their port glasses back to "heel-taps" at that worthy sentiment.

CHAPTER SEVEN

"How deep into the harbour, past the mole, *is* a 'show of force,' d'ye think, Mister Westcott?" Lewrie asked his First Lieutenant as HMS *Reliant*, followed by Parham and *Pylades,* stood in towards the middle of the entrance channel to Mole St. Nicholas. "Oh, Chalky, ye wee bloody pest . . . not now!"

The grey-blotched white cat had been loafing on the canvas covers of the quarterdeck nettings, now full of rolled-up seaman's hammocks, and took Lewrie's nearness, with a day-glass to his eye, a grand time to "board him"; right atop Lewrie's left gilt epaulet, and dig his back claws in deep so he could pluck the gilt-laced coat collar with a free paw, and snuffle Lewrie's left ear.

"Pleased with yerself, are ye?" Lewrie muttered, his head turned and his eyes almost crossed, nose-to-nose with the cat.

"I'll take him, sir . . . and, fetch a whisk," Lewrie's chief cabin steward, Pettus, offered, reaching out to take Chalky down and away.

"Aloft, there!" Lewrie bellowed to Midshipman Warburton in the main-mast cross-trees. "Anything to report?"

"No vessels in port, sir!" Warburton shouted back, a telescope to his own eye. "*Small* boats . . . at the quays, and drawn up onto the beach, sir! No French flags flying!"

Chalky was not taking his removal well; he made close-mouthed *Mrrs!*

of displeasure at Pettus as he was set down on the deck planking, then leapt back atop the hammock nettings to join Toulon, nose-to-nose, as if to complain . . . or pick a fight.

"It's early enough, sir, that we still have the land-breeze," Mr. Caldwell, the Sailing Master, pointed out. "It may prevail for an hour more, before the Trades take over. Or, less, depending?"

"Deck, there!" Midshipman Warburton called down anew. "There's a cutter under sail! Coming out towards the moles, sir!"

"What flag?" Lewrie shouted to him.

"Flag of truce, sir!"

"Signal to *Pylades*, Mister Grainger," Lewrie snapped over his shoulder to the signals Midshipman of the watch. "Put about to fetch-to. Ready about, as well, Mister Westcott, soon as the hoist is down. Soon as the way's off her, I'd admire was my gig ready t'row over to speak whoever it is in that cutter."

"Aye aye, sir!" Westcott replied, then began to snap out orders to helmsmen, brace-tenders, and the duty watch to prepare the ship for a slight wheel-about to put her bows into the wind off the hills, and bring her to relative rest.

"*Pylades* shows 'Acknowledged,' sir," Grainger announced.

"Very well . . . strike the hoist for the 'Execute,'" Lewrie told him, looking aft to squint at *Pylades*, which had already swung off to *Reliant*'s larboard quarter, about half a mile astern. Standing in on the early morning land-breeze, almost "Close hauled" already, yet *gliding* slow and swan-like on such a weak wind, it would not take much to bring both frigates to a halt.

Lewrie paced over to the starboard ladderway to the main deck, peering over the side, to assure himself that his Cox'n, Liam Desmond, had the gig manned and waiting for him.

"Fetched-to, sir," Lt. Westcott reported.

"I'm off, then. Mind the shop, Mister Westcott," Lewrie said as he made his way to the entry-port, where a side-party was hastily assembling to see him off, with trilling bosun's calls, Marine muskets at Present Arms, and doffed hats from the on-deck crew.

"We'll row over, just outside the breakwaters, and speak that cutter, Desmond," Lewrie said, once settled in the stern-sheets of the gig.

"Cat hair an' all, sor?" Desmond whispered from the corner of his mouth. "I've a damp scrap o' rag that'd do."

He'd not waited for Pettus to fetch up his hand-whisk to remove

Chalky's fur. With Toulon, a white-trimmed black cat, it wasn't quite as bad a chore, but with the littl'un . . . ! Even hanging his coat in the quarter-gallery toilet overnight did not save his uniforms from appearing "spotty" in broad daylight. He took off his cocked hat to inspect it as Desmond put the tiller over and called the stroke; expecting a parley with General Noailles, Lewrie had had his best-dress laid out for the morning, his best hat left in the japanned wood box 'til the very last moment, yet . . . ! "Aye, give me your rag, Desmond," he said with a sigh as he began to sponge down his hat and coat.

"Uhm . . . flag o' truce, sor?" Desmond asked in a soft voice.

"We don't have one aboard? Well, damme . . . ," Lewrie snapped.

S'pose this rag ain't big enough . . . or white enough, either! Lewrie thought. He dug out his own clean, somewhat larger white handkerchief and handed it forward. "Sykes . . . stick this on your gaff, if ye please."

"Aye, sir," the bow-man replied.

"Ugly-lookin' brutes, they is, sor," Desmond commented as they neared the stone breakwaters, and the oncoming cutter.

"Saint Domingue . . . Hayti . . . breeds 'em like mosquitoes, Desmond," Lewrie told him with a faint grin. "Haven't seen any other sort on this island . . . not in six years since I first clapped eyes on the bloody place!"

The oarsmen in the rebel cutter, lolling at ease as long as its lug-sail was up, were the usual ferocious-looking bully-bucks, garbed in loose tan shirts worn un-buttoned for the breeze, most with sleeves cut off at the armpits so their muscular bare arms could show, and the most of them sported ragged-brimmed, nigh-shapeless plaited straw hats on their heads against the sun. Most also wore cartridge-box straps or cutlass bandoliers crossed over their chests.

Astern, at the tiller, sat a younger, frailer-looking fellow of much lighter complexion; a Mulatto, in shirt, waist-coat, and knee-top breeches, with some dead French officer's sword, and a fore-and-aft bicorne. Beside him sat an even larger, darker man who scowled at them as if willing this party of strange *blancs* to drop down and die, that instant. He, too, wore gilt-laced cavalry officer's breeches, sword, a captured officer's coat, and little else, but for a small cocked hat crammed down on his head so hard that the corners drooped towards his shoulders.

"Arrêt!" the man snapped, his voice a deep, menacing *basso;* it was unclear whether he referred to his own boat or Lewrie's.

"Close enough, I think," Lewrie muttered to his Cox'n.

"Easy all, lads!" Desmond ordered. "Toss yer oars!"

The cutter's sail was quickly lowered, its tiller put over, and it swung as if to lay its beam open for a ramming amidships. Desmond heaved on his own tiller to parallel the rebel boat.

"*Bon matin, m'sieur!*" Lewrie called out, smiling. "*Comment allez-vous?*" He introduced himself, then waited for a response. "Ehm . . . any of you speak English? *Parle l'Anglais?*"

"*Va te faire foutre, vous blanc fumier!*" the big man snarled.

"A physical impossibility, *m'sieur . . . quel appellez-vous?*"

"I speak, *en peu, Capitaine,*" the young fellow at the tiller hesitantly, almost fearfully, said, his gaze flitting 'twixt Lewrie and his superior, as if expecting a blow for making the offer. There was a quick, rumbling pala-ver between them before the bigger man shoved the other, as if prodding him to speak for him.

"Colonel Coup-Jarret, 'e ask . . . what ees you' business 'ere,"

Colonel . . . "Cut-Throat"? Damme! Lewrie thought, appalled.

"We have come to see if all the French have fled your country, sir," Lewrie replied, as calmly as he could. "Or, if there are still some French we can kill. They are our enemies, as well, don't ye know."

The young fellow relayed that to Colonel "Cut-Throat," who gave Lew-rie a most distrustful glower, and spat overside before replying in a growl, more slave *patois* than French. Garble-garble-garble, as far as Lewrie could make out.

"Ze Rochambeau, 'e flee Le Cap . . . uhm . . . yesterday?" the young fellow informed them. "Noailles, 'e 'ave, uhm . . . *demi-douzaine? Demi-douzaine* . . ." The fellow looked terrified that he didn't know what that was in English, as if his superior would beat him for *not* knowing.

"A half-dozen, *oui?*" Lewrie offered.

"*Mais oui, demi-douzaine petit navires* . . . ships! *Small* ships! Noailles, 'e go to Havana. 'As depart-ed!" the scared young man said in a rush.

"Port de Paix?" Lewrie prompted.

"No *Française, aucun* . . . none. Umph!" as the bigger man gave him a thump on the shoulder. "Colonel, 'e say you go away, now! No more *blanc diables* mus' come to Haiti, *ever*! You go, now!" he said, taking on his su-perior's urgency and ferocity. "Ze whe . . . *white* devils 'oo come, z'ey will all *die* 'ere! Colonel Coup-Jarret, 'e swears z'is!" To punctuate the last, the Colonel pulled out a long *poignard,* or dagger, pointedly licked down the length of its blade, and grinned so evilly that Lewrie felt his blood chill.

"Well, ehm . . . thankee for the information, *m'sieur,* and we'll be go-ing back to our ship," Lewrie replied, performing a slight bow from the waist and doffing his cocked hat. "Enjoy your new country. Ta ta!' *Au voir*, rather."

Desmond got the gig under way and pointed out seaward, the oarsmen bending the ash looms perhaps a *touch* more strenuously than usual, which suited Lewrie right down to his toes.

"Noailles had already fled? Well, dash it, I say," Blanding said with a sigh as Lewrie and Stroud delivered their reports to him aboard *Modeste,* now the squadron was re-united and striding Sou'-Sou'west for Cape Dame Marie, and Jérémie.

"From what I gathered, sir," Stroud contributed, not wanting to stand about like a useless fart-in-a-trance, "Port de Paix's garrison were forced into Cap François long ago . . . and the rebels indeed have invested the Isle of Tortuga, as well. To keep the French from taking shelter there, where their small boats could not get at them with any hope of . . . well, vengeance, I'd suppose."

"Noailles didn't sail away all *that* long ago, sir," Lewrie pointed out, with a brow up. "It would seem that Commodore Loring did not maintain a constant blockade over any port but Cap François . . . where all the *valuable* prizes were." *If ye get my* meanin', he thought, and waited for the shoe to drop with Blanding. "Noailles, so I gather, had half a dozen vessels, all schooners, luggers, or such, with barely the capacity t'take off what little was left of his troops. God knows if he had room for women and children, too. I did not get ashore to see if the rebels had white prisoners . . . they met me by the breakwaters, and most like would've cut all our throats had we tried. Sorry."

"They say 'discretion's the better part of valour,' Captain Lewrie. No fault of yours," Blanding said, harumphing a bit, even so, at the disappointment of missing the French. "Havana, did they tell you?"

"Aye, sir."

"Well, da . . . blast my eyes," Blanding said. "And Kerverseau and Ferrand were allowed to sail away, as well . . . for want of watching? Can't put *that* in my report to Admiralty . . . dear as I wish to. Wasn't *our* fault the work was but half-done . . . and poorly, at that, by Jove!"

"Well, there's still Guadeloupe, Martinique, a few other isles still in French possession, sir," Lewrie tried to cheer him up. "The French colony of Surinam, down below Barbados? I just missed the expedition t'take it, back in '98. Is our Commodore, or Admiral Sir John Duckworth, still aspiring, and . . . acquisitive . . . perhaps we will be part of the next venture."

"We'll be blockading empty ports, Lewrie," Captain Blanding rejoined with some heat. "Consigned to vague, *far-distant* . . . bloody! . . . uselessness! Out of sight, out of mind, and don't come back 'til our rum's run out, and the water's brown with corruption. God . . . mean to say, *Heavens* above, but this is what success brings, if you ain't a well-known favourite! Spite-and-jealousy. *Spite-and-jealousy!* Pah!"

"Well, sir . . . the bald facts of our reconnoiters, the escape of the French whilst Cap François was blockaded . . . ?" Lewrie hinted. "Do we state . . . all of us . . . that, per orders, we discovered that the foe had managed to escape, with no blame laid on anyone . . . ? It might take Admiralty a year or two t'mull it over, but . . . such reports'd raise a *large* question, wouldn't they?"

"Bedad, Lewrie, but you're a sly one!" Blanding exclaimed, come over all beam-ish of a sudden as he grasped the eventual result.

Bedad? Lewrie thought, almost grimacing to stifle a smile; *He will end up with a whole new slate o' odd curses, 'fore his commission is done!*

"And . . . ," Captain Stroud sagely reminded them, "we've our prize-money from the Chandeleurs, *and* our share of the Commodore's prizes, to boot. Plus the greater glory."

"Stout fellow, Stroud! Dam . . . *stap* me if you ain't!" Blanding congratulated.

BOOK I

The rank is but the guinea stamp,
The man's the gowd for a' that.
-"IS THERE FOR HONEST POVERTY"
ROBERT BURNS (1759-1796)

BOOK I

CHAPTER EIGHT

*W*alking the streets of Kingston, Jamaica, or hiring a prad for a bracing ride in the near countryside, was a lot safer for Captain Alan Lewrie since the Beauman clan had dissolved. With Hugh Beauman's icily beautiful young widow now residing in Portugal, having inherited all, and sold up every last stick of the family's Jamaican plantations—and all their slaves—there was no one to hire bully-bucks to cut his throat in a dark alley, as they'd once threatened soon after Lewrie and his old friend, former Lieutenant Colonel Christopher "Kit" Cashman, had participated in that scandalous duel with former Colonel Ledyard Beauman, and his cousin Captain George Sellers, over who had been at fault for the shameful showing of their island-raised regiment near Port-Au-Prince, when the British Army was still trying to conquer Saint Domingue. Ledyard and his cousin had cheated; Cashman, Lewrie, and the duel judges had shot them down; and Hugh Beauman had been after Lewrie's heart's blood ever since. As a further insult, those slaves that he had . . . "appropriated" . . . had come from one of the Beauman plantations on Portland Bight.

With Hugh Beauman drowned in a shipwreck in the Tagus river entrances in Portugal, the parents long-before retired to England with all their wealth, the Beaumans' little empire had collapsed, absorbed by an host of indifferent others, their newspaper defunct, and their shipping business owned by others. Oh, there were still some distant kin on the island, along with forner employees and business partners, but without Hugh Beauman to direct the hatred, Lewrie was *almost* as safe as houses; the Beauman "syndicate" had evaporated, so Lewrie could dare to depart *Reliant* for shopping, and a shore breakfast, as he had this morning in a rare, and brief, respite from blockading duties.

Modeste, Reliant, Cockerel, and *Pylades* still cruised together as a squadron. There had been a week at anchor following the French surrender at Cap François, then a three-month stint at sea, prowling round the isle of Hispaniola, whilst the ships of the line and frigates of the Jamaica Station stayed busy invading more French island colonies, hoping for an encounter with a relieving French squadron.

Christmas and Boxing Day had come and gone, then New Year's Day of 1804, then Epiphany, Plough Monday, Hilary Term days for courts and colleges, and Candlemas, and, after all the excitement of the previous year, it was all rather pacific, and deadly-boresome. The newly independent Haitians did not try to export their slave rebellion to the rest of the West Indies, the weak French lodgements in the Spanish half of Hispaniola seemed to have given up on any attempt to flee to France, and the Spanish, the Dons, were behaving like their usual selves; that is to say, moribund. After getting stung rather badly as French allies they had drawn in their horns, and showed no signs of wanting any more to do with war.

With hurricane season over, the weather in the West Indies was delightful; with the heat of Summer dissipated, Fever Season was also gone, for a while, and it was all "claret and cruising" through steady Trade Winds, clear, sunny days, and only now and then a half-gale or afternoon squall. It was so very pleasant that Alan Lewrie was of two moods: either bored nigh to tears, or fretful that Dame Fortune would remember that it was her job to kick him in his arse, now and again . . . every time he felt smug and satisfied. Or had too much idle time.

During such lulls as this, without the heady spur of adventure and action, Lewrie could become, well . . . distracted. It was said that "idle hands are the Devil's workshop," and well Lewrie knew it! Given a week or so in port for re-victualling, replenishment, and re-arming, with the pleasures of a thriving harbour town a short row off in both ear-shot and eye-shot, and, given how little a frigate captain had to do when said frigate was both at anchor and flying the "Easy" pendant to show that she was Out of Discipline to allow her people to rut with their "temporary wives" or prostitutes . . . when aboard, able to *see* it and *hear* it as sailors and doxies coupled between the guns on the oak deck planks, danced, cavorted, and sang, well!

It did not help Lewrie's restless feelings to know that Lieutenant Geoffrey Westcott, his First Officer, had indeed discovered for himself a most lissome *jeune fille* from among the horde of civilian French refugees. Whether she was truly the penniless daughter of one of the most distinguished and wealthiest families of Saint Domingue, as was alleged, a corporal's widow, or a whore tainted with the one in 128 parts of Negro blood, a *sang mêlé*, and still considered Black in the old regime, she was hellish-handsome. Light brown, almost chestnut hair, enormous brown eyes, a fine brow and a swan-like neck, pouty lips, and a face nigh gamin or elfin in its loveliness . . . which put Lewrie dangerously in mind of his former mistress in the Mediterranean, Phoebe Aretino, or that murderous pirate-minx Charité de Guilleri. Phoebe had been a teen prostitute in the port city of Toulon during the British invasion of 1794, but was now "Contessa Phoebe" in Paris, the queen of perfumes. Charité de Guilleri had been a French Creole belle who, with her brothers and cousin, and some old privateers, had turned both pirates and revolutionaries with the purpose of freeing New Orleans and Louisiana from the Spanish; she had shot Lewrie in the chest, once, when he'd run them down and ended their game on Grand Terre Isle, at the mouth of Barataria Bay. Before that, they had been lovers . . . and damned if both of them had not been *grand* lovers! Which remembrance did Lewrie's equilibrium no good, at all.

How could one still evince a lusty itch for a young woman who'd hunted him down and tried to kill him for good, and had might as well have fired the shot that had slain his wife, Caroline, during the Peace of Amiens, in France in 1802?

Lewrie returned aboard *Reliant* just as Three Bells of the Forenoon were struck. The side-party was mostly the fully-uniformed Marines, the requisite number of sailors in shore-going finery, and those Midshipmen unfortunate enough to stand Harbour Watch; officers in port did not, and what Lieutenants Spendlove and Merriman were doing below in the gun-room to while away their idle time, Lewrie could have cared less. The crewmen of the Harbour Watch, those on the gangways and the weather decks, doffed their hats and stood facing him for a minute or so, then went back to their few duties, envying their mates below on the gun-deck, where they sported with their women.

"Anything out of the ordinary to report, Mister Grainger?" he asked the senior-most of the pair of Mids who stood the watch, a lad of fifteen.

"Two . . . two of the, ehm . . . women, got into an argument, sir," Grainger reported with a blush. "Bosun's Mate Mister Wheeler separated them, and ordered them off the ship, at One Bell, sir."

"Slashing away with belaying pins, they did, sir!" Midshipman Rossyngton, who was only thirteen, piped up. "Stark naked, both, sir!"

"Sorry I missed it," Lewrie said with a grin.

"Well, ehm . . . neither of them were what one would call 'fetching,' sir," Mr. Rossyngton ventured to say, with a precocious leer. "Rather old, and . . . fubsy, they were."

"Not t'yer *taste*, Mister Rossyngton?" Lewrie teased.

"Well, ehm . . . ," the lad flummoxed, turning as red as Grainger.

"Beg pardons, young gentlemen . . . Cap'm . . . but, there's a signal hoist aboard *Modeste*," one of the Master's Mates, Eldridge, interrupted, reminding them of their proper duties. He, his mate Nightinggale, and the Sailing Master, Mr. Caldwell, were their primary tutors in navigation, and an host of other seamanly work.

"Sorry, sir!" Grainger gawped, turning even redder, if that was possible, hurriedly raising his telescope to read it. "It is . . . 'Have Mail,' sir!" he crowed with an expectant "Christmas Is Coming" glee. "And . . . our number, and 'Captain Repair On Board.'"

"Buggery," Lewrie muttered, half to himself. He had hoped for a quiet morning to digest his succulent shore breakfast, sip on some of his cold tea collation, catch up with naval paperwork, play with the cats, perhaps read a chapter or two of a new book, and . . . take a good long nap, but . . . "Mister Rossyngton, pass word for my Cox'n and boat crew. Smartly, now!"

Will they be in any shape *t'row me over to* Modeste? he had to wonder as he waited. He had taken his gig ashore at Seven Bells of the Morning Watch, assuring Desmond and the others that he would hire a bumboatman for his return, so they could join in the sport belowdecks.

Sure enough, here came Liam Desmond, his Cox'n, still donning his short dark blue jacket, his tarred hat askew, and his long-time mate, Patrick Furfy, right behind him, still trying to do up the buttons of his sloptrousers . . . and reeling a bit.

"Sorry, lads, but I'm called away to the flagship," Lewrie told them as they hurriedly filed down the man-ropes and battens to the gig. "Hope I didn't interrupt anything *too* much fun."

That apology raised a stricken smile or two; most of them had been in full-throated song, nipping at smuggled half-pints of rum, and halfway to "connubial" bliss with their "wives" when called to duty.

All three frigates had sent boats to *Modeste* to lay hands upon their precious letters, newspapers, and packages. *Pylades*'s boat was commanded by a Midshipman, but *Cockerel*'s bore Captain Stroud himself.

"Mornin', Captain Stroud," Lewrie greeted him, once they had been piped aboard *Modeste,* in order of seniority.

"Good morning to you, Captain Lewrie," Stroud replied, looking excited, for a rare once, at the prospect of news from home. Most of the time, he was stiff-necked and taciturn, taking himself and his very first captaincy most seriously. "Mail, at last, hah!" he added. That was, perhaps, too *much* joy to show the world, so he quickly sobered his face and tone. "Would've sent a Middy or First Officer, but . . ."

"But, news from England is just too temptin', aye," Lewrie finished for him, secretly brimming with excitement and curiosity. "But, where is Captain Parham, young sir? And you are . . . ?"

"Allow me to name myself to you, sir. I'm Poole, sir," the Mid from *Pylades* said with a doff of his hat and a short bow. "Our Captain is ashore, sir . . . at a tailor's, and the chandleries."

"Captain Lewrie!" Lt. Gilbraith, *Modeste*'s First Lieutenant, said as he came forward to join them, doffing his cocked hat and making a "leg" to them all; business-like to Stroud and the Midshipman as he addressed them by name, but, oddly, more deeply to Lewrie. "We have begun to separate each ship's mail into bags, sirs . . . if you will attend me aft, in Captain Blanding's cabins?"

The Marine sentry announced their presence, and Blanding shouted a merry, and loud, "Enter!" to them. They filed into the cabins, hats under their arms, and bowed greetings to the squadron commander. Lt. Gilbraith went over to stand with Blanding, Chaplain Brundish, and Blanding's clerk and cabin servants, all of whom stood peering at the new arrivals with what looked like "cat that ate the canary" expressions, and a stiffness normally reserved for greeting an Admiral.

"'Tis a bit early in the day, gentlemen, but, given the celebratory nature of the occasion, allow me to offer you all a cool glass of Rhenish," Captain

Blanding said, beaming like a cherub, rocking or nigh-hopping on his toes over *something*. Lewrie knew him, by then, as a boisterous, mercurial fellow, but this was quite uncanny.

He's a handkerchief . . . has he been cryin'? Lewrie asked himself; *By the look of his red eyes, damme if he hasn't! What . . . ?*

"At a moment like this, I'd have wished that Captain Parham would have been able to join us," Captain Blanding went on as cabin servants scurried round with glasses and a bottle of wine. Damned if he *didn't* dab at his eyes, and blow his nose, rather loudly, to boot!

"He will be at the supper, surely, sir," Chaplain Brundish was quick to assure him. And damned if Brundish, scholarly, erudite and languidly calm in all weathers, didn't peer at Lewrie with a mixture of what seemed like awe and sly, secret amusement!

I've come into a fortune, and he wants t'touch me up for a loan? Lewrie was forced to think, wishing he could touch himself all over to make sure his breeches' buttons were done up, his shoes were on, or his neck-stock still in place.

Captain Blanding crossed to his desk and returned with a large parchment document, which he held out for them to see. There was a gilt seal, rather large, with a large blob of red wax, a seal pressed into it, and a red ribbon beneath the wax.

"This came to me by post . . . from London," Captain Blanding said with a tremble to his voice. "From Saint James's Palace. From our Sovereign, His Majesty King George." Blanding sounded as if he was about to croak like a frog in awe. "The King has seen fit to reward me for our victory over the French at the Chandeleur Islands by making me a Knight of the Bath, *and* a Baronet!"

"My word, sir!" Captain Stroud exclaimed.

"Huzzah!" Lt. Gilbraith, who was already in on the secret, said loudly. "An honour long overdue!"

"*Congratulations*, sir!" Lewrie cried, stunned.

"You . . . we . . . fought and won the only significant action with the French, last year, after all, sir," Chaplain Brundish pointed out with a laugh, though he'd known all about the announcement for several minutes already. "Of *course* the Crown would reward the victor!"

And by God if it wasn't, Lewrie thought. *The Naval Chronicle*, London papers which reached them such as the *Times* or the *Gazette*, had not featured anything approaching a fleet action since the war began again in May of last year. There were many reports of single actions against French National ships, some small-squadron encounters that had not resulted in any significant losses to either side, or many prizes taken; it was French merchantmen that had suffered the most, but they were profitable, and lacking in glory and honour. Their squadron and their fight at the Chandeleurs, which had resulted in all four French ships defeated and taken as prizes, *had* been the highpoint of 1803!

"To Captain *Sir* Stephen Blanding, Baronet!" Lt. Gilbraith proposed, now their glasses were full, and they seconded him with, "To Sir Stephen!" gave out loud growls of approval, and knocked their glasses back to drain them.

"Congratulations, sir!" Captain Stroud told him, going to shake hands.

"Hear, hear!" Lewrie added, happy to see the cabin servants go round to refill their glasses for a second toast. "Well earned, hey?"

"Ehm . . . we're not quite done, sirs," Captain Blanding tried to shush them. "There's something else to celebrate. Stanley?" he prompted Reverend Brundish, with a significant nod and wink.

"Ehm . . . Captain Lewrie," Brundish said, fetching forth a very large letter from *Reliant*'s heap of mail. "This has come for *you*." Brundish held it by pressing the tips of his fingers to two of its corners, waving it teasingly, and grinning widely.

It was a heavy creme-coloured bond, the calligraphy for sender and addressee large and "copper-plate" elegant. There was a red wax seal the size of a Spanish "piece of eight" coin to join the corners of the folded-over letter together.

"Uh . . . for me?" Lewrie gawped.

"No!" Captain Stroud cried. "Really?" Lewrie couldn't tell if he was astonished at what the letter might hold, or objecting.

"For you, sir," Brundish assured him, stepping forward to place it in Lewrie's hands, taking his wine glass to free both. It *was* from the Crown! Lewrie started to snag a fingernail under the wax seal to rip it free, then looked up, appalled, in need of help.

"Allow me to apply my pen-knife," Captain Blanding offered with a snort of delight. "A thing like that, you only receive once, and it would be a shame to ruin the seal by tearing it free."

"Insult to the Crown, what?" Brundish said, snickering.

"It's really a . . . ?" Lewrie could only gawp, going to the desk in the day-cabin, to watch Captain Blanding carefully lift the seal from three of the four corners. Once folded open, the creme-coloured paper proved to be but a protective sheath for the parchment inside, which Blanding let Lewrie open and read. Once, twice, then an even more dis-believing third time.

"Mine arse on a *band-box*!" Lewrie exclaimed at last. "They've made *me* a Knight of the Bath?"

"Oh, huzzah, sir! Huzzah!" young Poole cried. "Can't wait to tell Captain Parham!"

"Congratulations, sir!" Captain Blanding said, taking his hand and giving it a vigourous shake, whilst the rest of them cheered and hooted as if urging their choice of race horse in the last furlong of the Ascot or the Derby.

Why, though? Lewrie asked himself, though shuddering with glee and sheer stupefying surprise.

After a successful victory such as theirs, it was customary for *one* officer, the senior-most, to be honoured. At Cape St. Vincent it had been Vice-Admiral Sir John Jervis, "Old Jarvy," rewarded with the title of Earl St. Vincent. After Camperdown, it was only Admiral Duncan who'd been made a peer, and at the Nile, it was Nelson who had been rewarded.

The rewards for captains of the participating warships and the junior officers usually was promotion, or command of one of the prize ships taken. The fellow who'd carried word of the Glorious First of June battle in 1794, the frigate captain who'd carried word of Cape St. Vincent, *had* been knighted, but . . . why him, *and* Blanding, for the same battle?

'Cause I'm "Saint Alan the Liberator," "Black Alan" Lewrie, he sourly thought; *Hero of the Abolitionists like Wilberforce, or . . . I got knighted 'cause somebody in government's feelin' sorry for me for Caroline's murder by the French!*

It was hard not to grimace in anger and pain, and keep a sheepish grin of proper modesty on his face, after that realisation, even as he shook hands with the others and got pounded on the back; while the honour turned to ashes in his mouth!

Was it because he was . . . "well-known"? For a time, the Abolitionists had showered, papered, London and the nation with praiseful tracts of his theft of a dozen Black slaves from the Beaumans, long before the trial in King's Bench which had acquitted him. His black-and-white portrait had been on sale, selling almost as briskly as Horatio Nelson's for a month or two after, and God only knew how many of those, how many of the cartoons, how many illustrated tracts, he'd had to autograph for the adoring and supportive.

He had been turned into a *commodity* by the Abolitionist Society to further enthusiasm for the end of Negro slavery throughout the Empire, a larger-than-life *symbol*. And, in the Autumn of 1802, then in the Spring of 1803, in the run-up to the renewal of war with France (though he knew little of it on his tenant farm in Anglesgreen), there had been fresh tracts and portraits, sketches meant to *horrify* common people that the Corsican Ogre, Napoleon Bonaparte, would order the murder of a British naval hero and his wife over a trivial insult, or mis-understanding *taken* as an insult by the First Consul for Life of France. *Someone* in His Majesty's Government had cynically found him useful . . . again!

Aye, I'm well-known, Lewrie miserably considered as he took a fresh glass of wine. He was a successful frigate captain. He was a rogue, a rake-hell, too, and known for that to some. The latter repute *should* have can-celled out any fame from the first, so who had put the idea of knighting *him* in the Sovereign's ear?

If he ever had an *honest* shot at knighthood, it should have come in 1797, when he'd had *Proteus*, and had fought an equally-matched enemy frigate in the South Atlantic, a two-hour broadside-to-broadside slug-fest in the midst of a howling gale, to save an East India Company trade homebound for England, but . . . the Earl Spencer had been First Lord of the Admiralty at the time, Sir Evan Nepean his First Secretary, and both of them knew of his peccadilloes with other women, so there had been no hope, then.

Well, I do have allies, Lewrie told himself; *sponsors, patrons, and influence*. No one could hope to rise in English Society or a military or naval career *without* "interest," not politics, or the Church, or trade, or . . . ! There was his old school chum who'd been expelled at the same time as he had, Peter Rushton, now Lord Draywick, in Lords. In the Commons, there was William Wilberforce, Sir Samuel Whitbread, of the beer fortune, and many others of the progressive stripe; there was Sir Malcolm Shockley, married to Lucy Beauman, and in spite of her connexions to his old nemesis, friendly and supportive, too. Admiral the Earl St. Vincent? He was now First Lord of Admiralty, and he had always *seemed* well-disposed towards him, since the battle that had made him a peer; when Lewrie had been on half-pay, begging for a ship before the expedition sailed for the Baltic to swat the Rus-sians, Swedes, and Danes under Parker and Nelson, it had been "Old Jarvy" who'd allowed him an interview, then surprised him with command of HMS *Thermopylae* and her solo scouting mission into the Baltic, before the Battle of Copenhagen!

Lewrie suspected a reason even more distasteful: that somehow some agate-eyed manipulators in Secret Branch of the Foreign Office, people very *much* like Zachariah Twigg, found him *useful* to the Crown and to the Country, once more, and were even now playing up his name, and Caroline's death, to *enthuse* the populace!

Wonder if anyone ever refused *one?* Lewrie thought.

At least his knighthood was for a legitimate reason, he could tell himself, perhaps for *cumulative* duty? They handed the damned things out to poets, playwrights, painters, town mayors when a new bridge or town hall was opened, for God's sake! *Brewers,* iron barons, and *wool-spinning* tsars!

Might as well go along with it, he decided; *they won't offer twice, and . . . won't this put my father's nose outta joint? Think o' what Harry Embleton'll make of it, or my brother-in-law Governour?*

"Wet him down, instanter!" Lt. Gilbraith was crying, calling for more wine. "Won't be official 'til your presentations at Court, but, perhaps we could make a start at modest celebration, what?"

"I believe we could, Jemmy," Captain Blanding heartily agreed, lifting his glass in Lewrie's direction. "Sir Alan?"

"Sir Stephen!" Lewrie responded, though he lacked the twinkle that danced in Blanding's eyes.

CHAPTER NINE

A few more celebratory glasses of Rhenish put paid to Lewrie's plans for his late morning. In addition to the routine paperwork of a fighting ship, there was a new pile of directives from the Admiralty to be read through, initialed, filed away, or answered; he, and almost every Midshipman he had ever known from his early days, had been laid over a gun to "kiss the gunner's daughter" for the sin of reading one's personal mail, first, and neglecting Words From On High ... even were those words corrected sailing directives for the safe navigation of the Yellow Sea, which 99 percent of the Royal Navy would never even get close to, much less transit. To his cats' dismay, Lewrie and his clerk, James Faulkes, spent the rest of the Forenoon sorting it all out, and penning responses, too intent to play with them, shooing them off the day cabin desk and protecting Faulkes's feathered quill pens.

The musicians had struck up "The Bowld Soldier Boy" at half past eleven, at Seven Bells, and the Purser, Mr. Cadbury, Marine Lieutenant Simcock, and the Purser's Assistant/Clerk, Bewley (better known as the Jack-In-The-Breadroom), had escorted the painted rum cask on deck for the mid-day issue; Faulkes had gone antsy to miss it, forcing Lewrie to suspect that it was not just rejected love that had driven Faulkes to sea.

"Well, I think that should do it, Faulkes," Lewrie said at last, as the very last reply was sanded to dry the ink, carefully folded and sealed, then addressed. "Sorry it took so long. You might visit the galley and see Mister Cooke . . . he's always a pint of something hidden away. Did you miss the issue, he'll allow you a nip."

"Thank you, sir, and I shall," Faulkes said, departing.

"Well, lads?" Lewrie invited to his cats, who sprang atop the desk to prowl, bow their backs, yawn, and stretch, then nuzzle at his hands. "You just can't play with the pretty feathered pens, it isn't—"

"Hands is being piped to Mess, sir," Pettus, his cabin servant, said, cocking an ear to the silver calls on deck. "A glass of wine, sir?"

"Cold tea," Lewrie decided. "I've done that, this morning."

"Aye, Sir Alan, sir," Pettus said with a tight, pleased grin.

"Hey?" Lewrie scowled back.

"Well . . .'tis all over the ship, sir," Pettus told him. "Soon as your boat crew was dismissed, they were all bragging on it."

"It's not official 'til we get back to England, Pettus," Lewrie pointed out to him. "'Til then . . . 'Captain,' or a *plain* 'sir,' will suit. And, for a long time after. Damned silliness," he scoffed.

"Well, sir . . . I've served a vicar, and a bishop, but they don't hold a candle to a Knight of the Bath," Pettus said, almost sulking to be denied.

"You served a parcel o' drunks at that inn in Portsmouth, 'fore you came away t'rejoin, too," Lewrie said with a wry grin, "and, most-like one'r two o' them were *titled*, so it don't signify. Unless it'd look good on yer references, do ye ever wish t'leave my service."

"Why would I wish to do that, sir?" Pettus rejoined, in merry takings. "Being a knight's 'man' puts me a leg up over most other gentlemen's servants."

"Cap'm's cook . . . SAH!" the Marine sentry bawled, smashing his musket butt and boots on the deck outside.

"Enter!" Lewrie called back, rising to go to the dining-coach, and his table. "Come on, catlin's . . . tucker!"

Yeovill bustled in with a large, shallow wooden box-like tray, covered with a cloth. "Good mornin' to you, Sir Alan! We've somethin' special, to celebrate. And, somethin' special for the cats, to boot!"

Dammit! Lewrie groused; *This could get* irksome, *all this "Sir" shit . . . it'll be bowin' an' scrapin', next!*

He would have fired off a bit of temper, a swivel-gun's worth, perhaps, not an 18-pounder of "damn yer eyes!" but, when he beheld his dinner, he let it slide.

"All fresh from shore this mornin', sir," Yeovill boasted. "A parcel of shrimp, grilled in lemon and butter . . . drippy bacon salad, boiled field peas, and"—Yeovill pointed to each as he named them, revealing the best for last—"spicy jerked guinea fowl, sir! Oh, I've a mango custard for a sweet, too, sir . . . with vanilla, nutmeg, cinnamon, and cream."

"Well now, this *is* a grand treat, Yeovill," Lewrie agreed as he sat down. "Jerked, ye say? That's . . . ?"

"An island style of seasonin', Sir Alan, sir!" Yeovill beamed. "Peppers and chilies, sweet spices, all together. Zestiest, tangiest saucin' ever I put in my own mouth."

"A white wine, sir?" Pettus suggested. "You've still most of a crate of *sauvignon blanc.*"

"Cool tea," Lewrie reiterated. Long before in the West Indies, a neglected pot of tea, an unlit warming candle, had forced him to sip the rest; that, or toss it out the transom sash-windows and have his old cabin servant, Aspinall, brew up another. With lemon and sugar, it had proved refreshing, and Lewrie had had Aspinall make up half a gallon each morning, 'til the tropic sun was "below the yardarms" and he could switch to wine before his supper.

Yeovill had even laid aside some un-seasoned shrimp, de-tailed and peeled for the cats, along with strips of guinea fowl. Toulon and Chalky did not stand on seniority, naval or social, and dug into their bowls with gusto; Chalky had the odd tendency to purr while he ate!

And, after a few sampled bites from each dish, so did Lewrie!

After such a fine repast, it was even harder for Lewrie to keep his eyes open, but . . . there was personal mail to be read. He sorted it out into the most-likely agreeable, first, saving those from tradesmen and his least favourite kin for last.

His solicitor, Mr. Matthew Mountjoy, assured him that he owed no debts, with a long column of double-entry incomes and out-goes to tailors, chandlers, cobblers, hatters, and grocers showing that all his notes-of-hand turned in by them to Mountjoy had been redeemed to the ha'pence.

There was profit, too, now deposited to his account at Coutts' Bank. Admiralty Prize-Court had *finally* awarded him his two-eighths for the *L'Uranie* frigate that he'd taken in the South Atlantic . . . in 1798! She had not been "bought in" by the Navy right away, but laid up in-ordinary for survey and inspection, for years, before going into the graving docks, and the idle time had not been kind to her material condition. There had been another British two-decker "in sight" when she'd struck, so he only got £1,250 for her, but still . . .

But, there was Captain Speaks, and his furious demands for his bloody Franklin-pattern coal stoves that he'd purchased with his own funds for HMS *Thermopylae* before he'd come down with pneumonia in the Baltic and North Sea Winter, and Lewrie had relieved him of command.

Thermopylae was now in the Bay of Bengal, and might be for the next five years; her Purser, who had offered to ship them off to good Captain Speaks, had *not,* and was still aboard her. Any letter Speaks sent in search of his ironmongery took six months to reach her, with no guarantee that the letter might not be eaten by termites or Indian ants at Calcutta or Bombay before *Thermopylae* returned to port after a four-month cruise— longer if she could re-victual in a foreign port—and even a *prompt* reply would take six more months to make its way back to England. Since Captain Speaks very much doubted if the frigate *needed* heating stoves in the East Indies, he was *raving* to discover where they might have been off- loaded! Did he not get satisfaction, he threatened legal action, had retained a serjeant to press his case in Common Pleas, and etc. & etc., liberally sprinkled with dire suspicions that Lewrie was up to his eyebrows in collu- sion with a crooked purser! He would *not* be brushed aside in such a brusque manner!

> . . . *the Value of the Stoves Captain Speaks estimates at £35 each, and intends to seek a sum of £140, plus his legal Expenses. Do please write me on this head, sir, at your earliest Convenience . . .*

"Aw, shit!" Lewrie muttered, strongly considering his crock of aged American corn whisky for a moment. *He* didn't know what Herbert Pride- more had done with the bloody stoves, but, *Thermopylae* had paid off in December of 1801, and they'd have been damned welcome for the Stand- ing Officers, kiddies, and wives who would live aboard her whilst she was laid up in the Sheerness ordinary in Winter . . . of which the Purser, Mr. Pridemore, was a part! Perhaps he'd *meant* to ship them to the north of England, but had put it off 'til the Summer, and . . .

"Bugger 'em," Lewrie growled. The cats woke from their naps on the starboard-side settee table, the large, round brass Hindoo tray that was so cool to sprawl on during a tropic afternoon. With no invitation to play forthcoming, they closed their eyes, again.

Next, a letter from his father, Sir Hugo.

His rented farm was gone. The two-storey house he and Caroline had built in 1789 for £800, the brick-and-timber barn they'd erected to replace an ancient, tumble-down wattle-and-daub one with a roof of straw—bug-and rat-infested since the War of The Roses, most-like!—the storage towers for silage and grain, and the brick stables and coach house were now the property of his favourite brother-in-law, Major Burgess Chiswick, and his bride, Theadora; as were all his former livestock, except for a few favourite saddle horses and what crops had been reaped before the transfer of ownership.

"No more pig-shit . . . no more sheep-shit," Lewrie muttered with a touch of glee. "Good."

> *Less the payment of your last Quit-Rents, Phineas Chiswick, that six-toothed Miser!, offered a paltry £1,000, as Recompence for all your Improvements. As your Agent in this matter, I insisted that we would take no less than £2,000, and, since I learned that Phineas had valued the property at £5,000 for the outright Sale of it to the Trenchers, who would be footing the Bill for their daughter's Country Estate, forced him, at the last, to accept our Terms.*
>
> *Since you delegated to me the negotiations whilst you were away at Sea, I subtracted a sum of £200 as my Commission, and deposited the rest, £1,800, to your account at Coutts'. Trust that my share will be spent joyfully, if not wisely, haw!*

"And when did I agree t'ten percent, damn his eyes!" Lewrie fumed. Sir Hugo went on for several more pages. The Winter was a raw one, though the Thames had not frozen quite so solid as to allow the *proper* sort of Frost Fair. Zachariah Twigg had wintered at his rural estate, Spyglass Bungalow, in Hampstead, and had suffered several bouts with the ague. He was now fully retired from even his consulting work at the Foreign Office.

"Good!" Lewrie exclaimed loud enough to wake the cats, again. He'd been Twigg's pet gun dog since 1784, getting roped into neck-or-nothing, harum-scarum deviltry overseas, time and again, and if that arrogant, top-lofty, and sneering old cut-throat had retired, Lewrie could look forward to a *somewhat* safer career, from now on.

Sir Hugo had heard from Lewrie's sons, both now serving aboard their respective ships in the Navy. Hugh, his youngest, was a Midshipman aboard HMS *Pegasus,* under an old friend, Captain Thomas Charlton, a stolid, steady, and seasoned professional . . . though Charlton had a sly and puckish sense of humour, and a fond tolerance for the antics of Midshipmen. Hugh had taken to the sea like a cow to clover, and was having a grand time.

Sewallis, well . . . his oldest boy, and heir-apparent, had slyly amassed enough money to kit himself out, had forged a draft of one of Lewrie's early letters to another old friend and compatriot, Captain Benjamin Rodgers, and had finagled himself a sea-berth aboard *Aeneas,* a two-decker ship of the line. His one brief letter to his "granther" told a soberer tale of his self-chosen naval career, so far, but . . . Sewallis had always been the serious one. He was learning all of the cautions, "all the ropes," but said little of his fellow Midshipmen, confessing that times were hard on a "Johnny New Come" 'til he began to fit in. Sir Hugo suspected that he was coping main-well, but did not sound quite so joyful as Hugh. Had Lewrie gotten a letter from him, yet?

No, he had not, and there was not one in his latest pile. He expected that Sewallis would summon up the gumption to explain, sooner or later. *That'll prove damned int'restin'!* Lewrie thought.

On a happier note, Lewrie's former ward, Sophie de Maubeuge, now wed to Lewrie's old First Officer, Commander Anthony Langlie, had been delivered of a lusty baby boy, whom she had named Charles August, to honour her late older cousin, Baron Charles Auguste de Crillart, a French Navy officer who had been Lewrie's prisoner-on-parole in the Caribbean during the American Revolution, and Lewrie's Royalist ally during the siege of Toulon, the both of them being blown sky-high in the old *raʒee*-turned-mortar battery, *Zelé,* at the siege of Toulon. Charles had gotten his shrunken family aboard the captured frigate *Radicale* to flee when the port was taken by the French Republicans, avoiding the massacre of the Royalists, but had died when three French ships had chased her down on her way to Gibraltar. He had died not knowing that his younger brother and his mother had been slain, too, leaving Sophie his last, orphaned kin, and extracting a promise from Lewrie to see them safe with his dying breath.

Anthony Langlie and his brig-sloop *Orpheus* were, so Sophie told it, raising merry Hell in the Mediterranean, and had captured several merchant prizes!

London had been grandly entertaining that Winter, with several new plays and exhibits, Sir Hugo related; Daniel Wigmore's Peripatetic Extravaganze had put on a Winter season cross the Thames in Southwark, and had staged their comic plays and farces in a rented hall in Drury Lane; the delightful bareback rider/crack bow shot/*ingenue* actress, Eudoxia Durschenko—the delectable Cossack minx that had been hot for Lewrie, Sir Hugo teased!—was now about the town in the company of Lord Percy Stangbourne, a dashing Buck-of-The-First-Head, rich as a Walpole, intimate of the Prince of Wales, and a Lieutenant-Colonel of his family's home-raised Yeomanry Light Dragoons. They were both as horse-mad as if they *were* Cossacks, or Mongols!

"Good for her," Lewrie muttered, though with a tinge of loss; had it not been for Eudoxia's murderous, eye-patched expert marksman–lion tamer father, Arslan Artimovich, and his oath that the girl would *die* a virgin if he had to kill half the males in Great Britain, Lewrie *might* have given her a go.

There was a letter from his other brother-in-law, Governour Chiswick, who, with his long-suffering but sweet wife, Millicent, was now boarding his daughter, Charlotte, at their estate in Anglesgreen. Talk about cool and stand-offish! Governour's letter was as formal as a boarding school proctor's end-of-term summation on a student's progress. Governour *rated* her on her ladylike deportment, her advancing skills at singing, at playing the harpsichord and violin, her "seat" and "bottom" when riding her horse-pony, and the courage she showed on open-country rides at trot, canter, lope, and gallop. Charlotte "played well with other girls," though she did insist on having her way if not strictly reined back. Her table manners were exquisite for a girl her age, and she kept a scrupulously neat room, without the assistance of her maid, and she kept her clothes in good order.

Charlotte dearly missed her brothers, and did not understand why her father would so *cruelly* send Sewallis off to sea, when he was the eldest, who should have still been in school, preparing for a *civilian* career! She missed her old house, though she quite enjoyed to have her "uncle Burgess" and Theadora living there.

Worst of all, she would still weep when thinking of how much she missed her dear mother, Caroline, though the sunny days now outnumbered the glum ones. Charlotte had adored her Christmas presents from Sir Hugo, when he'd come down briefly from London.

Of missing her father, there was not one ward, at all. Though Lewrie had written her several times, there was no acknowledgement of her reading them, or receiving them, and . . . there was no letter from her to him enclosed.

The handwriting changed on the next page to Millicent's finer and more graceful hand, giving him a perky recital of all that Burgess and Theodora were doing with his old house, what colours they chose to repaint the rooms, which pieces of furniture they had retained, and an inventory of what they'd been given, or purchased, and how they had re-arranged. His office-cum-library with its many French doors and windows was now *such* a delightful, such a *splendid* garden room, awash in potted or hanging ferns, exotic Indian flowers and palmettos from the Carolinas in America, and one magnificent palm *tree* so reminiscent of Burgess's service with the East India Company army, and . . . !

Lewrie tossed it aside in disgust and sadness. As eager as he had been to flee the place, and escape Caroline's ghost, to be shot of all the hurtful memories, it still irked that what had been his sheet-anchor was now turned so topsy-turvy. If there had been *some* way for the children to have stayed on there, when home from school . . . !

"First Off'cer, SAH!" his Marine sentry bellowed.

"Enter," Lewrie glumly called back.

"My God, sir!" Lt. Westcott barged in, his hatchet face glowing with delight, and his usual brief flash-grin replaced with one that nigh-reached to his ears. "Captain Sir Alan Lewrie! Good God above, sir! Mister Spendlove and Merriman, both, told me of it, soon as I set foot on the gangway. My heartiest *congratulations,* sir!"

"Oh, don't *you* start!" Lewrie gravelled back. "*Blanding* earned his, I didn't, really, and I've no idea *why* I was included. It's all so damned silly."

"But, will you say the same at the shore supper, tonight, sir?" Westcott teased.

"*What* bloody shore supper?"

"Midshipman Bailey, of *Modeste,* SAH!" the Marine bellowed.

"That'll be the invitation, I'd think," Westcott said, chuckling. "Care to lay a wager on it, sir?"

"Enter!" Lewrie barked more forcefully, and a Midshipman from the flagship came in, hat under his arm, and bowing as if to a duke.

Christ, they are *bowin' an' scrapin'!* Lewrie sulkily thought.

"Captain Blanding's respects, sir, and I am to extend to you an invitation . . . to you and all your officers an invitation, that is, to join Captain

Blanding and his officers at a *f . . . fête champêtre*, this evening at Two Bells of the Dog Watch," the lad haltingly said, losing his rehearsed place several times. "It is to be held ashore, sir, at a . . . *restaurante* by name of The Rookery, and . . ."

"Any ladies allowed, lad?" Lt. Westcott asked, tongue-in-cheek.

"Ehm . . . I do not *know*, sir, no mention was made . . ." The Midshipman sneaked a peek at the written invitation to see whether ladies were to be included.

"The Rookery, Mister Bailey?" Lewrie asked. "I'm not familiar with it . . . why not 'The Grapes'? They do naval parties just fine."

And, The Grapes had been a dockside fixture, handily near the boat landings, since long before Lewrie's Midshipman days; *and*, they were used to rowdy behaviour and vomit.

"I am not familiar with it myself, sir," Midshipman Bailey confessed, looking as if he'd like to scuff his youthful shoe-toes together in embarrassment. "But the directions to it are here on the invitation, sir. Ehm . . . harbourside, further east along the High Street, a brick building with a courtyard, and a curtain wall before the entrances . . . 'tis said the rear dining rooms offer a splendid harbour view."

"God," Lewrie breathed, knowing exactly where this Rookery was; he and Christopher Cashman, his friends, and some obliging doxies had celebrated his victory and survival after the Beauman duel, the breakfast turning into a high-spirited, drunken battle of flying food and rolls. And, long, long before, it had had another owner. In 1782, he had gone there, once, a shiny-new Lieutenant.

"Baltasar's," Lewrie suddenly recalled. "An *emigré* Frenchman's fancy place . . . Baltasar's. I know it."

"Ehm . . . the invitation, sir. Sorry," Midshipman Bailey said as he stepped forward and laid it on Lewrie's desk, so timorously that he appeared to fear being bitten for being remiss; or, hesitant to approach a man newly exalted.

"Thankee, Mister Bailey . . . my deepest respects to good Captain Blanding, and inform him that I and my officers look forward to the . . . *fête champêtre* with great delight. Also express my thanks for his kindness," Lewrie told the lad.

"Aye aye, sir!" Bailey said, stepping back, all but clicking his heels or stamping shoes like a Marine, before turning to go. Once he was beyond the door, Lewrie turned to Westcott, giving him a wink and a looking-over.

"I'd think after a whole morning with your young lady, Mister West-cott, ye might wish t'give her a rest . . . give yourself one, too," Lewrie teased. "All that, *and* supper, would be more than plenty."

"'Twas an *entrancing* plentitude, sir, and thank you for asking," West-cott replied, chuckling in reverie. "*Mademoiselle* du Plessis was her usual delightful self, yet, one always longs for just a *bit* more."

Don't we just, Lewrie thought, grinning tautly.

"I'd expect you'd change shirts before the supper, sir," Lewrie said with mock sternness. "There seems to be some . . . reddish, coral-coloured powder on your collar. Rouge? Lip paste?"

"Coloured powder, sir," Westcott was glad to inform him. "She . . . *Mademoiselle* Sylvie, dabs it on to, ah, enhance her breasts, specifically the *areoli.*"

That's a new'un on me! Lewrie thought.

"Then it is indeed a pity that there's no mention of invitin' any ladies t'this celebration of ours, tonight," Lewrie japed, referring to the paper Midshipman Bailey had left. "Just as well, I s'pose. She'd be bored t'tears with all the salty talk, then scared when the bread rolls and pudding start flyin'."

"Well, that is a pity, sir," Westcott said, looking a tad downcast; or very, very *tired* after his energetic morning.

"Besides, sir . . . why drag your Sylvie to such a tarry gatherin', where ye'd have t'share her attentions with all the *other* young, un-married, and *deprived* Lieutenants?" Lewrie pointed out.

"To listen to their teeth grind, sir?" Lt. Westcott shot back with glee.

"Well . . . even if ladies *were* invited, the bulk of 'em'd be a pack o' fubsy chick-a-biddies," Lewrie said with a sigh. "And, there is the matter of whether *Mademoiselle* Sylvie would be suitable for our 'dash it, bedad' Captain Blanding. Acceptable to Chaplain Brundish, more to the point."

"Always tomorrow, then . . . do you allow me more shore liberty, sir," Westcott said, shrugging. "Or, perhaps tomorrow evening, after duties are done? Is The Rookery an elegant place, we could dine there."

"An 'all-night in,' Mister Westcott?" Lewrie leered.

"Oh God, please, *yes,* sir!"

"Go, Mister Westcott," Lewrie ordered, with a laugh. "Wipe yerself down, and warn the others t'shine. Can't let the repute of the ship down. Best kit, all that?"

"Aye aye, sir . . . going!" Westcott said, snapping to a loose sort of attention, and bowing his head before turning to depart, with a brief pause to ruffle the fur of the cats, who were napping like a pair of plum puddings atop the map board in the chart space; over the months, Toulon and Chalky had taken to him like a house afire.

Once alone, Lewrie had to dig at his crotch. He'd met the stunning Sylvie du Plessis once, and found himself "risible" at the recollection. And envious of Westcott's hellish-good luck!

I've become a tarry-handed, sea-goin' monk.*! he told himself.

So there he sat, vaguely listening to the sound of copulation and revelry on the gun-deck with the ship "Out of Discipline," then recalling that Lt. Westcott (the lucky bastard!) had made an off-handed comment that *Mademoiselle* Sylvie was a "Venus On The Half-Shell" in private . . . if one changed the hair colour from blonde to brunette of the model for that painting by . . . *some* bloody Italian!

High culture was not Lewrie's strong suit; he couldn't recall which Renaissance Dago had done it! But, he'd always panted over it, and would have bought a copy . . . if his late wife would have allowed.

In point of fact, his last, brief intimacy had happened the night before he and Caroline had fled Paris, mid-Summer of 1802. And he had lived an ascetic existence since, afloat or ashore. A grieving widower who *shouldn't* at Anglesgreen, then a Sea Officer who *couldn't* in this sea-going monastery of a Royal Navy frigate!

I'm a man . . . a natural man, he thought; *and it ain't natural t'go without. I never have* before, *by God!*

Suddenly, he found that he *could* entertain the idea of female company, again, yet . . . what *sort?* Jamaica was nigh-awash in "grass widows" whose husbands neglected them, but that would take *entrée* to Kingston Society, and take too bloody long, to boot. *Courtesans* like Mister Westcott's Sylvie? To take some woman like her "under his protection" would be expensive, and he'd be more-often at sea than in her company . . . almost as expensive as taking a second wife, with just as little sport resulting. Whores? Sadly, his last episode in London in his "half-pay" months following the trial, with no hope of gaining any new command, *ever*, had been depressing; poor little Irish Tess, who was so naive and hopeful . . . most-like his old friend Peter Rushton's new mistress, if God was just; at least he had money, a title, and a stand-offish wife who had presented him with two sons, and had no desire to risk another pregnancy, so . . . have at, dear!

In point of fact, Lewrie was at that stage where he could almost squirt semen from his ears if he sneezed!

"I could ask Westcott if Sylvie has a friend," he mused aloud. "Oh, *God*, no! *That'll* never do! But . . . what will?"

It was a quandary.

CHAPTER TEN

*H*MS *Reliant*'s brief idyll ended shortly after that *fête champêtre* (which indeed did feature flung food!) as the squadron prepared to sail off to prowl round Hispaniola once more. The Easy pendant was lowered, the outright whores and declared "temporary wives" were sent ashore in their jobbers' bum-boats, and the frigate scoured with vinegar, then smoked with clumps of smouldering tobacco to cleanse her of smuts, odours, and shore bugs. The last fresh water was pumped aboard from the clumsy, ark-like hoys; the last livestock and salt-meat casks stowed away on the orlop, and the officers' gun-room stores and captains' personal stores were replenished to the final crock of jam and the last pot of ink.

As with all the holidays, *Reliant* and the others would be at sea for Easter, as well, though the Reverend Brundish assured the captains that he'd planned a bang-up series of homilies for the occasion.

Not three weeks later, though, barely at the end of their second circumnavigation of Hispaniola, a group of three warships—one lighter frigate and two brig-sloops—intercepted them off Cape St. Nicholas with fresh orders.

"Any idea what they're speaking of, sir?" Lt. Westcott wondered aloud as Lewrie stood by the starboard mizen shrouds, one arm hooked round a stay to steady his day-glass.

"The frigate made *Modeste*'s number, after the private signals, then 'Have Despatches,'" Lewrie replied, intent on the mute flag-play between ships. "*Modeste* then made 'Captain Repair On Board' to her, and the frigate's gig is settin' out to her. Other than that?" There was a shrug to show his ignorance of matters beyond that. "Oh, here's a new'un . . . General to all ships . . . 'Course Sou'-Sou'west' and . . . 'Make All Sail Conformable To The Weather.' No, wait a bit . . . here comes another!"

"Captain Blanding runs off at the halliards, again, sir?" Lieutenant Westcott dared to jape, in a low voice meant for the two of them.

"Afraid so," Lewrie said with a snicker. "It's 'Form Two Columns' and . . . I s'pose that's the frigate's number . . . 'Take Station To Leeward.' Ready to come about to Sou'-Sou'west, Mister Westcott. I assume *we're* t'be the windward column."

"Aye aye, sir. Bosun, pipe hands to Stations! Helmsmen, ready to come about to Sou'-Sou'west!" Westcott ordered. "Man the braces and sheets!"

The frigate and her consorts had already hauled their wind for the meeting, to leeward of *Modeste*'s column of four warships, so the evolution was easily performed. *Reliant,* the leading ship, swung her bows no more than three points more Sutherly, braced the yards round, and eased the tautness of jibs, spanker, and stays'ls to take the Trade Winds on her larboard quarters.

"A reef in the main course, sir?" Westcott asked, looking aft to see *Pylades* falling astern a bit further than the required cable of separation. "We're striding away from *Pylades*."

"*We're* 'Conformable' to the weather, Mister Westcott," Lewrie laughed, hands on his hips and looking up at the set of *Reliant*'s sails. "Let Captain Parham clap on more canvas! It's a nice day t'let her step lively."

"Permission to mount the quarterdeck, sir?" Pettus asked Lieutenant Westcott, who had the watch. "Cool tea's up!"

"Aye, Pettus . . . come," Westcott agreed.

"Oh, good!" Sailing Master Caldwell chimed in, rubbing his paws together in expectation that he'd get a glass, too, as was the custom that had developed aboard, as Spring, and its heat, advanced.

In this manner, nearly forty-five minutes elapsed. The ship's bell struck Seven Bells of the Forenoon, and Marine Lt. Simcock's favourite tune, "The Bowld Soldier Boy," was heard as the rum keg came from below. The Master's Mates, and the Midshipmen, came up with their sextants and slates to prepare for Noon Sights, to be taken when the bell struck Eight Bells to end the Forenoon and begin the official Noon-to-Noon ship's day.

"One hopes you'll place us in the West Indies, today, Mister Munsell," Lewrie teased the thirteen-year-old Middy. "Should be very easy . . . what with Cape Saint Nicholas still in plain sight. And *not* in the middle of the Caicos Bank, hey?"

"Closer than usual, sir . . . he's improving," Mr. Caldwell said with a wink. Mr. Munsell was an eager, and tarry, lad, but still iffy when it came to the mysteries of celestial navigation and sun sights.

"Signal from *Modeste*, sir!" Midshipman Warburton piped up. "It is General . . ." Sure enough, two guns were fired aboard *Modeste*, to all to gather their attention, and precede a new signal to all seven ships. "Ehm . . . the frigate captain's gig is rowing back to her, sir," Warburton added, swinging his telescope down from the peak of the signal halliards to *Modeste*'s side.

"Oh, here it is, sir . . . 'Windward Column . . . To Alter Course to . . . West-Sou'west, Half West . . . Leeward Column . . .'"

"That's wordy, even for Captain Blanding," Lewrie commented.

"'. . . the Leeward Column Will . . . Wear About to Due South,' sir," Warburton read out slowly.

"Confusing, too, sir," Westcott pointed out. "Do both columns alter course together, when the hoist is hauled down, the lee column yonder had better be quick about it, or it will be *us* who tangle our bow-sprit with yon lead sloop!"

"Hoist the 'Query,' Mister Warburton, not 'Acknowledged,' and be quick," Lewrie snapped.

"Aye, sir."

"Lord, sir . . . he can't explain with a fresh hoist, without he lowers the one now flying, and that'd be sign for 'Execute'!" Lieutenant Westcott further worried aloud.

It appeared that Captain Blanding realised his unclear error, for yet another series of flags went up probably the last spare halliard aboard the flagship; it was "Leeward Column First."

"*Now* you may reply with 'Acknowledged,' Mister Warburton," Lewrie directed, letting out a whoosh of relieved wind. "And, thank God he had enough spares in his taffrail lockers t'say 'Leeward Column' twice!"

"The frigate captain's back alongside his ship, sir," Warburton reported.

A minute later, and he could inform them that that worthy, whoever he was, was back on his quarterdeck, and his gig led round to be towed astern.

"Mister Westcott . . . just t'be on the safe side, we'll continue on this course perhaps a whole minute after the 'Execute,'" Lewrie said to his First Officer in a close mutter. "Get a bit more separation to the South as they wear about. The rest of our ships *should* stand on in line-ahead astern of us. Mister Warburton, send to *Modeste* . . . 'Submit,' then 'Alter Course In Succession, Lead Ship First' and 'Query.'"

"Aye aye, sir!"

He won't like me for that, Lewrie told himself, peering aft to see what the flagship would reply . . . if she *could* at that moment; I'd *not care t'be second-guessed, publicly, either, but . . .*

"Signal's struck, sir!" Warburton cried, even before he could sort out the proper flags and bend them onto the halliards. He and his signalmen jumped to hasten it along.

"The lead sloop is wheeling to leeward, sir," Wescott said.

Sure enough, the brig-sloop was swinging to take the Nor'east Trades right up her stern, then swinging even wider to the West, with the winds on her starboard quarters, whilst the frigate and the trailing sloop stood on. The leading sloop could not complete a full turn over her own wake, but would harden up on almost Due North for a bit so the others could wear in succession, putting their helms over as they reached her disturbed patch of water where she'd begun her turn. All would stand on for a spell, then tack, in succession again, to end up with their bows pointed Sutherly for Jérémie and Cape Dame Marie, and passing well astern of *Modeste*'s column of ships.

"New hoist, sir . . . our number . . . 'Alter Course in Succession.'"

"Let's give it yet another minute, Mister Westcott, *then* we'll come about," Lewrie directed. "One one thousand . . . two one thousand . . . three one thousand . . ."

It was only when the second ship in the lee column swung away to wear about that Lewrie ordered his frigate to alter course. Like a pack of those strange beasts, elephants, *Pylades, Cockerel,* and *Modeste* changed course in *Reliant*'s swash, as if holding the tail of the first with their trunks, and plodding single-file round a bend of a narrow juggle trail.

"Your sextant, sir," Pettus said, after getting permission to mount the quarterdeck, again. His assistant, the fourteen-year-old waif of a cabin servant, Jessop, carried the precious box which contained Lewrie's personal Harrison chronometer, clutching it with both arms close to his chest as if it was part of King George's royal paraphernalia.

"Almost forgot all about it," Lewrie admitted as his chronometer was set beside the Sailing Master's and those of the few officers who could afford their own. He barely got his sextant out and held up to his eye, and drew the image of the sun down to the horizon, when the ship's bell began to chime at the last trickle of sand through all the hour, half-hour, and quarter-hour glasses up forward by the belfry.

"Time!" Mr. Caldwell snapped. "Lock, and record, sirs."

With sextants stowed away, the people on the quarterdeck broke apart into singletons or "syndicates" of two to figure out their readings with chalk on small slates, or with pencils on scrap paper. The Midshipmen huddled together, helping each other (or cadging solutions on the sly when they seemed more probable), to show the Sailing Master when summoned.

"Uhm . . . about here, sir," Mr. Caldwell said, making a mark on a chart pinned to the traverse board by the binnacle cabinet. Lewrie compared his own, as did Westcott, Spendlove, and Merriman, to the latitude and longitude discovered. Captain Alan Lewrie, he had to admit to himself, was only a *fair* navigator; the mathematics involved had not come to him as easily as it had to his contemporaries aboard his first ships. His feelings, and his bottom, had suffered daily during his time as a Midshipman 'til the right way had been "beaten" into his brain. Today, he was pleased to note that he was only a *few* minutes off in both longitude and latitude. Nonetheless, he quickly folded up his scribbled cyphering and shoved it into a coat pocket, nodding and harrumphing as if pleased to be in "agreement" with Caldwell, who *was* indeed a dab-hand navigator, worthy of Trinity House.

"Mister Munsell?" Caldwell asked. The lad offered up his slate with the air of a puppy about to be whipped for leaving piddles on the best Turkey carpet. "Oh, now *this* is novel, young sir. Your latitude is right, but, my *word*, sir . . . you have us nigh ashore on the coast of Cuba . . . round the Bay of Guantánamo! Better than yesterday, but . . ."

"Mister Westcott, sir . . . I relieve you, sir," Lt. Spendlove was intoning as he took over the watch.

"Mister Spendlove, sir . . . I stand relieved," Westcott replied, both doffing their hats.

"I'll be below," Lewrie announced, once Pettus and Jessop had his instruments secured.

"Signal from *Modeste*, sir!" Midshipman Rossyngton, who had replaced

Warburton on watch, reported. "All numbers, and, 'Captains Repair On Board.'"

"Well, no, I won't," Lewrie said with a sigh. "Be careful with 'em, lads. Mister Spendlove, pass word for Desmond and my boat crew."

He'll tear a strip off mine arse, see if he won't, Lewrie told himself; *In public, too . . . with* all *of us present!*

"If you'll come this way, sirs," Lt. James Gilbraith bade them, once all had been piped aboard. Lewrie had learned in the span of almost eleven months in Captain Blanding's squadron that Gilbraith was a weather vane for his superior's moods and intentions, so he watched him closely, and was relieved to note that Gilbraith was grinning so much like a "Merry Andrew" that it might mean there would be no storm of petulance coming his way.

"Welcome, gentlemen, welcome aboard!" Captain Blanding said as they were led into his cabins below the poop. He stood swaying to the motion of his ship with a glass of wine in hand, beaming most cherubic and happy, and Reverend Brundish stood off to one side, grinning, too.

"A glass for all, if you please," Blanding said to his leading steward, "and take seats, all. We've wonderful news. An arduous new task before us, but . . . wonderful news, all the same.

"Gentlemen . . . we're bound for Kingston," Blanding went on once wine had been supplied. "Captain Farquwar and his three ships are to replace us on the Hispaniola coasts, and we are to replenish, *then* . . . sail for England!"

"Well, I'll be . . . !" Parham began to cheer, then thought better of "I'll be damned!" and clapped his mouth shut. "Huzzah!" came from Captain Stroud. "At last!" was Lewrie's contribution.

"Don't be too excited, sirs," Blanding went on, "for on our way, we shall be the escort for a 'sugar trade' of better than an hundred merchantmen. Some will make for American ports, of course, but most will make for home. A thankless business, but . . ."

The great trades usually departed the Caribbean near the end of February, or the first week of March, two hundred, three hundred ships or more. It depended on the end of hurricane season, the richness of the sugarcane harvests and pressings for sugar, molasses, and rum; the indigo and dye-wood were second thoughts, as were the various spices of the

West Indies, like nutmeg and allspice, and the ground peppers of various heat.

This would most-like be the last late trade assembled, before the weather turned hot and the Fever Season began, nowhere as grand as the first, but it would still be a bugger to manage, as all convoys from the smallest to the largest were.

The merchant ships must be corraled together, all sailing from various ports to a pre-announced rendezvous. All must be herded into a loose pack, round which the escorting ships had to prowl, with some serving as "bulldogs" and "whipper-ins" to *keep* them together and in sight of each other, with all ships limited to the best speed of the slowest. Even before then, those ships departing Jamaica would have to be bonded, each master putting up the refundable sum, and signing articles promising to obey all instructions from the escort vessels, swearing that they would not break away and swan off until they were near their destinations.

The route would be arduous, too; beating into the wind through one of the passages out into the Atlantic, then heading Northerly to run up the East coast of America, taking advantage of the Gulf Stream current and the prevailing winds that swept clockwise round the basin of the Atlantic. Some ships would break away at the latitude of Savannah or Charleston, to enter the Chesapeake for Baltimore, or Delaware Bay for Philadelphia, whilst others would be bound for Boston or New York to trade their cargoes for Yankee goods. Cotton, tobacco, and rice predominated, along with hemp, tar, pitch, turpentine, and naval stores. Once a ship left a trade, it was on its own, whilst the rest would still be under escort all the way to various Irish, Scottish, or English ports.

It would be weeks and weeks of frustration, anger, and the urge to fire into the lot of them, for most merchant ship masters were used to going about their own ways, second only to God in their authority once out of sight of land, all as intractibly stubborn as mules. It was worse than herding witless sheep . . . or cats!

Merchant masters would balk at the restrictions, the slow going, and act as if there *weren't* a war on that required the Royal Navy that would always come to be thought of as tyrants, oppressors, martinets, or bullies . . .'til some French privateer or warship hove up over the horizon, at which point they'd follow their instincts to scatter like headless chickens, and blame their capture on the Navy's failings!

Despite how many French island colonies that had been taken after their return to French possession during the Peace of Amiens, there *were* still a few French warships lurking round the West Indies, and many privateers which sheltered in neutral harbours, re-victualled and fitted out before sortying for fresh plunder.

With Spain neutral, French privateers could operate from Puerto Rico, Santo Domingo, Cuba, and Spanish Florida with impunity. And the Americans . . . ! The damned Yankee Doodles still thought that the French "hung the moon," *years* after they'd helped them win their Revolution, despite the brief Quasi-War between France and the United States over the U.S. right of free trade with any nation, favouring none; and despite the bloody excesses of the French Revolution which should have appalled them. There were many Americans who counted their years by the French Directory calendar, with 1789 as the Year One, and harboured a Jacobin, "Sans Culottes" wish to address the inequities between "Common Men" and their richer, patrician leaders.

The Yankee Doodles nursed a continuing dislike for anything British (except for luxury goods) long after their freedom and independence had been won, too, and there were many who would turn a blind eye to a French privateer in their harbours between raiding voyages. After all, America had cut its baby teeth on privateering; their own captains and seamen might be envious of French privateersmen's success! Perhaps a blind eye might even be turned to prizes brought in and the cargoes sold as legitimate imports, and the ships auctioned off outside of the jurisdiction of formal Prize Courts!

This'll be a bastard, Lewrie gloomed.

"Has anyone an estimate of how large a trade it may be, sir?" Captain Stroud enquired, looking ready to be energetic.

"All things considered, perhaps prowlin' Hispaniola wasn't all *that* bad," Lewrie japed. "It's very . . . picturesque."

"Oh, tosh, sir!" Captain Blanding gleefully disagreed. "We've been away far too long, and none of us have any real wish to stay through Fever Season . . . whether your suggestions for citronella candles and oil lamps counter the fever miasmas or not. As to your question, Captain Stroud, I'd not expect much over an hundred ships, or so."

They tossed round the placement of their ships; would Blanding's larger and heavier-gunned *Modeste* lead, or trail; would it be best for *Reliant* or one of the 32-gunned frigates to serve as "whipper-in" astern; was the seaward flank of the convoy the place of most threat, or was the land side, should French privateers lurk in American ports as they sailed up that coast? And, would there be any re-enforcement to their four-ship squadron, perhaps even a brig-sloop?

It appeared that Captain Blanding would not be offering them a midday meal this time. After a last glass of wine in celebration the meeting broke up, and the frigate captains prepared to depart.

"Oh, Captain Lewrie . . . bide a moment, would you?" Blanding bade him.

"Aye, sir?"

Blanding waited 'til the others had gone, paced behind his desk in the day-cabin, and sat himself down, resting his elbows on the top.

"Dash your eyes, sir!" Captain Blanding angrily growled. That was such a change from his usual humourous temperament that it rocked Lewrie back on his boot heels! "Just dash your bloody eyes!"

"Sir?" Lewrie gawped, standing before the desk, hat in hand, and feeling like a schoolboy about to be tongue-lashed, *then* caned.

"Our manoeuvring today, sir . . . I *expected* that we had drilled enough over the better part of a year that you would *sense* my intentions, and act accordingly. Which you *did*, in a way, in that you stood on, realising that the new-come column *must* go about astern of us, to get clear for their course down towards Jérémie, and Cape Dame Marie! But, for you to hoist 'Query' and 'Submit' and make us look clumsy and cack-handed and *foolish* in the eyes of contemporaries, well! I'll not *have* it, sir!"

"I didn't know whether the new-come column *would* wear about as they did, sir," Lewrie rejoined. "Or, whether they'd luff up and lie bows to the wind to wait for us t'pass, or . . . Were *they* the windward column—"

"Your signal hoists made *me* look foolish, more the point, sir," Blanding snapped, cutting him off. "Now, perhaps I did err in placing them to loo'rd for our rendezvous, and perhaps my instructions were a touch confusing, but . . . a sensible course of action would have been to deem yourself the burdened vessel and hold your course, no matter, and let the *other* fellows figure out the best way round us without impeding us! Since I had no clue that Captain Farquwar would be relieving us on station, and would *have* to be the windward column to carry out his orders, it only made perfect sense to take them under our lee, on the most direct course from Jamaica.

"You take too much upon yourself, Captain Lewrie," Blanding admonished with a grave shake of his head.

"Sorry, sir," was all Lewrie could say in response. It would be pointless, and insubordinate to belabour the issue.

"Too many years of 'independent orders' and one-ship missions, I expect," Captain Blanding mused, suddenly sounding as if that was a sorrowful lack. "Just pay attention to my signals from now on, sir, and intuit my intentions from your experience of me. Some obedience . . . prompt obedience . . . would be preferable to discussion, especially after we pick up our trade. Its protection is vital, and I intend that not a single ship shall be lost to enemy action. Right, sir?"

"Aye aye, sir," Lewrie could only say; he'd found that the Navy preferred dumb reassurance with that phrase.

"I will second a pair of my lieutenants and my clerk to aid you once we reach Kingston, Captain Lewrie," Blanding said, his anger gone in an eyeblink, as if the matter hadn't arisen. "I will place you and *Reliant* as the principal vessel to whom the merchant masters pay their bonds and sign agreements. I've also a brace of Midshipmen who possess legible handwriting skills, should you have need of them, you have but to ask."

"Very good, sir."

"That's all, Captain Lewrie, you may depart," Blanding told him, remaining in his "seat of power" as Lewrie hoisted his hat aloft in a salute, looking in vain for acknowledgement of his gesture.

Wasn't too *bad,* Lewrie told himself once seated in the stern-sheets of his gig near Cox'n Desmond; *Not too much was torn off mine arse, 'cause I can still* sit *on it!* It still felt galling, though. He hadn't been reprimanded like that in years, no matter how mild!; *Damme, his signals* were *confusin'!*

In Blanding's place, Lewrie admitted to himself that he would've let the new-comers take station to leeward, too, but . . . when the time came, he would have ordered them to cross his column's stern in a very simple hoist. He shook his head, showing a grim smile.

Should I have tugged my forelock to the "lord of the manor" like a cottager? he asked himself; *or fluttered my sleeves and banged my head on the floor in a Chinee* kow-tow *like the "coral-button-men" did in Canton to the Emperor's trade minister?*

Lewrie imagined that being made Knight of the Bath and Baronet might have put paid to Captain Blanding's grand sense of humour and boisterous *bonhomie;* he was beginning to take himself seriously.

Was he in danger of doing the same thing? Lewrie rather doubted it; not even if he'd been elevated to the peerage. He had always had a feeling that he could stand outside himself and sneer at the poses that Society demanded of him, *knowing* that he was a fraud . . . and suspecting that sooner or later he would be caught out at it. He knew himself too well, warts and all, and was able to be frank about his lacks, and was able to laugh at his pretensions.

Trouble was . . . could Captain Blanding? It would be a pity if he could not, for, even after his reprimand, Lewrie still liked him!

BOOK II

L'Angleterre est une nation de boutiquiers.

England is a nation of shopkeepers.

–Napoleon Bonaparte

CHAPTER ELEVEN

*T*he trade ended up consisting of 109 merchant ships, some of them arriving from the minor, renewed traffic with the neutral Spanish Empire in the Americas, from New Granada on the Northern shoulder of South America, and from the Portuguese Empire of Brazil; from New Spain's ports of Tampico and Veracruz; and from the now-American port of New Orleans, in addition to the merchant ships departing Jamaica and the other British islands.

The route chosen was tortuous, leaving Jamaica on the Nor'east Trades *westwards* for the Yucatan Channel, round the westernmost tip of Cuba into the Gulf of Mexico, then beating up eastwards through the Florida Straits, strung out like a long, weaving python and tacking to either beam for days on end, making no more than five or six knots an hour, hobbled by the smallest and slowest at the tail-end. There was absolutely no way to protect them if a privateer sortied out of Havana or a Florida bay. In the Straits, and later on going North on a beam reach in the even narrower deep-water channel between Spanish Florida and the British Bahamas, the trade extended over five miles long, and if a foe attacked the tail-end, it would be only Captain William Parham's HMS *Pylades* that would be able to respond, and *hours* before any of the others could come about and dash to her aid.

Once North of the Bahama Banks, the trade made its best effort to stand Nor'easterly, to get as far out into deep waters as possible . . . where yet another parcel of merchant ships joined them from island colonies in the Windwards and the Leewards; ships from Trinidad and Tobago, Barbados, St. Vincent, and St. Lucia, ships from Antigua and St. Kitts and Nevis. They had been escorted by a lone frigate and a much older three-masted Sloop of War, but, damned if those two didn't turn round and toddle off home once they'd delivered their charges to Captain Blanding's, and the squadron's, care!

Those new arrivals had to have their *bona fides* certified, that their bonds had been paid and their signed agreements to the rules of convoying had been stamped and initialed "all tiddly" . . . by Lewrie and his officers!

It appeared that Captain Blanding's revenge was endless!

Had Alan Lewrie had his d'ruthers, and had *Reliant* been sailing alone, he'd have preferred the much shorter route Easterly and North-Easterly through the Windward Passage, but that decision had been made by the trade's Commodore, the senior-most and most experienced civilian master, elected by all the rest, and given the titular rank just a step below Captain Blanding for the length of the voyage.

And for each of those new arrivals, *Reliant*'s people had to make up fresh signals books to replace the ones they had been issued by the former escorts from Antigua, which kept Lewrie's clerk Faulkes, Mister Cadbury, the Purser's clerk, and the Midshipmen with good penmanship, scribbling away 'til every ship had a copy of Captain Blanding's orders.

"What was her problem?" Lewrie asked Lt. Westcott as he returned from one of the slower vessels at the tail-end of the convoy. *Modeste* had hoisted *Reliant*'s number, then sent Number 465, directing her to "enquire the reason for the ships astern, or those whose distinguishing signal is shown herewith, why they do not make sail agreeable to their situation." Number 465 also directed them to impress a man from each of the offending ships as punishment, but . . . Lt. Westcott had returned alone.

"Oh well, sir, the *Turtledove*'s main tops'l split right down the middle, and they had to bend a new one on," Westcott reported, calling for a measure of water from the scuttle-butt. "Not that the new one is a whit younger. But, that's not their only trouble, sir. She's a slow leak below, and, with only a dozen hands aboard, two of them boys, she can't spare too many from manning the pumps."

"Good God, who let *her* try a trans-Atlantic voyage?" Lewrie had to wonder aloud. The *Turtledove* was a short and bluff hermaphrodite brig, not over eighty feet on the range of the deck, with fore-and-aft sails on her foremast, and squares'ls on her main, and, frankly, looked as dowdy and ill-used as a Newcastle coal coaster.

"Oh, she's not, sir," Lt. Westcott pointed out, chuckling. "She's leaving us when we get level with Charleston, South Carolina . . . Saint Lucia to there, and back again. She'll probably be a 'runner' for the return passage . . . if she survives this one, that is."

"And the reason ye didn't press a man?" Lewrie asked, after he shook his head at her master's madness.

"Not a one of them worth the *trouble*, sir," Westcott told him, laughing outright. "The boys, some toothless gammers, and a spavined oldster or three? Her captain was the likeliest, but he's not a day under sixty. Call it . . . Christian charity, sir."

Before being accepted into a convoy, as the trades assembled in quarantine, they were *supposed* to be surveyed for seaworthiness, for a sufficiency of crew, spare spars, and sails, and for defences, but . . . evidently the Leeward Islands Station, knowing that such a decrepit old barge would *not* be bound for Europe, had let her off easy.

"Not if they get attacked, it ain't, Mister Westcott," Lewrie said with a mirthless bark of a laugh. "Does she have the defences to *qualify* as a 'runner'?"

"Half a dozen pistols, ditto for muskets, ditto for cutlasses and boarding pikes, and three very old two-pounder swivel guns, sir," Westcott told him with a grim look. "Though, I expect the discharges would deafen half the crew, and cause at least two of the gammers to drop stone-cold dead."

Lewrie paced to the taffrails of the quarterdeck to hoist his telescope to give *Turtledove* a good looking-over. All her sails were now back in place, the ripped tops'l only slightly lighter in colour than the rest; a fresh-cured deer hide tan against the aged parchment of her other sails. At least she now had a mustachio under her fore-foot, an evident wake creaming down her starboard side . . . though her angle of heel to the winds revealed a strip of sickly green underwater growth on her quick-work, as if her coppering had fallen off years ago and her master and owners hadn't bothered to heave her over on a beach to scrape off and burn off the weed and barnacles.

"Built slow, and losin' ground ever since," Lewrie decided as he shut his telescope and shook his head in wonder. "At least she's hoist-up a main t'gallant, and an extra stays'l up forrud. She *seems* t'keep up, now."

The last cast of the log that Midshipman Grainger had done had shown a meagre seven knots, and *Reliant* had had to take in canvas, else she would have strode away from her stern-most charges. She wallowed and sloughed, un-used to such slow progress, and once it became dark the merchantmen would take in sail for the night, making them bunch up and sheer away in fear of collisions, slowing the pace even further!

At dawn, Captain Blanding in *Modeste* would mount to his poop deck, scan about with a glass, and go into his daily apoplexy upon seeing how *far* the ships in the outer columns, the ships astern, had strayed, and then there would be Hell to pay, and half the morning wasted in chivvying them back into the fold.

"Christ, what a *shitten* business!" Lewrie groaned.

"Could be worse, sir," Lt. Westcott said, chuckling. "Do we not get a good lift as we pass through the belt of Variables, we could end set upon Cape Hatteras." He rapped his knuckles on the cap-rails atop the larboard bulwarks to ward off such a fate.

"You are *such* a joy, Mister Westcott," Lewrie said, groaning in mock dread, turning to cock a brow at his First Officer.

"As all the ladies say, sir!" Westcott quickly replied with an impish expression on his hatchet face, baring his brief style of grin.

"As *Mademoiselle* du Plessis said, sir?" Lewrie teased.

"Oh, well, sir . . . for a time, then tears . . . tears and lamentations," Westcott said with a dismissive shrug. "I fear my purse was all but empty after our last, short bout, and all I had to leave her was a five-pound note, but . . . she'll find another protector. Her sort will always survive."

"Another reason Lieutenants should *not* marry, or . . . ," Lewrie began to say.

"*Marry*, sir? Perish the thought!" Westcott said, shivering with mock terror, and uttering a *Brring* noise. "'Tis the ruin of many a man, in the Navy or not. No, no, sir! Not 'til I've been made Post. Even then I'd give it a long look and a hard try before committing myself to the *one* mort."

"Well, at least I can keep you out of woman trouble, so long as we're at sea, Mister Westcott," Lewrie said, chuckling at his second-in-command's irrepressible lust. "Once in England, though . . ."

"A 'temporary wife' in every port, sir . . . thank Jesus!"

"And Admiralty," Lewrie reminded him.

The watch bells interrupted them; eight of them struck in four pairs to signal the end of the Day Watch, and the start of the First Dog Watch, at 4 P.M. Up forward in the limited open space between the cross-deck ham-

mock nettings at the forward edge of the quarterdeck, and the binnacle
cabinet and double-wheeled helm, Lt. George Merriman was relieving Lt.
Clarence Spendlove of watch-standing duties. Happy Spendlove, who
would only have to stand a two-hour watch 'til the beginning of the Second Dog, and then have "all night in" and a long rest this evening, if the
weather co-operated and no crisis arose.

"You have the Middle?" Lewrie asked Westcott.

"I swapped with Merriman, sir. Just the one night," Westcott replied.
"If you have no more need of me, sir, I would wish to take a nap 'til supper
is served out."

"Carry on, Mister Westcott," Lewrie allowed him.

Once he was alone, Lewrie peered over the taffrails to see if the cutter
had been secured to a towing line, along with the launch and his gig. Convoying demanded the ship's boats be ready for service at all hours, if a
merchantman needed warning or assistance. *Blanding,* more to the point,
demanded prompt and plentiful use of the boats!

Lewrie put his hands in the small of his back, chiding himself to look
stern and "captainly" as he paced forward up the starboard side of the quarterdeck, then further onwards up the starboard sail-tending gangway, towards the bows, only halfway noting the neatness of the yard braces that
were belayed and hung on the pin-rails, how the excess rope was flemished
in neat coils on the gangway planking. His right hand idly rapped the
main-mast stays as he passed them, satisfying himself that they were properly taut . . . and fighting a grin of pleasure as he told himself that he was
fortunate to have Mr. Sprague as Bosun and Bosun's Mate Mr. Wheeler,
who were so particular and attentive to such things.

Lewrie went onto the forecastle and peered round the tautly bellowed
inner, outer, and flying jibs at their convoy . . . their awful and *bloody-
minded* convoy.

They had left Kingston, Jamaica, with eighty-odd merchant ships for
the Yucatán Passage, arranged in eight columns of roughly ten apiece,
with a cable of separation between ships in-line-ahead, and a cable of
separation between columns, a nice, neat travelling box that, to your lubberly layman meant . . . once he was told that a cable was 120 fathoms in
length—the convoy spanned a width of 1,920 civilian yards, and extended 2,400 yards from front to back. Easily guarded?

If only it was that simple!

Merchant masters naturally despised other ships getting anywhere
close to their own vessels, and the tendency was to shy off, widening the

gaps between columns to nigh two cables, and the distance between ships in-column about twice the desired space as well.

Going West from Jamaica had been the easy part, with all ships riding a stern wind, or a wind on their starboard quarters, but once they had turned Northerly to beam reach round the tip of Cuba, it was the leeward-lying columns, and the ones in the centre that had begun to fall behind, for the very good reason that the columns lying closest to the wind stole it from the others, and made better speed, pulling ahead despite frantic signals to reduce sail to conform with the rest, and the laggards ordered to crack on!

Then had come the long, slow slog to windward cross the top of Cuba and into the Florida Straits, and it was a wonder that Captain Blanding, or any officer in the escort, had a hair left on their heads, or voices left after screaming all the daylight hours in frustration.

To make way against the wind, a sailing vessel had to make long boards to either side of the prevailing breeze, and none but the few fore-and-aft rigged schooners or hermaphrodite brigs could point into the winds closer than sixty-six degrees off true. Any closer to "the eyes of the wind" and square-rigged ships risked luffing up and coming to a ruinous stop with their yards flung a'back.

The Trades were funnelled down the Straits from roughly the East-Nor'east; the convoy had to stand on larboard tack to the Sou'east to make progress, but sooner or later there was the Cuban coast and its shallows and shoals to consider, requiring that the ships come about, tacking to take the winds on starboard tack and steering North by East 'til the equally dangerous shallows of the Florida Keys loomed up, and they would have to go about, again.

In a perfect world experienced merchant mariners could perform that trick all at the same time, as soon as the Preparative was struck. But, first one had to get their bloody attention, make sure that every ship *acknowledged* that they *were* paying attention and was ready to come about, then do it together . . . which half of them were *not* and *did* not! The resulting stampede and chaos would have been hilarious, were it not hellish-dangerous.

Even the roar of one of *Modeste*'s 32-pounders would not arouse some of them. All escorts had to fire off guns in concert to awaken the worst offenders.

Once in the Straits, Captain Blanding had thought that he had the solution to the problem; his Sailing Directions issued to all merchant masters dictated that the eight columns would be narrowed to but four, and there had been several long paragraphs devoted to the evolution . . . which the civilian captains had not bothered to read 'til the very last moment, or were too illiterate to grasp in the first place.

It was like telling the village idiot how to re-assemble a clock, and hoping for the best! The order of sailing had gone to a width of 1,920 yards, and the length from the lead ships to the tail-ends of the columns to 9,600 yards, and to get them all sorted out into the four columns had taken the better part of a day, with ships swanning off on opposing tacks to avoid the ones astern, ahead, or to either beam to avoid collisions, with one column of twenty-odd ships thrashing along on starboard tack, Nor'east, the outer-most column to the North making a board to the Sou'east on larboard tack, and the two columns in the middle not sure whether to shit or go blind!

Lewrie was sure that Chaplain Brundish had taken himself below aboard *Modeste,* heart-sick that he had *not* cured Captain Blanding of his blaspheming, perhaps with wads of oakum and candle wax stuck into his ears so he could not hear the screams of the very best Billingsgate curses and imprecations bellowed by merchantmen and Navy officers to boot . . . amplified by brass speaking-trumpets!

A measure of relative calm had been restored once the trade had swung North up the narrow channel between Spanish Florida and the British Bahamas. It was only fourty-odd miles wide from the tiny Biminis and Great Isaac and Little Isaac to the Florida shores, so Blanding had left the convoy in four columns, too fearful, perhaps, of what further calamities would ensue should he try to put them back in the original sailing order. And when the Leeward Islands merchant ships had joined them above the Bahama Banks, in deeper and more open waters, they had been shepherded behind, ordered to take stations astern of the existing columns.

Lewrie extended his telescope again to look up those four long columns, then swung to the right to espy HMS *Modeste* out on the Eastern flank of the convoy. That was where the greatest threat usually would come, from seaward, and from windward, so a hostile warship or a privateer could use the wind to dash in, nip at the outer column, and snatch up a prize or two before the escorts could react.

"Usually," Lewrie muttered under his breath as he swung about to look for the other two frigates. Parham and his *Pylades* stood far ahead of the convoy, and a bit to seaward, searching for trouble and a first glimpse of strange sail. Stroud and his *Cockerel* guarded the larboard side of the trade, about mid-way down the left flank, and a good two miles or more landward.

A glance aloft at the angle of the yards and the streaming of the long commissioning pendant confirmed that the convoy *had* found a a slight lift. The winds, which had blown mildly but steadily from the East, now had a touch of East-Sou'easting to them. Two or three days more, and Lewrie could expect them to come from the Sou'east and allow all ships to alter course to the East-Nor'east, giving them all the sea-room in the world, hundreds of miles off Cape Hatteras and its shoals, for a long, curving passage to England, far from any searching foes.

And here I am . . . here's Reliant, *the "whipper-in" at the arise-end,* Lewrie told himself as he collapsed his telescope and took a last look about before heading aft to the quarterdeck once more; *just ploddin' along like a sheepherder. This wind continues t'back, the danger may come off our starboard quarters than abeam. It'll be a long damn' night!*

CHAPTER TWELVE

*T*he second rum issue of the day had been served out, Evening Quarters had been stood 'til the end of the Second Dog Watch at 6 P.M., and the Evening Watch took their stations on deck for the 8 to Midnight. The tarpaulins were cast off the hammock nettings and the off-watch crew's bedding was taken below.

Sunset, a rather pleasing one replete with all the ambers and reds and golds of semi-tropic seas, was rapidly fading, and the ocean was turning ink-black to seaward, still glittering with ebbing forge-light to leeward, and the winds, after a rather warm day, were cooling and most refreshing.

"A nice time to be at sea, sir," the Sailing Master, Mr. Caldwell, commented with a smile as he strolled the quarterdeck, puffing away on a short clay pipe. The Marine Lieutenant, Simcock, was taking the air as well, and enjoying one of his *cigaros*.

"Indeed it is, Mister Caldwell . . . Mister Simcock," Lewrie was glad to agree as he paced about by the windward bulwarks. He had shed his uniform coat and his cocked hat to savour the freshness and coolness of the evening, and to sprawl in his collapsible wood-and-canvas deck chair to enjoy the sunset. "So far, so good with our hen-headed charges, too. Nothing's gone smash, no one's strayed off, and none of them have rammed each other."

"Early hours, sir," Mr. Caldwell laughed. "Our merchant captains are possessed of a *ton* of foolishness."

"It's rather pretty, sir, even so," Lt. Simcock commented, and pointed with his chin forward and to starboard where the convoy lay.

And so it was; four long strings of sunset-tinted sails, with each sporting a pair of large taffrail lanthorns winking and rocking as the snail-slow hundred-odd ships gently hobby-horsed along, those lights casting shimmery patches of yellow-gold on the wave-tops. And at the change of the watch, when all ships, Navy or merchantman, had struck Eight Bells, the sound had come down to them like a faint and tinkly carillon. Much like their situation anent the bloody-mindedness of civilians, not one-tenth of their hour glasses or chronometers had agreed with each other, of course, so it had gone on for a while.

"We'll be losing some of our charges on the morrow," the Sailing Master was telling their Marine Lieutenant.

"Privateers? You're sure, sir?" Lt. Simcock asked with a gasp.

"The thirty-second latitude, sir," Mr. Caldwell told him with a chuckle. "Savannah, Georgia, lies almost directly on the thirty-second line of latitude, and Port Royal, Beaufort, and Charleston, South Carolina, lie a bit to the North of it."

"And thank God for their departure," Lt. Spendlove, now standing the watch, heartily stated, which made all three gentlemen laugh with delight. "The 'fewer the merrier,' to my lights."

"Ships bound for Savannah may run down the line of latitude, as they who cross the Atlantic for the West Indies do the fifteenth latitude, in search of the peaks of Dominica," Mr. Caldwell prosed on, glad to puff on his clay pipe and lecture, as he did with the Midshipmen at their lessons. "The lazy man's way, that. Does one know one's latitude, and holds the compass bearing, one's longitude is the only thing to be determined at Noon Sights. And . . . one can spot the mountains of Dominica from better than sixty miles, given a clear day."

"And the ones bound for Charleston get in sight of the coast, then turn North 'til they find it?" Lt. Simcock further asked. He was *not* one of those clever fellows who were quick with figures. That was why his family had purchased him a Marine officer's commission, and discouraged his wish to attend Woolwich and earn a commission in the Royal Artillery. At least aboard a warship, Lt. Simcock could still indulge in his enthusiasm for cannon and loud bangs.

"Oh, I'd suppose some of the least-skilled *may* grope their way to port in such fashion, but the experienced mariner would shape his course directly."

"There's many a master in the coasting trade back home who find their way from one seamark to the next," Lt. Spendlove contributed to the conversation. "People in the fisheries? They go out quite a ways to the good grounds, but all they require is a compass and a chip-log for Dead Reckoning."

"There's many a *merchant* captain who navigates that way!" Lewrie spoke up from his collapsible chair, with a snort of displeasure. "We have met a fair parcel of them, the last weeks."

That raised another round of agreeable laughter.

Lewrie rose from his chair as the last of the sunset guttered out, and only a top sliver of the sun lingered above the clear horizon.

"You have the ship, Mister Spendlove," he told his Second Lieutenant. "I'm bound below for supper. Send for me, should any more of those Yankee ships turn up to terrify our charges."

"Aye, sir . . . though *Modeste* may alert us, first, should one of them lurch up," Spendlove said in parting.

"Just in time, sir," Pettus told him as Lewrie walked over to his dining table to take a seat, pausing to pet Toulon and Chalky, who were already atop it, waiting for their evening meal to arrive from the galley. "A drop of something, sir? A claret? It will be rabbit, tonight, Yeovill tells me."

"Aye, thankee, Pettus," Lewrie agreed, noting that a bottle of claret already stood in the tall fiddles of the side-board, breathing.

"Yeovill feels un-appreciated, sir . . . the nights you don't invite others in," Pettus rambled on as he inspected a short-stemmed glass for smuts for the third time before pouring Lewrie a measure. "Likes to show off his culinary skills, he does."

"Sorry that I disappoint him," Lewrie said after a first sip of his wine. "I'd best have four or five guests tomorrow night, else he goes pettish. Hungry, are ye, lads? Lookin' forward to . . . *rabbit?*" he teased the cats. *That* set them off to quivery delight; they knew a few sounds or words like "sausage" or "jerky" and "treats," that would presage food, as well as they recognised their own names, and would come running (well, some of the time) when called.

Rabbit in particular; when fitting out and victualling in Portsmouth the year before, Captain Blanding had suggested that rabbits and quail, pigeons, and guinea fowl made a tasty alternative to salt-meats. Even before, in Anglesgreen, there were several large rabbit warrens on Lewrie's rented farm, so many that they'd get into the truck gardens and eat themselves silly in a single night. It was not allowed to hunt or snare them, for the land belonged to Uncle Phineas Chiswick, Lewrie's late wife's relative, but Patrick Furfy was a hellish-clever poacher, and somehow the rabbit population was reduced to a manageable level, and grilled rabbit or jugged hare turned up on Lewrie's table, and in the cats' bowls, with regularity. Oh, yes! They knew "rabbit" when they heard it.

"Cap'm's cook, SAH!" the Marine sentry outside the doors to the great-cabins bellowed, stamping his boots and musket butt on the decks.

In breezed Yeovill with the large oval metal barge in his hands. "Good evening, sir," Yeovill said; perfunctory, that, and equally sketchy was his greeting smile.

No, he ain't *happy,* Lewrie thought.

"Good evening, Yeovill!" Lewrie replied with forced enthusiasm. "Something smells delightful, I'm bound."

"Rabbit, sir," Yeovill answered, sounding a tad glum as he took the lid off the barge and began setting out smaller pots. "A one big enough for you and the kitties. First off, though, sir . . . a hearty bean soup."

Toulon and Chalky were teetering on the edge of the table, whiskers laid far forward, and their tails twitching. As Yeovill got within pawing distance as he served from the side-board, they stretched paws out to remind him that they were famished, too.

"Excellent!" Lewrie exclaimed as he sat down and whipped his napkin over his lap, though thinking the old saw *"There'll be foul winds from astern by morning"!*

"A lot of pepper sauce, the way you like it, sir," Yeovill added as he set a bowl of soup before him.

From Toulon and Chalky came hungry trills and outright wails of demand.

"If you'll pardon me, sir, I'll see to the eats whilst you eat your soup?" Yeovill asked, and lifted out a small pot from which he spooned shredded rabbit, rice, and un-seasoned beans into their bowls.

"Aye, go right ahead, Yeovill. They're starving," Lewrie said between spoonfuls. "Always glad t'see *you,* they are."

"Er, thankee, sir," Yeovill replied, with a tad more warmth than before, and a slightly broader grin. "The rabbit, sir, I roasted with salt, pepper, and a dash of Jamaican seasonings, then topped off with a large dollop of red plum jam, as you might with venison. There's sweet potato with butter, boiled peas and . . . baked cornmeal pones, to boot, sir!" Yeovill boasted. "What Mister Cooke showed me how to make without milk or eggs. One would go handsomely with the soup, this minute."

"Aye, it would," Lewrie agreed as Yeovill took the cloth cover off the separate bread barge and placed one on the side of his plate by the soup bowl. "Uhm! Hot and fresh! You're a wonder, Yeovill."

Christ, he's worse than dealin' with a wife! Lewrie thought as he bit into the pone; what the ship's freed slave Black cook called a hot-water-drop pone. It *was* good, though!

"Thankee for saying so, sir," Yeovill replied, pleased that his efforts had garnered praise. Yeovill had come aboard from an inn that had burned down, losing his position, and fancied himself a *chef* in the French *restaurateur* style; he'd even come with a large chest containing his own pots, pans, knives, and an host of sauces and seasonings.

For a man who knew his way with victuals, Yeovill was a *thin'un,* with a rough complexion and a shock of light brown hair so curly that it looked like friz . . . especially so since he had let it grow out into a seaman's queue; the hair bound back at the nape of his neck stood out like a bottle brush, or a frightened cat's tail.

"Oh, I'll be having five supper guests tomorrow night, Yeovill," Lewrie told him. "First Officer, Purser, Lieutenant Simcock, and two Mids. Thought I'd warn ye now, not wait 'til breakfast."

"Supper for six, sir?" Yeovill said, perking up devilish-glad. "Depend on me, sir!"

"Excellent!" Lewrie rejoined. "I knew I could."

"Well, I will leave you to it, sir," Yeovill said with a satisfied sniff, and a slight bow from the waist. "If Jessop can return the servers to the galley when you're done? Oh! Forgot to mention, but there's a wee apple turnover to go with your port and cheese, sir!"

"You spoil me, Yeovill, 'deed ye do," Lewrie praised further. Once Yeovill had left, Lewrie cast a wry grin at Pettus, who was filling a plate with his *entrée.*

"Aye, sir," Pettus agreed with a roll of his eyes. "But, he is a wonder, even so, sir."

Lewrie had dined later than usual, later than his officers, as was the custom. Barely had he finished a single glass of port and a meagre slice of cheddar that had not gone red-wormy yet, than the ship's Master At Arms, Mr. Appleby, and the Ship's Corporals, Scammell and Keetch, began their rounds to assure that all lanthorns and glim candles were doused for the night at 9 P.M., as soon as Two Bells of the Evening Watch were struck. He took himself on deck for one last turn, with his coat on this time against the cool wind and damp.

"Captain's on deck," Midshipman Houghton warned the others.

Lt. Spendlove shifted from the windward bulwarks to amidships of the quarterdeck to accommodate Lewrie's presence. "Evening, sir," he said.

"All's quiet, Mister Spendlove?" Lewrie asked, once settled by the mainmast shrouds.

"Mostly, sir, though . . . I was about to send for you to ask if I might post a lookout aloft," Spendlove hesitantly said. "The lookouts on deck . . . we've spotted several lights, the last few hours, sir. Ships passing Sutherly inshore of the convoy, at least three for sure. And, there *was* one ship bound South on the windward horizon."

"More American merchantmen?" Lewrie asked with a scowl, and one lifted brow. "How far off, the inshore ones?"

"Very possibly, sir," Spendlove replied, shrugging. "As to the ones to leeward of us, they seemed to be at least ten or twelve miles off, right on the horizon. The one up to windward, sir . . . ," Spendlove added, sweeping an arm out to starboard.

"Aye," Lewrie said, stepping up onto the slide of a carronade carriage, then atop the barrel to the top of the bulwarks, clinging to the thick tarry cables of the shrouds, and of half a mind to go out-board and clamber up the rat-lines for a better view.

For that mysterious set of ship's lights was still visible from the quarterdeck, and a higher vantage point might tell them more about the strange ship that displayed them.

"No signal from *Modeste*?" Lewrie asked, chiding himself for the uselessness of his question at once. If the flagship had been worried, there would have been blue-light fusees burning in her main tops, and signal rockets whooshing skywards by the dozen; alerting guns would be roaring and ruining his supper!

"None so far, sir," Lt. Spendlove told him in a neutral voice.

Most-like he's bitin' his cheek not t'laugh at such a hen-head question, Lewrie thought.

Coming down was harder than going up, in the dark; Lewrie went at it gingerly, so he didn't crack an ankle by jumping down. He was not as spry as he'd been in his Midshipman days.

"Aye, post lookouts aloft, in the fore and mizen tops," Lewrie directed, rubbing his hands with a cheap calico handkerchief to remove the cold tar that had stuck to him from the shrouds. "Have we night-glasses to spare?"

"Do I lend mine, sir, aye," Spendlove volunteered.

"Mister Westcott will be taking the Middle for Mister Merriman tonight," Lewrie remembered. "When he relieves you, my compliments to him, and he's to post lookouts aloft as well."

"Aye, sir!"

"Carry on, Mister Spendlove. Pay me no mind," Lewrie bade him. "I only came for the air." He paced aft down the starboard bulwarks, right to *Reliant*'s own glowing taffrail lanthorns, shielding his eyes from the brightness to peer seaward at the strange set of lights, with his hands cupped to either side of his brows.

Those lights were faint, and very far off, and about four or five points abaft of amidships. It was too dark to spot her sails to determine if the strange vessel was bound South, or was idling under reduced sail on a course matching their own . . . waiting for a chance to crack on and dash up to the convoy during the dull hours of the Middle Watch.

Still shielding his eyes, Lewrie crossed over to larboard and peered out at the other lights. From the height of the quarterdeck above the ebony-black sea, all he could determine of them was that one set of lights was only a point or two abaft, and the two South of her were even further astern of *Reliant*, and far astern of the bulk of the convoy. The newly-posted lookouts aloft might be able to see more of them, but only a little more.

As Lewrie watched, the Sutherly-most set of lights winked out, making him stiffen. Had she doused them? No, they winked to life one deep breath later—both that distant vessel and *Reliant* had sloughed into wave troughs at the same time, he realised—then winked out again, and did not re-appear, even as the frigate rose atop the waves.

Hopefully over the horizon, and innocent as a baby chick, Lewrie thought . . . with fingers crossed; *Damme,* forget *a decent hour or three o' sleep! I'll be up half the night in fret!*

CHAPTER THIRTEEN

*O*h, dear Lord, what a bloody . . . !" Lt. Westcott began to shout, then thought better of it. "They're all a pack of ninnies and . . . !"

"All I ask is you don't let us be rammed or trampled, Mister Westcott," Lewrie said, with his fingers crossed again, and a look of sheer stupefaction on his phyz.

A quarter-hour before the start of the Forenoon Watch at 8 A.M., *Modeste* had put up a flag hoist that would release the merchant vessels bound for Georgian or Carolinian ports. Unfortunately . . .

Civilian shipmasters were, in the main, not used to the customs of the Royal Navy. The flag signal, two-blocked at the peak of the halliards, *should* have been taken as the Preparative, put up early enough for even the dullest, sleepiest lookouts or mates of the watch aboard the trading vessels to have time to, One; *See* it. Two; Look up what it meant in their signals book and *read* it. Three; grasp what the Devil it *meant*. And Four; Act upon it when it was *struck down*, not before!

As soon as the signal went aloft, however, and two guns were fired to direct all ships' attention to it, some of the Americas-bound vessels hauled their wind that instant, going broader on the breeze; some with the winds fine on their starboard quarters, some others settling on a "soldier's wind" to the Nor'west with the breeze square on their sterns, and "both sheets aft." Yet a few others wore about to take the Sou'easterly wind on their larboard quarters, bound Due West for Savannah, Port Royal, and Beaufort.

"Two bloody hours to herd them back together . . . for this!" Lt. Westcott grumbled some more, astounded by the chaos that that Preparative hoist had engendered.

"Just fire into the most threatening, sir," Lewrie told him with his tongue firmly planted in his cheek, as the somewhat orderly nature of the convoy shredded in an eyeblink.

It was regrettable that those Americas-bound merchantmen weren't all in the landward columns; they were scattered throughout the convoy like raisins in a duff. To obey that signal, assuming they had *seen* it or paid the *slightest* bit of attention, they had to wheel about onto a new course, whilst the bulk of the ships bound for ports further North or for England stood on to the Nor'-Nor'east.

Well, they *did* 'til the ship that was waddling along two cables to windward decided to haul her wind and come down, or the ship wallowing ahead altered course, forcing the vessel down for the long voyage to wheel about to avoid a collision, too! Which wheel-about frightened the ship astern or to starboard to duck away as well, which laid her on a collision course with one of those departing ships that had come swanning leeward in dumb—very dumb!—obedience to that signal.

"Harden up windward two points, Mister Westcott!" Lewrie snapped as that idiotic, half-rotten *Turtledove*, which had been lagging astern all through the night, put her helm over to wear to Due West; as slow as she was, she would be beam-on to *Reliant* in another minute, as good as shouting, "Hit me amidships, I dare you!"

"Another two points!" Lewrie ordered half a minute later as the *Turtledove*'s sorry collection of gammers and clueless teens took an *age* to complete their wear-about to larboard tack, and was making as much a rate of knots as a drifting log.

"Thankee for the escort, *Reliant*!" her aged captain whinnied as the frigate shaved past her at long musket-shot. "We will take it from here!"

"I hope ye bloo . . . !" Lewrie began to shout back through a brass speaking-trumpet, but forebore. "I hope you have a safe passage!" he said instead. "You cunny-thumbed, cack-handed clown!" he muttered to himself.

"Oh God, I can't stand it!" Lt. Merriman said, holding his arms round his middle and wheezing with laughter. "What an idiot!"

"I say now, don't the columns look rather . . . queer?" Marine Lt.

Simcock, on the quarterdeck to take the morning air, pointed out. "One would think they'd seen a privateer, or something. Normal, is it?"

Reliant indeed had a fine view of sheer terror; after-most of the escorts, at the tail-end of those four long columns which were now haring off in penny-packets no larger than two or three, and all on disparate courses, they could witness it all.

"*Modeste* has struck her signal, sir," Midshipman Munsell reported. "The Execute is ordered."

"About bloody time!" Lewrie snorted. "Mister Westcott? We'll 'Spanish reef' the main course and tops'l for a bit, and get a way off her, else we'll tangle with the after-most ship of the windward column."

She was a large three-master, nigh the size of an Indiaman, and had ended up at the end of her column due to her lack of speed, and was looming up quickly. Her master and mates on her quarterdeck were peering astern with their eyes so blared open that Lewrie fancied that he could see the whites of their eyes at a full cable.

Hands aloft quickly clewed up *Reliant*'s main course and main tops'l to reduce the spread of canvas, and her own speed, turning the wind-full sails into lubberly bags, even as the merchantman's sailors scrambled aloft to shake reefs from her own sails and get a way on. It would make her fast enough to avoid collision with the frigate, but it would also push her along a knot faster than the ship ahead of her in column, which would "put the wind up" that one, forcing *her* to spread more canvas or turn alee, threatening whichever vessel lay ahead or to leeward of *her,* and . . . ! It was like watching an overly hopeful child's stack of wooden blocks come crashing down!

"Ehm . . . should someone have *planned* for . . . ?" Lt. Simcock hesitantly asked, looking about completely clueless. "Isn't there anything to be done?"

"Cross your fingers, Arnold," Lt. Merriman said, tittering with now-subdued amusement. "Say a prayer, if you like."

"Cross your legs and guard your 'nut-megs,' too, sir," the Sailing Master, Mr. Caldwell, guffawed. "Gawd, I haven't seen the like in all my born days! Like a pack of headless chickens!"

"About all we *can* do is sit back and watch it play out," Lewrie decided aloud. "And *if* no one goes aboard another, and *if* we don't have to render assistance, I expect it'll take 'til mid-afternoon to herd 'em back into proper order."

I could send Blanding a signal, with a humble *"Submit," but . . . I don't think he'd be very receptive,* Lewrie thought, trying *very* hard not to laugh out loud; *It's all up to him. Just an obedient old sailor, me. Yarr, and belike, har har!*

"We're safe, sir," Lt. Westcott opined. "We'll be clear of yon three-master in a minute, and up to windward of her, a bit."

"Very well, Mister Westcott," Lewrie replied. "Once clear, we will shake the 'Spanish reefs' out, and stand to windward of the convoy . . . t'keep the most of 'em from dashin' off for bloody *Africa*!"

"Ooh! *That* was a close'un!" Lt. Merriman groaned.

"Aah! I was *sure* they'd tangle!" Lt. Spendlove, drawn on deck by the commotion, said of another close call ahead of them.

"Aha! Signal rockets in the daytime?" Mr. Caldwell pointed out.

"Mmm! Pretty!" Midshipman Munsell enthused.

It was a miracle that all ships came through without a scratch in their paint, or a scrape down their hull scantlings. Twenty-five vessels left the convoy (wheezing with relief, cursing like Billingsgate fish-mongers, or fanning with their hats in shuddery "damme, I've cheated death, again!" laughter); that left eighty-four bemused or frightened-out-of-their-wits ships remaining, which Captain Blanding in *Modeste* tried to re-assemble. Lots of powder was expended in alerting guns, and every signal flag was employed from *Modeste*'s taffrail lockers before it was managed.

Blanding ordered the remaining ships to fetch-to and await his new directives. *Reliant, Cockerel,* and *Pylades* were ordered to "Send Boats"—not "Captain(s) Repair On Board"; their senior officer was most-like too abashed to face his juniors at that point—which took at least an hour or more.

"We're to what?" Lewrie asked, once Midshipman Houghton returned.

"We're ah . . . to enquire of all vessels their ports of call, sir," Houghton told him. "Captain Blanding has supplied us with the names and numbers he's assigned to each, and we're to sort them out in their order of departure from the trade, sir. He will re-assemble the convoy with all ships due to leave us for American ports into the lee-most column, or columns, sir. So they may haul their wind, and peel off as we approach the latitude of their destinations, sir, avoiding another, ah . . ."

"Oh, aye! Avoidin' *that* again!" Lewrie scoffed, dubious.

Wish he'd thought o' that beforehand, Lewrie thought; *damme, I bet* he *does, too. Or . . . I should've, if no one else did.*

Captain Blanding had vowed that not one of the merchantmen en-trusted to his care would be lost, and, despite that morning's debacle none *had* been. What happened to the lightly-armed "runners" that left the con-voy was not the Navy's responsibility, of course, but it looked as if keeping that vow would take several *tons* of luck . . . and Lewrie strongly sus-pected that they'd used a fair parcel of that luck up!

"Bosun . . . Mister Sprague? All ship's boats in the water, and manned!" Lewrie called down to the frigate's waist. "I'll send you in one, Mister Houghton, Mister Entwhistle, and Mister Warburton. Pass the word for them, pray, and I'll explain their duties once here."

"Ehm . . . Captain Blanding also wishes that the trade be ordered into *eight* columns, sir," Mr. Houghton went on, shambling his feet at being remiss in mentioning it.

Lewrie just goggled at him for a bit.

"Well, *that'll* keep ye busy 'til sundown, Mister Houghton. Oh, take joy of it, do, young sir!" Lewrie could not help from saying, and laughing right out loud, after a long moment.

Christ, what a shitten pot-mess! he thought.

They'd been given a list of names of the remaining ships, and the names of their masters, and would have to go aboard each one that was within sight in the rear of the convoy, assign them their proper new numbers, then tell them to assemble to leeward, if they were down for Wilmington, North Carolina, the James river, or the Chesapeake, or ports further North. Lewrie was mortal-certain that his Mids would be greeted with goggle-eyed, aston-ished stares, and splutters asking *how* they were to work their way leeward through the others.

Then, they would have to shepherd them to their new placings, *then* re-port to Captain Blanding in *Modeste* the names and numbers of the ships sent to the leeward columns so some clerkish-soul, likely Chaplain Brundish, could write it all down, with little ovals representing each ship, with ship names, numbers, and destinations jotted in *tiny* script beside each, to be checked off like landed crates from a cargo manifest as each departed them.

Hell, it might be dawn tomorrow *'fore we're back under way and in proper order!* Lewrie groaned to himself. It would be yet another very long night, and the chance of an enemy privateer showing up—Lewrie had let that threat escape his mind for some time—did not even bear imagining!

And what some curious and bemused American merchant ship that stumbled onto them during all that sorting out thought of the efficiency of the Royal Navy didn't bear thinking about, either!

Reliant was fetched-to, along with their convoy, rolling and wallowing most sickly. Lewrie's cook, Yeovill, came onto the larboard gangway from the galley up forward. He was not a good sailor with a cast-iron constitution if the ship was not under way. He "cast his accounts to Neptune" overside.

Damme, that says it all, don't it? Lewrie cynically thought.

CHAPTER FOURTEEN

*L*ewrie had over-estimated the time it would take to shake their convoy into its new sailing order; eight columns of ten merchantmen—with the last odd four tacked onto the tail-end—got formed by sunset, at the end of the Second Dog. The efforts of the escort ships had been aided by the boats from *Lady of Swansea,* the civilian "commodore" of the trade's ship, and several of that worthy's old friends who captained some of the bigger three-masters that regularly voyaged from the West Indies and back.

Lewrie suspected that what those experienced masters said among themselves, and passed along to every other vessel they could reach, went something very much like, "Listen, mates. This gilt-laced Navy pop-in-jay has less of a clue than a fart in a trance, so here's what *we'll* do . . . and bugger him!"

But then, Captain Alan Lewrie had been a cynical and sarcastic sort for years on end.

This sunset was not as spectacular as the one he had enjoyed the evening before. The wind was gathering strength from the Sou'east and the seas were a tad more boisterous. Though the skies were piled with white cloud during the afternoon, and the sunset was still pacific-looking despite the building thickness to the West, to leeward, there was a suspicious odour of fresh damp to the air, presaging rain, somewhere around them, sooner or later.

HMS *Reliant* still prowled the rear of the convoy, swanning from its larboard quarter to its starboard corner, continually making, shortening sail as it ran up close to the laggards, dashing off to investigate why a trailing ship did not press on, then quartering back to spur another to keep up—for the third or fourth time.

The ship's boats were still in the water, being towed astern by long painters, with tarpaulin covers to keep out the rain and splashed waves sure to come from swamping them, Lewrie took note as he made one last stroll round the quarterdeck before going below for his supper.

He looked forward once he fetched up at the cross-deck hammock nettings, studying their convoy, and shaking his head. It was now more manageable to escort. With two cables between each of the eight long columns, it now spanned almost a full two miles in width, and with ten ships in each column—less the four odd'uns—with two cables' separation between those, it was about two and a half miles long. Each of its flanks could be watched more closely by Captain Stroud's *Cockerel* to leeward, or Captain Blanding in *Modeste* to windward, and *Pylades* at the head of the box, and *Reliant* at its rear, had much shorter distances to go to confront any threat that loomed up in the night.

As slow as the convoy sailed, Mr. Caldwell, the Sailing Master, estimated that they were now close to the 34th degree of North latitude, and about 120 miles East of the Cape Fear in North Carolina. The winds had backed sufficiently and now came from the Sou'east, allowing all of the ships to reach across them on a Nor'easterly heading, assuring them good clearance of Cape Hatteras and the dangerous Outer Banks; and pray God the winds *stayed* out of the Sou'east, so that the bulk of the trade could reach the 40th latitude—where the New England–bound vessels would leave them—and steer Easterly across the North Atlantic.

"It'll be dark as a boot, tonight," Lewrie said to Lt. Spendlove, who had the watch.

"Aye, sir. And smells very much like rain," Spendlove agreed, "Though there was no sign of it to windward before sunset. The clouds were darkest to leeward of us."

"Keep a sharp lookout," Lewrie cautioned as he went below.

"Aye, sir. 'Tis a perfect night for raiders."

His supper guests were already in his cabins, and his steward, Pettus, had opened the wine cabinet for them. Lt. Westcott was sipping Rhenish, as was the Sailing Master, Mr. Caldwell. Marine Lt. Simcock had a brandy, and the Mids, Warburton and Grainger, were smacking their lips over sweeter sherries when Lewrie greeted them.

"We'd best not irk the Master At Arms, so, let's take our seats and dine," Lewrie suggested. "With luck, we may be done by the time he orders all lights extinguished, hey? You may serve, Yeovill."

"Aye, sir!" his cook perkily replied, eager to show off what he had cobbled together.

"Good ho!" Lt. Simcock enthused at the soup, a hearty beef and shredded bacon broth. "Quite zesty!"

"Indeed," Lewrie agreed after a first spoonful.

"I wonder if Captain Blanding sups this well, tonight, sir," Mr. Caldwell slyly said with a broad grin above his napkin, which was tucked into his shirt collar.

"Captain Blanding always dines well," Lt. Westcott added. "If he has the *appetite* this evening, though . . . ?"

"I doubt we'll discover whether he does or not," Lewrie told them, grinning himself. "You'll note that invitations to dine aboard the flagship've dropped off next to nothing, of late."

"Perhaps when we're in an English port, sir?" Westcott hinted with a wink. "One last get-together before the squadron's broken up?"

"If only," Lt. Simcock wished aloud, with a dramatic sigh.

"You wish such, Mister Simcock?" Lewrie asked.

"Convoying is not as exciting as our previous duties, sir," Lt. Simcock said with a shrug. "But, do we discharge the duty well, there is a chance that Admiralty will find us so *useful* at it that we'll be doing it forever."

"Oh, God!" Westcott said, cringing. "Heaven forbid!"

"We could *lose* a few merchantmen, perhaps, and . . . ?" Midshipman Warburton cheekily posed, half to his messmate Grainger and half to the table. Grainger looked ready to choke on his titters.

"Though it does seem to have its . . . *amusing* moments," Westcott said with a snicker. "The last two days, at least."

"With enough forethought, though, that chaos could have been avoided," Mr. Caldwell supposed with a frumpy, dis-approving air.

"*I* didn't think of it," Lewrie told them. "My one experience at convoying was with a 'John Company' trade to Cape Town, and they were all going to Calcutta, then Canton, together, so it never entered my mind that departing ships *had* t'be placed to leeward."

"We'll know better next time . . . if there is a next time," Lt. Westcott said with another mock-shiver and gag-grimace, which expression set Midshipman Grainger off again.

"Or formed in more than four columns, sir?" Mr. Caldwell asked with a derisive tone to his voice, ever-ready to lecture. "They were simply too hard to guard in such a formation, and we were very fortunate that no privateers popped up . . . so far."

"Well, I'd imagine that Captain Blanding thought that only four columns'd make our convoy more manageable in the straits we've passed through," Lewrie countered, finding himself defending Blanding, though he secretly agreed with Caldwell. "Especially on those legs of our passage requiring an hundred or more ships to beat to weather. As bad as they had to tack so often, think how much more catastrophic things could have been, with eight or *ten* columns bearing down on each other!"

"Now *that* would have been a picture!" Lt. Westcott laughed out loud. "We'd surely have lost a few, as Mister Warburton wishes, and then we'd never be saddled with convoy duty again, ha ha!"

My thoughts exactly! Lewrie thought with a taut little smile.

Pettus topped up their glasses, whilst Jessop and Yeovill fetched out the next courses. There was a sliced ham, smoked in the rural American fashion and purchased ashore in Kingston from a Yankee trader. Each guest got a fairly fresh baked potato and green beans, the beans dried for long-term storage on long strands that the ship's cook had laced from the overhead beams in the galley, what Americans from South Carolina that Lewrie had met in '98 had called "leather britches." A good soak and boiling with a ham hock or square of bacon fat brought them back to life, and served with shreds of scalded onion, well!

To liven up the meal, there was mustard, worcestershire sauce, the usual salt and pepper, and a liquid pepper sauce that Yeovill had discovered on Jamaica, as well as a creamy gravy, and some relatively fresh globs of butter for the potatoes. All the seasonings were more than welcome; after a few weeks at sea, on a diet consisting mainly of salt-meats, beans, peas, and dry ship's bisquit, anything that could add zest and tang to rations temporarily relieved the boredom, lingering on the tongue long after the meal was done.

Lastly came a rice custard, sweetened with honey, and sugar, and with some lemon juice, so sweet and tangy that the Midshipmen lapped theirs up in an eyeblink and looked longingly for seconds, Midshipman Grainger swearing that it was as good as his mother's lemonade!

"Now, had I more time this afternoon, sirs," Yeovill bragged as he

spooned out more for the youngsters, "I would have done you all an om-
elet apiece for a second course, with bacon, cheese, and a Spanish *salsa* . . .
all peppers, tomatoes, and such they put up in stone crocks with vinegar.
There was some in the soup, sirs, and I hope you found it savoury."

"Indeed I did, Yeovill!" Lt. Simcock assured him.

"The gun-room's chickens, or mine, Yeovill?" Lewrie asked with one
brow up in jest.

"Eggs is eggs, sir . . . what bankers on the 'Change in London call
fungible, once laid . . . and moved from nest to nest," Yeovill replied with
an inscrutable expression.

"Three cheers for Mister Yeovill, a most excellent chef!" Lt. Westcott
urged, lifting his glass on high.

"Hear hear!" the Sailing Master seconded.

"A glass with him!" Lt. Simcock proposed.

"Well, sirs . . . ," Yeovill demurred with false modesty.

"Aye, a glass with Mister Yeovill," Lewrie agreed, nodding to Pettus to
pour the fellow a glass of something. Yeovill chose brandy, and knocked it
back quickly, smiling fit to bust, as if he'd just had congratulations for the
meal from the King himself as they all joined him in a celebration drink.

Yeovill's job was done for the night; it was Pettus and Jessop who cleared
the table of plates, glasses, and utensils, snatched away the dampened tablecloth, and set out the port bottle, fresh glasses, and smaller barges containing sweet bisquit, nuts, and cheeses.

Once all their glasses had been charged with port, Lewrie looked
down the table to Midshipman Grainger, the youngest that evening, who
was seated at the foot of the table. He raised his glass of port and intoned,
"Gentlemen . . . the King."

Grainger paid no notice, busy stuffing sweet bisquit into his mouth, in
a squirrel-cheek contest with Warburton.

"Ahem?"

Warburton elbowed Grainger. "What?" Grainger objected.

"Gentlemen, the King," Lewrie repeated more sternly.

"Oh Lord!" Grainger said with a gulp, realising his error and quickly
grabbing his glass to raise on high. "Gentlemen, I give you . . . the King!"

"Sooner or later," Lt. Westcott japed, once the toast had been drunk to
"heel-taps."

"Dined ashore with some Army officers once," the Sailing Master recalled. "They stood for the King's Toast, of course, but . . . when a senior
officer proposed it, their Vice was too 'foxed' and distracted, and when the

President of the mess repeated it, *louder*, the poor chap looked round and said, 'The King? Here? Well, show him in,' haw haw!"

"I give you Thursday's toast, sirs," Lewrie went on. "'Here's to a bloody war, or a sickly season'!"

The best and quickest way to promotion and advancement, that, and a sentiment shared by all, the Mids most especially.

"Thank you for the invitation to supper, sir," Warburton said as the port bottle made its larboardly way to him again. "The memory of it *may* carry me through tomorrow's Banyan Day."

On Mondays, Wednesdays, and Fridays, cheese, pease, bisquit, and oatmeal were the main victuals, and hellish-disappointing, no matter how liberal were the portions. There was no mustard, no other sauce, that could make a Banyan Day tangy.

"For which we have Queen Elisabeth to thank," Mr. Caldwell said. "God bless her miserly nature."

"Kept the fleet aboard after beating the Spanish Armada, too," Lt. Westcott added. "Scurvy and fevers made a hellish reaping before they were released . . . and *paid*, d'ye see."

"The fewer heroes, the greater the glory," Lewrie japed with a cynical leer. "Don't believe there were any Spanish prizes taken, so there wasn't a larger share awarded to the survivors, either, so—"

Bang! of a musket stock; Slam-slam of the Marine sentry's boots, and a louder-than-normal shout of, "Midshipman Houghton, SAH!"

"Enter?" Lewrie bade, cocking an ear to the sounds of the ship and not liking what he heard. Bosun's calls were already shrilling.

"Mister Spendlove's duty, sir, and there's a strange ship attacking the lee columns! *Cockerel*'s fired off signal rockets!"

"Here's your excitement, Mister Simcock!" Lewrie said, rising quickly and dashing his napkin to the deck. "All hands, and beat to Quarters!"

CHAPTER FIFTEEN

*T*he night *was* black as a boot, but sprinkled with the fire-fly tiny gleams from taffrail lanthorns, gleams that seemed to be swinging more Easterly as the leeward columns of merchant ships shied from the threat of a raider in their midst. The *Cockerel* frigate was filling the air with up-swooshing pinpricks of bright amber lights of warning rockets, and her main-mast's upper-most tip showed a series of fusees burning bright blue in a diamond pattern. As Lewrie gained the deck, *Cockerel* fired off two guns, their discharges eyeblink spurts of white powder smoke, shot through with amber and yellow.

"Is she taking something under fire?" Lt. Spendlove was worrying aloud.

"Making the 'General' signal to the convoy, more like, sir," Midshipman Houghton commented as a Marine drummer began the Long Roll.

"Mister Westcott?" Lewrie called out.

"Aye, sir?"

"Steer Due North for the convoy's larboard quarter, and crack on sail," Lewrie ordered.

"Very good, sir. Quartermasters, come about to Due North. Mister Spendlove, I relieve you," Westcott snapped, drawing a breath for his next shout to the brace-tenders on either gangway.

"Aye, and thank you, sir," Spendlove said before dashing to his post at Quarters in the waist to supervise the guns.

Reliant rode the ink-black seas on a beam wind at that moment, rising and surging forward, then sloughing into a wave trough and butting through with a brief loss of momentum. The frigate trembled with what felt like a stallion's impatience at the start-line of a race as off-watch sailors thundered up from their mess and berthing deck for their posts, some in shoes but most unshod. Gun tools were dealt out, the arms chests were unlocked—that took a moment, for Lewrie had come to the quarterdeck without the keys, and had to send Pettus to fetch them—and the dull red battle lanthorns were lit down each battery, between the guns, reflecting hellish-eerie from the tubs of swabbing water. Even more tiny lights flickered to life as the slow-match fuses were coiled round the tops of the tubs and the ends lit to ignite the primer quills, should the newer flintlock strikers fail.

"Cast off your guns!" Lt. Spendlove was loudly ordering as the hands mustered by their pieces.

"Your sword and pistols, sir?" Pettus asked from behind Lewrie, almost making him jump.

"Pistols'll be more useful tonight, Pettus," Lewrie told him. "If there's need t'board anything, I'll snatch up a spare cutlass."

"Be back in a trice, sir, then I'll see the cats to the orlop," Pettus promised, then ghosted away at a dash for the great-cabins.

As *Reliant* altered course, the convoy's many lights swung away to starboard even quicker, tautening up to the wind at "full and by" to beat their way to weather, and safety.

"God, just *look* at 'em!" Lewrie muttered, groaning. "As bad as a flock o' witless sheep!"

The somewhat orderly columns that had stretched ahead of *Reliant* when she had sailed along astern of them were now seen from a new angle, and what Lewrie could see wasn't pretty. Viewed from the convoy's larboard quarter, and all ships scurrying away, he could make out *no* order to it, and was put in mind of the thousands of floating lotuses and tiny oil lamps wafting down the Hooghly river during some Hindoo festival when he had been at Calcutta, so long ago.

"The ship is at Quarters, sir," Lt. Westcott crisply reported a minute later, all his earlier gaiety vanished.

"Very well, Mister Westcott," Lewrie replied. "Now, does anyone *see* anything out there?" He put his hands on his hips and looked up to the mizen and the main fighting tops, which were now manned by spry younger topmen, sharpshooters, Marines, and lookouts.

"Aloft, there! Sing out, do you spot something!" Lt. Westcott shouted to them with a speaking-trumpet.

Lewrie walked to the forward edge of the quarterdeck for a look-see of his own. There was the gaggle of the convoy to starboard, and there was Captain Stroud's *Cockerel* a mile or so off the larboard bows, and there was a set of lights that he took for Captain Parham's *Pylades* much further off, fine on the starboard bows, but . . . other than those he could make out nothing.

"Deuced odd, sir," Lewrie heard the Sailing Master say to Lieutenant Westcott. "How could a privateer or frigate approach from alee? Windward's the preferred method."

"Is our raider a big, fast schooner, Mister Caldwell, striking from loo'rd, though, she'd be knots faster than any of the tubs we're guarding, and can go much closer to the eyes of the wind. A schooner *could* come up to us, close-hauled."

"Your pistols, sir," Pettus announced as he popped up, ghostly-like, once more. "Primed and loaded."

"Thankee, Pettus," Lewrie said, like to jump out of his skin, again as he accepted his double-barrelled pistols and stuck them onto the waistband of his breeches by the spring clips.

How the Hell does he do *that?* Lewrie wondered as Pettus vanished into the dark.

"Deck, there!" a lookout on the foremast shouted. "*Cockerel's* turnin' t'windward!"

Lewrie peered and squinted forward; sure enough, he could make out a change in *Cockerel's* lights. Her taffrail lanthorns were coming together, the starboard one overlapping the laboard, and the distance between her stern lights and her main-mast fusees becoming greater. By the glow of her fusees, he could barely spot some of her upper sail canvas.

"Whatever's out there, it's got past her," Lewrie barked. "And to windward of *us*! Harden up to windward, Mister Westcott. Lay her head Nor'east, again!"

We're a mile up to windward more than Cockerel, Lewrie schemed, hoping that *Reliant* might stumble upon whatever Stroud had discovered, first; *If there's a privateer 'tween us and the convoy . . .*

"Deck, there!" the main-mast lookout shouted this time. "Signal rockets to *starboard*! Rockets, *four* points off the starboard bows!"

"Make for the ship launching rockets, Mister Westcott!" Lewrie snapped.

"Aye, sir!" the First Officer replied. Lt. Westcott pointed out to the Nor'east as he spotted the merchantman in distress. "*Thus,* Quartermaster!" he directed the helmsmen, chopping his hand to indicate the course. "Harden up for a close reach, Bosun!"

Reliant turned up closer to the winds, her yards braced up for more speed, and the decks canting over to leeward a few more degrees. Barely had she settled on the new course than the lookouts raised the alarm again. *More* distress rockets were being launched by other ships . . . further up to the Nor'east!

"*Two* of 'em, damn their eyes!" Lewrie snapped, pounding a fist on the cross-deck railings. "That'un'll be *Cockerel*'s pigeon. We can only deal with the one off our bows."

And, since the convoy had turned away to flee so precipitously, the merchant ship that Lewrie *could* aid was more than a mile away, and if she had let fly all her canvas, it would take *Reliant* more than half an hour to catch her, and the raider, up!

"She's not firing any more rockets," Mr. Caldwell commented. "I expect she's run out of them, by now."

"Or, she's taken, sir," Lt. Westcott speculated.

"Whoops, I was wrong!" the Sailing Master said. "There's more!"

"From the same ship . . . or yet another one?" Lewrie wondered in rising frustration. "There's so many stern lights, it's hard to tell which one launched them . . . which one's launching *now*!"

"Poor *Modeste*," Lewrie heard Midshipman Houghton snigger. "She will be no help at all."

"Aye, Mister Houghton," Caldwell agreed, chuckling a bit, too. "She's not so much *leading* the stampede as she is being *chased*!"

"And can't come about without the risk of colliding with one of them . . . or causing a whole series of collisions," the Midshipman further supposed.

"*That* won't do Captain Blanding's choler any good, sir," Lieutenant Westcott, standing closer to Lewrie, muttered.

"It wouldn't do mine any good either, Mister Westcott!" Lewrie replied, wryly grinning and shaking his head. "I expect we'll hear all about it, come tomorrow."

"Hark . . . gunfire, sir!" Westcott said of a sudden, head lifted as if sniffing the air like a hound.

No one aloft or on deck had seen the gun flashes, and the sound came down seconds later, after the flashes guttered out.

"Where away, the gunfire?" Lewrie yelled aloft, but no one had a clue.

"I *think* it came from larboard, sir . . . up to the North of us," Westcott said with his head cocked over in puzzlement, and shrugging. "Among the stragglers from the lee-most column, most-like."

"Gunfire!" a lookout cried at last. "Deck, there! Gun flashes *t'larboard* . . . *two* points off th' larboard bows!"

"I see it, sir!" Midshipman Houghton cried. "*There*, sirs! One of the leading ships of the lee column!"

That was even *further* away than the two merchantmen that they'd seen firing distress rockets, making Lewrie frown in concern.

"Damme, could there be *three* privateers out there?" he griped. "If there are, let's hope that Parham and *Pylades* are close enough to help her."

"Pray Jesus we get to grips with *somebody*!" Marine Lt. Simcock fretted from his place by the starboard entry-port on the sail-tending gangway, where a file of his Marines stood swaying with their muskets ready and loaded.

"We'll *try* t'find you some *amusement*, sir!" Lewrie snapped back.

"Sorry, sir," Simcock all but whispered, much abashed.

It took nearly that estimated half an hour to catch up with the trailing ships of the fleeing convoy, and to get close enough to one of them to speak her.

"Hoy, there! This is *Reliant*!" Lewrie shouted to her from his starboard bulwarks.

"Hoy, the *Reliant*!" her master called back from the larboard side of his quarterdeck. "This is the *Avon*! Captain Quarles, here!"

"Were you the one firin' distress rockets?" Lewrie asked him.

"Aye! A big schooner come up from loo'rd and went aboard the ship astern of us, the *Peacock*!" Captain Quarles shouted. "Poor old Cap'm Venables was boarded and took before he could signal for help! I cracked on sail, and started firing off rockets to warn the others, but there was nothing I could do for them! What took you so long?"

"Eat shit and die!" Lewrie muttered, and took a deep breath to calm himself before replying. "Where is *Peacock* now, sir?"

"Last we could see of her, she and the schooner put about onto larboard tack and headed off Sou'-Sou'west! Didn't you *see* her, sir?"

"God dammit!" Lewrie spat, realising that the *Peacock* was lost for good. It had been the better part of an hour since *Avon*'s first rockets had been launched, since the privateer schooner had ghosted in and pounced, then tacked as soon as the boarding party had secured their prize. *Peacock* was a full-rigged, three-masted ship, and could sail no closer to the wind than six points, about sixty-six degrees. Slow as that process could be, she would now be *miles* astern of the convoy, and to dash off to rescue her would involve a very long stern-chase. If her lights were doused, Lewrie could only hope to lay his frigate on the same course of Sou'-Sou'west and thrash blindly after her in the utter darkness.

But, he could not do that. Once clear of the vicinity of the convoy, the privateer surely would head West for some American port to sell her off quickly, and trying to cut a course Westerly in hopes of stumbling across her and the privateer by mid-day tomorrow would be equally bootless. Besides, were there other privateers waiting to strike, he could not abandon the other helpless ships. He had to stay with the trade.

"Thankee, Captain Quarles! If the privateer schooner's gone, ye may be safe for the night!" Lewrie called over.

"Ain't you going after her?" Quarles demanded.

"I must stay with the convoy!" Lewrie shouted back. "And damned well ye know it . . . or should," he whispered for his own benefit.

"Oh, too bad," the Sailing Master said with a sigh. "But, we ain't like that chap from the Bible . . . the Good Shepherd?"

"If we aren't, Mister Caldwell, you can be damned sure that our Chaplain, Reverend Brundish, will *remind* us of it in his next homily," Lewrie said with a groan.

"How did it go?" Caldwell maundered on. "He went after the last wee lamb, instead of being satisfied with protecting the rest of his flock?"

"A parable, sir," Midshipman Houghton supplied. "It was one of Lord Jesus' parables."

"*Bugger* parables!" Lewrie snarled, stomping off aft before he fed his urge to strangle someone.

When it came time to round up the convoy at dawn, and chivvy them back into their proper columns after a long and fruitless night of wary patrolling, with the hands at Quarters and everyone sleepless and reeling, they could count up their losses.

Three ships had been plucked from the convoy during the night, by what was evidently a full three privateers, all of them schooners. The

masters of a few ships that had escaped close encounters and had manoeu-
vred clear related breathless tales of being hailed and ordered to fetch-to
by men who had declared their ships sailed with Letters of Marque and
Reprisal issued by France. Some of those who had demanded surrender
sounded French, but some sounded as English as plum duff!

Those losses had been galling enough, but to add to the misery there
were the ones that had been damaged during the convoy's panicky stampede to windward. The columns had shredded, wheeling away from the
threat, bearing up towards the next column to starboard, and order had
turned to shambles.

Another six vessels had gone aboard each other, tangling bow-sprits
and jib-booms in another's shrouds, or slamming hulls together and smashing chain platforms, which loosed tension on upper masts, and bringing
them down in rats' nests of sails, rigging, and spars. Those half-dozen not
only had to be found, limping along astern of the rest, but rendered aid
from sounder ships, or from the escort ships' stores, as well.

"A very rum show, by Jove," Captain Blanding mournfully said to his
gathered captains early that next afternoon. "A rum show, I must say!
And just how the deuce did they ever *find* us? Comments?"

No one wanted to touch *that* one. The sound of Captain Blanding stirring his cup of tea, that metal on china tinkling, was the loudest thing in
Modeste's great-cabins. Lewrie, Stroud, and Parham sat primly on collapsible chairs round Blanding's settee, where their commander sprawled in
untidy, and un-characteristic, gloom.

"Ehm . . . ," Captain Stroud finally broke the silence with a hesitant
noise. "Might they have known to be on the lookout for a Summer trade,
sir?"

"Uhm, possible, but . . . ," Blanding rejoined with a long sigh.

"Possibly the 'runners,' sir," Lewrie felt just bold enough to add. "They
were cruisin' the likely course a trade'd take, *somewhat* close to Hatteras,
and most-like stumbled into one of our ships that had broken away for Savannah or Charleston, asked a few questions of her master, and stood out
seaward t'find us."

"From leeward . . . on a night as black as my boots," Blanding mused
most miserably. *Tinkle-tinkle-tinkle*, went his spoon, though he had yet to
lay it aside and take a sip. His cup and saucer rested on his substantial mid-
riff. "And not one of our ships laid eyes on *any* of them, not even once!"

"Well, sir, once they'd taken a prize, they doused her lights," Captain
Stroud said. "As they had come in with all *their* lights out. Now, I thought

I caught a *glimpse* of something standing Nor'westerly, but . . . by then I was caught up close to the convoy, too busy searching for a much closer threat . . . and, it was only a fleeting glimpse of something darker than the night . . . far off."

Oh, I doubt that! Lewrie sarcastically thought, about to snort and scoff out loud. Stroud *would* have something to say that would make him look industrious and alert, even if the others weren't!

"After all the honour and glory we've won since sailing from Portsmouth last Spring, too," Captain Blanding said, with another of those long, theatrical sighs. "It is just too bad!"

"Well, sir," Stroud spoke up again, "we've taken rather a long jog East'rd since last evening . . ."

"Forced to," Captain Parham stuck in, grimacing.

". . . and our convoy will be East of the usual track, so if any more privateers are lurking about, that will make their hunt for more prizes much harder," Stroud soldiered on, with a quick squint of impatience directed at Parham. "It's good odds that we may escort the rest all the way to England with no more loss, sir."

Bloody toady! Lewrie thought; *He* had *to have been, t'be First Officer under that twit Fillebrowne in Myrmidon!*

"That very likely may be true!" Captain Blanding said, perking up a bit. "Thank you for the thought, Captain Stroud."

Stroud bowed his head in acknowledgement, with a taut, pleased grin on his face. Lewrie couldn't abide that.

"There is the problem, though, sir," Lewrie countered, "for our 'runners' bound for New England ports. If there are any *more* privateers on the hunt for prizes, our East'rd jog means the ships leaving the protection of the convoy have further t'sail on their own to reach the safety of an American port."

"There's that, aye," William Parham was quick to grasp. He all but winked at Lewrie as he continued. "Might it be necessary, sir, for the 'runners' who'll be leaving us . . . given the circumstances . . . to provide at least one frigate to see them safe?"

"Break up the escorting force?" Captain Blanding exclaimed in surprise, sitting erect and thumping his boots on the deck cover, loud as a gun. "Detach a fourth of our hard-pressed squadron? No no! It is simply not done! Should more privateers find us, where would we be, then, sir? Admiralty'd lop off my testi—"

"Ahem," Chaplain Brundish admonished with a wee cough. The task of keeping Blanding from blasphemy, Billingsgate language, and scandal-ous foul words surely had been a chore, the last few weeks. Brundish's warning sounded as if he sleep-walked through his watchfulness.

"You know what I mean, sir!" Blanding said, instead, harumphing and slurping tea to cover his slip.

No one eared for convoying, the Navy most of all, and there was many an officer charged with the thankless task who had become so frustrated and impatient with the snail's pace and the un-ending "herding" and "droving" that they had just flown a bit more sail than their wallowing charges and sprinted clear of them . . . if only for a few precious hours of dash and wind in their faces. Some few had actually kept on over the hori-zon, leaving their convoys un-defended! And, had been put before a board of court-martial.

"Bedad, those dashed Americans!" Captain Blanding grumbled, and slumped back into his settee. "Lewrie. You say the one privateer was re-ported to you, she put about and hared off Sou'west?"

"Aye, sir."

"For Savannah, Charleston, or a port in Spanish Florida, dash it," Blanding decided. "Where, with the collusion of the Dons, or the Yankee Doodles, her prize will be sold . . . where the French privateer may re-victual, perhaps *re-arm* herself, in perfect safety! Bah!"

"Damn all conniving neutrals, I say!" Captain Stroud snarled.

"Ahem," came a lazy admonishment from Brundish.

"Pardons," from Stroud, equally perfunctory.

"Bless me, for I do not understand the sea, and the ways of a ship upon it as thoroughly as you gentlemen," Reverend Brundish said with a shake of his head, "but . . . was there no way to chase after the privateer . . . privateers, pirates, whichever . . . and reclaim those three vessels they took from us, sirs?"

"Not without abandoning the rest to what could have been even greater loss, Reverend," Blanding said for them all.

"Best would be some of our cruisers to lurk off every neutral port to stop and search in-bound ships," Parham suggested. "Inspect their papers and seize every ship revealed as an enemy privateer, or a British ship they've made prize."

"Impossible, unfortunately," Blanding told him, sounding as if he was about to sink back into the Blue-Devils. "That would require a fleet twice as large as our present one . . . and would risk war with every nation that takes umbrage."

"There's risk enough of that, already, sir," Lewrie added. "We stop and search every ship we come across that sails independent, and press suspected Britons from their crews."

"Oh, that is simply too bad," Reverend Brundish said with a sigh. "I expect shepherds and drovers the wide world over face this sadness over the loss of their cattle, their camels, or sheep . . ."

No, don't let him speak o' sheep! Lewrie qualled inside.

". . . and puts me in mind of one of our Lord and Saviour's best-known parables . . ."

Damme, here it comes! Lewrie thought; *I bloody knew it!*

". . . the one about the Good Shepherd, who . . ."

Do I throw something at him, will that stop his gob?

"Best not," Captain Blanding said, making Lewrie gawp at him as if Blanding could read his thoughts. "Such can only assure me all the more of our failure."

"Oh. My pardons, sir," Brundish said, demurring.

Thankee, Blanding! Lewrie gratefully thought; *By Jove and By Jingo, and Bedad! But, bless ye for it! Dash ye!*

"We'll lose no more, gentlemen," Captain Blanding sternly told them. "We will keep all our ships together, with no detachments for any reasons. And, we will see all our charges safely to port in England . . . or else!"

That promised an arduous, sleepless, and long task!

And I won't have a speck o' fun 'til it's over, Lewrie thought.

Though he still had his cats, and his penny-whistle.

BOOK III

Let us be master of the Straits (of Dover) for
six hours and we shall be masters of the world.

–Napoleon Bonaparte

Baby, baby, naughty baby,
Hush, you squalling thing, I say;
Hush your squalling, or it may be,
Bonaparte may pass this way.

Baby, baby, he will hear you
As he passes by the house,
And he, limb from limb will tear you,
Just as pussy tears a mouse.

–British nursery rhyme
circa 1803-1805

CHAPTER SIXTEEN

*L*ewrie felt like breaking out his stock of champagne when some of the merchantmen departed the trade for the New England ports of New York, Boston, and Philadelphia, or the mouth of the St. Lawrence river to land their goods in British North America. And when those vessels resumed passage to Great Britain, he was cheered by the thought that it would be warships of the North American Station based in St. John's or Halifax that would be the ones to herd them.

The ships remaining were whittled down to a somewhat more manageable number—if the merchant masters kept what little wit they had together for longer than a four-hour watch—and the rest of the way was cross the open, rolling North Atlantic in mid-Summer; which passage wasn't all *that* bad, really, for the weather and the seas, though boisterous, at times, cooperated nicely to speed the trade Eastwards. If HMS *Reliant* had been voyaging under Admiralty Orders, the winds and the Gulf Stream would have let her reel off nine or ten knots per hour, and she would have bowled along like a diligence coach, logging nigh 240 miles from one Noon to the next.

With their many slow merchant tubs, though, six or seven knots, after a time, began to seem a giddy pace!

Then came Ireland and the Old Head of Kinsale, the harbours of Queenstown, Dublin, and Belfast, and more ships departed for a run into the Irish Sea, most making for Liverpool or Bristol, and Lewrie hooted cheery ta-tas to them ... *"Namasté"* in Hindoo, *"Adieu"* in Frog, *"Auf Wiedersehen"* in German, and *"Dasveedanya"* in Russian, mostly followed by, "Bugger off and die, ye bleak bastards!"

The trade reached Soundings as they bore up the Channel, and it was then Falmouth, Plymouth, and Portsmouth for more of the merchantmen with the number of columns and the numbers of ships in-column shrinking ever further, 'til they could espy the Dover cliffs, stand out to sea a bit further to avoid the risks of the Goodwin Sands, then finally sail up to the mouth of the Thames and let the trade make its way up-river to the London docks. The squadron bore away and made for the Nore and Sheerness, coming at last to weary, peaceful anchor.

"Your bloody turn! Better you than me!" Lewrie pretended to call to a frigate that was hauled to short-stays, ready to bring up her anchor, and was already shaking loose canvas to make sail. There was nigh an armada of merchantmen, an hundred or better, preparing for departure for overseas, all ships flying the horizontal yellow-and-blue flags indicating that it was a trade bound for America.

"May ye have joy of it, ye poor bastard!" Lewrie gaily called out. The captain of the departing frigate held a hand behind an ear, but it was too far for him to hear. He waved and smiled as if Lewrie had bade him good wishes, and Lewrie doffed his own hat and plastered on his best "shite-eating" grin.

"Beg pardon, sir, but the Bosun admires to have a boat lowered so he can see to the squaring of the yards," Lt. Westcott said at his elbow.

"Aye, Mister Westcott," Lewrie agreed. "Come t'think upon it, they all need a good soak t'keep their plankings swelled. Lower 'em all. And, give the Purser, Mister Cadbury, word that they're available. He'll be wishin' t'fetch fresh meat off from shore for the men. When he does, give him my boat crew for it, and your choice of Mid."

"Aye, sir," Westcott agreed, turning away to direct the raising of a boat from the cross-deck tiers with the main course yard.

"Yeovill, sir," Midshipman Grainger announced at the top of the larboard gangway ladder. "Permission for him to mount the quarterdeck?"

"Aye, come," Lewrie bade.

"We've run rather short of staples, sir," his cook told him. "I expect the Purser will be going ashore, and was wondering if I might be allowed to go with him, sir. Coffee, tea, sugar, cocoa beans, mustard, and such, sir, along with spices, sauces, and——"

"And boot-blacking, and stationery, ink, and sealing wax, along with raisins, currants, jams, eggs, and . . . you have a list?" Lewrie added.

"I do, sir," Yeovill assured him.

"See Pettus before you go, then, for he's my list, as well. If you think twenty pounds'd cover it?" Lewrie said. "Better yet, Pettus can go with you, too."

"Very good, sir!" Yeovill beamed. "And I'll be laying on something special tonight for your supper, sir."

"Uhmm, best wait 'til we see if Captain Blanding is of a mood t'treat us aboard *Modeste*," Lewrie cautioned. It had been weeks since Blanding had admonished him, and weeks since the early disasters with the order of the convoy. *Maybe he's over his pet, by now*, Lewrie hoped to himself.

"Oh . . . aye, sir," Yeovill replied, crestfallen that he might be up-staged.

The jolly-boat was in the water, by then, and Mr. Sprague was going down the man-ropes into it to assure himself that *Reliant* would present a mathematically exact picture to any scrupulous observer, all yards perfectly horizontal and even with each other, all stays, all of the running rigging, taut at the proper "tarry" angle.

"Deuced odd, Mister Caldwell," Midshipman Grainger was saying to the Sailing Master as he took the air amidships of the quarterdeck. "It's so quiet, and . . . still. I could swear my head is swimming!"

"Just you wait 'til you set foot ashore, young sir, haw haw!" Mr. Caldwell assured him. "There's nothing like better than two month at sea to dis-cumbobulate your equilibrium, don't you know."

Lt. Spendlove and Lt. Merriman were supervising the hoisting-off of the gig, now, with Bosun's Mate Mr. Wheeler doing most of the louder barking. Lewrie looked up at the commissioning pendant, at the set of the yards and the neatness of how the sails were furled and harbour-gasketed; it made *his* head swim a bit, too, and forced him to go over to the larboard bulwarks for a reassuring grip.

"Ahem, sir . . . the Purser wishes to mount the . . . ," Midshipman Grainger said.

"Come, Mister Cadbury," Lewrie bade. "I expected you earlier."

"If I could have a boat, sir, I will deal with the Victualling Board people ashore," Cadbury offered.

"My gig, sir, and my boat crew," Lewrie allowed. "See the First Officer for his choice of Midshipman."

"Thank you kindly, sir, you read my mind, I swear," Cadbury replied, most pleased.

"Yeovill and Pettus t'go with you t'see t'my needs," Lewrie ordered. "Get the best bullock ye can, and warn your clerk that once we have the boats in the water, I intend to 'Splice the Main-Brace' while you're still ashore. Keep a sharp eye on the boat crew, mind. Even if there's prize-money due 'em, there's sure t'be at least one of a mind to run."

"Aye, and I shall, sir!" Cadbury promised him, doffing his hat and heading briskly towards the starboard gangway.

House-keepin'! Lewrie thought with a sniff, looking over all the great lengths of running rigging that now lay on the sail-tending gangways in round flemishes, or was hung from the belaying-pin rails in equally symmetrical loops. The guns and their carriages were bowsed snug against the bulwarks at right angles to the stout timbers, and all the tackle associated with them stowed neatly beside them. The roundshot in the rope garlands beside each piece, the roundshot stowed in wooden racks round each hatchway in their hemispherical dimples, were scaled free of rust and freshly blacked as if ready for an admiral's inspection.

What was worn or faded would be put right over the next day or two of labour by all hands. *Reliant* would require fresh paint to make her new-penny shiny . . . assuming the dockyards had any, or would give them enough to get the job done without a letter from the King himself. Frayed stays and rigging would have to be re-rove or replaced in full, what gilt trim round her entry-ports, taffrails, and transom name-board that needed touching-up would have to come from Lewrie's own pockets. The boats would have to be inspected, and soft or wormed strakes would require fresh bosun's stores and new wood, along with even more paint. The man-ropes strung through the outer ends of the boarding battens and dead-eyed with fancy Turk's Head knots must be whitened, or replaced.

Then would come even more "house-keeping" to replenish her with rum, small beer, and wines, with livestock, and fresh fodder and clean straw for the forecastle manger; with tons of bisquit, kegs of salted meat, fresh-scrubbed and re-filled water casks. Expended powder and shot had to be replaced from Gun Wharf, and all that would be followed by the Purser's wares, his new bales of trousers, stockings, shirts, or neckerchiefs, short sailors' jackets and buckled shoes, new blankets and bedding, hammocks and small rope, tobacco, mustard, jams, sauces for each eight-man mess to purchase from their pay, and . . .

Lewrie reckoned it would be at least three days of work before he could even think to allow the ship to hoist the Easy pendant, and put the ship Out of Discipline for the crew's leisure. And if orders came on the fourth day, the *Reliant* frigate would be ready to answer them and put to sea, instanter, her people's rest and ease bedamned.

Mine own *bedamned,* Lewrie told himself.

At the moment, though, all he really wished was the freedom to go below, roll into his hanging bed-cot, and be left to sleep in peace 'til this time tomorrow! Had *Reliant* been sailing alone, or had their squadron been sailing in-line-ahead at night, Lewrie could reasonably assume that not *too* much could go wrong, and could snatch as many as four hours at a stretch 'til the next change of watch, but as escort to their convoy . . . well! It had been *so* much like herding sheep that their gambolling and straying hadn't allowed him more than a cat-nap between summons to the deck; they had done all but *leap over* each other in alarm, or crowd up to each other for security, then shy away to the far horizons, bleating like Billy-O!

"Ready to go ashore, sir," Pettus reported from the entry-port.

"You've my list . . . and my latest letters?" Lewrie asked.

"Aye, sir, and your funds," Pettus replied, looking very eager to set foot on solid land and prowl the chandleries and shops of Sheerness. The bleak naval town wasn't London, but . . . !

"Off ye go, then," Lewrie said with a cheerful wave.

Lewrie paced over to the starboard bulwarks, fighting the urge to *reel* like a drunken sailor; the ship was anchored and still, moving not an inch from dead-level, and what slight rising and falling from a harbour scend was negligible. What solid land would be like he didn't *dare* contemplate. Pettus would be taking ashore letters penned during the last two days onpassage up-Channel.

There was that continuing fuss over the Franklin-pattern stoves that Captain Speaks had left aboard *Thermopylae* in 1801, left with her Purser when laid up in-ordinary, and vanished. Might Lewrie's solicitor, Mr. Matthew Mountjoy, have news of them, or whether Speaks would be suing him in a Court of Common Pleas? Had his late wife's uncle paid him for the house and improvements of his rented farm, yet, and if he had, what was his latest balance at Coutts' Bank, and would Mountjoy remit him an hundred pounds to replenish his purse?

There was also his report of the voyage to Admiralty, as well as notice that *Reliant* was now in a British home-port, and what prize-money she'd reaped would be paid out to her crew . . . when?

There were long sea-letters penned a little bit each day during the long passage to be sent off to Admiralty to forward to his sons, Sewallis and Hugh, a letter to his father, Sir Hugo, a warning to the Madeira Club in

London that he *might* be up to the city for a few days and would be need-
ing lodging . . . they *couldn't* turn him down; Sir Hugo was one of the
founding members and financial backers! There were letters to his
brothers-in-law, Governour and Burgess Chiswick, with news of his arrival home for his daughter, Charlotte, who still lodged with Governour
and his wife, Millicent, in Anglesgreen.

Perhaps in a few days, he would have replies from some of them, with
fresh news of doings at home, and . . .

"Newspapers, Pettus!" Lewrie cried, leaning out over the bulwark to
shout down to the gig, which was already a pistol-shot off. "Lots of newspapers, every one you can lay hands on!"

"I'll get them for you, sir," Pettus promised with a cheery wave of his
own.

"Dig in, t'gither, lads," his Cox'n Liam Desmond, ordered his oarsmen.
"A hot stroke, Pat," he urged his long-time mate, Furfy, "and we'll show
these Sheerness lubbers man o' war'sman fashion . . . f'r good old *Reliant*,
hey, lads?"

"Beer, ale, an' porter in th' offin'!" Furfy was heard to grunt. "Stroke,
and . . . stroke, and . . . stroke!"

Better not *be,* Lewrie thought with a smile; *or not* too *much!*

CHAPTER SEVENTEEN

*T*he bum-boats had been circling like buzzards for several days before *Reliant*'s necessities had been seen to, and Lewrie had allowed her to be put Out of Discipline. As soon as the Easy pendant soared aloft and was two-blocked, every hand and Marine raised a great cheer, and gathered on the gangways to await the arrival of "temporary wives" and doxies.

"Ready, Mister Mainwaring?" Lewrie asked the Ship's Surgeon.

"Well, there's few signs of *early* cases of the Pox, sir, so . . . ," Mr. Mainwaring cautiously replied, then shrugged. He and his Surgeon's Mates, Lloyd and Durbin, would inspect the women as they boarded for a hint of being diseased, though . . . unless some girl's nose was rotting off and caving in, it was good odds they'd miss most of the symptoms of the Pox, and a week or so later, after *Reliant* was back in Discipline, there would be hands a'plenty in need of the dubious Mercury Cure.

" 'Tis fifteen shillings the man you'll earn, Mister Mainwaring," Lewrie reminded him, tongue-in-cheek. "If some of our people aren't poxed, already, there'll surely be a parcel of 'em for you to treat . . . and profit from, by next Sunday Divisions."

"Oh, I'm certain there are hands already poxed, sir," the Surgeon rejoined with a wry grin, "it's just that they dread presenting to me. Fifteen shillings is dear to them, and mercury clysters forced up the urethra are painful."

"Even after your talks?" Lewrie asked. He'd ordered Mainwaring to give all hands a lecture on the perils of the Pox and its signs . . . and had nudged the Purser to think of purchasing sheep-gut cundums for the men to buy and use. They'd not be as good as the ones from the Green Lantern in Half Moon Street in London—as protective as the round dozen stowed away in Lewrie's sea-chest—but perhaps they'd prevent *some* later sickness. Mainwaring and Cadbury were dubious that the ship's people would even be interested in purchasing or employing them, just as they had been when Lewrie had ordered them to obtain the citronella candles and citronella oils for lamps in place of the Navy-issue glims for lighting belowdecks in the West Indies to counter the nighttime miasmas and tropical damps that were thought to be the cause of Yellow Jack and Malaria. At least citronella cut down the swarms of pesky mosquitoes, so the crew off-watch could sleep soundly at night, and the lamps on the weather decks kept most of them at bay, too. The ship had suffered very few sicknesses during their year in the "Fever Isles," though Mr. Mainwaring put that down to their arrival in early Autumn, and their departure before the height of Fever Season.

It never hurt, though, for junior officers to humour the eccentricities of a ship's captain, no matter how daft. Captain Cook's Surgeon might have thought lemons, limes, apples, and pickled German sauerkraut daft, too, but *Endeavour* had had no scurvy on her long Voyages of Discovery!

"And we'll have no *gross* smuggling of spirits, either, will we, Mister Appleby?" Lewrie turned to enquire of the ship's Master At Arms, who, along with his Ship's Corporals, Scammell and Keetch, were to keep good order—or as much as could be enforced—during the riotous doings belowdecks.

"Count on it, sir!" Appleby barked, as eager as a bulldog.

"There's only so many places a doxy can hide a pint o' rum, or gin, so . . . perhaps Mister Mainwaring may find some for you, hey, Mister Appleby?" Lewrie japed, raising a snigger from them all as they contemplated how large a woman's "calibre" would have to be to accommodate *that*!

"No more than a dram vial, surely, sir!" Mr. Mainwaring countered, blushing a bit. "Else . . ."

"Else you find the reins t'your carriage, and ride out!" Lewrie hooted before turning away for the quarterdeck to leave them to it, and take a gentlemanly separation from the debauchery to come.

The bum-boats were butting up against the hull on both beams, despite the Bosun's warning that only the larboard entry-port was open to business, that the pimps and dealers in shoddy goods should already know that, and they should row round and queue up proper, or else. It became a scramble among the boats to be first to board, for the doxies to be first chosen, and tradesmen to be first with their wares, causing mild arguments, the sounds of which were quickly overcome with sailors' cheers and the giggles, titters, shrieks, and crude shouts of the women.

Lewrie took himself a bit further aft, towards the taffrails and flag lockers, putting on a grim, dis-interested expression, as if all of it was beneath him; though he *did* take more than one peek or two at the whores, the younger and prettier especially. He was the only officer on deck; officers did not stand Harbour Watches as a matter of course, and if his subordinates were not pretending dis-interest below in the gun-room, they were off ashore to pursue the same sort of pleasures as the hands, but more discretely. Midshipmen Grainger and Rossyngton, their youngest, paced the quarterdeck that morning . . . gawping red-faced and gape-jawed, their wee heads aswim at the sights in prepubescent lust.

It *was* distantly possible that one or two of the arriving polls were *real* wives who had found a way to travel to Sheerness once informed of where their husbands' ship had put in, or the lucky sailor was a Sheerness man to begin with. And it *was* possible that some women had come aboard only to sell their meat pies, sweet baked goods, and fruit, but . . . the bulk of them were local whores.

"Hoy . . . you on the quarterdeck, there!" a woman loudly bawled from the larboard gangway, just after passing the Surgeon's and the Master At Arms's inspections. "Izzat *you*, Cap'm Lewrie? Bugger me, if ye ain't! Cap'n Alan Lewrie, t'th' life, by Christ!"

Lewrie whirled about to peer at a blowsy, busty bawd with straw-blonde hair beneath a prim little blue bonnet. Her name had been . . . ?

"Nancy!" he cried back with a wide grin. "*Proteus*, durin' the Mutiny in '97? Damn my eyes, how d'ye keep, girl?" He made a quick way forward to say his "howdy-dos."

When the North Sea Fleet had mutinied in 1797, Lewrie's first frigate, HMS *Proteus*, had been fitting out and manning here at the Nore and had been caught up in it. The Committee of "the Floating Republic" had taken over a dockside tavern for their "shore headquarters," then decreed that the bum-boat trade could continue, and as many women who wished could come board the rebelling warships . . . perhaps they'd wished for the less-willing sailors to be kept mellow and pliant with the smuggled spirits, and sex. They'd hired bands and paraded with their blood-red flags through the streets of Sheerness, hoping to spread French-style Jacobin revolution throughout England to overthrow the King and House of Lords, disenfranchise the aristocracy, beggar the landed gentry, whatever odd notions that had come into their addled heads. But, when they ordered that no women would be allowed to *return* ashore, the mutineers had given Lewrie and his loyal men new allies.

When the sailors had run out of money for the doxies' "socket-fees," when the authorities had cut off the bum-boat trade and had run the parading mutineers from shore when the Army had shown up, Nancy, and her sisters, had struck a bargain to help Lewrie take back his ship and free the women to get back to earning a living. They had "dealt" with those mutineers who had laid aside their weapons, and their slop-trousers, to be pleasured on the mess deck with what came to hand; a long hat pin, a dagger, a sand- or shot-filled cosh, and other assorted protections natural to their trade, had done for most of the off-watch mutineers, with no mercy for people who could not, or would not, pay them or even share their rum ration with them or feed them a decent portion of their rations.

That bargain had been struck with guineas from Lewrie's purse, and the promise of more from his London bank; over an hundred pounds sterling in the account books to prostitutes "for services rendered" had sent his wife into a *snarling* huff . . . and his requests to both Crown and Admiralty to issue letters of official thanks had raised an host of senior eyebrows, to boot, but . . . he'd gotten his ship back!

Grudgingly, the doxies *had* gotten letters from Admiralty, even if the "patriotic efforts" had been worded most marvellously vague.

Nancy had put on a few pounds, but she was still a fetching mort. She took a short clay pipe from her mouth as he got close, and flung her arms round him, almost lifting him off his feet.

"Oh, 'tis been a long time since ye been t'Sheerness, Cap'm," she enthused, after setting him back down. "And an't ye a caution! I 'spect ye're a senior Post-Captain, by now, t'have such a fine, big frigate."

"It's good t'see you're still alive, and prosperin', Nancy," he replied. "The Navy still treatin' ye good? And, how's Sally Blue?"

"La, a war's always good t'my sort, Cap'm Lewrie," Nancy bragged, then turned more sombre. "As for Sally Blue, well . . . ye know how th' trade can be, Cap'm."

Lewrie winced at that news, recalling the little minx with the large, bright blue eyes of such a startling shade, and her long mane of glossy raven-black hair, a coltish teen who'd worked with an older woman who'd *claimed* to be her mother . . . and had possessed the unfortunate skill of being as fine a pickpocket as any in the British Isles, "Three-Handed Jenny" of London, included.

"Passed away?" Lewrie asked.

"Oh la, no, sir!" Nancy countered. "Sally lifted the purse of a rich'un she'd tumbled with, and got took up for theft. It was a close thing, her hangin' for it, but the rich'un pled f'r mercy, and she got transported for life t'New South Wales. 'Er Mam . . .'member her? Got a letter last year, sayin' h'it weren't half as bad as they say 'bout h'it . . . like ye skeered her with tales o' sea-snakes as long as yer ship, and all . . . and she's married a trooper sergeant!"

"Well, good for her!" Lewrie exclaimed, delighted that she had not died, as most poor whores did. "Even if she cussed like a Bosun, and couldn't help herself from liftin' everything in sight."

"Hoy, the boat!" Midshipman Grainger was calling overside to starboard, followed by, "Bosun, muster the side-party!"

"Thankee f'r rememb'rin' me, Cap'm," Nancy said as she turned to go about her business, coyly fiddling with her hair and rolling her hips. "Good f'r bus'ness, ye greetin' me so warm." She winked.

"Good enough for a Post-Captain, then good enough for a sailor with money, hey?" Lewrie whispered, winking back.

"Uhm sir?" Midshipman Grainger intruded. "I think the arrival is . . . I don't know *what* to do about him, sir. How many men to muster, and the Bosun . . ."

"An officer, Mister Grainger?" Lewrie asked.

"Don't know, sir!" Grainger said with a helpless shrug.

Lewrie crossed over to the starboard side. Bosun Sprague was peering at him, shrugging confusion. Lewrie leaned out to look down into the eight-oared barge that was ghosting up to the main-chains, at its sole passenger.

"What the Devil is *that*?" Lewrie gawped under his breath. "Turn-out for a Post-Captain might suit, Mister Sprague. Maybe he . . . it . . . won't know the diff'rence."

It wasn't a Navy officer, nor was it an Army man, either, though the visitor was garbed in a red coat adrip with gilt lace as profusely as a Turkish sultan.

There were some few Marines on watch in full kit with pipe-clay white belts and accoutrements, but they were posted in the bows and on the gangways to prevent desertion; they were under arms, but not available for a side-party. Neither were any officers with drawn swords . . . neither was Lewrie ready for *punctilio,* for he had had no need for his sword belt. Even with a long, intricate Bosun's call, their arrival's welcome would be sketchy.

Hope he likes informal, Lewrie thought; *whoever he is.*

He took comfort (some, anyway) in the thought that court bailiffs and attorneys didn't wear such clothing, and he wasn't going to be served papers!

It took an age for the visitor to make his way from the barge to the chain platform, then up the boarding battens; uttering grumbles all the way, and cursing under his breath. As his cocked hat with all the egret feathers appeared over the lip of the entry-port, the calls began. Sprague had to blow it twice before the fellow managed to get all the way up and stagger in-board with a whoosh of surly breath and a sour grimace of distaste as he peered about, owl-eyed.

"Welcome aboard, sir," Lewrie offered.

"I am come to speak with Captain Alan Lewrie," the very tall and lean older fellow announced, nose-high, and in a very plummy and clench-jawed Oxonian accent. "Might he be aboard, Mister . . . ?"

"I'm Lewrie, sir, And you might be . . . ?" Lewrie casually rejoined with a mystified grin.

The visitor seemed to start at that, and gave Lewrie one of those long, head-to-foot look-overs, then another, as if in dis-belief. It did not help that Lewrie was wearing his third-best hat, suitable only for stormy weather, his shirt sleeves and neck-stock, and sailcloth waist-coat and breeches, white cotton stockings, and an old pair of buckled shoes, whilst the visitor was dressed in silk and satin; his coat was red satin (with the aforementioned square yard of gilt lace), a white silk shirt and waist-coat, white satin breeches, white silk stockings, and shoes as light and insubstantial as a lady's dancing slippers. Under his over-sized cocked hat with all those feathers, he sported a formal powdered wig, and upon his chest and coat breast, he showed the sash and device of the Order of the Garter. To top off his appearance, he held a long walking-stick with a large gold top, more like a Lord Mayor's ceremonial mace.

"I am, sir, Sir Harper Strachan, Baron Ludlow, and equerry to the Court of Saint James's, and His Majesty, King George the Third," the visitor said as he made a particularly showy "leg" with a flourish of his hat cross his breast.

How's he keep the wig on? Lewrie wondered; *Glue?*

"Bugger that! Show us yer *tits!*" a sailor cried over the mild din of music and chatter.

"Oh," was all Lewrie could say in response, and whipped off his own hat to make a bow in kind. "Welcome aboard *Reliant,* milord. Your servant."

"I have just spoken with Captain Blanding, sir," Strachan went on, once he'd plopped his hat back on his wig and straightened back up, "to arrange with him his presentation at Court for his investiture in the Order of the Bath, and his baronetcy. The Crown would find it convenient did *you* be available to present yourself at the same time, sir."

"Oh, that," Lewrie gawped, for it had completely flown his ken, the last few months or so, and he had never really considered a knighthood earned. "I'd almost forgotten."

"Oh . . . *that,* sir? Slipped your *mind,* did it, sir?" Sir Harper bristled, his turkey-wattle jowls quivering, and his drink-veined cheeks reddening. "You hold a *knighthood* to be of so *little* moment, sir?"

"Meanin' that it was so long ago that Captain Blanding and I were informed of the honour, and we've been so busy of late, convoyin' a West Indies trade the last two months," Lewrie managed to babble in quick explanation. "Think of the expression 'herdin' cats,' sir, and that'll give ye the best impression of it. Back o' the mind, that?" he said with a helpless shrug. "Might I offer you some refreshment in my cabins, sir, and—"

"Do your quarters reek *less* than your ship, Captain Lewrie . . . which I *must* say you keep in a slovenly, nigh *mutinous* manner?" their haughty caller enquired, producing a large paisley silk handkerchief from a side pocket of his coat and pressing it to his nose.

"We're Out of Discipline, sir." Lewrie goggled at him. "Can't allow the people shore liberty, or they'd take 'leg bail' and run off, so *this* is their liberty . . . short as it'll be. As for the smells . . . all ships stink, sir . . . milord . . . even though we re-paint, scrub and scour with vinegar, smoke her with tobacco torches . . . ," he explained, heaving another shrug. "After a time, though . . . stink happens."

"Hmpf!" was Sir Harper Strachan's comment on *that,* looking about with amazement and outrage to see half-gowned women dancing with tars in the waist; the nanny goat half up on a gun carriage to get at one of the bread bags full of bisquit hung underneath the larboard gangway, and the assorted livestock in the forecastle manger. Even the musicians and the lusty songs seemed to irk him.

It didn't help that Lewrie's cats took that moment to arrive on the quarterdeck. Chalky, the younger and spryer white'un, patted at Lewrie's breeches for attention, then sprang aloft and scaled his leg and waist-coat, to perch teetering on his right shoulder, just as Sir Harper returned his gaze to Lewrie. His mouth plopped open.

"This is Chalky, milord," Lewrie lamely told him as Chalky put his cheek against Lewrie's to nuzzle and play-nip. "Came off a French brig in the West Indies in '98. Nice puss," Lewrie said as he half-turned his head towards the cat.

Feeling ignored, Toulon wandered up to paw at Lewrie's leg, too, mewing most plaintively. The Crown equerry stiffened in even greater distaste.

This is not *goin' well,* Lewrie told himself.

"That's Toulon, milord. Evacuated with me when he was a kitten in '94, so he's of an age by now," Lewrie further explained.

Toulon looked Sir Harper over, and ambled over to see if he'd be more amenable to "wubbies."

"You were sayin', milord . . . something about a convenient date?" Lewrie prompted as Toulon began to sniff at Sir Harper's ankles.

"Ah, yayss," Strachan drawled, "Captain Blanding has promised to make himself available for the weekly levee, next Tuesday, which will begin at ten of the . . . damme!" he yelped as Toulon laid a tentative paw on his silk stockings. "Get your creature away from me!"

"Here, Toulon . . . here, lad," Lewrie bade, clucking and snapping his fingers. "This coming Tuesday, milord?"

"Yes, this Tuesday next," Strachan snapped, shuffling away from Toulon, gently shoving with a dainty slipper to shoo him off. "At ten in the morning. In full uniform, and Court dress."

"Uniform *and* Court dress, sir? There's a diff'rence?" Lewrie asked. He was beginning to enjoy rankling the top-lofty shit.

"You will have lodgings in London, Captain Lewrie?" Strachan said. "A letter with the particulars could await you."

"The Madeira Club, milord . . . at the corner of Duke and Wigmore Streets. Might I bring someone along with me as a guest?"

"Hoy, Cap'm Lewrie! These look familiar?" Nancy took that unfortunate moment to open her bodice and shake her impressive poonts in his direction, to the cheers of his sailors as they hustled her below.

"*Not* one of your . . . !" Sir Harper began, aghast.

"Cats, sir?" Lewrie supplied.

"*Whores*, I meant to say, such as that . . . that . . . !"

"Merely an old acquaintance and ally, sir," Lewrie told him, wincing and wondering how much worse it could get.

"I *dare* say," Strachan sneered with another disdainful sniff.

"There's my father, sir, Major-General Sir Hugo Saint George Willoughby, retired," Lewrie said, "who resides in London. At such short notice, I rather doubt one of my brothers-in-law and his wife could attend, but if he could get away from his regiment in time . . ."

Lewrie would *not* invite his other brother-in-law, Governour Chiswick, not *this* side of Hell, anyway, even if he and his wife, Millicent, could bring his daughter, Charlotte, from Anglesgreen in a day. She was too young to appreciate it. He didn't need his disreputable old school chums, like Clotworthy Chute—who'd most-like fleece a naive peer of his year's rents, or grope up a lady-in-waiting—or even Peter Rushton, now Viscount Draywick, who sat in Lords and got drunk and diddled regularly and was prone to giggle at the most inappropriate moments. Both his sons were at sea, more's the pity. . . .

"The levee will include a great many who are to be ennobled or knighted, and will be bringing guests of their own, so it would be best did you limit your own . . . Sir Hugo Saint George *Willoughby*, did you say, sir?" Strachan looked as stunned as if he'd just been pole-axed at the knacker's yard, so stunned that he did not notice Toulon standing up to paw at his silk breeches. "Him?" Stachan goggled.

Damme, but my father does *get that reception whenever his name's mentioned,* Lewrie thought with a wry smirk; *He's* heard *of him, has he?*

Strachan, Lord Ludlow, gave Lewrie another of his disdainful up-and-down looks, as if to say that the acorn didn't fall far from the tree, and was the Crown aware of what a bad bargain they would be making by knighting the son of *that* rake-hell?

"The formal notice, and the requirements in our dress, shall be waiting at your lodgings at the Madeira Club, when you arrive in London, Captain Lewrie," Strachan intoned; hard to understand, though, with his handkerchief to his nose and mouth. "I would advise you come up to the city early enough to consult a tailor for the necessary items?"

"Thankee for the kind suggestion, milord."

"Good day to you, Captain Lewrie," Strachan said, performing a graceful and languid "leg" in *congé*, sweeping off his hat again. That was too much temptation to Toulon, who, though "of an age," still liked to play with strange things, and the egret feathers were simply too tempting, so he pounced at the perigee of the sweep. "Damn my eyes!"

"Good day to you, milord," Lewrie said, making a "leg," too, so he could hide his grin and stifle his laughter.

He'd quite forgotten Chalky, still teetering like a wren on a grass stem on his shoulder. With a petulant yowl, Chalky leaped for the deck . . . and found the hat and feathers intriguing, too.

"Side-party . . . departing honours," Lewrie snapped.

"Gaah, you hellish damned . . . !" Strachan snarled as he put his hat back on his head, now minus an egret plume that Chalky had tugged loose and scampered away with, closely followed by Toulon, who wanted a bat at it, too.

Baron Ludlow, Sir Harper Strachan, glared hot-blooded murder at Lewrie, his shallow chest heaving in anger, before turning away for the starboard entry-port, whilst the bosun's call trilled and trilled. He could not quite fathom how to leave, though, peering over to determine that the boarding battens were much too steep and shallow for a down-the-housestairs descent. Strachan tucked his walking-stick, mace of honour, or whatever it was under his left armpit, at last, while Bosun Sprague went into his third repeat of a call, shuffled about to face in-board, and groped blindly with one foot for the first batten with his hands gripping the inner face of the bulwarks.

"We *could* prepare a bosun's chair, sir, if you—"

"Garr!" was Strachan's comment as he managed to get both feet on the top batten, and shifted his right hand to the after-most main-mast stay.

"Oh, mind the tar, sir, we—!" Lewrie cautioned.

"Gaah!" Strachan re-iterated as the fresh tar got daubed on his fingers, before he re-discovered the man-ropes. It took him at least a very long minute before his hat was below the lip of the entry-port, and Bosun Sprague could take his call from his mouth and catch a deep breath.

"Did he make it into his boat, Mister Grainger?" Lewrie asked. "I'm afraid to look."

"Ehm . . . he did, just now, sir," Grainger reported, after a peek over the side.

"Poor *lubber*!" Midshipman Rossyngton whispered gleefully. "My *grandmother* isn't that clumsy!"

"Well now, Mister Sprague," Lewrie said, turning to the Bosun, "and wasn't *that* bloody disastrous? Congratulations on your lungpower, by the way."

"Thankee, Captain," Sprague replied, still looking a tad blown. "I gave him an admiral's salute . . . four times over, sir. The feller didn't get to the boat soon, I'd've trotted out the one to the King."

Lewrie went back to the cross-deck stanchions and hammock nettings at the fore end of the quarterdeck, where Toulon and Chalky were footballing their prize and play-pouncing on the feather. They looked up at him . . . seemingly very pleased with themselves.

"That's alright, catlin's . . . I still love you, despite that," he told them.

CHAPTER EIGHTEEN

*E*ven with the great improvements in the nation's road network, the prevalence of huge post-coaches and regular service, the growth of the canal system, and passenger barges, very few subjects of England, Scotland, Wales, and Ireland ever travelled much more than twenty miles from their home towns. It took money, and leisure time, for people to travel, so . . . though many wistfully hoped to see London one day, the number who did was but a fraction of the population of Great Britain.

Those who resided in London who ever traipsed west to the parks and The Mall, and the grandeur of the West End round St. James's Palace, would represent about the same small fraction, for most folk lived and worked, ran their shops and such, in familiar neighbourhoods where they felt comfortable, perhaps even safe, and might never stray more than two miles from them, whether the neighbourhood was what was coming to be termed "respectable," run-down and seedy but close to their employments, or a maze-like criminal stew.

The number of people of Great Britain who ever *entered* the Palace of St. James was an even smaller fraction. This cool but sunny morning, Alan Lewrie was one of them, for the first time in his life, and (mostlikely) the last, he reckoned.

He had come up from Sheerness as an idle passenger aboard one of the larger brig-rigged packets; ashore by gig to board her, cross the Medway and the Nore to the mouth of the Thames, and up-river to the city. He and Pettus travelled together, for he needed a "man" to see to his things. Captain Blanding took a larger entourage, including his cabin steward and personal servant; all depended on the packet's cook for their meals, which were quite toothsome since fresh food and fresh fish were available . . . as were lashings of drink.

The winds were contrary, as were the tides, so they all had to sleep aboard one night, Lewrie and Blanding given cramped dog-box cabins with narrow slatted berths, no larger than the accommodations that Lewrie had slept in when he was a junior Lieutenant. The berths were not the sort he was used to, either, for his did not swing from ropes bound to ring-bolts in the overhead deck beams, but was nailed to the inner hull plankings. Not only was the mattress as thin as a Devil's bargain, little more comforting than two quilts doubled over, but the lack of swaying motion was irritating, and kept him up half the night. He had been *rocked* to sleep like a babe in its crib too many years . . . stillness felt un-natural, and he envied Pettus and his hammock on the lower deck with the other servants!

The morning brought a hearty breakfast, though, with kippers and eggs, thick toast, and scalding tea, and enough hot water in civilian measures for a scrub-up and a shave, with the luxury of even more tea on deck afterwards, lazing in perfect idleness, even going so far as to *lean* on the bulwarks in lubberly fashion as the packet made the bend into Greenwich Reach and plodded along past the Naval Hospital, Observatory, and Deptford Naval Dockyards. If Captain Blanding had had trouble sleeping, he gave no sign of it, bubbling over with boisterous *bonhomie*, tucking away a large breakfast, then enthusing over all the new construction at Deptford, and expressing the hope that, once he had been honoured with his knighthood, one of the 74-gunned Third Rates on the stocks would soon be his.

"I thought you were immoderately proud of *Modeste*, sir," Lewrie commented, "and her turn of speed for a sixty-four."

"Oh, I am, Lewrie!" Blanding responded, laughing out loud. "But one aspires to greater responsibilities, a larger command, perhaps the charge of a squadron of Third Rates."

"I s'pose I'm too used to frigates, and their freedom," Lewrie confessed as a servant came round with a fresh pot of tea. "If Admiralty thinks me worthy of squadron command, I'd prefer it to be a frigate squadron, with me in *Reliant*, or another Fifth Rate thirty-eight."

"Well, I dare say you're a dashed good frigate captain now, sir," Blanding allowed, "and you've done very well by me, but . . . promotion and greater responsibility comes to us all, sooner or later, should we live long enough . . . and not come a cropper sometime in one's career. *Reliant*'s your third frigate?"

"Fourth, actually, sir," Lewrie told him. "Though I had *Savage* only a year or so . . . before the trial, and my being relieved, and got *Thermopylae* as a last minute replacement for her captain when he fell ill. I've a year and a half left in *Reliant* before she'll need to be put in the graving docks for a refit."

"Make the most of it, then, Lewrie, for there's most-like some Third Rate in your future," Blanding said with a shrug. "Your family will be joining you at Court?"

"Only my father, sir," Lewrie said. "He's the only one in the vicinity, given the short notice we got. Yours, sir?"

"Oh, there's the wife, and my eldest son . . . he's just taken Holy Orders, and is still angling for a good parish. I'm assured he will find a post as a vicar, not a rector."

Why's that not a s'rprise? Lewrie cynically thought. Church of England politics and "interest" was as fierce as any, and one's posting could be as profitable as a government office. Rectors were much like Lieutenants when it came to prize-money in the Navy; their share of the tithes, their salary, the size and profitability of the manse and the farm that came with it, the glebe, would keep a man in comfort, but it was the vicar who got the "captain's" larger share of the tithe, *and* a share of the tithes from the rectors under him. The Blandings were *ferociously* well-connected and well-churched . . . look at Reverend Brundish, for instance, Captain Blanding's personal Chaplain, who must be *very* well paid to come away from a profitable vicarage with all the huntin', shootin', dancin', fishin', and steeplechasin' in which he revelled! God knows the *Navy* didn't pay Chaplains pittance!

"My daughter will be there . . . she and the wife will take advantage of their time in London to expose her to Society," Blanding went on, winking and grinning as he added, "And find her a suitable husband if the market's good. Brundish'll accompany us, o' course . . . coached up to London two days ago, to prepare the ground, and see to the missus and my girl," Blanding added when he saw Lewrie raise a brow in question. "Care t'dine with us beforehand?"

God, that sounds tedious! Lewrie thought.

"Perhaps after, sir. I've people to see. Solicitor, my bank, Admiralty, and some old school friends," Lewrie begged off, hoping for a long delay before he would *have* to socialise with the Blanding clan. "And, there's the mystery of what Sir Harper meant by 'best uniform *and* Court dress.' One hopes his promised letter sent t'my lodgings will be explanatory . . . and not too costly."

"Where will you lodge, sir?" Blanding asked.

"The Madeira Club, sir," Lewrie told him, explaining that the place was a bachelor's refuge, respectable and clean, for the middling sort of gentleman. "Wonderful wine cellar and grand victuals, but not open to gambling. They retire early at the Madeira. You, sir?"

"Brundish's brother Charles is a bishop at Hampstead, and has graciously offered us the use of his London house," Blanding told him, "in Bruton Street."

Lewrie tried to place Bruton Street, and *thought* it was south of Oxford Street, safely distant from his lodgings, unless Blanding was intrigued by the name of his favourite coffee house, the Admiral Benbow, at the corner of Baker and Oxford streets, and blundered in.

And why am I not s'prised that Brundish is kin to a bishop? he asked himself.

"Aye, after might be best, after all, Lewrie," Blanding allowed with a sage nod. "Family to see, what? Doings to catch up on in my long absence? But! Once it's done, I'd much admire could you and your father join us for a celebration supper . . . after we go to Westminster Abbey or Saint Paul's to give thanks to the Good Lord."

They let my *sort in church?* Lewrie wondered, but agreed to his superior officer's suggestions, whether he cared for them or not.

"Thought we'd take a *cabriolet* this morning," his father said as Lewrie descended the steps at the Madeira Club to the kerb, where a light, two-horse carriage awaited with its weather-proofed convertible top folded down above the boot. "And ain't *you* a picture, what? Like a belle goin' to a ball, haw haw!"

One more reason I don't much like the old bastard, Lewrie told himself as a liveried footman opened the kerb-side door and let down the metal steps.

"Oh, stop yer gob," Lewrie growled.

"Get up on the wrong side o' the bed, this morning, did ye?" Sir Hugo St. George Willoughby gravelled as Lewrie got in. "Or are the breeches too tight in the crutch?"

Lewrie spread a clean-looking lap blanket on the leather bench seat before sitting down, just to be safe.

"At such short notice, they are a bit snug," Lewrie admitted as the footman closed the door and folded up the steps. "Daft, too dear, and if God's just, I'll only wear them this once. Silk breeches, mine arse!"

"Just like a belle's ball gown . . . daft, too dear, and good for only one appearance in a London Season," Sir Hugo remarked.

After landing in the Pool of London, taking a hack to the Madeira Club, and un-packing, Lewrie had found the ornate formal letter that Sir Harper Strachan had promised. Immediately upon reading it, he had begun to curse blue blazes. He would need a new pair of shoes in that idiotic slipper style, new white silk stockings, these damned silk breeches, and all the help the valet staff of the Madeira Club could offer alongside Pettus's best efforts. His best formal uniform coat, too long kept in a sea-chest, had to be aired out to rid it of ship-stink, but nothing could restore the gloss of its gold lace trim that had gone a sickly green at sea. A tailor who specialised in military and naval uniforms had to remove the old and sew on new, damned near overnight. Brushing it down, Pettus had gotten a whole handful of cat fur off it! He'd had to purchase two new epaulets to adorn his shoulders, too. A new silk shirt, a new black neck-stock, his best white waist-coat sponged down and pressed . . . the neck-stock, too, that very morning, after a wetting, a starching, and a time for drying before it was pressed with a hot iron.

"The latest thing, sir," the borrowed valet told him, winking. "And all the crack about town, these days. All the dandies are trying to emulate some fellow name of Brummell when it comes to stocks, whose own're marvels. Flat and sharp-edged, 'stead of ropy-looking after a bit. I'll bind it on last, if you don't mind, sir?"

He'd been in need of a haircut, long overdue, in point of fact, and a close shave that morning by another's skillful hand, instead of shaving himself. There had been a vial of West Indies scent for his smooth-shaven cheeks . . . and a discreet dash or two on his coat, which was still redolent of salt, tar, pea soup farts, and mildew. At least the scent was made from the leaves of the bay tree, and wasn't all that sweet.

The one item over which he almost balked was the wig. "Look, I only need it the once, for God's sake," Lewrie had told the wig-maker after trying several on, and discovering to his chagrin that with one of those follies on his head, his hat wouldn't fit! "I haven't worn a wig since 1780! I look like a 'Macaroni'!"

In point of fact, before his father had crimped him into the Navy that very year, sure that Grandmother Lewrie in Devon would turn "toes up" and leave a fair amount of her fortune to Alan and he could pay off his creditors with young Lewrie half the world away and all un-knowing, Lewrie *had* been a Macaroni fop, right down (or up) to the wee hat perched atop a too-big wig!

"Couldn't I just rent one for a day or two?" Lewrie had pled.

"Now what'd my reputation be, did I allow that, sir?" the wig-maker had disagreed. "Letting wigs out and them coming back with fleas, or lice, and the next customer getting infested? No, sir. It must be purchase only. You're to be presented at Court? I'll not put shoddy on you, sir . . . what would people say of me? Try this one, pray do."

He had found one that was sleekly swept back on both sides and allowed his hat to sit at almost the proper level, though Lewrie's own sideburns and the short four-inch queue that he wore bound with black ribbon at the nape of his neck were visible. The wig-maker had suggested that he pin it on with ladies' hat pins, just to be safe.

So that's how Strachan did it! Lewrie had marvelled. Sourly marvelled, really.

So there he sat in an open carriage, on display to the world in his new finery, with his hundred-guinea presentation sword at his hip, the one awarded by the East India Company for saving the small homeward-bound convoy in the South Atlantic, a few years before, when he'd still had the *Proteus* frigate. His gilt buttons were polished to mirror-like gleamings, those silly shoes blacked and buffed nigh to patent leather shininess, and all his clothes so restored, or new, that he feared the young imps of the London Mob would delight in covering him with dung and mud before they'd gone half a mile.

He stared at the sky, dreading rain, too. It had rained the day he'd arrived, though the last two had been dry, so maybe there would be no puddles to wade through when they alit at the palace.

If there are, will my father fling a cloak on 'em, like Walter Raleigh did for Queen Elisabeth? he sourly wondered; *I doubt that!*

"We'll have to be brushed down, once we're there," Sir Hugo said with a squinty look. "Damn powdered wigs. S'pose the palace flunkies and catch-farts know what they're about with whisks."

"Ever been?" Lewrie asked him as they headed south down Baker Street, turning right onto Oxford Street, and bound for the shortest and most direct main route down Park Lane along Hyde Park.

"The once," Sir Hugo allowed, picking lint from his coat. "When I got tapped and named a Knight of the Garter. Back when the King was saner than he is now, and 'Prinny' was a toddler. Horrid-stuffy, was 'Farmer George's' Court in those days. In Publick, at least. My sort, well . . . ye'll note they haven't had me back for a brandy since."

"Understandably," Lewrie japed with a smirk.

"Don't imagine *your* welcome will be a whit better, haw haw!"

Damme if he ain't got it exactly right, Lewrie thought.

CHAPTER NINETEEN

*W*hen rattling down Park Lane at a comfortable clip, their *cabriolet* had seemed fashionable enough for the occasion. The morning was clear and sunny, and those West Enders who had risen earlier than the norm were out in their own open-topped carriages, or on horseback for a canter through Hyde Park, to their right. Turning into Piccadilly, then turning once again into St. James Street, though, they found the way to the palace was lined with four-horse-teamed equipages, mostly closed, and with only their sash-windows down to acknowledge the season, all very much grander than their own. Sir Hugo began to work his mouth, squint, and grumble as they joined the long queue leading to the entrances, as if regretting his choice of conveyance.

"Might as well have hired a one-pony dog cart," he groused.

"Doesn't matter," Lewrie told him. He could have given a bigger damn if they had had to walk, at that point, or had they been trundled up in a rag-picker's wheel barrow. He'd *intended* to get a good night's sleep, but some members of the Madeira CLub (the younger, still-single ones) had proposed more toasts than usual, posed more "a glass with you, sir!" individual toasts that had gone on in the Common Room long after the uncommonly good supper, with all *its* toasting, and the port, cheese, nuts, and sweet bisquits. Major Baird, their "chicken nabob" who'd come back from India with a middling fortune in loot and was *still* seeking a suitable mate (when not pursuing stand-up "knee-trembler" sex with the wenches who haunted the theatres), had even discovered a stone crock of American corn whisky, and had urged Lewrie to imbibe with him.

To say that Lewrie was a *tad* hung over would be an accurate statement; a bit too "blurred" to feel impatient, out-classed by others' elegance, or anything much at all. Though there were some young women in the gawking crowd that usually thronged outside the palace on days when levees were held that were quite fetching. And, since Lewrie *seemed* to be Somebody of Note (he was in a carriage bound for the portico, wasn't he; an officer, wasn't he?), some of the bolder even cheered and tossed a flower or two. They surely wouldn't waste flowers at a closed coach, where the top-lofty nabobs kept their aloof distance!

"P'rhaps it ain't that bad, after all," Sir Hugo said, leering across Lewrie at a round-faced teenaged beauty who was all but bouncing on her tip-toes in excitement. Sir Hugo even tipped his cocked hat to her and grinned. Which grin seemed to put her off and make her frown. The sight of a beak-nosed old goat, liver spots and all, ogling her like a vulture would a neglected beef roast would have put any young woman off . . . even if he *was* dressed in a general's uniform, and might be as famous as the Duke of Cumberland after Culloden.

"Hmm. Pretty," Lewrie commented, after a glance. "How do you keep yer wig from comin' off when ye tip yer hat?" he asked.

"Glue," Sir Hugo said with a pleased sigh, sniffing the flowers he had gathered from the floor of the coach. "There's times when losin' my hair's a blessing . . . lots o' scalp for the paste, heh heh. It washes off, later," he added with a shrug.

The palace staff was very well organised. As each coach rolled up, one of the passengers, and the coachee, was handed a numbered ticket made of pasteboard. At the foot of the walk sat an easel with much larger numbers stacked up beside it, so that when the guests departed their number could be displayed to the throng of coaches waiting in a side yard, summoning the proper conveyance. The British Army should have been so efficient, but then . . . Army officers *bought* their commissions, and the palace staff were selected, and paid, for competence.

"Your invitations, sirs," a grandly liveried flunky demanded, chequed them off a list, and bowed them onwards to the imposing entrance.

Did one ask Captain Alan Lewrie what he recalled of St. James's Palace in later years, he could only shrug, cock his head to one side, and respond by saying, "Huge. Rather huge." His hangover might have had something to do with it. There were grand marble staircases, and sumptuous carpetting, huge head-to-toe portraits, many times lifesize, framed in overly ornate gilt. There was a positive *shit-load* of gilt, Lewrie remembered. High ceilings, replete with angels and cherubs above him, thousands of candles burning, furniture lining the hallways and gigantic rooms, too grand to really sit on, and one long hall after another; he reckoned that he might have walked half a mile before reaching yet another hall where the levee was held, which was already thronged with the rich, the titled, the elegant and dashing, and those who would be honoured . . . and hopefully *become* titled, and elegant and *interesting* because of it . . . at least in part.

"Anyone you know, hey?" Sir Hugo asked after another liveried and white-wigged servant had taken their hats and presented them with yet another set of claim tickets.

"Hmm?" Lewrie responded, peering about owl-eyed.

"Damn my eyes, are ye foxed?" Sir Hugo grumbled. "Did ye take on a load o' 'Dutch Courage' with yer breakfast?"

"Nought but coffee, lashin's of it," Lewrie told him. "Now, last night was another matter. No, I don't think I do know anyone. Don't even see the Blandings, yet. Do you?"

"None I know . . . but one'r two I'd *care* t'know," Sir Hugo said as he raised a brow and put on a grin to a willowy and languid dame in her forties, one with dark auburn hair and a "come-hither" grin, who was gliding by on the arm of a much older and tubbier man. She seemed to look the both of them up and down, then smiled and played with her fan against her cheek for a moment. Flirtatiously?

"I'm out of touch," Lewrie confessed. "Does that mean anything?"

"The key to Paradise," Sir Hugo muttered back. "She's took with one of us. Either that, or she had an itch needed scratchin'."

Yet another liveried fellow came up to them as they neared the tall and wide doors to the hall proper. He seemed to know what he was about, and was all coolly buinsesslike.

"Captain Alan Lewrie . . . Major-General Sir Hugo Saint George Willoughby, aha," he briskly said, "honouree and guest. In a moment, you gentlemen will be formally announced. Right after, Captain Lewrie, might you grant us a few minutes to explain the procedure, with some of the others? . . . Oh, good. Tea or coffee will be available, and there are sidechambers where any adjustments of your habiliments may be made . . . and last-minute needs may be answered in a 'necessary.' Once His Majesty has made his entrance, an equerry shall queue you up in order of honours to be presented."

"I'll take another number?" Lewrie asked, hoping that coffee would be shoved into his hands, instanter.

"In a matter of speaking, sir," the courtier told him, grinning. He was an older fellow who had obviously supervised these ceremonies so often that he could have done them in his sleep.

Another queue as couples, or parties of three or more, waited to be announced and admitted. There were old hands at it who'd been coming to the palace for ages, along with nervous, coughing, and "aheming" throat clearers of both sexes. Husbands squeezed wives' hands to reassure them; sons and daughters ranging from gawky teens to matronly women with flushed faces, all but squirming in un-accustomed finery to get more comfortable, some moving their lips over rehearsed phrases of greeting should they get a chance to be spoken to by their sovereign, and a pair of teen daughters practicing their deep curtsies, tittering at each other each time. There were men . . .

Christ, half of 'em look like brick-layers, or greengrocers! Lewrie thought in wonder; *They handin' out knighthoods for brewin' a good beer? That's how Sam Whitbread got his!*

On closer inspection, even those who already wore signs of rank, ladies in tiaras and elegantly clothed men with sashes and stars, were not all *that* elegant or handsome, either.

At last, the haughty major-domo thudded his five-foot mace on the marble floor and bellowed (elegantly!), "Major-General Sir Hugo Saint George Willoughby, and Captain Alan Lewrie!" That drew no particular note from those already in the hall, though Lewrie plastered a smile to one and all on his phyz and looked the room over. There were thrones at the far end, atop a raised dais, with a cushioned kneeler before it; all adrip with even more gilt, red, purple cloth, with the Union flag, the ancient royal banner, and the flags of England's subordinate lands, stood up behind. He admittedly gawked.

"If you would come this way, sir, ah," a plummy Oxonian voice bade. It was Sir Harper Strachan, Baron Ludlow, again, dressed in an even grander suit of court clothes, wielding his mace-like cane, and scowling for a second as he gave Lewrie another of those up-and-down appraisals. "Quite a change for the better, hah," he decided.

"Harper," Sir Hugo said from the side, nodding in thin greeting.

"Hugo," Strachan replied, just as coolly. There was evidently no love lost between them.

"Subalterns together . . . in The King's Own," Sir Hugo explained. "Ah . . . what memories," he sarcastically added.

Strachan wriggled his nose and mouth in a petulant manner, then languidly extended an arm to steer Lewrie to a side-chamber.

"Oh, there you be, Lewrie!" Captain Blanding said as he spotted him. "Top of the morning to you!"

"And to you as well, sir," Lewrie replied, bound for the side-board where a silver coffee pot stood steaming over a candle warmer. At last! After a sip or two of creamed and sugared coffee, he began to feel as if he was back in the land of the aware, and gave an ear to Strachan's introductions and explanations.

There was a coal baron who would be made knight and baronet, a senior, doddering don from Cambridge who'd written something or other impressive who would be knighted, an unctuous younger fellow who was to be made a baron . . . from the names and hints he dropped, Lewrie got the impression that pimping for the Prince of Wales was going to be amply rewarded in a few minutes. There was a fellow retiring from the Foreign Office who would also be knighted. Disappointingly, there were no other officers from the Navy. There were none from the Army either, but they hadn't done all that much but drill, drink, and dance since the Dutch expedition in '98.

When summoned, once the attendees had had half an hour or so to mingle, they were to queue up in descending order: the pimp, the coal baron, Captain Blanding, then Lewrie, followed by the don and the old Foreign Office ink-spiller. When announced by name, they were to make their way to a particular rosette in the carpet and perform a graceful "leg"—a deep, long one, Strachan insisted (there would be time for them to practice)—then move forward to the edge of the dais before the thrones and stop. Head bowed still, in proper humility when named to the King 'til the Sovereign approached them with the Sword of State, at which time they should kneel on the cushion. Once the rite was done, it *was* allowed that one might express a *brief* sentence of gratitude, before rising, bowing again, then walk *backwards* away from the throne, counting the large rosettes in the carpet 'til they reached the third (where they had begun) and deliver a final "leg."

"It is *not* done to break away and turn your backs on His Majesty,"

Sir Harper cautioned in a stern, clench jawed drawl. "So long as he is present—"

"Doesn't that make chatting someone up rather awkward?" Captain Blanding interrupted.

"One *may* converse with others, turned *somewhat* towards the Presence, but one must not face deliberately *away,* sir," Strachan said in irritation.

"Lask to 'em on a bow-and-quarter line, sir," Lewrie said with a tongue-in-cheek smirk. A third cup of coffee was doing wonders.

"Oh, good ho!" Blanding said with a happy, satisfied snort.

They could not quite catch what Sir Harper Strachan was saying under his breath, or quite make out the sound of grinding teeth.

"Palace staff will now assist you with your appearances," Sir Harper gravelled, "should you feel any adjustments are necessary."

"The 'necessary,' aye, by Jove," Blanding said, peering about for a door which might lead to a "jakes." He was pointed to a door to one side of the room, and eagerly trotted off.

"Might I assist you, sir?" a catch-fart in palace livery asked Lewrie, a wee minnikin who barely came up to his shoulder.

"Just whisk the bloody hair powder off, thankee," Lewrie told him. "Think I can manage the rest myself," he added with a nod at the door, behind which Blanding was urinating as loudly as a heifer on a flagstone floor and humming a gay air.

"Quite so, sir!" the wee fellow happily agreed.

Once back in the hall, Lewrie got introduced to Mrs. Blanding, the Reverend Blanding, and Miss Blanding; the Reverend Brundish he already knew. The son was already as plump as his father and mother, and affected an Oxonian accent as irritating as Strachan's. The daughter was somewhat pretty—she had not yet inherited her mother's slightly raw and rosy complexion. Once the "allow me to name to yous" had been done, Captain Blanding launched into a paean of praise for how Lewrie had been so energetic and clever during their service together, which forced Lewrie to put on his false modesty (a sham at which he was un-commonly good, by then). It appeared that their fusses over his many "Submit" hoists, and all the woes of the convoy, were quite forgiven.

"Such an *arduous* task," Miss Blanding piped up, sounding as she chanted. "As *daunting* as any labour of *Hercules,* to deal with so *many* un-co-operative merchant captains."

"Like herding cats," Lewrie rejoined with a grin and a wink.

"Or, much like the early years of King David, when he was but a humble shepherd boy," the Reverend Blanding the younger added.

Oh, Christ, here come the bloody sheep, *again!* Lewrie cringed.

"First to slay Goliath, then to see his flock to safety, aha!"

"Quite so, Jeremy, quite so!" Chaplain Brundish praised.

"The slaying part was a lot more fun," Lewrie told them.

"The French, of *course*," Miss Blanding said, her cheeks colouring a bit at her daring to speak in company, no longer reckoned to be a child, who should be seen but not heard. "Father wrote us of your *bereavement*, Captain Lewrie, and, dare I note the *satisfaction* that the victory over them I would *imagine* provided you?"

"Well, a touch of mine own back, aye," Lewrie gruffly answered.

He was saved by his father's arrival, with a glass of wine in his hands, and it was Lewrie's task to make the introductions all over again.

"You must be very proud of your son this day, Sir Hugo," Captain Blanding purred.

"Indeed, Captain Blanding, indeed I am," Sir Hugo boasted, rocking on the balls of his slippered feet. "Amazed, too, I must own, for I never thought he could direct his boyhood boldness into useful work . . . but, God help the French, hey? He ever tell you how he was sent down from Harrow, and why? Lord, but he was a caution in those days!"

"Why, no, I don't believe so, Sir Hugo," Blanding said, cocking his head to one side.

"My lords and ladies, gentlemen and gentlewomen . . . the King!" a functionary bellowed, with a thud of his mace.

Way was made to either side of the great hall, like the parting of the Red Sea for Moses; there was a fanfare, an end to the sprightly string music from the court orchestra, and a great deal of deep bowing and curtsying. Heads and gazes were lowered, but . . . some once-only guests like Lewrie did peek, as did the gossip-mongers, looking for a sign that King George was still in decent health, or fading fast; and to be sure, members of the Privy Council and the under-ministers of the latest Pitt administration searched for clues regarding the continuation of the present monarch, and their prestigious offices.

Well, he looks *sane*, Lewrie told himself; *but, there's no real way t'tell, is there?* Whilst he was still in the West Indies, one of his father's letters had noted that King George had opened Parliament in February by addressing the body as "my Lords and Peacocks"! Since Lewrie had never really

seen him in the flesh before—a parade of fast-trotting royal coaches jin-
gling through St. James's Square where Lewrie had grown up (admittedly not the good side of the square, much like his family's repute!), a
hat in a window, and a glance of a pudgy and serenely bland face for an
eyeblink—he had only the portraits in the gallery of Ranelagh Gardens
to go by, and if he'd met him in a shop in the Strand, he wouldn't have
known him from Adam!

The King *was* looking a tad rickety. He'd always been a hefty fellow,
as rotund as the late Dr. Samuel Johnson, as Captain Blanding and his
brood, but now the King's scarlet-trimmed and gold-laced dark blue suit-
ings looked as loose and free as a flagging jib.

"Queen's ill again?" he heard someone whisper. "Where's she?"

"And, here comes Prinny," another muttered.

"His Royal Highness, the Prince of Wales!" the major-domo cried.

Down the crowd went again in bows and curtsys, as a lesser fan-fare
sounded.

"Be the Regent soon, you mark my words," someone snidely hissed.

"God help us, then," a woman whispered back. And, once the King and
the Prince of Wales had passed them, and they could stand upright again,
the same woman remarked, "The Prime Minister's in no better condition.
He's played out."

"Well, we've Lord Canning and Lord Castlereagh," her companion
pointed out. "*And* a pack of ninnies. The William Pitt government now
consists of William, and Pitt, and the scribblers," he japed.

Sir Hugo's letter had expressed concerns that when William Pitt had
returned to office, he'd refused to find a position in his ministry for Add-
ington, whom he'd supplanted, and refused his own cousin and friend,
Lord Grenville. Pitt had even angered the Navy by turning out Admiral
Lord St. Vincent, "Old Jarvy," as First Lord of the Admiralty, just as his
campaign to root out corruption, malfeasance, graft, and double-dealing
in the Victualling Board and HM Dockyards had begun to solve some of
the long-standing problems. He'd replaced him with a man who could
have cared less, Henry Viscount Melville, Lord "Business As Usual"!
Government was run by an un-talented pack of nobodys.

"Looks a tad off his feed, don't he?" Sir Hugo whispered with a raspy
sarcasm. "Though Prinny's bulkin' up nicely, good as a prime steer."

"Where'd ye find the wine?" Lewrie asked.

"For you, that's for after," his father rejoined. "No matter do *I* get
squiffy, but you . . . you're the trick-performin' pony in this raree-show."

"Why'd ye bring up our Harrow bomb-plot?" Lewrie further asked.

Long ago, Lewrie at a callow sixteen, and a clutch of his fellow rake-hells at Harrow had decided to emulate Guy Fawkes's plot to blow up Parliament, and had obtained the materials with which to lash back at the school governor by blowing up his carriage house. They'd been caught right after, of course, Lewrie with the smouldering slow-match in his hands, and expelled. It was a feat to be dined out upon, but not a fact to be blurted out to a superior officer who might imagine that Lewrie still harboured pyrotechnical urges.

"Gawd, you're clueless!" Sir Hugo said with a snort. "See how Miss Blanding was makin' cow's-eyes? Ye told me they were stayin' in London t'find her a suitable match. Want t'be that poor bugger?"

"Oh, for God's sake, they *couldn't* . . . !" Lewrie objected.

"You're better off than most they'll find," Sir Hugo sniggered. "And a bloody hero, t'boot, with a knighthood and a bank full o' prize-money. Well, God help 'em with *that* project, and pity the poor fool saddled with *her*, soon as she pups an heir or two, and ends as round as her parents. Best they know your warts, right off."

"Captain Lewrie . . . sir," Strachan intruded with an impatient schoolmaster's "vex" to his languid purr. "*Might* you find the time to join us, sir? All are in place but for you."

"Oh . . . coming," Lewrie replied, following the equerry to the middle of the carpet to join the others. He stood by Captain Blanding, took a deep breath to settle himself, and did some last-minute tugging at his shirt cuffs and the bottom of his waist-coat to settle them.

"A *grand* moment," Blanding whispered to him, grinning like Puck. "A *proud* moment, nigh the finest in my life, Lewrie!" He was almost overcome with emotion and awe of the occasion. "Well," he quibbled, "there was my wedding day, and the arrival of the children, but . . . to be so honoured!"

"And Rear-Admiral sure t'come, soon after, sir?" Lewrie hinted.

"Oh well, aye, but . . . to stand before His Majesty, our Soveriegn, to converse with him!" Blanding went on, looking as if he would keel over in a faint, or whirl like an Ottoman Dervish and snap his fingers in glee.

Thud-thud-thud from a ceremonial mace, and a richly toned voice was calling for Captain Stephen Blanding of His Britannic Majesty's Navy to come forward. For a stout fellow, Blanding did most of that ritual well; deep bow atop the third rosette in the carpet from the dais, advance, stop, and bow again; it was the kneeling part that gave him a spot of bother.

A senior courtier stood by King George to hold an unrolled parchment for him to read from. "Captain Blanding . . . Captain *Stephen* Blanding . . . in honour of your stellar career as a Commission Sea Officer in our Royal Navy, and in grateful recognition of your splendid victory over a French squadron at the Battle of the Chandeleur Isles, we name thee Knight and Baronet," the King intoned, stumbling a bit over the words as if he missed his spectacles. Down came the sword to tap Blanding on each shoulder, and it was done. There *were* some words exchanged that hardly anyone ten feet away could catch, then Captain Blanding was up and bowing and backing away for the last bow on the proper rosette, and he half-turned to Lewrie, gaping with joy and with actual tears in his eyes.

Like he just got healed by Jesus, Lewrie thought, finding this ceremony, and the most un-godlike appearance of the King, a bit of a let-down. Blanding might be reduced to a quaking aspic, but for himself, Lewrie could only chide himself for a cynic and a sham.

"Captain Alan Lewrie, of His Britannic Majesty's Navy, will come forward!" the courtier intoned.

Third rosette; *Nice carpet,* Lewrie thought, looking down at it as he made his formal "leg"; *I like the colours.* Then it was head-up and stride forward, looking over both the King and the Prince of Wales.

A bit drifty, Lewrie thought of the former, noting how George III was turning his head about like a man looking for where he had left his hat; *Bored t'death,* was his thought of the Prince. *Was he got up too early this mornin', or do his nails really need a cleanin'?*

The last bow, then the kneeling, and the lowering of his head, but . . . he really *was* a tad curious to witness what was about to come, so he looked up without thinking . . . hoping that King George would be a *mite* more careful with how he slung that sword about.

"Captain Alan Lew . . . Lewrie," the King began, leaning to peer at the ornate document the courtier held out for him, "in honour of your stellar career as a Commission Sea Officer in our Royal Navy . . ."

Christ, can't anybody *pronounce it right?* Lewrie thought with a wince; *It ain't like* he's *a foreigner, is it?*

". . . grateful recognition of your inestimable part which led to victory over a French squadron at the Chandeleur Isles," the King said in a firm voice, though leaning over to squint myopically at the parchment the courtier held, then leaned back to conclude his words. "We do now name thee Knight and Baronet," he said, looking out over the hall, over Lewrie's head.

"Ahem?" the courtier tried to correct.

What the bloody . . . ? Lewrie gawped; *How's that? Did he just . . . ?*

King George looked down at Lewrie, then at the sword, with a bit of puzzlement, then tapped Lewrie once on each of his epaulets.

"Ahem?" from the courtier a little louder.

"Knight and Baronet," King George III reiterated in a mutter, as if making a mental note to himself. "Knight *and* Baronet!" he said once more, as if that sounded better. He returned his placid gaze out to the crowd once more, grinning as if quite pleased with himself.

"I, ah . . . allow me to express my gratitude, sir . . . Your Majesty, mean t'say," Lewrie managed to croak, sharing a glance with that courtier who was shaking his head, with his eyebrows up.

"What? Hey?" King George asked, looking back down at Lewrie as if he'd never seen him in his life, and how the Devil had *he* got there.

"Uh . . . that I'm proud and pleased to be so honoured, Your Majesty," Lewrie tried again.

"Well, of course you are, young fellow, and well-deserving of it, too!" the King rejoined, beaming kindly; addled as an egg, Lewrie deemed him, but kindly! "Now, up you get!"

Lewrie rose to his feet, his mouth agape as he performed a departing bow. Though his head was reeling, he managed to pace back with measured tread 'til he reached the third-from-the-dais rosette in the carpet, made a last "leg" with his hand on his breast, then half-turned to sidle into the larboard half of the crowd, looking for Sir Hugo and Captain Blanding. When he found them, safely deep in the second or third row of onlookers, he spread his arms wide and blared his eyes in a cock-headed grimace of "what the Hell just happened?" incredulity. He was in *serious* need of a stiff drink, something stronger than the wine that his father had discovered!

"Lewrie, did he say . . . ?" Blanding asked, looking aghast.

"'Deed he *did*, sir," Lewrie replied, shaking his head. "It must have stuck in his head from yours, and he did it by rote. I'm sure it was a mistake, soon t'be corrected."

Blanding's wife was looking huffy, as if Lewrie had both insulted the Sovereign and diminished the grandeur of her husband's investiture. Chaplain Brundish and the new-minted Reverend Blanding frowned as if someone—like Lewrie—had run stark naked through church, whilst Miss Blanding was making cow-eyes, as if actually impressed.

"Pity it won't stick," Sir Hugo drawled, looking wryly amused.

"Where'd ye find the wine?" Lewrie asked him. "And do they have brandy?"

Now the King was conferring honours on the Cambridge don, this time reading *much* more closely and sticking to the script. A polite round of applause followed. The Foreign Office chap got his knighthood—and no more!—and all applauded again, the tepid sort of acknowledgement preferred in Society; too much enthusiasm was deemed crude and "common." Once the last claps died, the string music began again, and people began to mingle, filling up the lane between. Trays of wine began to circulate, and Lewrie excused himself from the Blandings to beat up to a liveried servant with flutes of champagne, threading his way between people in his haste, nodding and smiling whenever one of them addressed him as "Sir Alan" in congratulations. He *almost* snagged a glass, but for the interruption of the senior courtier who'd first steered him to the side-chamber.

"A word, if I may, Sir Alan? May I be the first to address you as such?" he asked.

"About the, ah . . . ?" Lewrie asked with a knowing smile.

"Exactly so, sir. If you would be so kind as to come this way?"

He was led to the same side-chamber, where Sir Harper Strachan, Baron Ludlow, stood grimacing and working his mouth from side to side in agitation, as if he wore badly-fitted dentures.

"Hah! There you are, sir!" Strachan snapped, stamping his cane on the floor like a school proctor about to thrash an unready student, as if the gaffe was Lewrie's fault, and doing.

"Aye, here I am, milord," Lewrie coolly answered, wondering if he actually was in some sort of trouble.

"We feared you would get away before being presented with your patent, and your decorations, Sir Alan," the senior courtier said with an Oxonian drawl much like Strachan's, but much more pleasantly, as if trying to defuse the situation . . . or defuse Strachan. "If you'd be so good as to remove your coat for a moment, Sir Alan?"

Lewrie had not noticed before that a long side-board bore several shallow rectangular boxes, one of which the courtier opened. "Your sash, Sir Alan," he said, producing a wide bright blue strip of satin which he looped over Lewrie's chest from right shoulder to left hip.

Christ, this is for real! Lewrie realised as he put his coat back on, and the courtier brought out the silver-and-*cloisonné* star, which he pinned to the left breast of Lewrie's uniform coat.

"Most wear the sash under the coat, sir," the courtier informed him, "though there are some who wish their coats to be doubled over and buttoned, then wear the sash outside the coat, beneath the right epaulet."

"Risky for gravy stains," was the first thing to pop into Alan Lewrie's head.

"Oh, indeed, Sir Alan!" the courtier agreed, simpering happily.

"Grr," or what sounded like it, from Strachan.

"The documents will have to follow along, later, Sir Alan," the courtier went on. "They must be amended, do you see as will the preliminary work of the College of Heralds, to reflect your baronetcy."

"Amended? Mean t'say the King's slip'll . . . ?" Lewrie gaped.

"Sir Alan," Strachan interjected, high-nosed and arch, though *striving* for pleasance. "His Majesty, the Crown, does not *make* slips, as you term them. His Majesty does not *err*." That word sounded more like "Grrr" without the G. "And, *should* our Sovereign, ehm . . . get ahead of himself, then it *is* no error."

"Mine arse on a band-box!" Lewrie blurted, stunned. "Mean t'say I really did . . . the *King* really did make me a baronet, too?"

"That is the case, Sir Alan," the courtier said, beaming.

"He did," Strachan intoned, sounding imperious *and* angered.

"One must *assume*, Sir Alan, that His Majesty, on the spur of the moment, deemed your actions in the battle . . . the only noteworthy that occurred last year entire . . . *so* praiseworthy that he decided to name you Knight *and* Baronet in sign of royal gratitude," the courtier conjectured with a hopeful note to his voice. "And, *enfin*, what's done is done, and . . . to borrow the phrase from the Order of the Garter, *Honi soit qui mal y pensé*, what?"

Lewrie goggled at him, dredging through his poor abilities with French for a long second or two before he twigged to it. *Shame on him who thinks evil of it!* he understood, at last.

"Grr," again from Strachan, who *was* a Knight of the Garter.

"Mine arse on a . . . ," Lewrie croaked.

I'm in through the scullery door . . . or the coal scuttle, Lewrie thought, whilst the courtier beamed and nodded and Strachan ground his teeth. He shook his head in dis-belief that the King, who should have been better off in Bedlam by this point, could announce his marriage to his horse like the Roman Emperor Caligula, and the sycophants in the royal court would find an *excuse* for it, and ain't he the wag, though?

'Twixt the King, the shaky Prime Minister William Pitt, and Napoleon Bonaparte's threatened invasion, England's in a pretty pickle, he sadly thought; *pretty much up Shit's Creek!*

"Now I think I *really* need a drink," Lewrie told them.

There was a soft rap at the door, and a servant whispered that the rest of the honourees were assembled for their presentations. The senior courtier nodded and bade them be sent in.

With them, thankfully, came another servant with a silver tray of wine glasses, yet another with a magnum of champagne (a war with the French notwithstanding), so that Lewrie could snatch one and press the second servant to top him up while the others were receiving the marks of their new distinctions.

"Gentlemen, a glass with you all," Sir Harper Strachan said at last as the champagne circulated and Lewrie got his second. "Congratulations and happy felicitations on this day!"

After the toast, they were free to re-enter the great hall and circulate with their families and friends. Captain Blanding stuck to Lewrie for a bit on their way out.

"Sir Stephen, sir," Lewrie said with a wink and a nod, raising what was left of his champagne in toast.

"Sir Alan, haw!" Blanding responded in kind. "Ehm . . . did they set things right?" he enquired, leaning close and looking concerned.

"In a manner o' speakin', sir," Lewrie told him. "It seems the Crown don't *make* errors, else they'd have t'admit that His Majesty is soft in the head, again, so . . . it'll stand, can you believe it."

That froze Blanding dead in his tracks, with a stricken look on his phyz. "Well now, sir . . . that's simply . . . ehm." It seemed that Blanding *did* feel irked by Lewrie being elevated to his own level; as if his own investiture had been diminished, and robbed him of all the joy of it. He recovered well-enough to say, "Well now! Congratulations to you, Captain Lewrie."

"And mine to you, sir," Lewrie replied. "*You*, at least, more than earned it," he confessed.

"Ah, there's the wife!" Blanding quickly said, looking away.

"And you must show her how well you look in sash and star, sir," Lewrie said, looking for escape as much as Blanding.

"Aye, I shall. See you later, Sir Alan," Blanding said.

"Sir Stephen," Lewrie replied, tossing off a brief bow from the waist, and wondering if that promised celebration dinner and jaunt to Westminster Abbey or St. Paul's Cathedral was dead-off.

Once he found his father, Lewrie could not help giving him a toothy grin and saying, "I out-rank you, now. Do we ever dine out together, I'll precede you to the table."

"Mean t'say yer baronetcy'll *stand*?" Sir Hugo gawped, then was taken with loud laughter, the place and the august company bedamned. "Good Christ, but he must be deeper in the Bedlam 'Blue-Devils' than anyone thought. Sir Romney Embleton probably won't mind, but, damme, will young Harry throw a horse-killin' fit, begad!"

"Yes, he will . . . won't he?" Lewrie smirked, savouring how it would go down with that otter-chinned fool to have a second baronet in Angles-green when his father passed on, and he inherited the rank.

"I must write Sewallis at once, and tell him he'll be a knight when I am gone," Lewrie said. "Now, where's some more champagne?"

CHAPTER TWENTY

Now, how does *a baronet conduct himself?* Lewrie asked himself as he made a slow circuit of the hall with a fresh champagne in his hand, and an eye out for the nearest refills. And for the comely young women present . . . so long as it wasn't the Blandings' mort. Sir Hugo had strayed away in pursuit of the auburn-haired woman they'd spotted early on; he wished him joy of it, though he smugly thought that she'd not had eyes for *that* old rogue. It must be admitted that, now that he was knight and baronet, even a back-door variety, he began to enjoy the rare chance to preen. It wouldn't last, of course; within a few days he would be back in dreary Sheerness, back aboard *Reliant,* and in the *minutiae* of ship-board life, and his sash and star stowed away at the bottom of a sea-chest. The hall was not so crowded with people, nor was it as candle-lit as it might be for an evening event, that it had grown oppressively warm, and someone must have thrown up the many sash-windows and opened some glassed double-doors to let in the cool day's wind.

"Captain Sir Alan Lewrie, sir!" someone called out in a braying voice, forcing him to turn and peer about. A tall fellow with a full head of long dark blond hair was beaming at him, a fellow garbed in a uniform of some cavalry regiment, and epaulets of a Lieutenant-Colonel.

"Sir?" Lewrie said, smiling back. "You have the better of me."

"Percy Stangbourne, Sir Alan," the dashing fellow said, coming to shake hands vigourously. "Viscount Stangbourne, but everyone calls me Percy. Congratulations on your knighthood, Sir Alan, and gaining a baronetcy."

"Thank you kindly, my lord," Lewrie responded, an idea nagging at him that he'd heard that name before, but . . .

"I bring felicitations from a mutual acquaintance of ours, too, Sir Alan," Stangbourne teased. "Mistress Eudoxia Durschenko, of equestrian fame?"

Oh, he's the chap Father wrote me of! Lewrie realised, wondering if he would be called out for a duel by a jealous lover.

"You are acquainted with her, my lord? Percy?" Lewrie asked as innocently as he could (he was rather good at shamming "innocent," just as he was at portraying false modesty) yet thinking, *Honest t'God, your honour, sir, I never laid a finger on yer daughter . . . sister . . . wife . . . mistress! And why the Devil ain't he wearin' a powdered wig, too?*

"Mistress Eudoxia and I were fortunate enough to make our acquaintance during the last Winter interval, whilst riding in the park, and I have had the further great fortune to have obtained her father's permission to call upon her, Sir Alan," Lord Stangbourne blathered enthusiastically, like a teen in "cream-pot" love.

"He *did*?" Lewrie exclaimed, stunned. "If Arslan Artimovitch did, I'd have t'declare ye the luckiest man in all England!"

Probably showed him all his daggers, pistols, and his lions, to give him good warnin', Lewrie thought.

"So I consider myself, sir!" Stangbourne boasted.

"Seen them lately?" Lewrie asked.

"Off on their Summer touring," Lord Stangbourne said with an impatient shrug, "up to the reeky towns of Scotland and back." He had to swipe at the romantic mop of hair that fell over his forehead. "We do write, twice weekly. Mistress Eudoxia had spoken so admiringly of you, sir, and of your *splendid* defence of their ship when they were returning from Africa some years back, so . . . when I heard your name called, I simply *had* to meet the man who saved my intended, express my thanks, and take the measure of so bold a fellow, ha ha!"

See if I'm a rival? Lewrie cynically thought; *What? She's his "intended"? Is he daft? Young lords sport with actresses and circus girls, they don't bloody marry 'em!*

Lewrie recalled, though, how zealously Eudoxia's father guarded her innocence. Stangbourne would've *had* to propose just to get close enough to shake her hand or smell her perfume!

"Intended? Why, that's marvellous for you, my lord!" Lewrie pretended to be delighted. "Percy, rather. When next you write her, please extend my best wishes . . . even to her father. You'll wish her to leave the circus, o' course. Is her father amenable to that, too?"

"They see the sense of it," Percy Stangbourne said with another shrug, that one much iffier, as if he'd not dared broach the subject yet. "Ah, and here's my sister!" He brightened, waving to someone. "I say, Lydia, come meet the hero of the hour, that Captain Lewrie that Eudoxia told us about . . . the one who saved their bacon in the South Atlantic several years ago!"

Lydia Stangbourne looked a tad *less* than enthused at the mention of her brother's *outré* "intended," all but rolling her eyes. During the naming to each other, Lydia Stangbourne wore a placid, bland, and almost bored-with-the-world expression, her mouth a bit pouty. That was a bit off-putting to Lewrie, though she had an odd sort of attractiveness.

Instead of dropping him a graceful, languid curtsy in answer to his bow, though, she extended her hand, man-fashion.

Do I kiss it like a Frenchman, shake, or just stare *at it?* he wondered, compromising quickly by grasping her fingers. She found his response slightly amusing; one brow went up, her dark green eyes sparkled, and one corner of her lips curled up in what he took as a smirk.

"Sir Alan," she purred, looking him directly in the eyes.

"Miss Stangbourne, your servant, ma'am," Lewrie replied. There was no wedding ring to give him a clue, and if she had a lesser title than her brother the Viscount, he hadn't heard it mentioned. "Honoured to make your acquaintance," he added.

"Don't be *too* sure, Sir Alan," she responded with a toss of her head and a brief laugh, "we're both hellish-unconventional." A smirk and a rueful *moue* followed. "Just Lydia will suit, as just Percy does for my brother. At one time, 'the Honourable Miss Lydia' would serve, but that was a while ago."

"And hellish-informal to boot, haw!" Percy happily seconded.

"'Prinny' finds us amusing," Lydia said, inclining her head at the dais, and the Prince of Wales, which reminded Lewrie that Sir Hugo had written that Percy Stangbourne was an intimate of the Prince. His declared informality, and that acquaintance, might explain why neither of them was wigged or powdered!

Lydia Stangbourne was not a ravishing beauty in the contemporary sense, but Lewrie found her rather attractive. Her face was oval, with faintly prominent cheekbones, tapering to a firm but narrow chin and an average-width mouth, one with delicate, almost vulnerable, and kissable full lips . . . when they weren't haughtily pursed. Lewrie thought her a tad elfin-looking, though her nose, full-on, was too wide and large at first glance; but, when she turned her head towards a servant offering glasses of champagne, it then appeared almost Irish and wee. Lydia's eyes were dark emerald green, the brows above them thick and brown, and her hair was darker than her brother's, as dark blond as old honey, and faintly shot through with lighter gold strands.

In fashionable soft leather slippers, she stood too tall for Society's taste, three inches shy of Lewrie's five feet nine, almost as tall as his late wife. And she wasn't what Society wished in its womenfolk's form, either, for she was not pale, wee, round, and squeezeable. Her stylish light green gown clung to a sylph-like, willow-slim frame, her complexion hinted at "outdoorsy" pursuits, and her bare upper arms displayed a hint of muscle; her handshake had been more than firm, making Lewrie think that Miss Lydia did things more strenuous than pouring tea, embroidering, or punishing a piano.

"Shall we stroll?" Percy suggested, and with glasses in hand, they started a slow circuit of the grand hall, with Percy pressing for details of the sea-fight that had saved the Durschenkos, where were the Chandeleur Islands anyway, and what had happened there, as eager as a toddler to hear a scary ghost story.

"Percy, *must* Sir Alan recite *all* his battles?" Lydia chid him after a time, reverting to her earlier thin-lipped coolness. "You two could save that for another time. I am more interested in how Captain Lewrie gained his somewhat infamous repute . . ."

What the Hell's she heard? Lewrie wondered, ready to flinch.

". . . as a champion of William Wilberforce and the Abolitionist Society," Lydia went on, turning her head to bestow another of those direct-in-the-eyes looks with a brow up, and her lips curled in sly humour. "You were put on trial for stealing slaves, but acquitted?"

Is she twittin' me for fun? Lewrie asked himself, a bit irked.

"The tracts and the newspapers called you 'Black Alan,' did they not?" Lydia asked with what looked like a smirk.

"I wasn't fond o' that'un," Lewrie said, grimacing, "nor when they named me 'Saint Alan the Liberator,' either. I do despise chattel slavery, but I must confess that the whole thing began as a lark." He told them the bald truth of how he and Christopher Cashman had duelled the Beaumans on

Jamaica, and why, and how they'd arranged the "theft" of his dozen Black "volunteers," including the bizarre appearance of the seals that night as if in blessing, and what splendid sailors those rescued Blacks had become.

"*Seals*, Sir Alan?" Lydia posed, looking dubious, as if he was a superstitious fool, and Lewrie explained why people in the Fleet thought him blessed with a lucky *cess*; the "selkies" who'd appeared as seals at a sea-burial of a boy Midshipman from the West Country in 1794, and the seals that turned up in warning in the Adriatic, then those who had swum out to his frigate in a snow storm to guide the *Thermopylae* frigate into the Baltic in 1801.

"I *know* it's more co-incidence than fact, but stranger things than that've happened at sea," he concluded, with a disparaging grin.

"You seem to be a man of more parts than one would at first suspect, Sir Alan," Lydia commented, this time with a wider grin.

"Not a simple 'scaly-fish' stumpin' round his quarterdeck yellin' 'luff'?" Lewrie said with a laugh.

"We must have you to supper, if only to hear a tenth of it all!" Percy Stangbourne eagerly proposed.

"Indeed we must, Percy," Lydia quickly agreed, giving Lewrie another uncanny direct look, this time smiling promisingly and slowly fanning her lashes. "You will be staying in London for long?" She sidled an inch or two closer, her head slightly over to one side, and sounded as if his answer was vitally important to her.

"Only a couple of days, unfortunately," Lewrie had to tell her. "Admiralty, some other business, before I have to return to Sheerness. They tell me there's a war on, and the French are bein' a bother!"

"Dinner, today, perhaps?" Lord Percy proposed.

"I'm down for dinner with Captain Blanding and my father," he said, and damned unhappy he was to say it, too.

"Do I gather that that sounds as dreadful as supper parties with Wilberforce and Hannah More and their crowd?" Lydia japed, tossing her head back for a good laugh; on a very slim, graceful neck, Lewrie noted! "As much as one admires their good works, and their intentions . . . they are such a *tedious* lot!"

"Aye, I've been bored t'tears a time or two, myself," Lewrie happily agreed, laughing too. "Before my trial, it was almost once a week. And it's not just slavery they'll do away with. Fox-huntin' and steeplechasin', bear-baitin'n dog-fightin' . . . it'll be tasty food and *beer* to be done away with, next, I expect. Sling every child into what they're callin' a Sunday School, and wallop all glee from 'em?"

"Spiritous drink, music, and dancing, too, do you imagine?" she said with an intriguingly impish cast to her eyes. "What about supper this evening, Sir Alan? You're free, aren't you, Percy?"

"I would be delighted!" Lewrie quickly told her.

"We must show you off to London," Lydia said, tapping the star on his chest, next to his medals for Cape St. Vincent and Camperdown. "At White's, the Cocoa Tree, or Boodle's?"

"Almack's, too," Lord Percy boyishly hooted. "Make the rounds. And, I've a yen to try my luck again in the Long Rooms."

"Not too deep this time, Percy?" Lydia said, her face losing all animation, with a fretful expression.

"Last time, I garnered seventy thousand," Percy boasted. "Now, had I been gambling deep, it might have been a million, by dawn. *Do* say you will join us, Sir Alan, as our guest for the evening. My word, I still wish to hear at least some of your past battles, even though they may bore poor Lydia to tears, all that sailing stuff, and manly doings."

"Pooh, Percy, in Captain Lewrie's case, I very much doubt if I *could* be bored," Lydia rejoined; and there was yet another of her odd and encouraging looks, and a warm smile of amusement.

"Then I shall," Lewrie swore. He gave his address at the Madeira Club, got theirs in Grosvenor Street (*hellish*-fashionable, that!) and a promise that they would coach round and collect him at 8 in the evening. A handshake with Lord Percy, a bow to Lydia, then once more a clasping of hands with her, and this time her fingers trailed slowly cross his palm as they let go, and her enigmatic smile.

Well, well, well! Lewrie thought, damned pleased with himself; *Comin' up in Society, am I?* He had skirted round the fringes of the aristocracy in his childhood when they'd still had the house in St. James's Square, and at his various public schools, then encountered a few more of the peerage in the Navy; in the main, he'd never been all that impressed or in awe of Lord Thing-Gummy types. They were either competent, or lacklustre bores, either likable dunces or rogues, or vicious little tyrants with no time to spare on "the lower orders."

Lord Percy, Viscount Stangbourne, seemed to be a decent sort so far, and his sister . . . ! *How* does *one go about seducin' her kind?* he puzzled; *Or would that be too aspirin' for a lackey like me? Hmmm,* he pondered further; *bound t'be bony, and not much by way o' tits,* but. . . .

CHAPTER TWENTY-ONE

*G*ad, yes, but Viscount Stangbourne gambles deep, and has a most uncanny knack o' winnin' most of the time," Sir Hugo informed him once they set off in their *cabriolet* from the palace. "He can afford to . . . they're *swimmin'* in 'tin.' I'd advise ye t'stick to Shove-Ha'penny or bowls, for neither of us ever had a head for serious gaming."

"A pound or two at Loo, perhaps," Lewrie assured him, marvelling at how the cheery sunlight winked off his star.

"That's what ye always promised, and how much o' yer debts did I end up coverin', what?"

"Then I'll toady and cheer *him* on," Lewrie replied. "His sister is rather interesting," he added, striving for *mild* interest.

"The infamous Lydia? A scandalous baggage," Sir Hugo snickered. "Fetchin', I'll allow, but . . . ye didn't read about it? She was in all the papers, about three years ago."

"What was it about?" Lewrie asked, a bit more intrigued.

"Her parents settled two thousand pounds a year on her when she came to her majority . . . the brother twice that 'til he inherited everything when they passed. The fortune hunters lined up by the battalion," his father began to explain. That sum made Lewrie grunt in amazement; one could have a fine, gentlemanly life, in some style, too, on about three hundred a year . . . before the war, and the taxes, at least!

"She was hellish-hard to please, but finally wed at last, four years ago," Sir Hugo continued. "The fellow, Lord Tidwell, was only a baron, below the Stangbournes in the peerage, but his title was an *old* one, and Percy's only the *third* Viscount, d'ye see, though the groom's people were *nigh* as well off." Like any Englishman, Sir Hugo delighted in the doings of "The Quality" and was snobbish about the order of precedence in the peerage; there was some juicy gossip there for sure. Divorcement charges and counter-charges and testimony of adultery were printed, bound, and sold as mild pornography!

"Didn't take, though," Sir Hugo explained. "It turns out that Tidwell was a *very* nasty item, with a taste for more perversion than *I* ever knew existed!" Sir Hugo, in point of fact, had been one of the founding members of the Hell-Fire Club, and knew more than most!

"I rather doubt *that*!" Lewrie shot back with a leer.

"Wish me to continue, hah?" Sir Hugo gravelled, leaning back to one side of his seat. "Fellow was flyin' false colours, it seems, so it wasn't more than eight months into their 'wedded bliss' than she up and decamped to the family house in London, then to the country, and got her brother t'hire on lawyers. Well, Percy's in Lords, and their borough is most like a 'rotten' one, so their Member in Commons filed her a Bill of Divorcement, quick as ye could say 'knife.' Oh, it was just lurid . . . ! Brutality, waste of her dowry, reducin' her to little more than 'pin money,' adultery, demands for carnal acts *no* decent woman should put up with?" Sir Hugo was not quite *drooling*, but he did massage his hands against each other vigourously.

"Soon as hers hit the agenda, Tidwell filed one against her . . . alienation of affection, refusal of proper congress, and adultery, too," Sir Hugo related, cackling in glee. "And the charges were the titillatin' marvel, two years runnin'! She'd've had people's sympathy for her lookin' elsewhere for affection, seein' as how she claimed he was poxed to the eyebrows, *and* a secret sodomite, and she feared for her health, but for how *many* other men were alleged, d'ye see, so . . ."

"That'd make her what, thirty or so?" Lewrie asked.

"About that, perhaps a tad older," his father said, impatient to continue. "Parliament finally saw things her way, and granted her the divorcement, t'his cost, and she got t'keep all her jewellry and paraphernalia. She's still in bad odour in Society, but still *in* Society, whilst Tidwell's retired to his country estates . . . rantipolin' ev'rything in sight but his horses and huntin' dogs, and rumoured t'be so poxed he has t'carry a bell t'warn people off like a leper. 'Prinny' back yonder, she and Percy are in his circle, and I heard he'd've made a sally at her, 'til the King warned him off. And, I heard that she snubbed him, too . . . so she must've been talked to by one of the palace catch-farts . . . or has more sense than I imagined of her."

"D'ye think all the charges were true?" Lewrie asked, intrigued, and finding that those too-snug silk breeches were even snugger in the crutch, of a sudden.

"It's good odds she and her attorney gilded the lily, but in the main, I expect they got Tidwell to a Tee," Sir Hugo snickered. "As to Tidwell's charges, they might be true, too, but he brought it on himself and has no one else t'blame. Why? Fancy your chances with her, what? Ye find her all *that* fetchin'?"

"Fetching, aye," Lewrie admitted with a wry smile, cocking his head to one side. "But, she'd most-like laugh my sort to scorn, did I try," he scoffed. "Someone raised so rich and privileged, *born* to the peerage, well . . . I'm a boot-black in comparison. And, I'm sure that there's some still chasin' after her with an eye out for her fortune, so . . ."

"Know what they say, though," the old rake-hell rejoined with a nasty cackle, "ye sup on roast beef and lobster mornin' noon and night . . . ev'ry now and then bread, cheese, and beer is toppin' fine, ha ha!"

"So. Where are we bound?" Lewrie asked, noting that their *cabriolet* had just passed through Charing Cross and was bound east for the busy, bustling Strand. "Saint Paul's for a long kneel-down, and a homily-long prayer from young Reverend Blanding? It appears Westminster Abbey's out. We've long passed that."

"Don't know about that part, but *you're* dinin' with 'em at that splendid chop-house in Savoy Street you went on and on about, and thankee for tellin' me of it. I, on the other hand, will coach on home for my townhouse, then dine with a lady I met at the levee, and a *most* handsome mort she is, too! You'll beg off for me, will you, there's a good lad."

"What? Don't tell me ye made progress with that auburn-haired wench that quickly, with her 'lawful-blanket' there!" Lewrie gawped.

"Not her . . . a 'grass-widow' whose husband's regiment's been posted to the Kentish coast, in case Bonaparte *does* manage t'get his army cross the Channel. Aha!" Sir Hugo cried as the carriage neared Savoy Street. "Coachman, draw up here, so my son may alight."

"What? What the Devil . . . ?" Lewrie carped.

"You can whistle up another conveyance once you've eat, right?" Sir Hugo said as the assistant coachee got down to open the kerb-side door and lower the folding steps.

"I'm saddled with the Blandings, alone, while you . . . ?" Lewrie fumed.

"Your friends, not mine," his father said with a snicker, tapping his walking-stick impatiently to force Lewrie to alight.

"I can always count on ye, Father," Lewrie said once he was on the pavement, heaving a long-suffering, resigned, and I-should-know-better-by-now sigh. "You will always let me *down!*"

"Ta ta, lad! *Bon appétit!*"

Lewrie had changed to light wool breeches that fit more comfortably and a sensible pair of shoes with gilt buckles for his evening out. Lord Percy Stangbourne had swapped slippers for highly polished cavalry boots. "Don't I look dashin' and dangerous, hey?" he'd hooted, showing off his elegantly tailored uniform, in which he *did* look very dashing, indeed, and revelled in it.

Lydia Stangbourne came gowned in a champagne-coloured *ensemble* that surprised Lewrie with its lack of translucence. Oh, its under-sleeves were sheer, but it was not as revealing as young ladies, and a fair share of older ones, preferred these days. The top of her gown began almost at the tips of her shoulders, and it *was* delightfully low-cut in the bodice—a grand sight, that, though Lydia was not *amply* endowed—but her gown was rather conservative compared to the rest of the women who dined at Boodle's. She had seemed happy to see him, and during the coach ride her face had been animated and nigh girlish. Once there, though, that softness had evaporated, and Lydia had worn almost a purse-lipped pout, a royal "we are not impressed" expression.

The Stangbournes—Percy particularly—seemed to be regular customers at Boodle's, for their party had been greeted with the enthusiasm usually associated with the arrival of a champion boxer or jockey. Liveried flunkies took their hats, walking-sticks, or cloaks with eagerness to serve, and even before they had left the grand foyer for the main rooms, flutes of champagne had appeared. A dining table had been awaiting their arrival, but it had taken nigh ten minutes to reach it, for their entry had turned into what felt like a royal procession. All the young and "flash" sorts, and a fair number of older ladies and gentlemen, had simply *had* to come and greet them with much beaming, bowing, hoorawing, curtsying, and tittering; so many Sir Whosises and Dame Whatsits, Lord So-and-Sos and Lady Thing-Gummies, being introduced to Lewrie—and so many japes and comments passed between them and Percy—that he had felt quite overwhelmed . . . and, after a bit, irked to stand there like a pet poodle and listen to subjects he knew nothing about sail round his floppy, fuzzy ears! And have them scratched now and again, like "Ain't *he* a handsome hound, now!" tossed at him.

Another thing that had irked him after a while: scandalous or not, Lydia Stangbourne still drew admirers and "tuft-hunters" by the dozen. He'd lost count of how many young fellows he'd met and shaken hands with, all of whom had looked him up and down and had seemed to dismiss his presence as a potential rival; they all seemed to be civilians, of course, elegantly, stylishly garbed.

And, once returning to their own tables, *laughing* at him behind his back, *sneering* at him for a jumped-up inarticulate "sea-dog," not worthy to be in *their* select company! His ears had begun to burn.

Lydia had sported that bored, pouty look, as if raised to play "arch," though she had smiled briefly when greeting admirers and had chuckled over their jests. *What the bloody Hell was I hoping?* Lewrie had thought . . .'til Lydia had shifted her champagne glass to her left hand and had slipped her right arm into his. *Hullo? She bein' kind?* he'd speculated, imagining that she had sensed his unease and was just playing the polite hostess, as a *duty* to ease the "outsider's" nerves!

Once seated, though, she had turned lively, smiling and laughing and seeming as rapt as her brother as Percy dragged tales of derring-do and battle from him, an explanation of his "theft" of those dozen slaves, and the fleet actions he'd participated in. Given a chance to preen, even to a small audience, Lewrie had begun to feel more at ease, as the supper progressed, keeping things light and amusing.

"And are you married, Sir Alan?" Percy had asked. "Even though I hear that many sailors don't 'til they attain your rank. Was Dame Lewrie unable to attend the levee this morning?"

"My . . . my late wife, Caroline, was murdered by the French two years ago," Lewrie had sobered. "We'd gone to Paris, during the Peace of Amiens, a second honeymoon, really . . ."

"Good God above, *why*?" Percy had demanded, his mouth agape.

"You poor man!" Lydia had exclaimed.

"The shot was meant for me," Lewrie had told them, laying out how he'd angered Napoleon Bonaparte by presenting him captured swords in exchange for the prized hanger Bonaparte had taken from him after blowing up his mortar ship at Toulon on 1794.

"You've *met* the Ogre?" Lord Percy had further cried.

"Only twice, and neither time was enjoyable," Lewrie had said, having to explain that first encounter long ago, and how he'd refused parole and had had to surrender his sword, to remain with his men and the Royalist French with him, who surely would have been slaughtered on the spot, had it not been for the arrival of a troop of "yellow-jacket" Spanish cavalry to whisk them away to safety.

"Don't know if it was *really* me and the dead Frogs' swords, or something else that rowed him, but, he set agents and troops to hunt us down and kill us. We *almost* got clean away, almost into the boat, but, some French marksman . . . ," Lewrie had tried to conclude, but all the memories had come flooding back, and he had stopped, chin-up and his face hard.

"My most *sincere* apologies for broaching the subject, sir . . . *but,* to have been face-to-face with the Corsican Tyrant, the Emperor of all the French, well!" Lord Percy had cried, much too loudly, and had proposed a toast, again much too loudly, to Lewrie's honour. And, by the time for dessert, port, and cheese, the same people who had been introduced once had come to their table for another round of greetings, their names and faces just as un-rememberable as the first time.

Then, with supper done, Lord Percy would not take "no" for an answer 'til they'd made the rounds at Almack's, and at the Cocoa Tree too, to show Lewrie off and name him to everyone they knew as the hero who had bearded Bonaparte twice, and lived to tell the tale!

Lewrie began to feel like a prize poodle, again, for a whole other reason!

CHAPTER TWENTY-TWO

*L*ewrie wished he had begun to play-act yawns and beg off after Almack's, but there he was in the Cocoa Tree, one of the fastest gaming clubs in London, nodding, bowing, and smiling (a tad forced by then, his smiles) to yet another parcel of simpering "hoo-raws." Percy was dead-set on entering the Long Rooms to find a game, and Lewrie had to follow along.

"Do you care for a flutter of the cards tonight, Sir Alan?" he asked, craning his neck to find an empty chair and a game he liked.

"I've really no head for gambling, mil . . . Percy," Lewrie said with a grin and shake of his head. "Got my fingers burned and learned my lesson before I went into the Navy."

"Are you *sure* you're English, sir?" Lydia teased, tossing back her head to laugh, her arm under his once more. "Why, wagering is the national disease!"

"Got cured of it," Lewrie told her, chuckling.

"I wager the wagers Alan makes against the French are deeper than any *I've* ever made!" Lord Percy hooted. "Wager *wagers*, hey? Well, you two can support me whilst I take a risk or two. I say, there's an opening for *vingt-et-un*. Smashing!"

"Keep your head, Percy," Lydia cautioned her brother. "You've taken on nigh your daily half-dozen."

"A gentleman who can't manage half a dozen bottles of wine per day is no proper gentleman, Lydia," Lord Percy scoffed. "She's of a piece with you, Alan . . . do the stakes near an hundred pounds, Lydia'll go all squeamish and quaking. There must've been a *miser* in the family tree long ago, and she inherited, ha ha!"

"Let us know whether you're winning or losing large, Percy," she told him with a wry tone. "Scream or groan, and we'll come running to your rescue. Captain Lewrie will surely join me for more champagne?"

"By this time o' night, I'm about ready for a pot o' tea," he had to admit to her, feeling well and truly "foxed."

"Now I *know* you're not English, Captain Lewrie!" Lydia teased again. "There must be a West Country Methodist, or a Scottish Calvinist, in *your* family tree."

"Well, my mother's family *is* from Devonshire," Lewrie quipped.

"A pot of tea, then . . . with Devonshire cream," Lydia decided, smiling most fetchingly, and with lowered lashes.

They found a comparatively quiet corner table in the outer public halls, and ordered tea with scones and jam, which didn't even seem to faze the waiter; odder things had been called for at the Cocoa Tree.

Over several restoring cups, which cleared some of the fumes in Lewrie's head, Lydia led him through his background; how his mother had died in childbirth, and Sir Hugo had come back to take him in. . . .

"*That* Willoughby?" Lydia almost gasped. "The 'Hell-Fire Club' Willoughby? Good God, Sir Alan, he's almost as scandalous as I!" She laughed in delight, then lowered her head to peer hard at him, cocking her head over to one side. "Do you take after your mother, now, or do you take after *him*? Do you share *his* proclivities, even *my* less-than-good repute might be in jeopardy!"

"Just a simple sailor, me, Lydia," Lewrie japed.

"You're aware . . . my divorce and all that?" she asked intently.

"Father told me a bit, this afternoon," he admitted, shrugging. "Sounds as if you got saddled with the Devil's first-born son."

"He was, and he is," Lydia told him, looking a bit relieved by his answer, "and I'm well shot of him. You have children?"

And Lewrie had to explain how both his sons were in the Royal Navy, and how Sewallis had managed to forge and scrounge his way into a Midshipman's berth, which much amused her. His daughter, Charlotte, well . . . "She's with my brother-in-law and his wife in Anglesgreen. Never heard of it? Halfway 'twixt Guildford and Petersfield, a little place. Best, really.

My father's country place is there, but there's no one to care for Charlotte . . . even if Governour thinks it was all my fault, our going to Paris, and Caroline's murder, and . . . the last I saw of Charlotte, over a year ago, she blamed me, too."

"You don't have a seat, yourself?" Lydia asked, her voice going a touch cool for his lack.

"Caroline and I were her uncle Phineas's tenants. We ran up a house, built new barns and stables, but, after her passing, I couldn't stand the place . . . all hers, d'ye see . . . and *then* Uncle Phineas decided that my other brother-in-law, Burgess Chiswick, and his new wife needed a place of their own, and turfed me out, so he could *sell* it to Burgess's new in-laws, the Trencher family," Lewrie explained. "Now, my father's place is home . . . do I ever get a chance t'go there, what with the war and all. Twice the acres, twice the house, even if Sir Hugo opted for a one-storey Hindoo-style *bungalow*. Rambles all over the place, and even has an ancient Celtic hill-fort tower, later a Roman watch tower, he's partially rebuilt. Mine, when he passes, but—"

"Lydia, darling Lydia!" a man interrupted, coming to loom over their table. "Pardons, sir," he added, very perfunctorily, as if the presence of another man was of no concern, and good manners were not necessary. "How delightful you look this evening, my dear!" the gallant continued. "The colour of your gown makes you simply ravishing!"

"Why, hullo, Georgey," Lydia rejoined, turning arch and bored-sounding once more, extending her hand to be slobbered over. "Alan, may I name to you George Hare. Georgey . . . allow me to name to you Captain Sir Alan Lewrie, Baronet," Lydia said, pointedly using Lewrie's Christian name, and Hare's diminutive.

"Pleased to meet you, sir," Hare replied, tossing off a brief bow from the waist before turning his attention back to Lydia.

"Yer servant, sir," Lewrie gruffly responded, striving for the blandest note, as if the fellow made no impression, though he felt an urge to slap the interloper silly, or demand what the Devil he was doing by intruding. *Damme, does she know* everyone *in London?* he fumed.

"Lydia, my dear, have you given consideration to my invitation to Lady Samples' supper party on Saturday? It will be ever so gay an affair . . . music, dancing, and *écarte?*"

"Unfortunately, I cannot attend, Georgey," Lydia said with the weariest drawl, drawing back her hand. "Percy and I thought of going to the country for the weekend. Some time *en famille, n'est-ce pas?*"

"Well, perhaps a brisk canter through the parks before then," Hare suggested with a hopeful expression.

"We shall see, the weather permitting," Lydia said, all but feigning a yawn. "I can promise nothing."

"Ehm, well . . . does it not rain, I'll send a note round," the fellow pressed, knowing he was being snubbed but determined not to show it, and stubbornly determined to arrange a meeting with her. "Yer servant, sir . . . your undying, humble servant, Lydia," he said, bowing himself away.

"Such an *unctuous*, beastly boor!" Lydia huffed once he was gone. "Can he not *see* how heartily I despise him? My apologies, Alan. Your grand night should *not* have been interrupted by such a toadying, money-hunting . . . oily *pimp*!" she all but spat, her face fierce with anger.

"I gather his sort turn up rather a lot?" Lewrie said, feigning an amused grimace, though he wasn't much amused; it *had* been irksome!

"*Some* more subtle than others," Lydia told him, making shivers of disgust, then smiling faintly. "My mis-fortune at marriage . . . that is the reason I dread re-entering *that* particular institution," Lydia said with a head-cocked shrug before peering intently into his eyes. "Though try telling that to all the swaggering jackanapes who can't *imagine* a woman who *won't* swoon at the sight of them! To be single, I am thought un-natural . . . a condition only cured by throwing my self, and my dowry, into some new man's dungeons! To be re-enslaved!"

"Then don't," Lewrie told her with a grin. "Enjoy your life."

"Georgey Hare's one of the worst," Lydia went on, stunned for a second by Lewrie's bald directive. "His family's decently well-off, and he's a thousand *per annum*, so he can *play* at the law. . . ."

"I don't like attorneys, much," Lewrie japed. "Except when in need o' one."

"Oh, let us speak no more of Georgey, or his slimy ilk," Lydia said with a huff of exasperation, slumping into her chair and looking pouty-sad. "I know!" She perked up, instantly turning mischievous and leaning over the table towards him. "Do we wait upon Percy, it will be *dawn* before he leaves the Long Rooms. Winning or losing, he can't be dragged away by a team of bullocks! Will you trust me, Sir Alan, to find some place more amenable to quiet conversation?"

Could we really *be "aboard"?* Lewrie devoutly wished to himself, amazed by her daring. "God, yes!" he quickly agreed.

"Then let us go," she said, determined.

.   .   .

"Are you . . . comfortable, Alan?" Lydia asked in a whisper as she lay beside him, her head propped up on the pillows and her forearm.

"*Most* comfortable," he told her, stretching and sighing blissfully, half-turned towards her with his right arm under her pillows. "And damned grateful, thankee very much!"

Her long dark blond hair was down, and her grin was impish and in-fectious. By the light of a single candle on the night-stand, her green eyes sparkled like emeralds as she regarded him, as if inspecting him for warts. She grew sombre for a moment.

"I mean . . . are you comfortable with your . . . estate in life?" she amended, waving her free hand in the air. "Do you aspire to . . . ?"

"D'ye mean t'ask if I aim for wealth?" he countered, sitting up a bit. "Never gave it much thought, really. No, really!" he insisted to her *moue* of dis-belief. "Look . . . I've my father's house and land when he passes, and he came back from India a 'chicken-nabob,' so I'll not have t'go beg-gin'. In the meantime, there's my Navy pay, and I've been more fortunate than most when it comes to prize-money. There's a goodly sum in the Three Percents, inherited plate, jewellery and such, and a tidy sum at Coutts'. I'm *not* after yer money, if that's what you're wonderin'. Aye, I'm 'com-fortable,' as ye say, Lydia. 'On my own bottom,' as the Navy says. Do you fear I am?"

"It's what I fear from every man," she confessed, cuddling up onto his chest to drape herself atop him.

"Well, the proof's in the pudding, as they say," Lewrie said, a bit miffed that she would even ask, though he still stroked her bare back and shoulders with delight. "Of course, that'd require that you'd allow me t'know you better."

"You do not think you know me a *trifle* better than you did this morn-ing, Alan? Yesterday morning, by this time?" she lazily teased, shifting a slim thigh over him in response to his stroking.

"And I'd admire to know a lot more, Lydia," Lewrie told her as she raised her head to look at him.

"I would admire that, too," she whispered, earnestly, intently staring at him for a moment before sliding up to kiss him deep, with her breath still musky from the after-glow of their lovemaking.

He had *hoped*, but hadn't been too sure where they were headed. They had tried a less-fashionable tavern, and though it was still open for business so late, it was too full of half-drunk young couples who were much too loud. Her coach had taken them to her family house in Grosvenor Street, after which she'd called for coffee, cream, and sugar from the sleepy few servants still awake, and dismissed them for the night. They had sat close upon a settee, turned towards each other, inclining their heads closer and closer as they'd whispered and laughed, and . . . then she'd drawn him to his feet and had led him on tip-toes in stockinged feet to a spare bed-chamber, giggling at their daring 'til locked in . . . and Lewrie's fondest wish had been realised.

Lydia was very slim, as slim as Tess the Irish lass in "Mother Batson's" brothel in Panton Street, as girlish-slim as his late wife had been when they'd first wed, her flesh firm but so silkily soft, as if he ran his fingertips through fine-milled talcum powder. Their un-dressing had been slow and tentative, despite Lewrie's urgent and fierce wants after two years of celibacy since his return from Paris; he didn't wish to frighten her off at the last moment. On Lydia's part, she had shown a shyness that Lewrie wouldn't have expected in a woman so out-spoken, or one with an allegedly scandalous past. There had been just the one small, dim candle to light them under the covers, with Lewrie's back turned as she'd slipped beneath them, and her head partially averted as he did so; she hadn't come to his side 'til the sheet was pulled up to their chins, and he had slid a light hand over her taut but tantalisingly soft belly.

Might be just the once, so make the most of it, he'd cautioned himself, savouring every moment as if it was the very last they would share, that he would have with any woman, slowly sliding down her body to worship her graceful neck, her ears, her breasts, and her stomach, at last to the tops of her slim thighs, her belly, and her fine corn-silk blond fluff, then even further down. . . .

Hoping against hope, Lewrie had brought along four of his Half-Moon Street sheep-gut cundums; there was an awkward moment to don one and return, but by then Lydia had been more than eager, her bottom lip almost trembling as she drew him down to her with a kitteny mew. Again, despite the brute lust roaring in his head, he'd begun slow, pausing a time or two to contain himself . . . before Lydia had begun to urge him on to a canter, to a gallop, with breathless wee cries of, "Yes, oh yes!"

Too much wine, too late at night, Lewrie couldn't fathom how, but the world had evaporated from his senses. The mattress and sheets might as well have been a cloud, and the only things that existed were their bodies and their joinings, and then Lydia had been grasping and raking his back, clinging with upraised thighs, crying out as guardedly as she could to avoid waking the house staff, and Lewrie could let go, groaning like the timbers of a storm-wracked ship, and wishing he could roar like a lion in triumph and mind-frying pleasure!

"What's the time?" Lydia asked in a whisper, breaking off from kissing his mouth, his shoulder, and rolling off him a bit to peer at a mantel clock, with her hair mussed most prettily, and some longer strands dangling over her face.

"Uhm . . . a bit after four," Lewrie told her after a squint of his own. "Should I be going, before the house wakes?" He felt like crossing his fingers to hear her answer, for he certainly didn't wish to go!

"Not quite yet," Lydia said, swiping her hair back in place and bestowing upon him a sly, impish, and teasing look as she settled back half atop him and resumed her kissing. "We're the *idle* class, Alan. We take cocoa and toast at ten, and don't stir out 'til after noon, do you know. At least Percy has his regiment, his clubs, coffee houses, and a seat in Lords, when he bothers to attend. The servants don't stir 'til half past five. Or so our butler tells us."

"No sleep-walkers on staff, are there?" Lewrie japed.

"All sound sleepers, for all I know of them," Lydia told him, chuckling. "There's still time . . . for us. If you wish, that is? If you find me pleasing?" Oddly, that struck Lewrie's ear as a *plea* to be found pleasing, and pretty.

"Aye, by God I *do* . . . and there's no other place I'd rather be right now for a . . . for a bloody knighthood!" he told her, which caused them both to laugh, almost loud enough to wake the house for a bit, 'til he drew her down to him and held her close, and their lips met in sweet, light brushings, curled with glee at first.

"Make love to me, Alan," Lydia whispered, urgently, but sounding shy, as if amazed at her own daring to even ask.

"Make love to *me*, Lydia," Lewrie whispered back, his own voice grave and earnest, peering intently into her eyes and wondering why he had ever thought her *less* than hellish-handsome. With her hair down, and her bored and arch expression blown to far horizons, she was very lovely . . . to him, at least; which was all that mattered, wasn't it? Here, this moment, she even seemed vulnerable. Not a stiff member of the aristocracy, but an ordinary woman with wants and needs.

And so she did, and he did, make love one more time before he had to go, more hungrily this time, more fiercely, thrashing and panting to an almost simultaneous bliss. Then lay entwined and cuddling and kissing and gently stroking 'til the mantel clock reached 5.

"Where did we leave our shoes?" Lewrie muttered, his head well fuddled by then, as he peered about the parlour; they hadn't been in the bedchamber.

"We left them by the settee," Lydia whispered back, giggling. "How remiss of us."

"How embarrassing that could've been," Lewrie said as he found his and sat to slip them on.

"Oh, I am loath to let you *go,* though I must!" Lydia declared as he got to his feet again, and she came to embrace him, dressed only in a silk robe, almost as soft as her flesh, and warmed by her warmth. Lewrie slowly ran his hands up and down her slim back, down to her narrow hips and wee bottom, purring in her ear. "I must. *You* must, else . . . it's almost half past five."

" 'Parting is such sweet sorrow' . . . ," Lewrie said, chuckling.

". . . 'that I should say goodnight 'til it be morrow,' *yes*! And all that, *but* . . . !" she insisted, laughing again and breaking away to lead him by the hand to the foyer, and the front door. "I'll not send you out into lawless London un-protected, Alan. Here."

"Well, hullo!" Lewrie said; she had handed him a wee one-barrel pocket pistol to shove into his uniform coat.

"Even here in the West End, there's foot-pads aplenty, and I'd not wish any harm to come to you," Lydia assured him. "Mind, now . . . I expect you to *return* it!" she teased, her eyes alight.

"Let's set a time for that," Lewrie said with a grin. "Supper tonight? There's a grand chop-house I know in Savoy Street. Hellish-fine wine cellar, and *emigré* French *chefs,* t'boot. Eight-ish? And no clubs after. As few of your host of admirers as possible."

"Sir, I would be delighted to accept your kind invitation," she said, dipping him a graceful curtsy, grinning back. "But, you must go at *once!*" Lydia insisted, play-shoving him to the door.

There was just one wee problem with his leaving; the door was locked tight, and though several bolts could be withdrawn, there was no key in sight!

"*Un emmerdement*, as the Frogs'd say," Lewrie whispered. "Don't think askin' yer butler'd do much good, would it?"

"Oh, God!" Lydia breathed, opening every drawer in the massive oak side-board table where the mail, page-delivered notes, and calling cards ended in a large silver tray. "Here's one!"

"Too small . . . that's surely for one of the drawers. Let me look," Lewrie offered, infected by Lydia's urgency. "Aha!" Far back in the lowest drawer there was a *huge* housekey, strung with a hank of ribbon and a pasteboard tag. "This'un's big enough for the Bank of England." He inserted it, gave it a turn, and let out a happy sigh as the main lock clanked open.

Thank God for efficient house-keepers! Lewrie thought as the door yawned open to the front stoop and the street with nary a creak; the hinges had been well-oiled!

"You're off to your Madeira Club?" Lydia asked as he stepped out to the stoop, clutching her robe about her more tightly. "I will send round a note."

"Hmm?" Lewrie asked, wondering why a note was necessary, if he had set the time when he would coach to collect her.

"My treat . . . a surprise," she told him, smiling inscrutably. "Here . . . your lodgings? Neither is suitable, are they, Alan?"

"Damme, but you're a grand girl, Lydia!"

"Now shoo, scat! Begone! And thank God it isn't raining!" she urged, swinging the door shut yet blowing him a kiss just before it closed completely.

Damme if she ain't *a grand woman!* Lewrie told himself as he plodded east down Grosvenor Street, looking for a carriage, beaming and whistling "The Bowld Soldier Boy," the tune used when the rum issue was fetched on deck aboard *Reliant*. At half past five A.M., it was not quite dawn, but milk-seller wenches with cloth-covered buckets yoked over their shoulders were already stirring to cry their wares to the waking houses. Horse- or pony-drawn two-wheeled carts and traps were clopping along, their axles squealing, filled with fruit or vegetables, and young girls yawned as they carried baskets of fresh flowers. The tin-smiths and tinkers were out, the rag-buyers and -sellers halloed their goods. Knife sharpeners, bakery boys with their trays of hot loaves and rolls, old women with baskets of eggs, venomous-looking, un-shaven men with fletches of bacon . . . the street vendors of the city were already out in force.

And all found it amusing to see a Navy Post-Captain, a man with the sash and star of knighthood, walking when he could ride, and the fellow appeared stubbled, mussed, and perhaps even a trifle "foxed"—did he even know which part of London he was in?

Lewrie took great delight in doffing his hat to the vendors, offering cheery "good mornings." He could not recall being happier in years!

CHAPTER TWENTY-THREE

A hot bath and a close shave, a hearty breakfast and six cups of coffee, and Lewrie still felt like Death's-Head-On-A-Mop-Stick, but . . . there were things to meet and people to do, to make the most of his brief time in London. There was the College of Heralds, where grave people who put a lot of stock in such arcane things as coats-of-arms hemmed and hawed, suggested, and queried him over what he would like, or what was suitable to his career, to paint on a parchment, and . . . "the, ah, fees will be so much, and might you wish to pay by a note-of-hand, or a draught upon your bank, Sir Alan?"

No fear the Crown'll run short o' "tin," Lewrie sourly thought; *They must do a whoppin' business handin' out honours, if they cost the recipients so bloody dear! I could buy a* thoroughbred *for that much!*

With the promise that preliminary sketches, in full colour, mind, would be forthcoming, Lewrie toddled off for dinner, then a visit to his bankers at Coutts' for more cash, and a review of his accounts. He was pleasingly amazed that the Prize-Court on Jamaica had completed their surveys of the four French warships they had taken at the Chandeleurs—captured warships always seemed to breeze through quickly since the Fleet was in such need of new ones—deciding on a sum of £50,000. Lewrie's frigate's share was a fourth of that, and his own two-eighths amounted to £3,125! Nothing to sneeze at, for certain! He left £1,000 in savings and transferred £2,000 to the Funds, where it would earn a tidy £60 per annum. He pocketed the remainder, with plans to splurge, quite frankly.

Later, passing a bookseller's bow-window display, he was taken by the sight of not one but two books written by his old steward and cabin servant, Aspinall! He dashed in and flipped through their pages, which were un-cut, so he only saw half. Just as Aspinall had promised, one was an illustrated guide to all the useful knots employed aboard a ship, and the other a compendium of music and songs popular in the Royal Navy.

"Good God!" Lewrie exclaimed as he read the dedication in the first one about knots.

> *To my old Captain of HMS* Jester,
> *Sloop of War, and the Frigates*
> Proteus *and* Savage
> *An Officer of un-paralleled Energy,*
> *Courage, and Skill, whose determined*
> *but pleasant Nature won the Affection*
> *and Admiration of every Man-Jack,*
> *Capt. Alan Lewrie, RN*

"Damme, that's gildin' the lily, ain't it?" Lewrie muttered.

"A most useful guide, that, sir," the bookseller told him, "yet one that instructs even the humblest beginner. We've done quite well with it, as well as the music book. In the coming year, we plan to bring out yet another, on the making of intricate items of twine, which the author informs me that sailors will do in their idle hours, as gifts for their dear ones."

"On 'Make and Mend' Sundays, aye," Lewrie said, unable to resist boasting, "He's dedicated this'un to *me*, it seems."

"*You* are that Captain Lewrie, sir? My shop is honoured!"

"I'll have three copies of each," Lewrie quickly decided. "I've sons in the Fleet," he explained. "You are the publisher, or . . . ?"

"I am, sir," the bookseller told him.

"So Aspinall's in touch with you, regularly? Then you have his home address, so I could write and congratulate him?" Lewrie asked the fellow. "And, might I purchase some paper and borrow a pen, I'd like to write a short note, first, that you could send on at once?"

"Done, sir, this very instant!"

At least someone from the old days is doin' well! Lewrie gladly thought as he strolled out with his purchases. When Aspinall had left his service, the

lad's plans for the future and making a way in civilian life had sounded a
tad iffy, but . . . so far he seemed to prosper. Lewrie didn't think that he
would have enough time in London to look him up for a natter; the best he
expected would be a reply sent to his lodgings.

Damme, I should've bought a set for Desmond! Lewrie realised; *If he's still
in the American Navy*. He was *forever* forgetting Desmond McGilliveray, the
bastard son he'd quickened with Soft Rabbit, a Cherekee slave he'd been
forced to "marry" by his Muskogee Indian hosts during the American
Revolution, on a doomed expedition up the Appalachicola river in Spanish
Florida to woo the Muskogee and Seminolee into war against the Rebel
frontiers. Their guide, half-Muskogee himself, had given the child his own
name after the British survivors had left, and taken Soft Rabbit for his
own. And, when they had both died of the Smallpox, little Desmond had
been delivered to the McGilliverays in Charleston, South Carolina, and
raised as White. During the so-called Quasi-War 'twixt America and
France, the American Navy and the Royal Navy had secretly co-operated,
and Lewrie had been completely stunned to meet the boy, hear him speak
of his Indian mother by name, and realise who he was!

Well, he don't write me *all that often, either,* he mused.

A stop in at Lloyd's coffee house for tea and a place to use his pen-knife to
slit the pages so he could read the books later, and wonder of wonders,
there was his old school friend from Harrow, Peter Rushton, Viscount
Draywick, holding forth with a table of gentlemen on the reality of the
threat cross the Channel, and what was the Pitt administration doing about
it, et cetera and et cetera.

"Alan, my old!" Peter yelped, tipping his chair back onto four legs and
rising to greet him. "Sir Alan, Knight and Baronet, can you feature it, haw!
Read of it, and congratulations, indeed! Comin' up in the world like one of
those infernal French hot-air balloons!"

"Peter! How the Devil d'ye keep?" Lewrie cried, pumping his hand.

"Main-well, Alan, main-well, I will allow," Rushton said with a smug
and satisfied smirk. "In town long, are you?"

"A day or two more, perhaps, then back to Sheerness. I hear there's a
war on, and the French are bein' a bother," Lewrie replied. Hell, that jape
pleased once! "How are things in Lords? Met someone you should
know . . . one of yours, Percy Viscount Stangbourne?"

"Hell of a fellow!" was Peter's opinion. "Simply mad-keen to have a go

at the Frogs with that regiment he raised, and the grandest sportsman going. Has bottom at the gaming tables, let me tell you! Got a head on his
shoulders, too . . . quite unlike half the twits that sit in Lords. He actually
stays awake, pays attention, and damme if he don't make plain sense when
he speaks up. Quite unlike *me*, Lord knows, haw haw! Here, let's take a
table and have a glass or two."

"How's Clotworthy?" Lewrie asked, once two glasses of brandy appeared. "Still up to his old tricks?"

"Prosperin' quite nicely," Peter told him, with a wink and a nod over
Clotworthy Chute's chosen profession, that of a charming "Captain Sharp"
who specialised at separating new-come heirs and aspiring "chaw-bacons"
from some of their money by playing the knowing guide to every pleasure
and absolute necessity of life in London, sharing a very pretty penny with
all the tailors, hatmakers, renting agents, and furniture and art dealers to
whom he steered the gullible. "Of late, the lad's gone *honest* . . . sort of.
Artworks, statuary, furnishings, and the sort of classical tripe people used
to bring back from their Grand Tours of the Continent." That stunning
news was delivered with another wink and a nod. "Have you the time, you
should see his new shop."

"Bronze Greek or Roman statues made a thousand years old in one
week in a salt-water bath, hey? I saw him pull that off in Venice! He has a
genuine talent, and a damned fine eye for the real article, I'll give him
that," Lewrie said with a laugh. "If I don't see him before I leave, give him
my very best regards."

"Oh, I shall. So. If you haven't been dined out on your newest bau-
bles," Rushton said, pointing at the star on Lewrie's coat, "yet, I mean
t'say . . . we should dine together, tonight. My treat."

"That'd be grand, Peter, but I'm promised," Lewrie had to tell him.

"Not with your father," Rushton said with a shiver.

"With a lady," Lewrie corrected him, hoping to leave it at that.

"Oh ho! Anyone I know? Or, would care to know?" Peter leered.

"She *may* be known to you," Lewrie hinted, off-handedly.

"Well, it can't be that Rooski wench, Eudoxia Durschenko. Her circus
and all's on tour for the Summer," Rushton said, puzzled. "Off somewhere
far north and nasty, where the locals offer sheep dung for admission, haw!
And, I hear Percy Stangbourne's mad for her, anyway. Who else do we both
know you could hunt up on short notice, hmm . . . my word, that's a poser."

"And it ain't Tess . . . or a parlour guessing game," Lewrie rejoined
with another laugh. "How is Tess, by the way?"

"Still utterly *delightful,* old son!" Peter boasted. "Found her a very good place, convenient to Parliament . . . it can be *days* between real business . . . and I must confess I've become rather fond of her. I thank you for introducing us, and feel forever in your debt for it . . . even if the wife won't."

"Spoilin' her proper?" Lewrie teased. "And, you're welcome."

"Oddest thing . . . she seems pleased and content with the simplest things. Doesn't pout for gew-gaws, and all that, as your run-of-the-mill courtesan or mistress will. Simple, conservative tastes, and . . . comes of bein' bog-Irish poor so long, I s'pose," Peter said with a shake of his head in wonder. "Should I give *her* your regards?"

"Only if you think it best," Lewrie told him.

"Really, now . . . who *is* the lady in question?" Rushton said more animatedly, leaning forward on his elbows and leering. "You leave me most perplexed."

"A gentleman never tells, Peter," Lewrie gently chid him.

"The *Devil* they don't!" Rushton hooted with glee. "If one can't boast, then what's the point o' chasin' quim?"

"My lips are sealed," Lewrie said, shaking his head "no."

"Well, if you won't you won't," Rushton said with a sigh as he leaned back and took a sip of his brandy. "I s'pose you'll be back at sea in a week, anyway, with no time for sport, so whoever she is, take what joy you can before. Keep the French in line, on *their* side of the Channel, there's a good fellow."

"Crossin' the Channel ain't like puntin' down the Avon," Lewrie dismissively said. "I haven't spent all *that* much time in it, but it's a nasty piece of work, one day out o' three, and a right bastard on the fourth. Hellish-strong tides sweep up and down it, and a contrary wind can whistle up when you're halfway across. It's hard to feature just *how* the Frogs intend t'manage it, at all."

"You've not been following the papers, old son," Rushton objected, shifting impatiently in his chair and leaning forward again. "Where the Devil have you *been,* you haven't kept up?"

"West Indies," Lewrie told him with a grin.

"Soon as the war began again, last May, Bonaparte started shifting nigh an hundred thousand troops to the coast, and began building an armada of boats . . . might've launched it all *before* May. There's umpteen *thousands* of boats of all descriptions, barges, gunboats, sailing craft, rowing craft as big as Cleopatra's that might be able to carry whole batteries of artillery, limbers, caissons, forge waggons, *and* the horses!" Rushton hurried to explain. "They tell us in Parliament that they're massin' 'em round Boulogne, Dunkirk, and Calais, mostly, for the shortest trip cross the Dover Straits, but they're buildin' 'em in any port or river, from Brest to Amsterdam. I tell you, old son, Bonaparte means to try it on, sometime this Summer we're told to expect, and if 'Boney' does, then all our Sea Fencibles, Yeoman militias, and our pathetically small army won't be able to handle 'em!" Peter gravely insisted, jabbing a forefinger on the table top. "We can build all the Martello towers we wish, but the French will just sweep round those and head for London, laughing all the way."

"What the Hell's a Martello tower?" Lewrie asked, frowning.

"Looks like a big, tall drum, with lots of guns, but they're too far apart from each other to deny the ground between 'em, and the garrisons're just large enough to defend themselves, penned up inside."

Lewrie would have asked Rushton what a Sea Fencible was, too, but that might have been confessing a tad too much ignorance. He supposed someone could inform him, sooner or later.

"Can't exceed the *budget*, after all," Rushton sneered, tossing back a dollop of brandy. "The nation's survival mustn't reduce the subsidies to our *good* allies, the Austrians!

"Now, when he was still First Lord of the Admiralty, Earl Saint Vincent assured us the Navy could handle things . . . told us, 'I do not say the French cannot come, my lords, what I say is that the French will not come *by sea*'! Reassurin', 'til that dodderin' Pitt reclaimed office and turfed him out for Lord Melville, who most-like don't know what an *oar* looks like. God, for all we know, Alan, the French *might* float over in really *big* hot-air balloons and land soldiers right in Whitehall. We've heard they'd experimented with the bloody things . . . s'truth!" Rushton barked, in response to Lewrie's stunned look. "The bloody snail-eatin' bastards might have *two* hundred thousand men in arms round Boulogne," he said on, leaning on his elbows again, looking wearied and depressed. "We all just hope that you and the rest of the Navy *can* handle 'em when they come. I *like* bein' a philandering rake-hell, with lashings o' 'tin' and a lovely mistress t'spend it on, Alan. A *free* English gentleman, who'd prefer t'die in my bed, and not get beheaded by a French guillotine. All that stands between us right now are our stout 'wooden walls.' And salty sods like you!"

That rant had been a tad too depressing for the both of them, so Lewrie had not stayed at Lloyd's much longer after that one brandy was drunk. He

walked back to the Madeira Club, hoping for a long nap to restore his flagging energies, but . . . it wasn't Lydia's promised note that the day-servant
who manned the desk and cloak room held out to him. It was a letter from
the First Secretary to Admiralty, William Marsden, requiring him to report at his earliest convenience upon the morrow to be briefed upon "certain confidential matters pertaining to the threat of possible invasion."

"Good Christ, I guess it's serious!" he muttered.

CHAPTER TWENTY-FOUR

*O*h Dear Lord above," Lydia Stangbourne muttered, setting down her tea cup and sighing resignedly. "The bloody papers, the bloody scribblers!"

She was back in the gossip columns again, as was Captain Sir Alan Lewrie, Bart. Though no names could be mentioned, anyone in London who followed the news could figure out who was involved.

> *Last evening, a dashing Naval Person, recently made Knight and Baronet, was seen in the company of a Lady best-known to our readers for obtaining a Bill of Divorcement, which was an infamous marvel in our pages two years running. Perhaps the Lady in question may teach the heroic "Sea-Dog" some new parlour Tricks, or, has our Jason obtained a fresh sheet-anchor for his good ship* Argo?

If it had been the *Times* or the *Gazette*, the jape might have been printed in Latin or Greek, though both papers were not immune to such smirks in English, these days, she realised, laying the newspaper aside. She shook her head and let out another sigh, thankful that the damnable "observer" had only seen them together at supper, not later as they entered Willis's Rooms for the night.

"Hallo, sister, and aren't you a picture?" her brother, Percy, commented as he came breezing into the small, informal dining room, as chipper as ever.

"Good morning, Percy," Lydia said, forcing a smile on her face . . . and folding the paper so that that item would not show. "Cook will be delighted that you came to breakfast on time, for a change. Have a good night, did you?"

"Smashing night!" Percy crowed, sweeping his coat-tails as he sat down. There was a pot of coffee for him on the side-board, and a servant poured a cup for him at once. "Good ho! Bacon *and* kippers! I'm famished. Thank you, James," he said as his plate was delivered. After creaming and sugaring to his taste, and a first sip, he went on. "Yes, the cards were with me . . . at Almack's, not the Cocoa Tree. The change was good for me. Oh, I was down about five thousand for a bit, but finally broke even, and then a couple of side wagers put me a thousand to the good. What did you do with *your* evening, and was it enjoyable?"

"Most enjoyable," Lydia said, colouring a little at the memory. "I went to supper with Captain Lewrie. He knew of this perfectly *fine* chop-house in Savoy Street, and you simply *must* go there, Percy! They have . . . it's like an 'all-nations' dram shop in a way. *Emigré* French *chefs,* a Neapolitan who specialises in fish dishes, even a *Hungarian* who prepares the most *marvellous* medallions of veal or lamb, something called a *ragoût,* one they call a *goulash,* and there was an appetiser of smoked oysters in a sweet, hot sauce that was heavenly!"

"With Captain Lewrie?" Percy said, his fork paused halfway to his mouth, took his bite, chewed, then got a sly, teasing look. "Damn my eyes, Lydia. Has the gallant Sir Alan caught your interest?"

"He is most charming and amusing to me . . . without the unctuous smarm of most of the men I know," Lydia replied, going arch, bland, and imperious. "He's a most admirable fellow. Soon to leave us, more's the pity. Admiralty's ordering him back to Sheerness on the morrow . . . a confidential matter, was all he could tell me of it. He should be at the Admiralty this minute, being told what it may be."

Lydia strove to make it all sound of no real concern to her . . . concealing the smile that threatened to betray her as she thought of when, and where, Lewrie had told her of his letter from the Navy, and what they had been doing minutes before.

"He *hasn't* thawed the coldness of your heart?" Percy japed.

"I do *not* have a cold heart, Percy," Lydia rejoined with a languid drawl. "But, after that beast, Tidwell, I've a wary one. Had our late parents not settled so much on me, and upon you, my wariness might not be necessary. Or, my fear that one day you will squander it entire on one bad turn of the cards. Should you render us both penniless, I'd have to settle for one of those . . . those!" She produced a real shiver of disgust. "Who most-like would not *have* me, did I not fetch them a fortune!" she tossed off with a brittle laugh.

"Oh, don't start on that, Lydia, not *this* lovely morning," her brother protested. Both looked to the windows that looked out upon the back garden; it was a misty morning of light rain, and they both had a laugh over it. Percy took another bite or two, then returned to coffee, looking over the rim of his cup. "I didn't get the impression that our heroic Captain Lewrie was all *that* well-to-do. Perhaps he's just one *more* of your avaricious suitors? Wary, wary, wary, pet!"

"We've known him for not quite two whole days, Percy," Lydia scoffed with another light laugh, busying herself with her tea. "I've seen no sign he intends to woo me, and besides . . . wooing's rather hard to do when one's a thousand miles out to sea, or halfway round the world!"

"Well, there's that . . . though you could do a lot worse," Percy tossed off, intent on a nicely smoked kipper and his scrambled eggs.

"He said something over supper last night," Lydia continued with her own attention on her own breakfast, "that may aid you getting your regiment posted to the coast."

That was a lie; she had brooked the subject to Lewrie.

"Oh, really!" her brother said, perking up.

"If Horse Guards seems loath to accept, might it not help to go down to the coast and meet the general in charge, or ask for an audience with the Lord-Lieutenant for Kent?" Lydia laid out. "Were *they* aware of a regiment of Yeoman Cavalry so well horsed, equipped, and trained, and readily available, might not a request from *them* to Horse Guards turn the trick for you?"

And a regiment so hellish-*expensive*, even for people with their wealth and incomes! As much as Lydia approved of Percy's new "hobby," for it got him out in the country and away from the gaming tables, the few times her brother had *let* her see the accounting ledgers, with his typical male "tut-tuts" about why a *woman* would wish to, or was able to *understand* them, she'd been simply *appalled* at the costs. If they did not go "smash" due to Percy's gambling, then his "toy soldiers" would *drag* them down to poverty!

She was thirty-one, whilst Percy was twenty-seven. There had been a brother born between them, but he'd not lived a year, and after Percy, their mother had not produced another. She felt older-sister-protective of him, but frightened, too, by how boyishly he'd fling himself into things. Kicking his heels in London, he could gamble every night of the week but Sunday; with his regiment called up and out in the field, living rough, soldiering would put a stop to all that, for the duration of the emergency, Lydia hoped.

She reckoned that he could just as well have gone shopping and purchased whole brigades made of *lead*, foot, horse, and artillery, and been just as content arranging them on the long formal dining table!

The pity of it was that so many people who mattered, the Prince of Wales included, who already had regiments named as "His Own," had told Percy what a dashing and patriotic thing he was doing that it was far too late for him to turn the endeavour over to someone else to let them bear the expense. His pride, his repute in Society, would suffer! And that was just as un-imaginable as Percy swearing off gambling!

"That's a shrewd thought, by Jove!" Percy exclaimed. "Your Sir Alan Lewrie's a sly one, no error, to have thought of it. An *admirable* idea, hey? Get it? An 'admiral'-able idea from a Navy officer?"

Well, Percy found it amusing.

"He is not *my* Sir Alan, Percy," she pointed out. "Though, it may be good to strike while the iron is hot. He will have to coach to Sheerness tomorrow. We could go with him. Offer our own coach, then stay to tend to *your* business." She tossed that off between sips from her cup, as if it was spur-of-the-moment.

"Tomorrow?" Percy frowned. "With Lewrie?"

"Quite *early*, I'd imagine," Lydia mused, gybing him for his slug-a-bed ways. Despite the vigour of her night, she had been back in her own bed by 2 A.M., and had risen, remarkably refreshed and enlivened, at 8. Almost *singing*, she would own.

"Crack o' dawn, all that?" Percy queried, furrowing his brow and pulling a face. "No, no, it couldn't be done tomorrow. There'd be need of letters written, first, the ledgers to gather . . . next week, *maybe*."

"Well, if you will not, Percy," Lydia said, feeding a strip of bacon to their springer spaniel, who'd been begging and whining, "then I will take the coach and offer conveyance to Captain Lewrie, myself."

"You'd *what*?" her brother exclaimed, appalled. "Alone? All the way to Sheerness, then *back* without a man to *protect* you?"

"I am almost your equal at shooting, Percy," she breezed off as if it was no bother. "Father taught us early and well, do you recall? Our coachees are good shots, too. They *should* be, since you've recruited them into your regiment," she pointed out with a smirk, and one of her eyebrows up. If Percy could not be cozened into it, then she would be brazen; she gave him a very level and determined look.

"To the *further* ruin of your reputation, and it might not be . . . ," he said, scowling.

"Percy, good Lord . . . ," she said, "do I ruin my reputation even more, that may be a *good* thing. The parents of my damned admirers at last could put their feet down, I'd no longer feel hunted like a stag through the woods, and be spared all the grasping *bother*!" she blurted, laughing in his face.

She busied herself with a bite of buttered toast, chewing while Percy got his wind back.

"What decent family would have the likes of me, anyway, Percy," she went on with a self-deprecating chuckle. "Were it not for my 'dot,' they'd most-like tell their young men to find someone a lot more attractive, more . . ."

She would have added a scathing "Assuming your gambling *leaves* me anything" but thought it was the wrong time to nag.

"Oh, Lydia, I don't know *where* you ever got the idea you're not attractive. Why . . . you're as fetching as most," Percy tried to assure her, though it was back-handed and clumsy. And it *irked*!

Lydia could have *told* him where she'd gotten the idea! Their father had loved her dearly, though he'd naturally hoped for a boy and heir. Despite having a girl-child as his first-born, he had delighted in amusing her, talking to her, and calling her "my little funny face" or "you little monkey face" with the tickles and treats and affections that made her squeal with joy; it had been as dear to her as if he had said "my little princess." 'Til other children began to taunt her as "Miss Monkey Face!" most cruelly, and she'd seen the why in her mirrors.

Her father had not been handsome; perhaps that was why he had married so late in life. He'd been all craggy-faced, with prominent cheek bones and bushy brows, and a Cornish beak of a nose, and as tall and rangy as a Clydesdale. Her mother, though . . . no matter his looks, he *was* immensely wealthy in lands, rents, and investments, and *titled*, a proper peer, whilst her family had been nigh as well-off, but commoners. Like had called to Like when it had come to land and wealth, and she'd brought almost an equal portion, along with her great beauty, of the sort that Society had applauded and worshipped.

"Lydia, I swear, you're as thin as a rope, dear child! You eat like a sparrow! Do you *wish* to be called a 'gawk'? No man will have you, then!"

she'd said once, with a brittle laugh. And the once that Lydia had over-heard them discussing her, her mother fretting that "she is such a *plain* child. Pray God she blossoms late, as some do, before being presented at Court, and to Society for her first London Season, else we must consider settling a large sum upon her to tempt the *right* sort of young gentleman!" And Lydia had been heart-broken.

Her *debut* at eighteen had been a miserable affair. Though her parents had deemed her pretty, by then, and her looks *had* rounded and softened to the point that she could, now and then, think herself adequate, even what little hope she'd had of success had been dis-appointed.

Young girls of her status in the peerage, young girls from the squirearchy or the newly-risen middling class, all properly schooled in music, manners, dancing, and "womanly attainments," paraded at the many events . . . it had been the prettiest who had found success, and young men's approval. Her dowry had been £500, a goodly sum to go under some young gentleman's "coverture," yet . . . it had been the pretty, the ravishing, the *cute*, who'd shone at all the drums, routs, supper parties, the operas, symphonies, and subscription balls, whilst her own luck had been lacklustre.

Lydia had refused to try again at nineteen or twenty, preferring their country estate and her horsewomanship.

At twenty-one, she'd been dragged back to London, this time with £2,000, and the change had been remarkable, and to her, sickening. That Season it had been the young beauties who had been ignored, whilst Lydia had been inundated in invitations and flatteries. Disgusted with the grasp-ing hypocrisy, she'd treated the young beaus quite badly, but . . . no matter how arch and insulting, how flippant or scornful, she'd treated them, the greediest would *abide* her, declaring her bold, out-spoken, and intriguingly *modern*!

Lydia shook herself back to paying attention, squirming again at those memories; Percy was still blathering on about something.

" . . . then break the journey at Shooter's Hill. Take a basket of goodies and dine *al fresco* atop it, hey?" he suggested, quite wistfully. "I swear, the sweetest, cleanest air ever did I breathe was at the top of Shooter's Hill. Or, is that on the north bank, near Tilbury and the forts?"

"You've your geography wrong, Percy," Lydia corrected him. "It's a bit past Greenwich, on the south bank of the Thames . . . on the road to Chatham, and Sheerness. Why? If you're not going 'til next week?"

"Well, if you're so dead-set . . ."

"I am," she coolly replied, sugaring and creaming fresh tea.

"First light tomorrow?" He grimaced. "God, I'd have to retire at *sunset* to get out of bed that early!"

"I am told that diligent soldiers are sometimes *required* to do so," Lydia teased.

"Can't let you gad off so boldly, what'd people say of you, or me for allowing it?" Percy said, shrugging surrender. "Should anything befall you . . . highwaymen . . . or worse, well."

"Percy, do you mean you intend to accompany Captain Lewrie and myself?" she asked, relieved that he would weaken so quickly.

"I s'pose I could, yes," her brother said, half his attention taken by the spaniel, who found him an easy mark, as well. "We will both go. Perhaps he can tell me more of his sea stories on the way to Sheerness. Begad, do you think they *have* a decent lodging house?"

"You are the best brother in the world, Percy!" Lydia said as she rose to go to his end of the table and give him a hug, and tousle his long hair.

Well, he had his good points, she thought as she returned to her seat, secretly thrilled. With Percy making three, there could not be any more intimacy, though she wished she could scheme a way. Those few hours over two nights were more pleasurable, pleasing, and passionate than any she had known in her little experience. She could, however, spend a *few* more days with Lewrie to learn more about him and his life at sea, of which she knew next to nothing; perhaps even be invited to go aboard his ship and see him in his proper *milieu*. And, stave off the loss of his presence just a bit longer!

Lydia determined to write to Lewrie's lodgings, informing him of their offer of a more comfortable coach than any he could hire, of which *he* knew nothing yet . . . then caution *him* to take credit for the idea to help Percy find employment for his regiment! It was just as un-seemly to be a clever woman as it was to be a single one!

CHAPTER TWENTY-FIVE

*L*ewrie had been delighted by the Stangbournes' offer, though it made for cramped quarters in their coach. There was Percy's valet and Lydia's maid, and Pettus to do for Lewrie, plus two coachmen and a footman, little more than a lad whose sole duty seemed to be tending to the folding steps and the coach doors, and general fetching and toting. It would not do for the maid to ride outside, so one man-servant ended up on the coach roof, like the cheap seats aboard a huge diligence coach, and the luckier two crammed into the outside rear bench above the boot, which bore more luggage than Lewrie's whole family would need did they dash up to London for their Spring shopping, and spend a week at it!

The sky was clear for their *pique-nique* atop Shooter's Hill and it had been pleasantly warm. When Percy was off tramping up to take a gander of the semaphore tower and its method of working, Lydia had given Lewrie a snippet of newspaper.

"In case you haven't seen this," she'd whispered, looking away shyly. "I hadn't *thought* I would draw unwelcome comment upon you. If you find it embarrassing, then I am sorry I—"

"Mine arse on a band-box!" Lewrie had guffawed, though, to her great relief. "With any luck, people will think it was Captain *Blanding*! And his wife will give *him* Hell."

"You are not . . . ?" Lydia had gasped, with a wide grin.

"Not a bit of it!" Lewrie had assured her. "What Blanding and his brood and his Chaplain think of me doesn't matter a toss, and if Wilberforce and *his* lot take me off the 'champion' list, then I'll be spared a parcel of dreadful-boresome suppers!"

His reaction had pleased Lydia greatly, and they'd sat on the quilt close together, hands closer, fingers twining, and both wishing they could embrace and kiss. Her smiles had been lovely and promising, sometimes wistful, sometimes impishly bold, as they'd prated mostly of nothing, wishing that the hovering servants and the enthusiastic Percy could vanish like Will-of-the-Wisps.

They'd found lodgings suitable to their needs at the very same hotel that Lewrie had used long ago when fitting out HMS *Proteus* for the West Indies, close to the merchant docks and a view of the Little Nore in 1797 . . . the same hotel where Theoni Kavares Connor had stayed, for nigh a week, unfortunately, and did they dine there together, Alan sincerely hoped none of the staff would recall him from that time, and ask of his former mistress (the mother of one of his bastard children) and how she kept!

Then, he hired a boat to bear him out to *Reliant*. It had been gratifying to be piped aboard not to the usual bare-headed stances of attention from all hands on deck at the moment of arrival, but by the loud cheers and whistles of *Reliant*'s people as soon as they had seen the sash and star. *They* had been victorious, *they* had won it all for him to wear, and a proud reflection upon them and their frigate, as he had told them that instant, before going aft and below.

His cats had been delighted to see him after the short absence, and his cook, Yeovill, had been equally delighted when he had been informed that he would be preparing at least one sumptuous dinner for a Viscount and his sister. The great-cabins, though . . .

"Scrub and scour, Pettus," Lewrie had ordered, sniffing at the corners. "The cat's box especially, fresh sand for the morrow . . . *and* the quarter-gallery."

"Baking soda, sir," Yeovill had suggested. "A box of it in the sand, sir? Cancels odours, it will. I've lots of it, sir."

"We've still some citronella candles, and lamp oil, too, sir," Pettus had reminded him. "That smells fresh and sweet, it does."

"Pass word for Desmond and Furfy t'help with the cleaning, and all, Pettus. We'll start straightaway," Lewrie had ordered, looking over his modest furnishings and wishing that he could replace or re-furbish half of it overnight. Or, should he, he'd reconsidered. This was how he lived, and—odours aside—this would be what he would show the Stang-bournes. He could always explain that the Royal Navy had a dim view of captains who lived *too* comfortably; bare-bones Spartan was preferred.

He had dined ashore with the Stangbournes, of course, leaving Yeovill even more time to prepare his feast, but had been back aboard just at Four Bells of the Evening Watch to make arrangements for their reception aboard the next day at Noon. Fresh sand and snow-white man-ropes for the entry-port and boarding battens; a bosun's chair to be prepared for Lydia of a certainty, and for Percy, too, if he proved to be clumsy or had a slip; it would *never* do to drown a peer! Lastly, he had the largest ship's boat, the cutter, readied for the next morning. Lt. Westcott had suggested it rather than his shorter gig, and had had the cutter scrubbed out and some of its paint touched up, earlier.

It had *not* rained, though there was a vast awning slung above the quar-terdeck lest it did. Lord Percy *had* managed to scramble up the battens, Lydia had been *delighted* to be hoisted high over the bulwarks and depos-ited on the starboard sail-tending gangway, alighting with an un-ladylike whoop of glee! The tour of the ship had gone well, even if belowdecks had still borne a faint reek of too many people crammed in too close, and the smells of salt-meat casks drifting up from the orlop. They'd emerged up forward by the foredeck hatch and steep ladderway, right by the sickbay and forecastle manger, then had strolled aft past the bowsed-up guns to the base of the main-mast and into his great-cabins for a drink before dinner.

"Somehow, I do not picture you, Sir Alan, a fellow of such bellicose nature, having cats as pets," Lydia had teased him, forced by the circum-stances, and the presence of other dinner guests, to fall back upon her ini-tial formality. At that moment she'd had the impetuous Chalky in her lap, arching and trilling to her lace-gloved stroking, and with Toulon standing by her right, paws working on the settee cushions and about to jump and join them.

"Captains live aft, alone, Miss Lydia," Lewrie had told her, a prisoner to formality, too, in his speech, at least, though his manner was unchanged. "Might dine a couple of people in each night, but for the most part, well . . . they're good, amusing company."

"Even does Chalky like to nip," Lt. Westcott pointed out with a laugh. "Learned *that* to my harm."

"My last captain preferred chickens, ma'am," Midshipman Rossyngton piped up, turned out in his best. Lewrie had had to invite all his Commis-sion Officers, of course, but only had chairs, or places, for two more guests, and had chosen the two youngest Mids, even though Mister Ent-whistle was an "Honourable," and the youngest son of another peer.

"Hunting dogs, ma'am," Midshipman Munsell had added shyly. "He was big on hunting, and fetched off half a dozen of his favourites. It was Bedlam."

"And messy, I'm bound, hey, Mister Munsell?" Lewrie had japed.

"When one of them, ah . . . on the deck chequer or his carpets, he would call his servant . . . 'Smithey . . . dog, uh . . . stuff!' " Munsell had blurted, catching himself a second too late; but all had been amused.

"Ye don't get that sort o' mess, with cats," Lewrie had said.

"Or, the barking in the wee hours, I'm bound?" Lydia had posed to Munsell, drawing a shy nod of red-faced agreement, pleasing the lad right down to his toes.

Yeovill had out-done himself. There had been a soup he'd called a Spanish treat, served cool to suit the weather, loaded with peas and maize kernels, rice, and pureed tomatoes in a spicy beef broth; Yeovill was very high on rice! Next had come quail (old to Lewrie by then but new to the Stangbournes) with fresh asparagus sprigs drizzled in *hollandaise* sauce and cheesy hashed potatoes. The fish course had been a medley of mussels and peeled shrimp, with buttery wee brussels sprouts; all served with piping-hot rolls and a cool and light *sauvignon blanc*. There'd been a mid-meal salad of wilted lettuce, drippy bacon, and *vinaigrette*. Last had come a small chuck roast with boiled carrots and roasted potato halves, boiled onions, and bottles of *bordeaux*. And, to top it all off, Yeovill had whipped up another of his lemon custards.

"Your cook's a bloody wonder, Sir Alan!" Percy had exclaimed to-wards the end. "I've half a mind to hire him away from you. Do you dine this well at sea?" he'd marvelled, shaking his head.

"Don't force me to out-bid you for his services, milord. And, no, not after the first week when the fresh victuals run out, or go bad," Lewrie had hooted back. "I fear even good Mister Yeovill has to use his creativity and imagination after a while. Even I will be reduced to salt-meats and our famous weevilly ship's bisquit!"

By 2 P.M. he'd seen them back ashore for a needful nap, and had re-turned aboard to tend to ship's business, and a nap of his own. The Stang-bournes would return the favour at their lodgings.

Supper ashore was at half past seven, but Lewrie turned up just at seven, this time in his second-best uniform coat, without the sash and star of his new knighthood, or his medals either.

"Would you care for a stroll before supper, Lydia?" he asked. "The sunset's rather nice, this evening, and from my more pleasant doings with the French, I've discovered that they place great faith in a stroll before eating to sharpen the appetite."

"Why, thank you, Captain Lewrie, and I should be delighted," she responded. "Percy, we will only be a quarter-hour, half an hour at the most," she'd told her brother, who had half-risen from his chair before twigging to what she meant; that the invitation was for two, not three. He'd sunk back with a sly grin.

Outside their inn, the shadows were lengthening, the sunset so grand that though their view to the west was blocked, it extended out eastwards to reflect on the hulls of the many warships in harbour, on the sails hung slack aloft to air them and prevent mildew and rot, and shimmer reddish-golden off the Little and the Great Nore anchorage that was, that evening, at least, at slack water and seemingly still, alive with only mill-pond ripples and stirred by light airs.

Merchant ships lay along the quays by which they strolled, her arm tucked inside his, and their hands linked. Jib-booms and bow-sprits jutted high overhead from some which lay bows-on alongside piers built at right angles from the quays, masts and spars and furled canvas soaring aloft even higher amid their mazes of shrouds and running rigging, silhouetted against the greying dusk. Lading was done for the day, so the bustle of waggons and carts, and the rumble of wheels no longer forced people to shout to converse. The last sea birds were winging overhead, or perched on bollards, some peeping or gulls mewing. A few ships had their taffrail lanthorns and work lanthorns lit, while out in the roads, lights could be made out aboard the anchored ships, and it was all rather peaceful. Faint laughter, some song, and strains of musical instruments could be heard coming from the sailors' taverns along the dockside street.

"What an odd world you live in, Alan," Lydia said at last. "The ships, and all these mysterious . . . whatevers you pointed out to us . . . sheets and braces, jears, and I don't know what-all you called them. I expect it would take a lifetime to learn it all."

"I think I had one week t'learn them, else I was bent over the barrel of a gun and thrashed on my bottom with a stiffened rope starter," Lewrie cheerfully confessed. "It's called 'kissing the gunner's daughter,' and I kissed her quite *often* 'til I got 'em all right. Do ye know, the first time they threatened that, I thought the girl must be a *really* 'dirty puzzle' if they meant it as punishment!"

With just the two of them, at last, Lydia could lean back her head and laugh out loud, then place her right hand on his upper right arm and lean closer to him as they walked slowly along, as if trying to snuggle. They shared fond smiles, which Lewrie found himself wishing could go on far longer.

"You've changed coats," she noted. "This is not as fine."

"And once we sail, my everyday coat is even sorrier," he said. "The good one, then this'un, will go deep in a sea-chest, along with the star and sash. No call for 'em at sea, unless some admiral dines me aboard his flagship."

"Along with what passed in London?" she rather meekly pressed.

That drew him to a stop so he could turn and face her. "London was a welcome idyll, and a *memorable* one. I don't recall all of it, such as the palace and all, but . . . but I most *certainly* will remember the best part, *your* part. Dare I say . . . *our* part?"

"God, how I wish to kiss you!" she whispered.

"Then let's do!" Lewrie urged, putting his arms round her.

"Do I look like a sailor's . . . doxy, do you call them . . . this way?" Lydia said with a happy, throaty chuckle after she threw her arms round him and shared a long, deep kiss with him.

"It's a seaport, and I don't *give* a damn if *you* don't!" Lewrie laughed. "Never a doxy, not *you*, Lydia . . . a captain's *lady,* is what people will think. And a damned handsome lady, at that."

"Even one so scandalous?" she teased after kissing him again.

"Oh, bugger that," he shrugged off. "What's scandalous about riddin' yourself of a beast? I'd hope . . . well."

"Hope what, Alan," she purred, looking up at him a bit, her eyes alight.

"That what's begun would continue . . . hard as that may be with me at sea," he confessed, feeling a physical surge of warmth filling his chest. "With *Reliant* to operate in the Channel at least for the rest of the year, it won't be months between letters, if you . . . mean t'say, if I could have your permission t'write, and . . ."

"Of *course* I wish you to write me, as often as possible!" she declared. "Just as I swear that I will respond to each, and write to you, even should yours be delayed, or you are too busy. Really, Alan, after what *has* passed between us, it's hardly possible to mis-construe *me* as a spinster-girl whose parents' permission you must ask, now does it?" She hugged him closer, laughing again. "Though I appreciate the thought, mind," she wryly added, her smile japing but fond.

"Often as possible," Lewrie promised as they resumed strolling along, crossing the cobbled street to the wide wooden beams of the seaside quays.

"Tar and salt . . . the seashore smell," Lydia mused. "When we went to Brighton for the Summer ocean bathing, I always delighted in its freshness."

"Quite un-like what a *ship* smells like," he japed back. "That reek that greeted you, in spite of all we could do? The manger, our mildew, our wet woolens, our pea-soup farts and sweat? I thought you might heed a scented handkerchief, for a minute or so. The way your nose wrinkled?"

"Well, I must own to *slight* notice," she confessed, chuckling again, concentrating on the toes of her shoes for a moment. "But, I *do* crinkle my poor nose when amused, or . . . gawping in awe of all that you showed us," she said, looking back up at him again.

"Rather a *nice* nose," Lewrie fondly told her.

"Oh, tosh! Now you're being kind," she demurred.

"No, I'm not," Lewrie baldly stated.

Three watch-bells chimed from the nearest merchantman, lying alongside the quays, quickly followed by the chimes of dozens more as half-hour glasses ran out a bit later.

Lydia looked to him, part in puzzlement, part in appreciation.

"Such a lovely sound . . . though a lonely one," she commented, her head cocked over to listen to the last, distant *dings*.

"Three bells . . . half past seven," Lewrie told her. "I s'pose we should be headin' back, before Percy gets worried and comes lookin' for us. Our supper will be late bein' laid."

"I do not mind our being late," Lydia said, hugging him again. "Nor do I much mind Percy fretting. The last few years he's become quite good at fretting over me, more's the pity. Yes, we must return to the inn . . . but slowly, please?"

"Aye, milady," Lewrie agreed.

"Aye," Lydia echoed as if savouring the strangeness of the word.

"Then there's a good pirate's 'aarrrh,'" Lewrie added. "I use it now and then, for fun."

"Aarrhh!" she cried, trying it on and finding it thrilling. "I rather like the sound of those bells. They chimed all through our visit aboard your ship. Whatever do they mean, though?"

"Well, a ship's day begins at Eight Bells of the Forenoon Watch, at Noon," Lewrie explained as they strolled arm-in-arm, half snuggled down the now-dark street, "and each half-hour, a ship's boy turns the sand-glass and strikes one bell for each half-hour that passes 'til he reaches eight, four hours later. We name each four-hour watch—"

"So *much* to learn of your world!" Lydia said, almost gasping. "You must tell me as much as you can, and direct me to books where I can discover more!"

"It's much like learnin' Russian, or Greek, I warn you!" Lewrie cautioned her. "Sailors' cant is contrary and sounds like nonsense to a lubber like you."

"A lover?" she chuckled.

"Lubber . . . not even a 'scaly fish,' yet," Lewrie told her.

"And when you return, might you quiz me on what I have learned? Might you bend *me* over a gun and make me . . . 'kiss the gunner's daughter' with a what did you call it?" she enthused, skipping ahead of him a step or two, their hands together.

"A twine-wrapped length of rope . . . about this long," he said, freeing his hands long enough to indicate a length of eighteen inches. "A stiffened rope starter a Bosun'll use on the slow-coaches."

"Mercy, sir! *That* long, is it?"

"Perhaps, do ye *have* t'be . . . bent over a gun, I could discover something *else* that'd serve," he said with a leer, a bit startled by her boldness . . . but liking it very, very much!

"Yayss, I surely think that you could," Lydia drawled, coming back to tuck herself against him as they walked on towards the welcoming lanthorns of the inn.

Just damn my eyes, but I like this woman! Lewrie happily told himself as they dared to embrace and kiss just once more before they had to go in, a kiss that lasted and lasted, but could not last long enough.

BOOK IV

We are come to a new era in the history of nations; we are called to struggle for the destiny, not of this country alone but of the civilised world.... We have for ourselves the great duty of self-preservation to perform; but the duty of the people of England now is of a nobler and higher order.... Amid the wreck and the misery of nations it is our just exultation that we have continued superior to all that ambition or that despotism could effect; and our still higher exultation ought to be that we provide not only for our own safety but hold out a prospect for nations now bending under the iron yoke of tyranny of what the exertions of a free people can effect.

-PRIME MINISTER WILLIAM PITT (THE YOUNGER)
ADDRESS TO PARLIAMENT, SUMMER 1804

CHAPTER TWENTY-SIX

*I*dyll's over," Lewrie muttered, once he had signed for a thin set of ribbon-bound and wax-sealed orders *hand-delivered* direct from Admiralty by a taciturn older Lieutenant; the fellow knew nothing and said little more, then departed to catch the morning coach to London before it left without him.

Lewrie ripped the ribbons upwards, breaking the seal, and unfolded the orders. For a brief moment, his eyes strayed to another, smaller sealed note on his day-cabin desk, one from Lydia Stangbourne. Which would he *prefer* to read first? But, there was no helping it; he puffed out his lips in irritation as he turned back to the orders.

" '. . . take upon yourself the charge and command over HMS *Fusee*, Bomb (Eight), Lieutenant Joseph Johns (Three) . . . ,' " he read under his breath, almost mumbling. "There's *three* Joseph Johns in the Fleet?" he wondered aloud. "Who would've thought it? Ah . . . 'has aboard at this time Mister Cyrus MacTavish, Esquire, and his Chief Artificer to perform certain experiments with the devices that Mister MacTavish has designed and fashioned. You will render all aid and support to the timely experimentation, and trial implementation of said devices against French harbours and gatherings of craft amassed for the possible sea-borne invasion of the British Isles. You will see that your officers and men become cognisant of all mechanical details of said devices to support such experimentation and possible implementation with all despatch. You will provide both escort and material support to Lieutenant Johns, his vessel, Mister MacTavish, and his Artificer in this endeavour . . .' " Lewrie wondered if that meant he had to dine them all in each night, and serve them their grog ration, too.

"What the Devil . . . 'You are also most strictly cautioned that this endeavour is of a most highly secret nature, and you are not only to protect HMS *Fusee,* the devices, and their designer and fabricator from capture by the enemy at all hazards, but you are also strictly charged to restrict the secret of the existence of said devices from any naval personnel or civilians not directly involved in the afore-said experimentation.'

"Well, there goes shore liberty and any more chance o' puttin' the ship Out of Discipline t'ease her people. Whew!"

Which step to take first? Brief his officers on the so-far unseen mysterious "devices," or go find this *Fusee* bomb and speak with Lieutenant Johns, this MacTavish fellow, and his un-named artificer?

Did he have time to read Lydia's note? No. With a long sigh, he swept both secret orders and *billet-doux* into the top right-hand drawer of his desk and locked them away.

"Shove me into my coat, Pettus, and pass the word for my boat crew," he ordered.

It took a shore call upon the Port Admiral to discover exactly where HMS *Fusee* was anchored, then required a long row into the Medway and through the protective boom to discover *Fusee,* which streamed to the tide near the old receiving ship HMS *Sandwich,* which old three-decker *still* emitted the same old reeks of impressed misery that he'd encountered when manning his first frigate, HMS *Proteus,* in 1797.

For a vessel engaged in a secret endeavour, her Harbour Watch was remarkably slack; Lewrie's gig was only an hundred yards off before someone woke up and hailed them. The scramble to man the side for the arrival of a Post-Captain *could* be called comical, were it not so serious.

"Captain Alan Lewrie, come aboard to speak with your captain," Lewrie announced to the single Midshipman present. *Fusee*'s crew was about the bare minimum, not over fifty hands all told, so no more than one Midshipman was required.

"Here he comes, sir . . . Lieutenant Johns," the older lad said, almost in relief, as a tall and lean fellow in his mid-thirties turned up on the bomb's quarterdeck.

"Joseph Johns, your servant, sir," the fellow said, doffing his hat with a jerky half-bow from the waist. Lt. Johns was scare-crow thin, with a prominent Adam's apple, a long wind-vane of a nose, and noticeable cheekbones. He looked to be a perfect non-entity but for a pair of eyes that seemed aflame with enthusiasm. "We've just received directions from Admiralty that you would be in charge of us, and of our . . . ehm," he added, jutting a pointy chin forward to his bomb's foredeck, where two thirteen-inch sea-mortars would usually be emplaced in side-by-side wells, heavily re-enforced with great baulks of timber to withstand the shock of their upwards discharge, and the down-thrust of recoil. Now, the wells were shrouded by what looked to be a scrap tops'l so large that it might have come off a frigate. Looking in that direction gave Lewrie the impression that the canvas shrouded six great water casks; he also took note of a long and heavy boom rigged to the base of the bomb's foremast, and a hoisting windlass so it could be employed as a crane . . . *forward* of the mast, not aft.

"Pardon me for seeming remiss in searching you out, sir, but as I said, orders came aboard not half an hour past," Johns went on.

"Mine preceded yours by no more than an hour, Mister Johns. It is of no matter," Lewrie allowed, clapping his hands into the small of his back and craning his neck to look upwards. "I had a converted bomb in the Bahamas, 'tween the wars, but *Alacrity,* as a gun-ketch, had her masts equally spaced, like a brig, and the mortar wells were fore and aft of the foremast. Your *Fusee* resembles a three-master that's missing her entire foremast, and sports but main and mizen."

"The newer construction allows both mortars to work in concert, sir, bows-on to a target, 'stead of anchored beam-on, and *becoming* a better target," Lt. Johns laughed. "I admit the new ones look queer, but with much larger jibs and fore-and-aft stays'ls, they *will* go up to windward at least a point closer."

"But still make lee-way like a wood chip?" Lewrie wryly asked.

"No worse than the older class, sir, but . . . aye," Lt. Johns said with a fatalistic shrug. "Bombs are notorious for it, unfortunately."

"Any chance that so much lee-way, when engaged in the, ah . . . experiments mentioned in my orders, might cause any problems, Mister Johns?" Lewrie asked, lowering his voice like a conspirator plotting mayhem . . . what *sort* he still hadn't a clue.

"Well, sir, I *would've* preferred a vessel with deeper 'quick-work' and less lee-way, but the wells are handy for the, ah . . . things, and *Fusee's* lower freeboard will aid in their . . . deployment," Johns replied, looking "cutty-eyed" and furtive, all but laying a cautioning finger to his lips. "But, you must meet Mister MacTavish, the fellow who devised the, ah . . . items, sir!" Johns perked up. "His ideas are visionary. They could revolutionise naval warfare, sir! This way."

"All that? Hmm," Lewrie most dubiously said. "Lead on, then."

"You've sufficient ship's boats, Captain Lewrie, might I ask?" Lt. Johns enquired as he led the way to a small companionway and a very steep, but thankfully short, ladder leading below.

"Two twenty-five-foot cutters, my gig, and a jolly-boat," Lewrie told him, taking off his hat and ducking, but, "Ow!" he yelped.

"Mind the deck beams, sir," Lt. Johns warned, much too late. "I have found a cautious crouch best serves, sir, when belowdecks." A trice later, and Lewrie found himself in the gloom of a very dark and small joke of a "great-cabin." Lt. Johns's own quarters right-aft were screened off by deal partitions and a louvred door; down each beam were four "dog-boxes," and along the centreline stood a rough planked table with sea-chests for seating, much like the orlop deck cockpit of bigger ships, where Midshipmen, Surgeon's Mates, and Master's Mates resided.

Two men sat slouched on their elbows at the table opposite each other, poring over sheaves of drawings and plans, which were rolled up hastily at Lewrie's appearance as they turned to glower at him.

"Captain Lewrie, sir, allow me to name to you the designer of our, of the . . . Mister Cyrus MacTavish, and his senior artificer and fabricator, Mister Angus McCloud," Johns announced. "Gentlemen, allow me to name to you Captain Alan Lewrie, of the *Reliant* frigate."

At least only the one *of 'em popped out of a haggis,* Lewrie told himself; with two Scottish names mentioned in his orders, he'd expected a lot worse.

"Captain Lewrie, your servant, sir!" the urbane-looking one said as he cautiously got to his feet and came forward to offer his hand to Lewrie. "MacTavish, sir, formerly Major in the Royal Engineers."

MacTavish was lean and fair, with an almost noble face, dressed in a plain dark blue coat, buff breeches, and top-boots.

"And my right-hand man, Angus McCloud," MacTavish pointed out.

If he'd dressed in kilt, cross-gartered plaid stockings, and a Scotch bonnet, McCloud could not have looked more "Sawney," his grizzly beard included; Lewrie hadn't seen one on a man in ages. The man wore a slate-grey tweed suit of "ditto," the fabric so rough that *sparrows* might have woven it from straw and twigs. McCloud was much older than his employer, grey and bristly curly-haired, with tanned and leathery rough features. He continued scowling. "G'day t'ye, Cap'm," was all he had to say, with a short nod, still seated.

"Gentlemen," Lewrie replied. "For the moment, you have the advantage of me. My orders did not specify exactly what it is we're to *do*, or what your devices do."

"And with good reason, sir!" MacTavish said with a bark of good humour. "Do the French learn what is in store for them, it would make our trials much more difficult, not to say impossible. Does the term 'torpedo' mean anything to you, sir?"

"Ah . . . some sort of eel, or ray?" Lewrie asked, shrugging his ignorance. "A fish o' some sort?"

"Will you take coffee, Captain Lewrie?" Lt. Johns offered.

"Yes, join us and I will enlighten you, sir," MacTavish grinned. Once all were seated, and Lewrie had a mug in his hands, the man went on with a sly and boastful grin. "There's all these bloody barges and boats the French have built, not counting the *prames* and *chaloupes* of varying sizes and armament built as gunboats to provide escort to the invasion, when it comes. So many that the French have had to anchor them outside the principal invasion ports, up against the breakwaters in row after row, waiting for the moment when the troops and artillery go aboard them."

"Like trots o' peegs, a'nuzzlin' a sow," McCloud supplied with a gruff tone.

"Now, with that the case, Captain Lewrie, how would you get at them?" MacTavish asked, already smiling with impending glee to reveal *his* solution.

"With bombs and sea-mortars, gunfire, and fireships, I s'pose," Lewrie replied, sure that his answer would be wrong. "A cutting-out expedition on dark, moonless nights?"

"Ye canna geet yair frigate that close t'shore," McCloud piped up. "Bombs canna expec' calm waters, e'en can *they* get inta shallower waters, an' th' Frogs' gunboats'd put paid t'yair fireships an' a' yair puir sailors ye send rowin' in."

"Well, Angus, when the time comes, are we successful, there'll be all those in concert, *but* . . . with the addition of my torpedoes . . . my *cask* torpedoes, aha!" MacTavish cried triumphantly. "Those things shrouded in the mortar wells, sir? We've half a dozen ready to go and more being fabricated even as we speak. When the time comes we intend to launch them by the hundreds on a French port, and blow all of their *caïques* and boats and barges to kindling!"

"Uhm . . . how?" Lewrie had to ask. It *sounded* fine, but . . .

"Imagine, sir, an assault launched in the dead of night without an in-kling of danger," Mr. MacTavish continued, squirming impatiently on his seat. "Ship's boats tow my cask torpedoes in close to shore, cock the deto-nating mechanisms, start the clock timer, and set them to drift in on a mak-ing tide. Channel tides are rapid, inexorable! Now . . . silently, un-seen, for they ride very low in the water, *waves* of them waft inshore, right up to those *caïques, péniches,* and barges, as quietly as mice!"

"Dinna forget th' grapnels, an' th' spikes," McCloud dryly added.

"They bob up alongside the French boats," MacTavish further en-thused, sketching out the assault with the tips of his fingers flutter-creeping towards a box of sweet bisquits on the table top. "Grapnels and old bayo-nets snag or spear into the hulls of the boats, the first warning that any-thing's amiss to the few French sailors aboard them to watch over their anchor cables and the lines which moor them together, hah! Then, when the clock timer winds up the trigger cords, and those few Frogs' best ef-forts to dis-lodge them prove fruitless, up they *go* in gigantic *blasts,* ah ha!" he cried, raising his hands, his fingers spreading further to simulate soaring chunks of debris.

"Float in on the tide," Lewrie said back, shifting uneasily on a hard sea chest. "That could take a while, even on a Channel tide. Your clock timer mechanism . . . ?"

"We determine the speed of the tide, set the timers to account for it, judge the distance at which the torpedoes are released, then prime them and off they go," MacTavish told him, beaming.

"Uhm, Channel tides flow *into* their ports, aye, Mister MacTavish . . . but, there's a strong tide up or *down* Channel to consider," Lewrie had to point out. "Is the bottom smooth, tide-washed sand and mud, or is it rocky, which sets off strong eddies? It's not as if all your cask torpedoes will just drift *straight* in. Some will swirl about and might end up a mile from where you want them."

"But the *bulk* of them surely will succeed, sir," MacTavish said with complete assurance in his devices. "Boats will be lost to them, some dam-aged and force the French to replace them, and once a few blow up without warning, think of the *panic* they will engender. What French sailor would dare to sleep aboard his *caïque* or *péniche* if the presence of death may come with each sunset?"

Think of the panic in the boat crews who tow the damned things in, ready to explode! Lewrie sourly thought.

"*How* close ashore to the anchored boats would boat crews have to get before releasing them?" Lewrie asked.

"Well, that would depend on the run of the tide, Captain Lewrie. I should imagine that each boat will have a Midshipman with a passable skill in mathematics," MacTavish said, shrugging off the problem. "Some of your, what-do-you-call-them . . . Master's Mates, able to judge the height of the boats' masts, and perform simple trigonometry to determine the distance, the speed of the tide, and set the clock timer accordingly."

Boy Midshipmen with good *mathematics?* Lewrie wondered; *Now* there *is a snag! A veritable paradox!*

"As to the matter of suitable boats, sir," Lt. Johns brought up once more. "We've only a small gig and an eighteen-foot jolly-boat on our inventory. To tow them in quickly, then make their way out just as quickly, it would be best if we had some boats larger than your two cutters . . . thirty-two-foot barges with two masts for lug-sails and a jib would be best. Or at least twelve-oared barges."

"We'll ask of the dockyard," Lewrie told him. "I'm sure they might have some spares. What *condition* they're in, well. If we need authorisation, who do we mention? Are we under Lord Keith and North Sea Fleet? Droppin' a powerful name sometimes helps."

"No worry, then, Captain Lewrie," Mr. MacTavish said with a top-lofty smirk. "We have letters from Lord Melville, personally signed, authorising *any* expense or requisition. Might *they* do?"

Mine arse on a band-box! Lewrie thought; *What do I want, what does* Reliant *need . . . and how much can I get* away *with?*

"I expect they'd do main-well, Mister MacTavish," Lewrie allowed. "Uhm . . . could I see these wonders? Not the plans here, but the real articles?"

"Aye, weel . . . ," Artificer McCloud grumbled, rubbing his beard.

"But of course, sir! This instant!" MacTavish quickly agreed.

"Hmm . . . rather big," Lewrie commented once the canvas shroud had been drawn back just far enough to expose one of the devices to his eyes. To all outward appearances, the "cask torpedo" was a large water butt, about four feet tall and fat in the middle, tapering at each end to shallow hemispherical lids, not the usual flat wooden lids set into the ends two or three inches below the rims. Any large tun, cask, or barrel made to hold liquids was constructed with extra care, of course, so that the staves fit together so closely that only the slightest bit of seepage occurred. In this case, seepage inward would be the ruin of the device, so it had been slathered all over in tar, then wrapped with more tarred canvas.

"Th' bottom's heemispherical, ye'll note," McCloud pointed out, "sae thayr's space feer th' ballast, tae keep eet ridin' oop-right een th' water."

"And the upper hemisphere is a void, a space for air," MacTavish added. "That is where the clock mechanism sits, along with the pistol which ignites the charge at the proper time. When one is about to let one go, one first pulls the line with the blue paint on the last inches of the line . . . that will start the clock. The red-painted line cocks the primed fire-lock of the pistol. The clock gears drive a circular wooden disk, which has several dowels projecting from it. The trigger line is bound to one of the dowels, and, as the clock turns the disk, the line is drawn taut, 'til it pulls the trigger of the pistol, and . . . bang!" he gleefully concluded. "The gunpowder and the pyrotechnicals ignite, and *adieu, Monsieur* Frog, ha ha!"

"How much gunpowder?" Lewrie asked, getting up on his tip-toes to peer over the top of the torpedo, taking hold of one of the hoisting ring-bolts. "And how low in the water will it ride? I notice the top is not tarred, but painted black. And, how do you *set* the clock at the last minute?"

"One hundred and twenty pounds of powder," MacTavish told him.

Lewrie stepped back a foot or two!

"D'ye mean it's loaded, *now?*" he gawped.

"Weel, o' course eet's loaded!" McCloud said with a short snort of amusement. "But, the pistol's nae primed, nor cocked, an' th' *clock* ain't runnin'. Eet's safe as sae many bricks!"

"So . . . when the time comes to prime the pistol's pan, set the clock timer, and ready it to go, how *do* you, if the top's sealed?" Lewrie asked, growing a bit more dubious of the whole enterprise, and feeling a faint shudder of dread in his middle.

"As to that, Captain Lewrie," MacTavish said soothingly, "one must remove the bung set into the very top. The hole is wide enough for your average man to reach down into it, set the clock timer for the minutes judged best, pull the lock back to half-cock and prime the pan, then draw it to full cock . . ."

Oh, Jesus! Lewrie groaned inside; *Pity the poor fool who does that from a wallowin' rowin' boat!*

". . . pull the trigger lines to set it all in motion, then drive the bung back in place," MacTavish went on, not noticing Lewrie's look of utter dread. "The torpedo will float with the top six inches free of the water, and, should waves slop over it, the bung will keep things dry enough for as long as the clock runs."

"Mind noo, ye'll hae *t'wind* th' bluidy thing, feerst!" McCloud hooted, then turned to spit overside.

"That's why the top is painted black, to hide it from a casual observer or lookout," MacTavish breezed off. "The ring-bolts will do for hoisting out from this vessel, and for towing lines from the boat which takes it in close. The old socket bayonets will be fitted over muzzle stubs from old Tower muskets, and the same for the grapnels . . . all the metal fittings screwed in and washered, and tarred inside and out. But, we'll do all that before they're hoisted out."

"So, right now we're sittin' on seven hundred twenty pounds of gunpowder," Lewrie said, shaking his head, "and if anything goes amiss, we could take out old *Sandwich* yonder, the Medway Boom tenders, and an host of unwary workers?"

"Nae countin' th' spare kegs o' powder stored below," McCloud said, his head cocked over and nodding genial agreement with Lewrie's estimate.

"Mister Johns, I think it best if you move *Fusee* out into the Great Nore anchorage near my ship," Lewrie suggested.

Not too bloody near, thankee! he thought.

"Of course, sir!" Lt. Johns replied, stiffening with eagerness to be about the start of their "adventure."

"We'll take my gig in tow, and bring my boat crew aboard for a bit," Lewrie added. "Alright with you, sir?" he had to enquire, for it was not his ship, and Lt. Johns was *Fusee*'s commanding officer.

"Very good, sir! Bosun, pipe all hands to Stations for taking in the anchors!" Johns bellowed.

Lewrie's Cox'n and his gig's oarsmen came tumbling aboard from the boat, and a long tow-line was bound to her stem bollard for towing astern. It would be a nice rest for them, instead of another long row of several miles. They began stretching and chattering, peering about at the oddness of a new ship, a type which most of them had never seen.

Patrick Furfy, "stroke oar" and Liam Desmond's long-time mate from their Irish village, took out a short stub pipe and began to tamp shag tobacco into it.

"Furfy!" Lewrie snapped, looking aghast. "No smoking! If you please," he added once he saw the surprise on Furfy's face. "Not 'til we're back aboard *Reliant*."

And off this *"Vesuvius"!* Lewrie determined.

CHAPTER TWENTY-SEVEN

*I*t was another of those fine Summer sunsets, the wind from off the North Sea just cool enough to rid the great-cabins of the warmth of the day as it wafted down through the opened windows in the coach-top overhead and through the half-opened sash-windows in the transom.

It was two days since Lewrie had discovered *Fusee* and her lethal cargo, and one day after Mr. MacTavish and Lt. Johns had briefed *Reliant*'s officers and Midshipmen. That had *seemed* to go well; did one consider "struck dumb" and "appalled" proper reactions. Lt. Merriman and Lt. Westcott had shared stunned looks, but would "soldier" along; Lt. Spendlove, *Reliant*'s Second Officer, though, had expressed his distaste for the torpedoes, calling them "infernal machines" and unworthy of a gentleman-warrior. "If they're to revolutionise warfare at sea, sir, it will be a *brute* form of revolution. Does this war go on long enough, we'll be shelling enemy cities, next," he'd said, shaking his head in sadness. Oh, Lt. Spendlove would carry out his duties to the Tee, he'd quickly assured Lewrie, but he'd rather hoped that MacTavish and his torpedoes would prove a failure. Close blockade was the very thing, to Spendlove's mind, just as the former First Lord of the Admiralty, the Earl St. Vincent, had determined.

This evening, Lewrie would not be dining in Lt. Johns, MacTavish, or McCloud, nor any of his own people, either. He and the cats dined alone, Toulon and Chalky atop his table with their separate bowls of victuals.

With no one to impress, Lewrie could dress comfortably in an old pair of slop-trousers, old buckled shoes and cotton stockings, and just his shirt and loosened neck-stock. Once Pettus removed his soup and began to fill a plate with the *entrée*, Lewrie could take the note from Lydia Stangbourne from a pocket and unfold it to read once more.

She hoped that his assignment in Channel waters for the rest of the year would allow them to see each other again, *more* often, and even *very* often! Should he be called to London, that would be grand, and it would *not* involve round after round of gaming clubs; should he be back in port long enough, he must write her at once, and she would coach down so that they—

Thud! went his Marine sentry's musket on the deck. "Midshipman Warburton . . . *sah!*"

"Enter," Lewrie answered with a frustrated growl. There were a few times when solitude was welcome, and this was one of them!

"Mister Houghton's duty, sir, and I'm to tell you that there is a boat hailing us, with a visitor," Warburton announced.

"From *Fusee?*" Lewrie asked, scowling.

"From shore, sir . . . he appears to be a civilian," Mr. Warburton told him.

Percy, come t'have my guts for toppin' his sister? Lewrie wondered. No matter. "I'll be on deck directly. Thankee, Mister Warburton."

"Aye aye, sir."

Lewrie frowned, dabbed his mouth, and rose from the table, hiding Lydia's note in a trouser pocket once more, silently damning all callers who'd disturb his supper, or ruin his good mood.

"Good God!" Lewrie said, though, once his visitor had boarded. "Where the Devil did *you* spring from? Hallo, Peel."

"Sir Alan Lewrie, sir!" Mr. Peel—"'tis Peel, James Peel"—replied, doffing his fashionable thimble-shaped hat and bowing as grandly as he would at Court; laughing, though. "I bow to your grandeur! I'll even *kow-tow* at your magnificence!"

"Now that'd be a sight," Lewrie barked, laughing back and going to shake hands. "The last I heard from you two years ago was a letter from somewhere in the Germanies."

"Well, soon as the war began again, things got a bit hot for me and my line of work, so the Foreign Office found something else for me to do closer to home. Damn my eyes, Lewrie, how do you keep?"

"Main-well, considerin'," Lewrie replied. "Care for a bite or two of something? Or would ye care t'watch *me* eat while you sip a bit of brandy?"

"Just a dab or two of what you're having . . . and the brandy!" Mr. Peel japed.

When Lewrie had first met James Peel in the Italics in 1795 or so, he had first taken him for a side of beef sent to bodyguard that old cut-throat from the Foreign Office's Secret Branch, Mr. Zachariah Twigg. Peel was big enough for that duty; he was not quite six feet tall and "beef to the heel," all of it lean muscle. And he could certainly *look* threatening with his very dark brown hair and eyes, a pair of strong hands, wide shoulders, deep chest, with the lean hips of a panther. A brainless bully-buck Peel was most certainly not, though, for he'd come from a distinguished family of the landed gentry, had a quick and clever mind, and at one time, before his cheating at cards in his regimental mess had caught up with him and forced his resignation, Peel had been a Captain of Household Cavalry—though even the Curraissiers thought that he "rode heavy." Peel had been Twigg's man in the West Indies during the slave rebellion on Saint Domingue/Haiti, and had aided Lewrie against the Creole rebel pirates in Louisiana, and again during the Franco-American Quasi-War of 1798–99.

"A growin' lad needs his tucker," Lewrie commented, watching the fellow eat part of his own supper and empty half the fresh-baked rolls in the bread barge.

"Ehm . . . you aren't come from Mister Twigg with another of his harum-scarums, are you?" The fingers of his left hand were crossed to ward off that very occurrence, under the tablecloth.

"No, the old fellow's done with spy-craft, and we're the worse off for it, but . . . it comes to us all, sooner or later," Peel said.

"Fading, is he?" Lewrie replied. "I recall my father mentioning he'd had a bad Winter, but when that was . . . ?" He shrugged.

"Had several bad Winters," Peel said between bites of pork chops. "His physicians finally told him to avoid London and its air like the plague, and Winter at his country estate in Hampstead. Oh, he'll come down to London in the Spring, when the coal smoke's not as heavy, but for the most part, he's up at 'Spyglass Bungalow' spoiling his grand-children something sinful."

"Thank God," Lewrie commented, letting out a pent breath and un-crossing his fingers. "If he *had* wished to rope me in, I'm spoken for any-way. Something just as lunatick as any Twigg dreamed up."

"You mean your cask torpedoes?" Peel asked with a sly smirk.

"Don't know what you're talkin' about, and besides . . ." Lewrie tried to wave off; with a fork full of mashed potatoes, in fact.

"Lewrie . . . recall! I'm Secret Branch?" Peel japed. "We know all about them, and I wish you the best of good fortune with them."

"You're here to check up on them?" Lewrie asked.

"God, no, not me!" Peel said, laughing. "That would be some anxious Admiralty sort, and he won't pester you 'til you've had at least a few trials. No . . . I was making the rounds with Admiral Cornwallis of Channel Fleet, Admiral Lord Keith's squadrons in The Downs, and one or two others, regarding the estimated numbers, types, and strengths of the in-vasion fleet Bonaparte's building. Uhm, might I get a top-up of this excel-lent . . . whatever it is?"

"A single-*château bordeaux,* sir," Pettus informed him as he did the duty. "The Captain brought several back from the Gironde."

"You've numbers?" Lewrie asked. When he'd called upon the Admi-ralty in London, they'd given him the descriptions and some sketches of what they *thought* the various French invasion vessels looked like . . . but no idea of how they were armed, or how many he would face.

Peel gave him a cock-browed look, and a head-jerk at Pettus.

"Pettus . . . one of those 'take the air on deck' moments," Lewrie told his cabin steward. "And take Jessop with you for a bit."

"You are aware of the types?" Peel asked in a low voice once he was sure they were alone.

"There's *guilots,* to transport horses and artillery batteries," Lewrie ticked off on his fingers, "there's some three-masted hundred-footer gun-boats, what they call *prames* . . ."

"With twelve twenty-four-pounders," Peel stuck in. "Though they build them so quickly, and of such light materials, that *prames* can't stand against a frigate. Go on," Peel urged with a sage nod.

"They showed me brig-rigged *chaloupes,*" Lewrie said, waiting.

"Three twenty-four-pounders and an eight-inch mortar," Peel said.

"I'm told there are some lesser gunboats, two- or three-masted luggers, even cutter-rigged small ones?" Lewrie asked, pausing again for informa-tion.

"Might face only one twenty-four-pounder and an army field piece in the smallest Dutch-built ones, perhaps some older naval guns of lesser calibres in the French-built," Peel enlightened him. He was picking his teeth as he did so.

"Then there's all those damned *pénishes* and *caïques,* all of 'em luggers, to carry troops and supplies," Lewrie continued. "Admiralty said there were hundreds of 'em."

"About seven hundred gunboats and escorts of various types, and their plans are for over two thousand transports," Peel told him with a grave look. "I'm told, though, that both Admiral Cornwallis and Admiral Lord Keith estimate that it would take two or three tides to get *all* of them to England, and with Channel Fleet, our North Sea Fleet, and The Downs combined against them, given enough warning when they at last decide to try it on, we could *massacre* them. The French just don't have *that* many experienced sailors, and most of their guns will be manned by *soldiers* with little knowledge of naval gunnery."

" 'Less it's a dead-flat calm, when they come, their artillerists will find floatin', bobbin', and wallowin' boats just *won't* sit still as solid ground, where they learned their trade, aye," Lewrie determined, almost ready to whoop with glee, and a wish that the French *would* try. "And, they can't send 'em out to the slaughter without the support of their Navy, and we have their proper warships bottled up in Brest and Rochefort, or in The Texel in Holland."

"They might get out, yes . . . but I doubt they will enjoy it!" Peel said with a snicker, topping up his own wine from the side-board. "After all, the Frogs must man those squadrons' guns and retain enough sailors to handle the ships . . . *and* reserve even more skilled artillery men for the harbour and coastal batteries that 'Boney' has had erected all along the Channel coast, to boot. Is God just, the French *may* plan to have their infantry aboard the gunboats work their own guns to defend *themselves*! Perhaps they work to a tight budget?"

"Two for the price of one?" Lewrie snickered back, reaching to refill his glass, too.

"There is another matter, though," Peel admitted at last; Lewrie became wary in an eyeblink, for this was the way that Mr. Twigg had begun to introduce his previous schemes. "There are, according to one of our . . . sources in Paris . . . several hundred *more* invasion craft to figure with."

"You've still agents in Paris?" Lewrie asked, stunned.

"One or two," Mr. Peel confessed most slyly. "Once the war began last May, Bonaparte clapped a total embargo on correspondence going in or coming out of France . . . almost every book, newspaper, or letter's read . . . but we've managed. We have our ways, after all. So far, we only have vague descriptions, no sketches, of this other type of craft, but everyone would dearly love to lay hands on one. You'll be working along the French coast? Good. Do you ever come across what looks like a water-beetle with sails, you snap it right up."

"A water-beetle," Lewrie said with a dubious frown.

"There's a *M'sieur* Forfait, been made inspector-general of the invasion fleet. One of Bonaparte's pet mathematicians and scientists? Forfait earned his spurs designing and building shallow draught barges and such for use on the Seine. Some people in London think the entire idea's as daft as bats, but . . . he is a *skilled* mathematician, so we can't dismiss his work out-of-hand."

Mister MacTavish is a skilled engineer, too, and look what he's *come up with!* Lewrie sourly thought.

"There are two types described," Peel went on, leaning closer. "One's about thirty-six feet by fourteen or fifteen feet, and will only draw about three feet of water. The second's about forty-six feet in length and sixteen or eighteen feet in breadth. That one is said to draw a little less than four feet of water, when fully laden. Eighty or an hundred soldiers aboard . . . a twenty-four-pounder gun mounted in the bows, and, from the description *may* resemble two serving platters joined together, the top one inverted, and very flat-bottomed. There are slanted berths for the soldiers in the rims of the lower platter, and they're *supposed* to be rigged like a Schweling fishing boat . . . whatever the Devil *that's* supposed to look like. Any clue?"

"Never seen one in my life," Lewrie told him with a shrug.

"Anyway, the most intriguing part of the written description is that there's a long box atop the upper platter that runs the length of the boat, tall enough to allow the soldiers aboard to sit below it and be sheltered from fire," Peel said, grimacing with mock dis-belief. "Four or five abreast, and twenty or so deep, so they can sit there in the same formations they'd form in the field . . . Napoleon Bonaparte is very fond of the column when attacking opposing lines. Not keen on it, myself, but it's seemed to have served him well, so far. Now, what we are worried about is whether that protective box, and the wide slope of the upper hull from the waterline up, might be *armoured* somehow. If the French *have* re-enforced these boats, they might be the principal craft to drive themselves right onto the beaches, and be proof against shot from any of our field guns or horse artillery batteries. Our fellow in Paris describes the damned things as three-fifths of their length flat, with a rise of eight feet at the ends. They could come ashore like so many walruses!"

"Armoured? With iron plate, d'ye mean?" Lewrie gawped. "That'd make 'em top-heavy as Hell. Centre of gravity, metacentric height . . . all that?"

"*You've* been reading technical books?" Peel teased.

"Ye listen to others long enough, well . . . ," Lewrie shrugged off. "If they're armoured, they'd be drawin' a lot more water than three or four feet, Jemmy. I'll allow that the breadth of their hulls'd buoy 'em up a good deal, but not that much. And if they're that heavy, it would take a lot more sail area than a fishing boat's t'drive 'em."

"The report says that they only require a crew of five or six seamen," Peel said, dredging half a roll through the juices and gravy on his plate for a last bite. "And some sort of paddle arrangement to propel them if the wind fails. What sort? The work done by soldiers? Really, Alan . . . if you see one, go after it, MacTavish's experiments bedamned."

"I'll try and do my best." Lewrie grinned back. "Anything else? Pick up the Golden Fleece? Slay Medusa while I'm at it?"

"What's for dessert?" Peel asked, laughing heartily.

"I think my cook said there's a bread pudding. Are we done on confidential topics, I'll have my steward return," Lewrie said, rising to go to the forward door to his cabins to speak with the Marine guard so he could pass word for Pettus and Jessop.

"Rather humble fare for a knight and baronet," Peel mused once he'd returned to the dining-coach. Lewrie opened a covered dish.

"It comes with caramel sauce," Lewrie said, after sticking one finger into the dish and licking it. "And don't *you* start! It's all a sham, anyway. Awarded for sympathy, not anything I *did*. The closest I ever got to something of note was years ago in the South Atlantic when we took the *L'Uranie* frigate. And the baronetcy . . . hmpf! King George was havin' an off day, let's leave it at that. Unless ye wish to hear the whole story."

"Is it amusing?" Peel asked.

"Completely," Lewrie assured him.

"Then do tell!"

CHAPTER TWENTY-EIGHT

*I*t's grand that Spain's stayed out of the war, so far," Peel said after supper. They had gone on deck to the taffrails of the quarterdeck so he could light up a slim *cigaro* and blow smoke rings at the night. "Do they decide to re-join the French against us, the price of tobacco will soar, and the quality will decrease. Say what you will of American tobacco, but I still think the best is from Spanish colonies."

"Wouldn't know much about that. Never developed the taste for it," Lewrie said with a shrug, lounging most lubberly on the after-most bulwarks. He looked over to *Fusee*, about half a cable off to larboard. "They wouldn't let you smoke over there, not with all the powder aboard her. We're *much* more hospitable," he added, grinning.

"Think those things will work?" Peel asked.

"No idea," Lewrie replied. "I s'pose we'll soon find out. The wind's fair enough for us to set out tomorrow morning, and let us test the first batch. Though, after what we've learned of them the last few days, I think my chances'd be better were I a French *matelot* sittin' on an anchored barge than bein' in the launchin' boat."

"Well, if MacTavish's don't, there's other designers' ideas to try out," Peel imparted with a knowing nod and wink. "There's a fellow name of Robert Fulton . . . an American, who's come up with a variation on the torpedo. Man's just *brimming* with ideas. He claims he could build a ship driven by a steam engine. Dead-keen on steam engines, he is."

"No thankee!" Lewrie scoffed, after a second of surprise. "Correct me if I'm wrong, but don't steam engines need big *fires* under the boilers? Fire, on a wooden ship? Brr!"

"Not only that, this Fulton fellow said he could also build a *nautilus*, a submersible boat that could sink down twenty or thirty feet and stay down for the better part of an hour," Peel further told him. "A small crew, three or four, I forget which, paddle it forward in some way."

"And do *what* with it?" Lewrie gawped, then shook his head. "The very *word* 'sink' makes my 'nut-megs' shrivel. Sounds suicidal, t'me."

"That's what Admiralty thought, too," Peel said with a snicker. "He offered both, just after the war began again last May. I gather that Fulton couldn't sell his ideas to his own navy, and couldn't raise sufficient private funds in his own country, so he flogged his schemes on this side of the Atlantic. The last card up his sleeve was the idea of explosive torpedoes, though I believe that the submersible boat and the torpedoes would have worked together, the boat towing the torpedoes under an anchored ship, and the torpedo exploding when it came into contact, whilst the submersible paddles away on the other side."

"Not with a timing mechanism?" Lewrie grimaced. "That would take some sort of *hair-trigger* pistol, and *any* hard knock'd set it off. You wish crew for *that* thing, best look in Bedlam!"

"Admiralty's judgement, too," Peel said, shrugging, pausing to take a deep puff on his *cigaro* and exhale a jet of smoke. "Mind, now. All these daft schemes are William Pitt's doing. Soon as he got back into office as Prime Minister, he pressed for offensive action, and not sit idle, waiting for the French to invade. Admiral the Earl Saint Vincent was against them, but who knows about Lord Melville. The damned things *may* turn up to be tested, do we give events long enough, or they grow dire enough."

"Christ," was Lewrie's sober comment to that.

"Better us than the French, I suppose," Peel said, laughing some more. "Before he came to London, Fulton tried to sell his schemes to Bonaparte. Went to Paris during the Peace of Amiens and got an audience with the 'Ogre' himself . . . and thank God 'Boney' thought Fulton's ideas madder than a March Hare, too."

Lewrie tried to picture what the French would have done with a submersible boat and a towed torpedo. Could people be found with more martial ardour than sense to crew the things in the first place? Then this anchorage at the Nore would lie open to a creeping, unseen danger. Portsmouth, Plymouth, Great Yarmouth, or Harwich . . . He had to shake his head to rid himself of the image of a peacefully anchored and sleeping warship suddenly smashed open by a titanic blast, then heeling over and sinking in minutes, aflame from bow to stern!

No thankee! At least a steam-driven ship'd give you a fightin' chance, and stay atop *the sea!* Lewrie thought, wondering uneasily where all this inventiveness would lead. Warfare at least had a *few* gentlemanly rules— not that Lewrie had *always* paid heed to them when needs must—but, in the main both sides went into battle with assumptions that things would go honourably, fairly, and . . . sporting, like knights of old at a joust. If inventiveness mated with desperation, though . . .

No, with any luck, such things won't work well enough to become normal, or acceptable, Lewrie told himself.

"Penny for your thoughts," Peel prompted upon seeing how silent and pensive Lewrie had become.

"Wonderin' what Fulton's torpedoes are like, compared to ours," Lewrie dissembled; it wouldn't do to sound fretful, even with a friend. That would be "croaking," and might give Peel the impression that he'd no faith in MacTavish's torpedoes and would not do his utmost to test them fairly.

"Smaller, I gathered," Peel told him, flicking an inch of ash over the stern. "Small enough to be rolled over the side of a boat . . . spherical, made of copper. I think they're to be deployed in pairs, with a line buoyed with cork blocks like a fishing net, between them. Other than that, the clockwork timers and cocked pistols to set them off are similar to MacTavish's. This very moment, there's probably a captain like you charged with experimenting with Fulton's version. A competition 'tween the two versions, if you will.

"And of course, old man," Peel sarcastically added, assuming an Oxonian accent, "can't let the old-school side down, you know! Better the winner is British, than a benighted 'Brother Johnathon' from *New* England, what?"

"Yoicks, tally-ho, and all that?" Lewrie smirked.

"Win for 'The Roast Beef of Old England,'" Peel laughed back. "Unless the damned things turn out to be a pile of manure."

CHAPTER TWENTY-NINE

*T*he first cask torpedo was tried out in English waters, just off Mersea Island and the mouth of the Blackwater river, where the North Sea tides ran particularly strong, and the ebbs left miles of exposed mud flats. *Reliant* stood guardian to the *Fusee* bomb as she worked her way within a mile of shore as the tide began to flood, and it was Lieutenant Johns and Mr. McCloud who saw to its priming, its lowering into the waters, and its towing behind one of their new thirty-two-foot barges.

Lewrie had himself rowed over to *Fusee* to watch, and stood with Mr. MacTavish whilst the evolution was carried out.

"They will be setting the timer . . . drawing the cocking line to the pistol . . . and letting it go!" MacTavish narrated, a telescope to his eye, like to jump out of his skin with excitement. "McCloud and I agreed to set the clockwork for half an hour. No specific target, just a trial of all the various elements, you see, sir."

He'll piss his breeches, does he have t'wait for half an hour, Lewrie cynically thought, a telescope to his own eye. The twelve-oar barge was wheeling about, fending off from the torpedo with a gaff and re-hoisting its lug-sails . . . in understandable haste, he also noted.

MacTavish, for all his seeming urbanity, *did* closely resemble a squirming, tail-wagging, circling puppy which would piddle in excitement. He collapsed the tubes of his glass and became rivetted to his pocket-watch, a fine one that had a second hand in addition to the usual minute and hour hands. The fellow paced, stewed, fretted, peered at his watch, and fussed with the set of his coat and waist-coat, his neck-stock, and (unconsciously) his crutch.

The barge returned, Lt. Johns and McCloud came upon deck, and the boat crew led her aft for towing. Long minutes passed. As a half-hour slowly ticked by, Lt. Johns and McCloud caught the fidgets, too, coughing and ahumming and now and then putting their heads together with MacTavish for urgent whispered conversations.

Lewrie looked at his own watch. If MacTavish was right, their torpedo would explode in five minutes. He lifted his telescope again, looking for the device, but could not find it any longer. That black-painted upper hemisphere hid it from sight most effectively, even with a slight chop and bright sunlight shining off the white-glittering wave tops; the damned thing should have had a ring of revealing foam around it. *Unless it had sunk, of course*, Lewrie thought.

"Ehm, sirs . . . ," *Fusee*'s Midshipman piped up, coughing into his fist for attention. "Sirs? Ahem? That trading brig coming out from the river. Should we warn her off, or something?"

Lewrie wasn't the only one who raised a telescope, or scrambled for one. Sure enough, a small two-masted merchantman was rounding the point east of Bradwell Waterside and standing out to sea, sails trimmed to broad-reach the Nor'easterly breezes.

"Could she be anywhere near your torpedo, Mister MacTavish?" Lt. Johns fretted aloud.

"What was the rate of the tide, Mister McCloud?" Lewrie asked the artificer. "In half an hour, could it have . . . ?"

"Nae muir than four or five knots, I judged eet, sae . . . ," McCloud tried to shrug off.

"Pencil and paper!" MacTavish cried.

"My slate, sir?" the Midshipman offered.

"Think we *should* warn her off?" Lewrie suggested.

"Warn her, aye, sir!" Lt. Johns hurriedly agreed.

"How?" Lewrie further asked. "You have signal rockets?"

"We could fire a gun!" Johns barked, turning to order his small crew to man one of *Fusee*'s puny 6-pounders.

"And what'll they make o' that?" Lewrie snapped.

"I . . . don't know, sir!" Lt. Johns replied, stunned to inaction.

"Five knots' drift for half an hour, that's two knots' progress . . . on a course roughly Northwest . . . ," MacTavish was mumbling half to himself, a stub of chalk squeaking loudly on the Midshipman's borrowed slate. He paused to raise an arm to where he judged the torpedo first had been released, his other arm to mark a rough course of drift; then he fumbled to trade slate and chalk for his telescope once more. "Well, damme, I think . . . yes, it'll be wide of the mark. *Sure* to be wide of the mark."

Once clear of the shoals, the little merchant brig hardened up a point or two to the winds to sail on a beam reach, angling further out to sea, as if to pass well to windward of the anchored bomb and frigate, without a clue or a care in the world.

"Safe as sae meeny houses," McCloud predicted, his thumbs stuck in the pockets of his waist-coat. "We'll miss her by a mile or—"

BOOM!

A gigantic column of spray and foam liberally mixed with dark clouds of exploded gunpowder sprang up from the sea . . . tall enough to tower over the brig's mast-head trucks, between her and the shore.

"Oh shit," Lewrie breathed.

Hope her owner has insurance, he further thought.

"One half-hour to the minute, sirs," the Midshipman meekly said.

"My *God*!" from MacTavish.

"Weel, hmm," from McCloud.

A shiver in the sea from the explosion was transmitted to *Fusee* to rattle her blocks, up through her hull to the tiny quarterdeck, to make the oak planks shudder for a second or two.

"What have we done? Dear Lord, what have we done?" Mr. MacTavish was almost whimpering, about ready to tear his hair out by the roots.

"Weel, eet *deed* wirk, sir, sae . . . ," McCloud tried to comfort him.

Lewrie took another long look. The merchant brig had hardened up to a close-reach; it was the wind pressing her sails that made her heel over more steeply, not the blast of the torpedo. She sailed off to their right-hand side, revealing that titanic column of spray and foam that was collapsing upon itself like a failing geyser, at least a mile inshore of the brig, but closer to the mouth of the Colne river than the centre of Mersea Island, as MacTavish had planned.

"That'll put the wind up him," Lewrie commented sarcastically. "Perhaps the whole coast. Mister MacTavish, did you or Admiralty warn the locals of your trials?"

"Well, of course not, Captain Lewrie!" MacTavish snapped back. "They are to be secret!"

"Well, it don't look too secret, now," Lewrie told him with a wry grin as he lifted his telescope once more. What fishing smacks that had been out off the coast were haring shoreward. Signal rockets were soaring aloft from Clackton-on-Sea, and a semaphore tower's arms were whirling madly, the large black balls at their ends passing on a message to somewhere most urgently.

They were a bit too far offshore to see or hear the alarm their torpedo's explosion had caused, but Lewrie could only imagine they had stirred up a hornet's nest; militia drums would be rattling, mustering bugles would be ta-rahing, and the womenfolk would be dashing about in a dither, sure that the mysterious blast had been a fiendish French device, sure sign of imminent invasion!

"Good Lord, sir, do you imagine that the locals might think our torpedo was a . . . ?" Lt. Johns gasped, aghast at the implications.

"I'm going back aboard *Reliant*, Mister Johns," Lewrie told him, wishing he could wash his hands of the entire endeavour, that minute. "I think the best action on our part would be to slink away . . . very quietly and quickly, and practice saying', 'Who, me?' "

"And declare my torpedoes a failure, sir?" McTavish said with a snort; now that the brig had escaped all harm, he was back on his high horse.

"It did work, sir," Lewrie rejoined, "But I don't think more trials on *our* coast are a good idea. You wish to try them in the conditions they'll face if accepted? Better we go mystify and frighten the French, in a real Channel tide-race."

"Well, right, then . . . in the Channel, yes," MacTavish relented. "Yes, it did work, didn't it?" he declared, beginning to strut a bit in pride of his invention. "Boulogne, perhaps. The harbour where they're marshalling their forces."

"Uhm, perhaps someplace less well-defended, first," Lewrie said. "Let me think of something. For now, Mister Johns, get under way and follow me at two cables' distance. We're off for France."

"Aye aye, sir!" Lt. Johns enthused, all but licking his chops.

And get as far away from the results of our handiwork as we can! Lewrie thought.

CHAPTER THIRTY

*A*re you quite sure this is a good idea, sir?" Lt. Westcott had to ask one more time, just before Lewrie departed the ship. "I could go in your place."

"Our people are still leery of the damned things, sir," Lewrie replied, patting himself down for essential items before going down to one of their cutters, where his Cox'n, Liam Desmond, and his boat crew awaited him. "I can't ask any of them t'deal with 'em if someone does not lead the way. Don't worry, Mister Westcott . . . do we launch enough of them, your turn will come."

"Very well, sir," Westcott said with a resigned sigh. "Best of luck, sir."

"Thankee, Mister Westcott. *Reliant* is yours for the time being. Keep her off the mud," Lewrie said, first formally, then with a laugh. He doffed his hat, then descended the man-ropes and battens to the boat, leaping the last few feet to stumble into the arms of his oarsmen, and then scrambling aft to its stern-sheets, by Desmond.

"Shove off, bow man," Desmond ordered, his voice muted in conspiratorial fashion. "Out oars, starboard, and make a bit o' way . . . out oars, larboard, and pull t'gither! Set the stroke, Pat."

Reliant and *Fusee* had closed the French coast after full dark, creeping in with leadsmen in the fore chains sounding the depths to a distance of two miles offshore, where both had anchored to single bowers, both vessels completely darkened. Despite the mugginess of a warm Summer night, all the oarsmen had been ordered to wear their dark blue jackets and tarred black hats, just as Lewrie had donned his old plain coat and doubled it over his chest to hide the whiteness of his shirt. The night was so dark that the only way Desmond knew how to steer for *Fusee* was to make out the foam breaking round her waterline.

The shore was much easier to see, even two miles off, for the towns of St. Valery sur Somme and Le Crotoy were lit up with street lanthorns or storefront lamps, one town to either side of the mouth of the Somme river and the deep bay axed into the shore between them. It was easier, too, to make out the many riding lights of an host of anchored *péniches* and *caïques* in the small harbours and up either bank of the river; so many wee riding lights that the flotillas resembled an extension of the towns that had flooded down the shoreline to fill the entire bay.

"Mister Merriman still behind us, Desmond?" Lewrie asked, looking astern.

"Seems t'be, sor," Desmond replied after a quick peek for the splash of oars—darkened oars, not their usual natty white and gay blue. Even both cutters' hulls had been smeared with galley soot.

Lewrie patted himself down once more, seeking his small boat compass, the hilt of his hanger, and his pair of double-barrelled pistols, his powder flask and leather pouch for spare cartouches. How he could *read* his compass without a candle would be another matter.

"Hoy, the boat!" someone called as they neared *Fusee*.

"*Reliant* Number One!" Desmond called back.

"Aye, come alongside to larboard!" the voice yelled back.

Desmond put the tiller over to swing the cutter round *Fusee*'s stern. "Easy all," he ordered, to ghost near her sides.

"That you, Captain Lewrie?" Mr. MacTavish asked in an exaggerated whisper from one of the barges that sat rocking and wallowing by the converted bomb's bows.

"Here, sir!" Lewrie called back, forcing himself to sound eager.

"We've four torpedoes ready in the water, ready for towing as soon as you're ready to receive them, sir," MacTavish said, sounding gleeful.

"Christ!" Lewrie muttered, imagining four of the beasts primed and ready, their spikes and grapnels, affixed, bobbing close together!

"Hoy, the boat!" again from the quarterdeck.

"*Reliant* Number Two!" Lt. Merriman announced as his cutter came in sight, ghosting up behind Lewrie's.

"I will see to one of them, Midshipman Frederick the second," Mac-Tavish continued as loud as he dared, as if a French guard boat was within hearing distance. "McCloud's instructed him thoroughly in its operation, and it's simple enough, after all."

Says you! Lewrie sourly thought; *Is that the lad's name?*

"Our two are ready for towing," MacTavish went on. "Lieutenant Johns will pass you your tow-lines. Sure you have everything in hand, sir? Row in abreast, about one hundred yards apart, and release them as one?"

"If we can *see* to do that, aye," Lewrie told him.

"Well, er . . . ," MacTavish flummoxed.

Didn't think that quite through, did ye? Lewrie scoffed to himself.

"I've a small hooded lanthorn, and if I spark my flint tinder that may create a signal," MacTavish extemporised quickly. "I will be the one to judge the heights of the masts, and the proper time to set them free. When I signal, set your timers for fourty-five minutes."

"Bow man, hook on," Desmond ordered, steering the cutter under *Fusee*'s larboard side just long enough for a towing line to be thrown down to them and secured to a stern cleat. "Ready, sor."

"Make way, Desmond, and get us clear of the others. To starboard of *Fusee*'s barges."

"Aye, sor."

"Jaysus, Joseph, an' Mary," stroke-oar, Patrick Furfy, muttered as the tow-line paid out to the point that the massive torpedo put a strain on it, slowing the cutter to a crawl. He freed one hand long enough to make a sketchy cross over his chest.

As delightful as *Reliant*'s sailors had thought the idea of blowing Frenchmen to Kingdom Come, the explanation of how they would have to deal with the torpedoes' inner workings had made many of them look queasy and "cutty-eyed." Primed pistols to be cocked? Clocks set at the last moment, too, right alongside 120 pounds of gunpowder? *Brr!* If their officers or their senior Midshipmen did it, that was one thing, but if the time came for a massive attack with dozens of them, and it would possibly be *their* duty to set the clocks and prime the pistols and get away, that was quite another! Which was why Lewrie was here in *Reliant*'s lead cutter. Whether *he* cared to be, or not!

Lewrie could see two faint grey smears off to his left as the two barges slowly stroked away to form half of the line-abreast, white-painted hulls sooted to blend in with the sea and the night. He turned to look aft again, and made out Lt. Merriman's cutter just beginning to stroke free of *Fusee*'s sides.

"Let's be about it, then, Desmond," Lewrie told his Cox'n. "We will form line-abreast with those two boats to larboard."

"Aye, sor," his usually cocky Irish Cox'n grimly replied.

The oars creaked in their canvas-wrapped tholes in unison, and the cutter surged to each long stroke, rocking and wallowing between to the chops and rolls of the sea, rising and dipping to the scend with a faint sound of surging water down its flanks. The hands dug in and uttered faint grunts to drive forward, the cask torpedo's towing line raising a groan of its own, dragging against the rowers' efforts as if the cutter was tethered to a stone landing stage. So slowly it seemed that the time went by, with the lights of Le Crotoy and St. Valery drawing no closer, the anchored trots of invasion boats remaining tiny and distant, with the threat of a cruising gunboat lying just beyond their sight 'til one might suddenly loom up, demanding identification, with its guns run out and ready for firing!

Then, in a twinkling, Lewrie thought them *too* close to the enemy boats, as if he'd managed to nod off for long minutes and was presented with being at close quarters, awakened by some Frenchman crying, *"Qui va là?"* or the bark of a gun! He could make out individual shops and houses ashore, spot waggons in the streets, espy people strolling about, and the *péniches* and *caïques* anchored in their dozens were so close that he could almost make out details in their rigging!

Close enough, dammit? he asked the aether, turning to peer out to larboard for MacTavish's signal, for a spark from his flintlock and tinder lighter, or the covert flash from his hooded lanthorn, but there was nothing to pierce the darkness. He couldn't even see either of *Fusee*'s barges. If it had been up to him, he'd have signalled for the torpedoes' release five minutes before! Off to starboard, there was no sign of Lt. Merriman's cutter any longer. So when . . . ?

"Izzat a spark, sir?" an oarsman whispered.

Yes, and just thankee, Jesus! Lewrie crowed to himself, for he could see it, too, as MacTavish cocked and fired his igniter over and over.

"Easy all, Desmond," Lewrie whispered to his Cox'n. "Furfy and Hartnett . . . haul on the tow-line and bring the thing alongside."

"Aye, sor!" Furfy softly replied, crossing himself once more.

Without forward motion, the cutter wallowed and rolled fitfully as the great cask was pulled up astern, right to the cutter's transom. Lewrie laid his hat aside and leaned out as far as he could reach to take hold of it, but those spike bayonets and the grapnels fended the torpedo off like an aroused porcupine. It butted against the cutter's rudder with loud thuds, keeping it even further away!

Well, this *is hellish-awkward,* Lewrie silently fumed.

"Let's haul it round alongside the larboard quarter," Lewrie ordered. That spared the rudder, but the bayonets still kept it too far away; the only way that he could see to remove the large bung-like tompion from the torpedo's hemispherical top and reach down *inside* to set and activate its mechanism would be to leave the boat altogether and clamber *on top* of it . . . and if he fell off, he would surely drown, for Lewrie could not swim a single stroke! The last time he had been forced into the sea was at Toulon in 1794 when his mortar ship exploded, flinging him sky-high, and his cabin steward, Will Cony, had buoyed him up and towed him to the nearby beach!

"See if you can turn it halfway round, Furfy," Lewrie snapped in frustration. "Spin it so the grapnels lay fore-and-aft, and take off two or three of the bayonets."

"*Touch* it, sor?" Furfy yelped, wiping his big hands down both thighs of his slop-trousers. "*Me,* sor?"

"Aye, *you,* sir!" Lewrie insisted. "The bayonets fit over the barrel stubs like they do on yer own muskets. Furfy . . . the bloody thing can't go off 'til I've *set* it!"

"Bear a hand, Pat," Liam Desmond snapped, leaning over the side. "You too, Hartnett. Pass the gaff back here. Thomas, hook onto one o' the liftin' ring-bolts t'steady th' bastard."

They got the torpedo turned and removed three of the bayonets, which allowed the massive bulk to thud right against the cutter's hull, sounding like a large wooden bell despite the need for silence. Lewrie turned his head to see that the larboard-side oarsmen not involved with the torpedo's turning and steadying shrank back to starboard.

"Let's see, now," he muttered, leaning far out despite how close they had hauled it, grasping one of the ring-bolts with his left hand, and groping at the tompion with his right. "Damme, that's snug!"

The tompion which kept the inner works dry was a flush fit into the low-domed wooden top, with only a small brass ring-bolt in the centre, only large enough to pass a thin rope through it, or one finger! Lewrie clawed the tompion's edges with his fingernails, but that was of no avail. There was nothing for it but to lean out even further from the dubious safety of the cutter, chest pressed against the torpedo's top and his legs from the knees down *inside* the boat so he could take hold of the ring-bolt and try to pull upwards. "Well, shit, finally! Here, Furfy."

He handed the tompion back to Furfy, the nearest seaman, who acted as if Lewrie had just offered him a lit *grenado* bomb!

He still couldn't reach inside, though.

"Hold it close alongside, lads, and *very* bloody steady, hey?" Lewrie whispered harshly to his sailors as he groped for the far edge of the torpedo to haul himself out half on top of the bobbing, rolling beast. "Hold my legs, Desmond."

Even though he had managed to reach inside, the night was nigh as black as a boot, and even a tiny glim candle was right out of the question; too much gunpowder, and too many damned French patrols! He stuck one arm down inside, fumbled about, and found the clockwork mechanism. The only hand, the minute hand, was straight up at "midnight." Lewrie gently pushed it down to what felt like a quarter past. Oops! As the cutter and torpedo bobbed opposed to each other, he had to fiddle some more to make sure that he hadn't pushed the hand down too far! Now, where were the two trigger lines? He found them, drew them to their full lengths, and pulled his arm clear.

God, forgive a sinner! he prayed, then jerked them both, hard.

Both mechanisms sounded off together, making him gasp in fright; there was a hellish *clank!* as the fire-lock on the pistol drew back to full cock, and a bladder-emptying *whirr-tick!* as the snugly wound clock began to function. After a few panting breaths to calm himself—and realise that he *hadn't* been blown to atoms!—Lewrie coiled up those lines and dropped them to a far corner of the torpedo's interior.

"Right, Furfy. Hand me the bung, again," he bade. Sliding just a bit more into the cutter, he carefully placed it atop the torpedo's top, rattled it round into the hole, and tried to push it back down.

"Christ on a crutch! Mine arse on a bloody *band-box*, it won't seat!" Lewrie spat. Had it swelled in the few minutes it had been out? The tompion was only halfway home, and the priming and the powder in the pistol barrel which fired the larger charge would be soaked as the torpedo bobbed its way inshore, with the chop sloshing over it!

"Hand me an oar, somebody. I'll have t'hammer it home!"

Every sailor in the boat croaked, taking in great gasps of air! Someone—it might have been the bow man—let out a wee whimper!

But they passed him an oar, which he shortened up on as he slid back into the cutter, feeling an immense sense of relief, it must here be noted!

He turned the loom of the oar flat to the tompion, lifted it, then gave it a couple of hard whacks.

"Our Father, who art in Heaven, hallowed be . . . !"

"Does it look flush yet, Desmond?" Lewrie asked.

"Oh, flush'z yer dinin' table, sor, *aye*!" Desmond whinnied, seconded by a chorus of hearty agreement from the rest.

"I don't know . . . ," Lewrie speculated, using the loom of the oar to prod the rim of the tompion; if it slid smooth, that was fine, but . . . he reckoned there might be an inch to go for sure water-tightness.

Well, it ain't gone bang yet, so . . . , he thought, rising to stand in the boat, with Furfy clinging to his legs to steady him; or cringe in terror. Lewrie slammed the oar down on the tompion one more time, much harder, causing a deep empty-barrel thud from the torpedo, a thud that sounded very much like *Doom!* Several sailors stuck fingers in their ears and squinted their eyes tight shut!

"Look flush now, Desmond?" he asked again.

"I, ah . . . wouldn't know, sor," Desmond croaked.

"Wouldn't want water gettin' in and ruinin' it, right?"

"Perish th' fackin' thought, sor!" Desmond assured him.

"That should do it, I think," Lewrie decided, passing the borrowed oar back forward. "Let's free the gaff and the tow-line and get away from it. Bugger the bayonets. Just toss 'em over and get a way on."

Only the forward-most larboard oarsmen could get their oars in the water, whilst the starboard-side rowers were free to work. The tow-line was tossed free, and the cutter began to move again.

"It's followin' us!" someone cried.

With only the full bank of starboard oars at work, the cutter was circling round to its left despite Desmond holding the tiller hard over to larboard to steer away; they were circling the torpedo, and it was still right alongside!

"We're spiked to it!" Furfy pointed out, most anxiously.

"Must've spun about and stuck a bayonet into the hull," Lewrie said, hoping that MacTavish had spent a *goodly* sum on his clocks! "Get us free. Gaff, here! Shove the bastard off!"

"Un-screw the bayonet from the barrel stub!" another suggested.

"Won't come free! Th' bitch's rollin' too much t'get a grip!"

"Arms and legs, over the side and push, lads!" Lewrie snapped. "Heave, heave, heave!"

" 'At done it, sir!"

The torpedo at last drifted a few more feet away, bobbing like a gigantic cork, the lights from the town and anchored invasion boats glinting off its painted top and steel grapnels and bayonet blades.

"Ain't natural . . .'tis Devil's work, them things!" a sailor whispered to his mate as they got both banks of oars working in unison and made their escape. Lewrie opened his pocket compass and held it close to his face but could not quite read it. On the way in, before they had left *Fusee*, the course had been Sou'-Sou'east, and the reciprocal to take them back near the converted bomb vessel *should* be Nor'-Nor'west, but . . . he looked astern to the lights of St. Valery and Le Crotoy. "Keep the towns on our starboard quarter, Desmond, and that'll take us somewhere near *Fusee*."

"Aye, sor," Liam Desmond replied with a firm mutter and a nod. Now they were getting away from their infernal device, he sounded in much calmer takings. By the faint whispers and brief flashes of his sailors' teeth, the cutter's crew seemed much relieved, too, some even uttering very soft laughter.

Jesus, what a shitten mess! Lewrie thought, letting out a sigh, relaxing himself, falling into an exhausted lassitude. That happened to him, now and then, at the conclusion of battle aboard ship, or the end of a person-to-person fight with his sword; the intensely keen concentration at either left him so spent of a sudden that he sometimes needed a good sit-down to regain his strength, and his wits. Lewrie shook himself back to full awareness, and groped round the sole of the cutter for his hat. It was soaked, of course, and trampled into ruin, but he clapped it back on his head.

And what was the time when the damned clock began to run? he suddenly thought; *You bloody* fool, *ye didn't note it! How'll I know if the bastard blows up on time? Shit, shit, shit!*

"Coffee, sir?" Lt. Johns's cabin steward offered.

"Aye, more than welcome," Lewrie replied, accepting a battered pewter mug of scalding-hot black coffee, waving off the further offer of goat's milk or sugar. They had found *Fusee* by steering blind 'til espying the long, irregular skirt of foam breaking round the anchored bomb's waterline. MacTavish and Midshipman Frederick had come along a few minutes later, and lastly, Lt. Merriman's cutter had approached, coming alongside to starboard, having steered too wide and to seaward for a time.

"Cup for you, too, sir?" the steward offered Merriman.

"God, yes!" the cheerful Merriman (so aptly named) answered.

"Four minutes by my reckoning, for mine, McCloud!" the inventor, MacTavish, said to his artificer in a loud whisper.

"Pardon, sir, but, did you have any trouble with yours?" Lieutenant Merriman softly asked Lewrie. "Mine was a total bastard."

"A complete shambles, aye," Lewrie muttered back, "gettin' it alongside with all those bloody bayonets, gettin' the tompion out, and fumblin' in the dark, then gettin' the bung back *in*? We got spiked to the damned thing for a bit, too."

"Aye, sir. I can't see *how* the torpedoes can be managed in the dark. And, if we launch them in daylight, it will have to be done so close inshore that the French shore guns and gunboats shoot us all to flinders," Lt. Merriman told him, shaking his head. "I don't know . . ."

"Launchin' 'em by the dozens," Lewrie muttered back. "I can't picture our sailors gettin' it done right, night *or* day. They're too damned complicated t'set and prime."

"About time, gentlemen! It's about time!" MacTavish enthused, drawing all participants, officers and sailors, to the bulwarks to peer shoreward. That was anti-climactic, though, for at least three more minutes passed before the first explosion.

There was a distant and dull *Boom!* as a torpedo at last went off, shooting a geyser of spray and foam into the air, and sounding no louder than the slam of an iron oven door. And much further out to sea than the tide should have taken it, according to MacTavish's last-minute estimations. It had not gone much more than half a mile.

"Hmmm, I'd have thought . . . ," MacTavish fretted, then drew out a sheaf of papers from his coat and tried to decypher them in the dark.

Even more long minutes passed before the second torpedo burst, and they almost missed that one, for though this one *had* drifted in to roughly the proper distance to reach a trot of *caïques*, the geyser of spray, foam, and gunpowder smoke looked little taller than the splash of a 32-pound shot dapping along from its First Graze, and the sound of its expected titanic explosion was little more than a *fumph!*

"Not all the charge went off?" Lt. Johns said, crushed. "How could that be?"

"*Someone* was remiss as to snugly replacing the tompion, and the sea got in," Mr. MacTavish accused.

Mine, most-like? Lewrie sheepishly thought, but would not allow that to stand.

"If seawater got to the pistol's priming or powder charge, it wouldn't have gone off at all, Mister MacTavish," Lewrie told him. "I expect it was the main charge below that got soaked, somehow, and went off like a squib."

"Th' casks're tighter'n a drum, an' *tested* fair leaks, sair!" McCloud the artificer bristled back, twitching his jaws so hard that his scraggly beard rustled. "Paid ower weet tar an' bound in tarred canvas. They *canna* leak!"

"Evidently that'un did, Mister McCloud," Lewrie rejoined. "Or, being stored at sea for a week or so, the damp got to the gunpowder."

"Two to go, though, gentlemen. All's not lost, yet!" MacTavish insisted.

But the trial evidently *was* over, for after a full hour waiting for the other two to explode, long past the time when they had been set to go off, there were no more geysers or bangs.

"I don't understand," MacTavish said, bewildered. "According to my calculations . . . ! I am certain that I prepared *mine* properly, if no one *else* managed to follow such simple instructions . . . !"

"Let's get under way, Mister Johns," Lewrie ordered, yawning. "I'm amazed the French haven't found us, yet, and we must be clear of the coast by dawn."

"Aye, sir," a crest-fallen Lt. Johns agreed.

"There's still two to go, I must point out to you, sir!" Mister MacTavish peevishly demanded. "There's still darkness!"

"Ain't in the cards, Mister MacTavish, not tonight it ain't," Lewrie told him. "I'm charged with keeping you two, your torpedoes, and anyone involved with 'em, out of French hands, and we've pressed our luck as far as I think it seemly t'go, tonight. We're off."

And I need some bloody sleep! Lewrie told himself.

CHAPTER THIRTY-ONE

*T*he morning after their assault on the mouth of the Somme river, *Reliant* and *Fusee* were forced to return to Sheerness. Lt. Johns had made an inspection of the remaining torpedoes and found that their clockwork timer's inner workings were so corroded by salt-air damp that they would not run; likewise for the fire-locks of the igniting pistols. A lack of mineral oil to protect them from rusting would have guaranteed a failure. In private, Lt. Johns had also confided to Lewrie that both the clocks and the pistols were of the cheapest manufacture, cast-offs or rejects of such low quality that they appeared to be the first failed efforts of new apprentices. "Trust Scots to pinch and bemoan a *groat*, sir, a penny bedamned," Johns had muttered, most sadly disappointed.

MacTavish and McCloud, he'd also reported, had gone off on each other, each blaming the other for the failures, and the artificer sent off in a huff, sacked from his position. MacTavish would have to see to the construction of new torpedoes himself, find a new artificer to oversee the work, and most definitely not spare HM Government's money this time on the timers or pistols!

Lewrie had begun his report to Admiralty the morning after the trials off the Somme, and completed it just before *Reliant* had come to anchor in the Great Nore. He dis-passionately described the complicated method of priming and activating, the difficulty with the tompion and the use of them in the total dark, along with the risks involved if deployed during the day; the shoddy materials used in the first place, and the great risk of damp getting to the powder no matter how snugly the torpedoes were sealed, due to being stored above-decks exposed to weather, then slung over the side and towed long distances all but submerged. It was no way to treat gunpowder, if one wished it to stay dry and go *Bang!*

His clerk and one of his Mids with a good copper-plate writing had made copies, one for MacTavish. Lewrie expected he would hear the fellow's screeches all the way down-river from Woolwich once he read *his* copy!

In the meantime, though . . .

"Excuse me, sir, but I wonder if I might have a word?"

"Aye, Mister Merriman?" Lewrie said, looking up from his stroll of *Reliant*'s quarterdeck to savour the Summer sunshine.

"It's about the torpedoes, sir," Lt. Merriman began.

"*Those* bastards!" Lewrie said with a dismissive snort.

"Indeed, sir," Merriman said with a wry grin of agreement. "I and Mister Westcott were talking things over last night, and we were wondering if there would be any more trials with them. If so, we think we've come up with a way to improve them. Sea-anchors, sir!"

"Sea-anchors?"

"One uses a sea-anchor to keep a ship's head to wind in stormy weather, but . . . was a sea-anchor used in a strong tideway, would not a drogue *pull* the torpedo shoreward faster? Just bobbing about like they did, we had to get within a mile, with the timer set for fourty-five minutes, but . . . if we could launch from farther out, we could almost do it in daylight, and be out of range of most shore guns," Lt. Merriman said, bubbling over with enthusiasm.

"Might as well put a mast and a lugs'l on 'em, sir," Lewrie rejoined, feeling gloomy of a sudden to imagine that there *would* be one more round of trials with the damned things! "Or, just shove tons of powder into a fireship and let it *sail* itself in."

"The First Lieutenant brought the idea up, too, sir," Merriman replied, falling alongside of Lewrie's in-board side as he paced aft to the taffrails. "If the drogues won't improve the torpedoes, then perhaps a *small* fireship, a fire-*boat*, might serve the purpose."

"There's the problem of damp, though," Lewrie pointed out.

"Aye, sir, and on that head we asked Mister Mainwaring the Surgeon if he knew of any earth or element that would absorb damp," Lieutenant Merriman rushed on, all eagerness. "He cited sodium chloride, sir . . . whatever that is."

"Fire-boats . . . as in *ship's* boats, Mister Merriman?" Lewrie asked, pausing in mid-stride.

"Exactly so, sir! Every dockyard's full of them, or they can be readily bought," Lt. Merriman continued. "One could place a floor above the ribs and keels, a bulkhead forward in the bows, and deck it all over, with just a cuddy to allow for setting the timer and priming the pistol igniter just before the crew abandons it. Perhaps even construct interior beam partitions to form a box cabin which would secure the powder charge, sir? Fill the voids between the hull and partitions with this sodium chloride whatever to soak up the damp, perhaps even line the entire box with tin, or lead, or . . . something . . . to keep it all dry, and a cheaply purchased fire-boat could sail in under its *own* power. Why, they might not even *have* to be set alight, and could sail in in the night with the French none the wiser 'til they explode . . . and a cutter or barge could carry a lot more gunpowder than one of the cask torpedoes, sir!"

"You've sketches, Mister Merriman?" Lewrie asked, beginning to be intrigued. *Anything* would beat MacTavish's casks all hollow!

"Uhm, Mister Westcott said he would essay a sketch or two, sir," Merriman explained. "He did not wish to present them to you 'til he and I were perfectly satisfied, but he also said that I should speak to you about the possibility."

"Hidin' his light under a bushel basket, is he?" Lewrie japed.

"Well, sir, if our idea seems plausible, Mister Westcott thought that the fire-boats should be deemed as secret as the torpedoes, hence we should show them to no one else but you, for now, sir," Lieutenant Merriman said in a more guarded way.

"When you and the First Officer deem 'em ready, bring 'em aft to the great-cabins, Mister Merriman," Lewrie told him. "And mum's the word 'til then. Carry on."

"Aye aye, sir," Merriman said, doffing his hat in salute.

Gawd, another *daft idea!* Lewrie thought once Merriman had gone; *Even* more *gunpowder . . . a ton or so? Brr! Still . . . an explosive boat doesn't depend on the tide alone. Lash the tiller and it'll steer itself. I wonder . . .*

He heaved a sigh, realising that if Admiralty found Westcott's and Merriman's concept practical, both officers might be sent off to develop the boats, costing him two damned competent men. If he wrote too en-thusiastically, Admiralty might even think *him* clever enough to oversee the project and take *Reliant* away from him and give him a shore post at some dockyard!

Admiralty thinkin' me clever? Lewrie scoffed, though; *That'll be a cold day in Hell! I'd fight that, even did "all night in" with Lydia come attached!*

It was mid-afternoon before Lewrie heard back from Lieutenants West-cott and Merriman, and he was, in point of fact, writing a letter to Lydia Stangbourne and looking forward to a good nap once that was done and sent ashore to be posted—in emulation of his cats—when his Marine sen-try loudly announced their arrival. "Come!" he bade, and Westcott and Merriman trooped in, cocked hats under their arms and a packet of draw-ings in their hands, carefully rolled up and bound with twine to guard against their contents being revealed prematurely.

"Tea for all, Pettus, and then take yourself a long idle hour or so on deck," Lewrie called out. Pettus poured them all tumblers of Lewrie's pat-ented cool tea from a pitcher, set out lemon slices and a sugar bowl, then departed, taking wee Jessop with him.

"Quite refreshing, sir, thank you," Westcott said after a sip.

"What have you come up with, then?" Lewrie pressed, shifting with some eagerness in his chair as they sat round his dining table. "If it ain't torpedoes, it's welcome."

"Oh, aye, sir!" Lt. Westcott laughed, baring, his teeth in a wide grin. He un-did the knots in the twine and un-rolled a short stack of folio-sized sheets. "The first, sir, is the overall outer design with ends, overhead, and beam views. Mister Merriman and I reckon that we'd need at least a twenty-five-foot cutter to get the job done, though a thirty-two-foot barge could carry more sail on its two masts, and more gunpowder, depending . . ."

"On how big a bang you wish, sir!" Merriman finished for his compan-ion, with a laugh. "You'll note, sir, that the decking-over to keep the pow-der charge safe from spray and slop is slightly arched. To channel a heavy sea off like water off a duck's back."

"How'd the sailors hoist sail, then, if it's arched?" Lewrie puzzled, frowning over the drawing, which was as fine and detailed as any he'd seen in a dockyard office. "Wouldn't *they* slide over the side, *with* the water?"

"Ah, you'll note that the decking ends just inside the gunn'ls, and two inches below them, sir," Lt. Westcott explained with another grin. "So the cap-rail of the gunn'l forms a low rail to brace their feet as they tend the sheets and halliards."

"Uh-hum!" was Lewrie's comment to that thoughtful provision. It appeared that his two Lieutenants had given the matter more thought than the recently departed and un-lamented Mr. MacTavish had his casks.

"The decking-over extends right aft, almost to the stern-sheets, sir," Merriman said, taking up the explanation of the plans. "There's the cuddy-like hatch to allow access to the box cabin, through which the powder kegs will be loaded, and the clockworks and pistol can be set." He used a pencil to tap the pertinent parts.

"That way, sir, the kegs could be kept dry and safe from accidental discharge in the tender's magazines 'til needed," Lt. Westcott added. "Now, the next sheet, sir, depicts the interior appointments, and the lining and beam partitions to hold the dessicant."

"Dessicant?" Lewrie puzzled.

"That's Mister Mainwaring's 'break-teeth' word for blocks, bags, of sodium chloride . . . *salt*, sir!" Merriman said, chuckling. "*Very* scientific, that, for stuff that'll soak up humidity and any leaks."

"There's another . . . humidity," Westcott stuck in, winking.

"See how much we're learnin'?" Lewrie japed right back.

Damned if the interior sketches were not merely fine builders' plans, but they had done three-quarter-view drawings, too, shaded in varying tones of light and dark, as meticulous as a wood-cut illustration printed in a reference book, or a serious newspaper article!

"I did not know that you two were such talented artists," Lewrie praised them, leaning far over the table to admire their work.

"Well, sir, the rough preliminary sketches were my work, but Mister Westcott is the real draughtsman," Merriman confessed.

"Indeed he is!" Lewrie exclaimed, leaning back. "I once asked if he was musical, and when he said 'no' I assumed his true talent lay in seafaring."

And women, Lewrie reminded himself; *most definitely women!*

"But, I s'pose we all have our side-lines t'keep us occupied in our off-watch hours," Lewrie went on.

"Thank you, sir," Lt. Westcott said, grinning and bowing at the waist whilst seated. "George here, though, wrote the proposal, and I dare say that you will find it equally meritorious, Captain. Merriman has a way with words."

"It's included, sir," Merriman said, almost shyly.

"I look forward t'readin' it," Lewrie said. "But, once cocked and all, what happens to the boat's crew . . . and how many men?"

"As to the second sir, if I may, we estimate that only one Midshipman would be required to command and steer the boat in, sir," Lt. Merriman replied, shifting in his chair to scoot closer. "Each of the boats would need two hands to tend the sails, then spell the Mid for as long as it would take for him to start the timer and cock the pistol, then . . . as to the first matter, sir, we envision that each explosive boat would need a gig or jolly-boat to trail it in, then take off the crew . . . once the tiller is lashed and the sails trimmed for the last time," Lt. Merriman explained. "Though it is possible that if a flotilla of boats are launched, only three or four oared and masted barges could recover all the hands from a round dozen."

"A Lieutenant or two to command overall, sir, and take charge of the recovery boats," Lt. Westcott added with a shrug.

"Um-hmm!" Lewrie said in appreciation, looking up at the overhead and deck beams for a moment. "Given the risk of losing the both of you to this proposal, should Admiralty approve it, it must be sent on to them at once. Secretly, but speedily. I'll read the proposal this evening, then call upon the dockyard Commissioner, first thing in the morning, to have the drawings and all forwarded to London by the fastest, most secure courier . . . along with my own strong recommendation for the plan's urgent consideration.

"What bloody good *my* backin'd do, well . . . ," Lewrie scoffed as he patted his hair and tossed his shoulders and hands up in a shrug of his own. "At least we'll get it put forward and see what they'll make of it, one way or the other."

"All we ask, sir!" Merriman enthused.

"Thank you for approving, sir," Lt. Westcott seconded. "We're sure that this is a much more useful idea than what we've seen so far."

"Good God, Mister Westcott!" Lewrie barked in amusement. "What *ain't?* And, congratulate Mister Mainwaring on his jape about . . . salt!"

CHAPTER THIRTY-TWO

*R*eliant spent another two idle days anchored in the Great Nore with no orders, and Lewrie was just about to let the ship be put "Out of Discipline" for forty-eight hours when another grim-faced Admiralty courier turned up with a fresh set of sealed orders, marked "Captain's Eyes Only." He signed for them, bade the courier a good journey back to London, then went aft and below to read them.

"Good God, who do I have to murder t'get out o' this?" Lewrie gravelled once he'd opened the be-ribboned and wax-sealed packet. He was "required and directed to make the best of his way" to Portsmouth Dockyard for further . . . "trials." This set of orders was even shorter and more enigmatic than those that had preceded the trials with the cask torpedoes. Evidently, people at Admiralty worried that letters of too verbose or revealing nature could be intercepted by French agents in England, or treasonous Britons in their employ.

There was a second one-sheet letter from the Honourable Henry Legge, a fellow billed as Commissioner Without Special Functions, a title new to Lewrie; that'un was just bloody galling!

"'. . . choice of Mersea Island and the Blackwater River estuary an imbecilic choice, resulting in wide-spread panic among His Majesty's subjects' . . . ye didn't tell us *where* t'try 'em out in the first place, ye nit-pickin' . . . !" Lewrie fumed under his breath. "'. . . had the cask torpedoes functioned as designed in your rash and precipitate attack upon the French invasion fleet then gathered at the mouth of the Somme the nature of future attacks *en masse* would have been revealed to the foe prematurely, as would the existence of said torpedoes, which the Lords Commissioners for executing the High Office of Admiralty severely and strictly charged you to protect at all hazards!' "

"Ye *said* t'try 'em out on the Frogs, damn yer blood!" Lewrie spat. "*Somebody's* tryin' t'cover his arse!"

He opened his desk to fetch out the original set; there it was in black-and-white, as plain as the canvas deck chequer. He was to conduct trial implementation of the damned things against French harbours and gatherings of invasion craft!

" 'Due to the extremely secret nature of the devices, it is not feasible *at this time* to warrant formal charges laid against you,' at this *time?*" Lewrie gawped. They'd considered hauling him before a court-martial board for doing what he'd been *ordered* to do in the first place?

" 'Upon reading, you will destroy this letter and your previous orders to prevent any knowledge of the devices' existence, and upon arrival at Portsmouth you will turn over your latest set of orders directing you there to continue trials to the Port Admiral for his safekeeping'? The bloody Hell I will," Lewrie agrily whispered, rolling them all up into a tight cylinder and re-wrapping them with the ribbons attached. He shoved them to the back of the lowest locking drawer in his desk, sure that he might need to present them if a time came when the torpedoes were perfected and used in mass attacks, the secret would be out, and they *could* put him to court-martial!

"Damn 'em all," Lewrie grumbled, then took a deep breath before donning his coat and hat and going on deck. The First Officer, Mister Westcott, was by the first larboard 9-pounder on the quarterdeck in his shirt sleeves, a sketch pad and a charcoal stick in his hands, chatting with the Purser, Mr. Cadbury, who was seated upon a second 9-pounder's breech-end, mumbling to himself as he balanced his books in the fresh air and mild mid-morning sunshine. "Good morning, Mister Westcott."

"Good morning, sir," Lt. Westcott replied, abandoning his artwork.

"May I see? Damme, but for the lack of colour, that's *Reliant* to the life," Lewrie commented. "Is the ship ready for sea in every respect, Mister Westcott?"

"Well, aye, sir," Westcott replied, looking puzzled.

"There are a few items to come aboard from the dockyard and the chandlers, sir," the Purser stuck in with a worried look on his face.

"Paid for, or promised, Mister Cadbury?" Lewrie asked.

"On order, sir, but not yet paid for," the Purser replied.

"You can make up the lacks from Portsmouth sources," Lewrie said. "We're ordered there, instanter. I see the winds are from the West."

"Roughly, sir, aye," Westcott said, looking up at the commissioning pendant atop the main-mast, then taking a quick squint about the harbour. "We do have a working-party ashore, though, Captain."

"Recall them at once, stow away whatever it is they're there for, then get the ship under way by Noon," Lewrie ordered.

Paying off from the winds once the anchors were up would be an easy chore, as would the long starboard-quarter slant out to sea. To turn roughly West-Sou'west to make passage to Portsmouth, though . . . that would be a long, hard slog almost into the teeth of the winds and take at least a day more, with a night spent standing "off and on" the coast 'til it was light enough to attempt an approach into port.

"I'll see to it directly, sir!" Westcott vowed.

In his best uniform, with sash and star of his knighthood, and the Cape St. Vincent and Camperdown medals round his neck, Lewrie reported to Admiral Lord Gardner ashore . . . with some trepidation, it must be admitted, since Lord Gardner was reputed to be a dyspeptic and irascible officer of some age, a tetchy man who did not suffer fools at *all* gladly, and, Lewrie had heard, some described him as "composed of paper and packthread, stay tape and buckram," for his over-attention to every little detail, no matter how niggling. Lewrie was forced to sit and wait in the great man's ante-room for an hour before being allowed an audience.

"And you are *who*, sir?" Admiral Lord Gardner testily enquired as he gave Lewrie an up-and-down inspection.

"Captain Sir Alan Lewrie, my lord, the *Reliant* frigate. I was ordered to Portsmouth and told to deliver my orders for transfer from Sheerness to you for safekeeping," Lewrie replied.

"You waste my time with this, sir?" Lord Gardner snapped. "Most pop-in-jay captains announce their arrival to me by letter!"

"Uhm, it's a matter of secrecy, my lord . . . concerning trials of certain, ah . . . devices?" Lewrie tried to hint.

"What sort of devices?" Gardner sourly demanded. "Secret, you say?"

"Well, my lord . . . if you have not been told of them, I cannot dsecribe them to you," Lewrie answered. "No one not engaged with them is to be allowed to—"

"*Bedamned* if you cannot, sir! What sort of foolishness is this tripe? Niles? . . . Niles! Come here at once, I say! There's a lunatick in my office ravin' about secret devices!" Gardner erupted, then hailed for an aide. At the top of his lungs, too,

Might as well give it to the town criers, too! Lewrie thought with a wince; *Yoo-hoo! Frog spies! Harkee t'this!*

A door to a side office adjoining opened and a genial-looking Post-Captain who looked to be in his early fifties entered, his brows up in query. "You called, my lord?"

"*This* imbecile . . . what the Devil's your name again? This officer claims he's ordered to give *me* his transfer order to keep it secret, and goes on about *devices*!" Lord Gardner ranted.

"Alan Lewrie, sir," Lewrie offered, hoping that this new fellow knew more than his superior. "The *Reliant* frigate?"

"Guessin' the name of your own ship, sir?" Lord Gardner sneered.

"Lewrie, Lewrie, Lewrie," the Post-Captain muttered, "*Reliant,* aha!" he concluded with a snap of his fingers. "May I see them, sir?"

Lewrie handed his orders over whilst the newcomer hummed a gay tune under his breath as he read them.

"Sir Alan, sir," the Post-Captain said at last, stepping up to offer his hand. "George Niles, Flag-Captain, and your servant, sir."

"And I am yours, Captain Niles," Lewrie responded in kind.

"'Fraid he's the right of it, my lord," Captain Niles told his superior. "Those infernal things built at Gosport? Captain Lewrie's the goat charged with their testing, and Admiralty *does* wish us to see that his orders are kept safe, lest Bonaparte get the slightest inkling of their existence. All very 'mum's the word.'"

"Then why could he not just *say* so?" Lord Gardner snapped.

"I expect he's cautioned to not say a thing about them to anyone not aware of them to begin with, my lord," Captain Niles jovially informed the Port Admiral. "The fewer in on the things, the less odds that someone would blab, my lord."

"Does Admiralty not trust *me*, Niles?" Lord Gardner yelped, still wroth and in high dudgeon.

"Merely 'need to know,' my lord," Captain Niles pooh-poohed to calm the fellow. "I'll see to Captain Lewrie, if I may, sir. There are his orders, here, to file away . . . more like *squirrel* away? If you will come into my office, sir, I do believe there are separate orders specific to your ah, mysterious duties."

"Thank you for rescuing me, sir," Lewrie told Niles once they were in his side office with the door closed on the Port Admiral's.

"His bark is much worse than his bite, Sir Alan," Captain Niles told him with a sly grin. "Unless one *deserves* a nipping, and then he *can* latch on like a bulldog and gnaw a limb or two right off, ha ha! Yes, I have them here, sir. 'Captain's Eyes Only,' and all that nonsense. Here you are, sir."

Lewrie took the folded-over, wax-sealed, and ribbon-bound letter from Niles, which was also marked "Most Secret and Confidential" in bold writing.

"Do *you* know what it's about, sir?" Lewrie dubiously asked.

"Even if I did, I'd forget it the moment you leave my office, Sir Alan," Niles said, chuckling. "I will admit to curiosity, though. You are not the first officer to call upon us with secret orders waiting for him, you know. The other fellow, Captain . . . well, I gather you and he are to work together on whatever it is that Our Lords Commissioners deem so vital. Mind, I forgot him and *his* packet as soon as *he* left my office, too, ha ha!"

"Then I shall be on my way at once, Captain Niles, so you may forget my arrival, as well!" Lewrie japed.

"Goodbye, then, Captain 'Whoever,' and good fortune," Niles said with another sly look and a glad hand.

Lewrie was back aboard *Reliant* just a tick before 11 of the morning, and got himself comfortable before opening his newest set of sealed and secret orders. With a tumbler of cool tea with lemon juice and sugar near to hand, he broke the seal and read them.

They were much like the first when he'd learned of those cask torpedoes; he was required to take upon the charge and command of the trials, to serve as escort and guardian of the hired-in-for-the-purpose collier *Penarth*, commanded by one Lieutenant Douglas Clough . . .

"*Penarth* . . . ain't that Welsh?" he puzzled with a frown. "Sure t'be, if she's in the coastal coal trade. And this Douglas Clough? A Scot? Lord, I hope he's better than the last two. I *think* Penarth is close t'Cardiff. 'Aid to the best of your abilities the officer placed in charge of the trials' . . . no, it *can't* be!"

"Midshipman Grainger, *sah*!" the Marine sentry bellowed.

"Enter," Lewrie bade, quickly stowing away his letter.

"Captain, sir, there is a boat coming alongside, with a Post-Captain aboard," Mr. Grainger told him. "The First Officer has been alerted, and the side-party mustered."

"I will come on deck, Mister Grainger, thankee," Lewrie said, already almost sure who it was that had come calling.

He arrived on the quarterdeck, standing near the beginning of the starboard sail-tending gangway and the entry-port, waiting to see if his suspicions were true. As the upper tip of the standing "dog's vane" on the caller's hat peeked over the lip of the entry-port, the bosun's calls began to tweedle, the hastily gathered Marines and sailors saluted, and a grim, jowly face emerged beneath the hat, then the upper body of a stocky, paunchy Post-Captain who wore his own hair in a grey fluff either side of his ears, with a long old-style seaman's queue over the back collar of his coat.

"Cap'm Joseph Speaks . . . come aboard to speak with your Captain Lewrie," the fellow announced in a loud voice as he doffed his cocked hat to one and all, scowling or grimacing most un-congenially.

"Welcome aboard *Reliant*, sir," Lt. Westcott rejoined.

"Welcome, Captain Speaks," Lewrie seconded, stepping forward with his own hat lifted. *So that's what he looks like*, he thought.

"Cap'm Lewrie?" Speaks said, taut-lipped, drawing out "Lewrie" a second time as if in disgust.

"Aye, sir," Lewrie replied, bland-faced.

"Where in the Hell are my bloody iron stoves?" Speaks barked.

CHAPTER THIRTY-THREE

*H*onest t'God, sir, that's the last I saw of 'em," Lewrie told the older fellow as they sat in *Reliant*'s great-cabins with a pitcher of cool tea before them on the low brass Hindoo tray table before the starboard-side settee. "What Pridemore did with 'em's *his* doin', and I haven't a clue where he, or the stoves, are now."

"*Thermopylae* was sent off to the East Indies last May when the war started up again," Captain Speaks gravelled, "and Pridemore, one of her Standing Officers, went with her. What the Devil anyone would need heating stoves in Calcutta or 'Sweatypore' boggles the mind, but *someone* owes me for them," he doggedly insisted.

"It's possible that Pridemore leased a couple to the Standing Officers of other laid-up ships, sir," Lewrie speculated, "or sold 'em outright, expectin' that you'd not recover? They could've gone to a scrap-iron monger, or the dockyard offices, on the sly, but I . . . you *have* been in touch with my solicitor in London, Mister Mountjoy?"

"All stand-offish petti-fogging and legalese," Captain Speaks said, almost snarling. "Look here, sir . . . we can settle this like gentlemen. They're worth fifty pounds each on today's market. . . ."

"They were worth thirty-five pounds when you bought 'em, sir," Lewrie gently objected, sure he was getting gouged.

"Noted there's a war on, sir?" Speaks snapped back. "The price of

261

iron's up, and civilian iron goods are in shorter supply, so did I wish to replace them, that's the going price. You give me a note-of-hand for two hundred pounds, and we'll call it quits, and it'll be up to you to redeem the sum from that sharp-practiced 'Nip-Cheese' Pridemore. Sue *him* in a Court of Common Pleas!"

I am *bein' gouged!* Lewrie felt like yelping.

"And how's your parrot, sir?" Lewrie asked instead, to delay his agreement, which he would *have* to make. "Still gabbin' away?"

"Hellish-fine, and of no matter, sir!" Captain Speaks rejoined. "I hate to state it this way, Captain Lewrie, but I am senior to you by five years on the Navy List, and your immediate superior in this endeavour with the torpedoes, so consider how much better we will rub along with each other with the debt settled . . . without my having to take *you* to Common Pleas, hey?"

"But it wasn't my fault!" Lewrie insisted, immediately thinking how lame that sounded, as if he was back at a school from which he was not *yet* expelled.

"You trusted the wrong person, and yes, it is," Speaks growled.

"Oh, very well," Lewrie said after a long moment and a great, resigned sigh. He could afford it, after all; it wasn't like the loss of two hundred pounds would leave him "skint." He took a long sip of cool tea to slake a suddenly-parched throat, rose, and went over to his desk to scribble out a note-of-hand to Speaks. "You'll still have to send this on to Mountjoy, in London. He's my shore agent and estate agent," he told the testy older fellow. "There's not a jobber who'll give you full value in Portsmouth . . . they're all retired Pursers," he wryly japed. He fully expected that Speaks would hand his note to a local banking house, get his money in full, then *they* would send the thing on to Mountjoy, who'd turn it in to his bankers at Coutts', and everyone would be square. "Here you are, sir," he said as he returned to the settee. Captain Speaks took it, squinted hard at it as if suspecting a ruse, then grunted, nodded in satisfaction, and shoved it into a side pocket of his uniform coat.

"You'd done that at the very beginning, Captain Lewrie, and we would have each saved a pretty penny on stationery and postage," the heavyset chap commented, baring his teeth for a moment in a triumphant grin. "Now, sir . . . you know what a torpedo is?"

"We've just finished a round of trials with cask torpedoes, as designed by a Mister Cyrus MacTavish, sir," Lewrie told him. "And an awful waste o' time and materials they were."

"Good, then, you understand the basic concept," Speaks replied. "What we will deal with are *catamaran* torpedoes, a different kettle of fish, entirely."

"Catamarans," Lewrie said, sounding highly dubious. Catamarans were work-stages used alongside a ship's hull to scrub, clean, or paint, to tend to the maintenance of channel platforms, dead-eye blocks, and mast shrouds. They were little more than two great baulks of timber for buoyancy, with planking nailed across them.

"Much bigger than the casks of which you speak, sir, and with much more powder aboard than that upstart American, Mister Fulton's, copper sphere torpedoes," Speaks informed him. "That's why we've the *Penarth*. She's all sorts of capstans, windlasses, and standing jib-arms for unloading tons of coal in cargo nets at one go. She's an old and ugly bitch, but she'll suit my purposes. Our purposes, rather."

"What the Devil are *they* like, sir?" Lewrie enquired, hoping to get down to business and put the money out of mind; and that Captain Speaks would be fair-minded enough to consider the matter over and done as well. When he'd replaced him, *Thermopylae*'s officers and warrants had spoken highly of him, and his concern for the hands' welfare. The fellow was touted as the typical "firm but fair" sort.

"Are all your officers and Midshipmen aboard at this minute, Captain Lewrie?" Speaks asked, instead.

"All but my First, sir, Lieutenant Westcott," Lewrie told him.

"Damme! Recall him at once," Speaks ordered. "It'd be better were they all on hand for a demonstration, all together, so we do not have to go over it in dribs and drabs."

Westcott won't care for that, Lewrie thought with a tiny secret smirk; *He's most-like up to his ears in some chit's tits, by now. Did he leave his whereabouts? I can't recall.*

"I'll see to it, sir, though it may take some time to hunt him up," Lewrie said. "Lieutenant Westcott said he had relatives down from home, and may be showin' them the sights." A fib, not a lie, that!

"No later than Four Bells of the Day Watch, then, Captain," Speaks demanded. "Or on your head be it, what?"

"Aye, sir," Lewrie answered, thinking that this sharp-tongued and impatient man was not *quite* the genial and easy-going Speaks that had earlier been advertised. "Faulkes?" Lewrie asked of his clerk. "Did Mister Westcott leave his shore address with you?"

"Yes, sir."

"Pass word for my boat crew, and go ashore and recall him. Do express my sincerest apologies, but he is needed back aboard at once."

"Yes, sir," Eaulkes replied, eager to get off the ship for two hours or so himself.

"Good taste in cabin furnishings, Lewrie," Captain Speaks said after Faulkes dashed out. "Quite . . . comfortable, I'd imagine."

That sounded like a back-handed condemnation, another way to say that Lewrie's great-cabins were a touch *too* fine, not the Spartan bare-bones indifference to personal comfort expected by the Navy.

"Thankee, sir," Lewrie said, watching Speaks rise and go aft towards the transom settee.

"You carry your *wife* aboard, sir?" Speaks asked, espying that wide-enough-for-two hanging bed-cot.

"I am a widower, sir . . . two years ago," Lewrie told him, with a slight dis-approving edge to his voice.

"Good God, are those cats?" Speaks further growled, spotting Toulon and Chalky, curled up together on the coverlet. "Mousers, I'd hope?"

"Passing-fair at it, sir, but mostly company," Lewrie replied. "You've your parrot, I've my cats. They're nigh mute, but amusing."

"I despise cats," Speaks huffed. "Can't abide them. Give me a good dog, now . . . that's another matter."

What else'll *he find fault with?* Lewrie sourly wondered.

"Your ship, sir!" Captain Speaks said, turning to face Lewrie. "When I came aboard she *looked* 'ship-shape and Bristol Fashion.'"

"We try t'keep her all 'tiddly,' sir," Lewrie blandly said. "I find that the French make that difficult, now and then."

"So much like my old *Thermopylae*," Captain Speaks said, seeming to mellow at the mention of his last command. "Of the same Rate, and weight of metal. You were at Copenhagen."

It sounded like a petulant accusation.

"Aye, sir."

"Got a chance to fight her," Speaks said with a grunt.

"We did, sir. And went up the Baltic to scout the state of the ice and enemy harbours on our own," Lewrie answered. "We rejoined the fleet the night before."

"Lost good Mister Ballard," Speaks sadly mused, pacing about the cabins as if they were his own. "Arthur was an excellent First Officer to me. Would have made a fine Captain, had he lived. I liked him very much. Though you didn't know him as long as I—"

"He was my First Officer in the *Alacrity* for three years, sir, in the Bahamas, 'tween the wars," Lewrie interrupted.

He goin' t'blame me for that, too? Lewrie angrily thought.

"I did not know," Speaks gruffly said. "Well, sir! Be sure to be aboard *Penarth* by Four Bells, and Lieutenant Clough and I will show you what we're to work with, and familiarise your people with the procedures."

"Very well, sir. I'll see you to the deck," Lewrie offered as he went for his hat, which he'd left on the dining table.

"No need, sir," Captain Speaks quickly said. "I might take one or two minutes to savour being aboard a frigate, again."

"You'd wish a brief tour, sir?" Lewrie asked.

"No, no, don't wish to bother your people," Speaks insisted.

"No bother at all, sir, and since I'm goin' on deck, too . . . ," Lewrie said, but Speaks was already halfway to the doors to the weather deck. He had to trot after him, then pass him as Speaks idled on the outer deck between the guns. Lewrie was at the top of the gangway by the break of the quarterdeck by the time Speaks made a slower way up the ladderway. "Side-party for departure honours, Mister Houghton," Lewrie ordered his senior Midshipman from the corner of his mouth.

Captain Speaks paused at the top of the ladderway, hands in the small of his back and gazing forward to the forecastle, taking in all the bustle of *Reliant*'s hands, the mathematical exactitude of all the yards and maze of rigging. Speaks heaved a deep sigh, which came out as a throat-clearing grunt, then became all business-like as he doffed his hat in departure. The bosun's calls tweedled, muskets and swords were presented to see him over the side, right to the last moment when the dog's vane of his hat dropped below the lip of the entry-port.

Poor old shit's jealous, by God! Lewrie told himself; *I have a command, and he don't . . . not a real'un.*

Captain Joseph Speaks would have recovered from his pneumonia by April of 1801, but Admiralty had not offered him another warship, and then the Peace of Amiens had *kept* him ashore on half-pay. Mid-May of last year had seen at least an hundred ships put back in commission, but . . . none of them were his, and when finally recalled to active service, what had he gotten? Not a frigate or warship commensurate with his seniority, but a *project*!

No wonder he's turned sour as crab-apples! Lewrie realised.

CHAPTER THIRTY-FOUR

*B*efore boarding one of *Reliant*'s cutters for the long row out to *Penarth*, Lewrie had time enough for a private moment with Lieutenant Westcott.

"Should Captain Speaks make mention of it, some of your family are down to Portsmouth to see you, Mister Westcott," Lewrie muttered to him. "Which took you ashore. He might have a 'down' on ye, else."

"Thank you for covering for me, sir," Westcott said with a wide grin, not one of his usual quick flashes.

"And was a good time had by all?" Lewrie japed, with a leer.

" 'All' *did*, sir," Lt. Westcott cheerfully confessed, "and we'd have had a better, had Faulkes not found me. The lady's most obliging and fetching, a recent widow of an apothecary. Sold up the business to another, but didn't manage to gain all *that* much security. Thank God she can still afford to send the son off to a schoolmaster . . . *with* his dinner pail. Hours and hours on her hands, alone, most days?"

And yours on her, Lewrie told himself, chuckling at the image.

"Whatever shall I *do* with you, Mister Westcott?" Lewrie teased.

"Swear I'm an abstinent and celibate Christian, should bully-bucks come and ask for me, sir!" Westcott rejoined. "And that I'm not here!"

· · ·

Penarth was a two-masted brig, fitted with shorter mast stubs to serve as crane supports, one aft of her foremast, the other forward of her main-mast, from which jib-arms could swing. She had much more freeboard than *Fusee*, the result of a much deeper hold for the coasting coal trade, and slab-sided, with none of the tumblehome designed into warships to reduce top-weight; her boarding battens were vertical, and a hard climb right *over* her bulwarks to an in-board set of steps, with no proper entry-port.

"Welcome aboard, sirs," her "captain" said. Lt. Douglas Clough was indeed a Scot, but without a Highland "sawney" accent. He was red-haired and pale-complexioned, though, his hair, when he doffed his hat, frizzy and tightly curly-wavy. Clough was an odd-looking bird, for his forehead receded at a pronounced slant from a heavily beetled ridge of brow, his large, stubby nose almost matching the angle of his head so that it appeared that they were one precipitous slope.

"Captain Speaks has spoken . . . has explained the nature of the cata-maran torpedo to you, sirs?" he asked.

"Only that they are a *form* of torpedo, sir," Lewrie said for all.

"Let's show them, Clough," Captain Speaks grunted.

"This way, sirs. We keep them in the hold, out of sight. Nice and dry 'til deployed. If you will all follow me?" Clough bade.

Someone had done some modification work on *Penarth* to lengthen her main midships hatchway, perhaps turning two into one, and removing some cross-deck bracing timbers. They clambered down yet another very steep ladder into the belowdeck gloom, lit only by a pair of lanthorns built like the light rooms found in a warship's powder magazines.

"Here they are, sirs," Lt. Clough proudly announced, pointing to two large boat-like objects, one to either side of a narrow aisle running fore-and-aft. The objects were covered with tarred canvas on the outside, taper-ing bluntly at either end, and put Lewrie in mind of gigantic *cigarros* of the same colour as aged tobacco leaf.

"What *are* they?" Midshipman Rossyngton wondered aloud.

"Catamaran torpedoes, young sir!" Captain Speaks snapped back.

"We've eight aboard at the moment," Lt. Clough explained. "Two here, two more forward on this temporary deck, and four more below in the lower hold. A catamaran torpedo is twenty-one and a half feet in length, much like a ship's boat in size, three and a half feet in beam. They taper to blunt ends, with a slight rise a'low and a rise aloft, ha ha! The main mid-section is basically a sealed wooden chest, with the interior lined with lead to make it water-proof, and all the seams soldered to prevent any leakage once they're in the water. They're flat on the bottom and the top, though they do have a slight curve to their sides."

"Much better than any creation but Fulton's copper spheres," Captain Speaks told them, as if they were his own idea.

"If they're sealed, sir, how does one manage to set the timer and cock the igniting pistol?" Lt. Merriman, who had had more experience than the others with such devices, enquired, clambering up onto a cradle in which one of the torpedoes sat for a closer look.

"See that stand-pipe in the top?" Clough pointed out. "There's a water-tight tompion at its mouth. When one removes the tompion, the starting lines are attached to it, and all one has to do is give both a good, hard yank, and one is in business, sir."

"Aye, we've dealt with that before, sir," Lt. Westcott said to their host, "but . . . how do you *set* the clock? You can't get a hand down that pipe."

"They're already set, sir," Clough replied with a confident grin. "Some for as short as fifteen minutes, some for half an hour. The pistols are loaded and primed, as well."

"Mean t'say, they're ready *t'go?*" Lewrie gawped, aghast, with a shrivel of his "wedding tackle."

"Soon as you yank the cords, sir," Clough told him.

"And they're already filled with gunpowder?" Lt. Spendlove said with a worried frown.

"With such a tiny access point as the stand-pipe, sir, there is no way to load them at the last minute," Captain Speaks spoke up. "Aye, they're loaded."

"Ehm . . . how *much* gunpowder, sir?" Midshipman Warburton asked.

"Fourty kegs, young sir," Clough announced.

"Jesus!" one of the Mids whispered.

"All up, they weigh two tons each," Captain Speaks said. "We must use *Penarth* and her stout hoisting gear to lift them out and put them in the water. A two-decker seventy-four was not available," he added, almost making a jest; a very dry one.

Four hundred bloody pounds *o' gunpowder?* Lewrie goggled, horrified. Unconsciously he stepped back from the torpedo he'd been inspecting, but there was another of the monsters at his back. He looked up to the patch of sky framed in the large hatchway *most* longingly, as he tried to grasp the idea that he was standing amid thirty-two hundred pounds of explosives, all just waiting for a stray spark. MacTavish's poor cask torpedoes couldn't hold a candle to these!

"Set at fifteen minutes only, Lieutenant Clough, it would be necessary to tow them in quite close before releasing them," Spendlove the skeptic said, his face grim. "Even a strong tide run didn't take our previous experiment in as quickly as we wished. Unless they have a method of motive power you'll be telling us about?"

"They float in on a making *tide*, sir!" Captain Speaks grumbled. "The boat-like *shape* of their hulls is what will make them faster than any damned cask, or set of spheres!"

"Or, they'll swirl end-for-end like twigs in a mill-race," was Lewrie's skeptical comment. "Or turn beam-onto the tide like logs."

"Beam-to the tide, sir," Lt. Merriman added with his head laid over to one side in contemplation, "there's more surface area, like a two-decker's hull freeboard, for the tide to push against. It *might* waft them in a bit quicker, but . . ."

"Drogues, Mister Merriman?" Lt. Westcott quipped with a wink.

"And a fixed rudder, perhaps, sir." Merriman grinned back.

"What the Devil are you talking about?" Captain Speaks asked.

"Will the civilian designer or fabricator be sailing with us, sir?" Lewrie asked Speaks.

"I'm given to understand that he will not," Speaks told them, frowning over whether that mattered. "Busy building even more of the things, I imagine. Why do you ask, sir?" he asked, rather archly.

"Mister Westcott and Mister Merriman gave the matter a bit of thought after our first, unsuccessful trials with cask torpedoes, sir. They came up with an idea for un-manned ship's boats, decked over and rigged to sail in," Lewrie explained. "These catamaran torpedoes are a *form* of boat, as Mister Clough said, a semi-submersed one. I wondered if we could . . . make some modifications to them without express permission from their designer, or would we have to wait 'til whoever it is mulls our ideas over and approves them, sir."

"Modifications?" Captain Speaks gravelled, grimacing as if the word was a sort of blasphemy. "What sort?"

"First of all, sir, a fixed rudder at the, ah . . . whichever end one names the stern, sir," Lt. Merriman eagerly contributed. "An oar or sweep extending from the stand-pipe down the top and over the end? That might help them stay on course once released. And a sea-anchor rigged from the bow-end, deployed and allowed to fill, and its tow-line to go taut before the torpedo is set free would *drag* the torpedo inward, sir!"

"Since one can't rig a mast and sail on it, sir—," Lieutenant Westcott attempted to add, but Speaks cut him off short.

"I am tasked . . . *we* are tasked to make experiments with the torpedoes as built and delivered to us, sirs!" Speaks snapped. "We will make a go of what we have to work with. We will prove them useful, as they are, sirs! Got that?"

"We do, sir," Lewrie replied, speaking for all again.

"Now, should they not produce the desired results in their current form, we *might* suggest improvements to their designer and the yard at Gosport," Speaks relented and allowed, a long moment later. "For now, though, let's be about the task at hand. Lieutenant Clough and his people are ready for sea. Are you as well, Captain Lewrie?"

"I am, sir," Lewrie told him.

"Last-minute lading to be concluded by the end of the First Dog today, and we shall sail by dawn tomorrow, the wind depending," Speaks ordered. "We shall be trying them North of the Channel Isles, mostly off Guernsey. Too damned close to spying French eyes for me, but . . . those are my orders. We done, gentlemen? Have Mister Clough and I satisfied your curiosity?"

Not in the slightest, Lewrie uneasily thought, but was forced to say that he and his officers were ready and willing.

"Excellent!" Captain Speaks barked, in happier takings, leading the way to the weather deck, fresher air, and a dubious sort of safety.

"Ehm . . . Captain Speaks seems dead-keen on them, does he not, sir?" Lt. Westcott said once they were back aboard *Reliant* and standing on the quarterdeck together, a bit apart from Spendlove and Merriman.

"Driven," Lewrie glumly agreed, cautious to not be heard making unfavourable comments about a senior officer; it just wasn't done!

"One hopes they go boom as advertised, sir, on time and all that . . . ," Westcott went on in a guarded mutter, heaving a leery shrug. "If they don't, one also hopes Admiralty *allows* modifications. If not, I fear that Captain Speaks takes the project *too* seriously, sir?"

"Privately, Mister Westcott, we may *think* what we wish, but for the hands, we'll just to have to 'soldier on,'" Lewrie told him, tapping a finger on his own lips. "Make the best of it without quibbles?"

"'Growl we may, but go we must,' aye, sir," Westcott said with a resigned sigh.

"It'd be best did we not even growl, sir," Lewrie japed.

"Aye, sir, aye, sir, two bags full!" Westcott quipped back, and clicked his heels together as he raised two fingers to his hat.

If they don't work . . . and I'm pretty sure they won't, Lewrie thought as Westcott and the others made their way below to take their ease for an hour or so; *there'll be Hell t'pay. And do we raise our suggestions again, will Speaks be desperate enough t'listen, or will he snap* all *our heads off?*

CHAPTER THIRTY-FIVE

I suppose this beats convoying, sir," Lt. Westcott said before he departed the anchored frigate for his first taste of picking up one of the catamaran torpedoes to tow it in, prime it, and release it.

"We may look back on those days as idyllic, aye," Lewrie said. "Off ye go, then. Don't get yourself 'hoist by your own petard.'"

"By God I'll try, sir! Ready, Mister Houghton?"

"Eager to go, sir!" their eldest Midshipman perkily replied.

"Ah, the enthusiasm of the young!" Westcott laughed.

The afternoon before they sailed from Portsmouth, they had seen Captain Blanding once again, as *Modeste* had departed for The Downs to gather a fresh West Indies–bound trade. Their old comrades-in-arms of last year, Parham in *Pylades* and Lt. Hyde in *Cockerel*, had sailed with him, re-enforced by a brace of brig-sloops. Blanding's two-decker 64 flew a red broad pendant, a solid red pendant marking Blanding as a substantive Commodore, no longer a senior Post-Captain, so that might have been a good-enough sop to his ego, along with his knighthood and baronetcy . . . even if the duty assigned him would be sheer drudgery and frustration. Bound for the West Indies in late Summer, too . . . he'd sail into the start of hurricane season, by the time he arrived, and mostlike would have to winter over, or risk a late-Autumn departure at the very height of the storm season!

Dreadful as all that would be, Lewrie almost envied him!

"Coffee, sir?" Pettus asked once he'd gained permission to come up to the quarterdeck. He held Lewrie's battered old black-iron pot by the bail and one towelled hand underneath it, with a string of pewter mugs clanking together from his elbow.

"Aye, Pettus, thankee," Lewrie answered, taking a mug.

"*I'd* take a cup, Pettus," Lt. Spendlove cajoled.

"Then here you go, Mister Spendlove," Pettus cheerfully agreed. "Black only . . . what the French call *noir*."

Lewrie went over to the starboard bulwarks to watch Westcott's and Houghton's thirty-two-foot barges row over to *Penarth,* which was anchored about two cables off. One torpedo was already in the water, and the second to be tried this morning was being hoisted out, its grapnels at either end—Lewrie could not quite deem them bow or stern!—attached as soon as it emerged from the deep hold and rested on deck for a bit.

Both ships lay West-Sou'west of Guernsey, and St. Peter Port, about two miles offshore, anchored by best bowers and stern kedges to keep them beam-on to the island, though the holding ground was "iffy," and the strong Channel tides were already in full flood, making thigh-thick anchor cables groan in the hawse-holes. If a French warship did appear, they would have to cut their cables and lose their anchors in a rush so that *Penarth* and her secret torpedoes could escape, and the frigate to engage the foe to save her. Lewrie would have liked them to have remained under way for the first trials, or at the least come to the wind fetched-to, but Captain Speaks had insisted, fearful, perhaps, that the tide would carry both ships into too-shallow water and take the ground, right behind their own torpedoes, or almost atop them when they exploded! *If* they exploded.

The second torpedo swayed high over *Penarth's* bulwarks, inching upwards and outwards in fits and starts as her crew grunted and heaved on capstan and windlass bars. There was a goodly sea running, and for a time it looked as if the collier's rolling would swing the torpedo so far outboard that the weight would over-set her, and God help the men tailing on the steadying lines to check those swings!

At last, though, the jib-arms and fore-course yard dipped far enough to lower the torpedo out of *Reliant's* sight, below her starb'd bulwarks, and Lewrie let out a sigh of relief. If the torpedo slammed against *Penarth's* hull hard enough, would that set the pistol off?

He heard a long "whew!" nearby, and turned to see Lieutenant Clarence Spendlove, still with a wince on his face and his eyes wide.

"Perhaps they'd do better towed by the collier from the outset, sir . . . if they are as water-tight as they claim them to be," Spendlove said with a dubious shake of his head. "Anything but a flat calm . . . ?"

"Then the sight of 'em'd let the secret out of the bag, Mister Spendlove," Lewrie said, "and scare the Hell out of everyone in Portsmouth! *And* with good bloody reason!"

"There is that, sir," Spendlove agreed, chuckling a little. He sobered quickly, though. "If they prove successful, and we launch them by the dozens against the French, though, sir . . . by the hundreds, what will the world make of them, sir? What will they say of us, of Great Britain, for using them? That we're clever, or that the torpedoes are infernal engines?"

"Frankly, Mister Spendlove, novel ways t'blow Frogs t'Hell are fine with me," Lewrie told him with a wry grin and a shrug expressing disinterest in the world's opinion. "The onliest problem I have with 'em is that none of the devices we've seen or heard described to us are worth a tinker's dam, and if we *do* launch 'em by the hundreds, we'll look hellish-desperate, and the *failure'd* give us a black eye. Mark my words, sir, fail they will. The duty assigned us . . . well, at least it keeps us from more convoy work, and it *does* keep us close to port. Almost like day-sailin', or yachtin' like the royal family!"

"Fresher victuals, aye, sir," Spendlove said, perking up a bit, relieved to know that his captain somewhat shared his distaste for the devices . . . if not for the same reasons as he held.

"And nigh-daily mail service, Mister Spendlove," Lewrie added, thinking of Lydia Stangbourne's latest chatty letter.

Lewrie took a sip of his coffee, then wandered over to the larboard bulwarks for a bit, grimacing at the sight of the bow and stern anchor cables slanting away at noticeable angles from the bow hawse-hole and the taffrail hawse. The wind pressed upon *Reliant*'s hull, on her freeboard, and the tide-race shoved at her "quick-work" below the waterline, together. He'd posted a Midshipman at either cable to keep an eye on the angles, and their tautness, for the first sign of slippage, but was still worried. He looked up to the mast-heads where lookouts were posted to sing out at the first glimpse of French snoopers. They were alert, intent on their portion of the horizon, but silent so far. *So far so good,* he thought, with fingers covertly crossed.

"Mister Westcott and Mister Houghton are setting out from the collier, sir," Lt. Merriman reported.

"Very good," Lewrie said, returning to the starboard side. He got there just in time to espy the two barges standing out, clear of *Penarth*, lug-sails and jibs squeaking aloft and beginning to fill.

Much as Lewrie had loathed going too far aloft since his Midshipman days, he had to. With a telescope slung over his shoulder he mounted a carronade slide, then its barrel, to the cap-rails of the bulwarks and swung out into the main-mast stays and rat-lines, slowly and deliberately making his way almost to the cat-harpings below the fighting top. Boot heels snug on the rat-lines and one arm looped to a stout stay, he turned to face outboard and extended the telescope.

At first, *Penarth*'s masts were in the way before the two barges got a goodly way on and began to bound towards the island. Lewrie had to laugh out loud to spot both the "beef to the heel" Lt. Clough and the stocky older "gotch-gut" Captain Speaks high aloft in *her* rigging, their own telescopes extended!

Reliant was rolling, making it difficult to keep the boats in his ocular; the urge to pull out his pocket-watch to check the time, and to keep his precarious hold aloft, and keep the telescope aimed at the same time, was a bit awkward, but . . .

Both barges were lowering their sails, at last, and hands began to haul the torpedoes in close alongside. The ant-sized Lt. Westcott and Midshipman Houghton clambered atop the torpedoes to remove those tompions, both clinging for dear life to the stand-pipe as the things rolled and wallowed, and the choppy sea broke over them.

In for a soakin', and dry breeches, once back aboard, Lewrie thought as he watched them scramble. Seconds later, and they were in a clumsy rush back aboard their boats, and in understandable haste to quickly get away from those now-primed fourty kegs of gunpowder! As they gained their boats' safety, each man displayed a bright yellow signal flag, wig-wagging to beat the band for a few seconds, in sign that they were successful. Tow-lines were cast off, and sails began to sprout; tillers were put hard-over, and the boats began to ghost away from the freed torpedoes, rapidly gathering way and coming about to beat "full and by" back towards *Penarth* and *Reliant*.

"What's the rate of the tide, Mister Rossynton?" Lewrie called down to the Midshipman he had posted with the chip-log.

"Ehm . . . four and three-quarter knots, sir!"

Lewrie stayed in the shrouds long enough to make sure that the boats had made sufficient clearance from the torpedoes, even if they malfunctioned and blew up prematurely, then stowed away his telescope and carefully turned his body to face the shrouds and make his way to the deck.

"It will be a long slog back," Lt. Merriman was telling Midshipman Entwhistle, "short-tacking home dead downwind of us."

"Is someone keeping the time?" Lewrie asked, safely in-board and on solid oak planking once more.

"Aye, sir," Merriman told him. "By pocket-watches and glasses. Though we don't know which of our boats was in charge of the one set for a quarter-hour, or the half-hour." Merriman had a watch with a second hand, as did Entwhistle, and a ship's boy standing nearby had turned a set of sand-glasses as soon as the yellow signal flags had been displayed. The boy swiped his runny nose on his shirt sleeve, almost dancing a jig as he divided his attention between the timing glasses and the sea shoreward, impishly grinning in anticipation of a very big pair of bangs.

Lewrie put his hands in the small of his back and paced along the starboard bulwarks to the taffrails and back, chiding himself to act "captainly" and stoic, for a rare once. He tried humming a tune for a bit, but thought that a bit *too* much a sham, and left off. He resisted looking at his watch again as long as he could, then . . .

As soon as he pulled it from his breeches pocket, there came a *stupendous* roar, and he looked up to see what looked to be a *mountain* of seawater and smoke jut skyward!

"Huzzah!" the ship's boy squealed, hopping up and down in glee.

And, "Huzzah!" from *Reliant*'s crew, most of whom were standing by the starboard rails, or in the rigging like so many starlings on a bare tree's limbs.

"That's the quarter-hour one, to the minute, ha ha!" Lieutenant Merriman gloated. "Tremendous! Simply tremendous, hey, Clarence?" he asked Spendlove. "God, look how tall and big a blast it is!"

"Rather big, aye, George," Lt. Spendlove agreed rather glumly. "However . . . it was released about a mile from shore, as I adjudged by sextant, and even with nigh a five-knot tide to drive it, it still only made half a mile, by my reckoning." Spendlove had a slate covered with trigonometric equations (he was a dab-hand navigator and mathematician), which he showed to one and all. "It appears that even this strong making tide is not enough to carry the things within range to do much real damage."

"There's still the half-hour one," Merriman pooh-poohed, too taken with the seeming success of the first torpedo. "If it travels twice as far as the first, we could see clouds of mud in the explosion, in shoal water, which would represent the depths of water in which the French barges and such are reputed to be anchored outside their ports."

And, as Lt. Westcott's and Midshipman Houghton's barges came alongside a quarter-hour later, the second torpedo exploded just like the first, on time but roughly half a mile to starboard of where they *expected* it to drift. It was impressively loud and tall, but no one could espy any of Merriman's expected mud.

"Some vagary in the tide, perhaps," Lt. Merriman puzzled.

"Wide of the mark, yes, George, but . . . far short of where one would expect it to drift. Still too far offshore, even released within a mile of the island," Lt. Spendlove patiently countered. "And in full view and gun range of the French batteries, had we tried it out against them."

"Well, perhaps Captain Speaks will let us try my drogues on the next batch," Merriman rejoined, shrugging it off. "They'd be easy to rig up."

"Signal from *Penarth*, sir," Midshipman Grainger reported. "It is 'To Weigh Anchor,' sir."

"Very well, Mister Grainger. Ah! Mister Westcott! And how was your little jaunt?" Lewrie asked his First Officer as he came back to quarter-deck. "Ye look a tad *moist*," he teased him.

"'Tis a soggy duty, sir, having to ride the back of the damned thing like a boy on an ox," Lt. Westcott wryly told him, flashing one of his brief white-teethed grins. "Out of the boat, into the boat . . . I missed my leap and got soaked from the waist down."

"Ye'll have to let the wind dry ye off, Mister Westcott. No goin' below for a change of clothing," Lewrie grinned as he told him. "For now, let's get our anchors up and get the ship under way."

"Aye aye, sir," Westcott ruefully replied. "I expect that my breeches'll drain, do I undo the knee buttons."

There were no more trials that day, or for the next two, for the winds and seas got up, making the hoisting-out of more torpedoes too dangerous. The two ships stood off-and-on Guernsey, out to mid-Channel, and back again in shifting winds, rolling grey seas, and now-and-then showers of rain. It was only on the third day that the sky cleared and the seas abated, allowing a full day of trials with four catamaran torpedoes, two in the morning and two in the afternoon. All four reliably blew up on time, but nowhere near enough to shore, nor anywhere near where they were expected to drift from the points at which they were released.

They stood back out to sea for the evening, and *Penarth* put up a hoist that Lewrie was sure Speaks detested; he *requested* permission to come aboard *Reliant,* instead of ordering Lewrie and all of his officers and Mids to come aboard *Penarth* for a conference.

"We'll have all but the officer and Mids of the watch to dine, Yeovill," Lewrie warned his talented cook. "Maybe a good feed'll make the fellow feel a tad better. Do your best."

Not ten minutes later, one of *Penarth*'s boats made the crossing to *Reliant,* and both Captain Speaks and Lieutenant Clough were piped aboard.

"Sorry for the intrusion, Captain Lewrie," Speaks began as soon as he gained the quarterdeck, "but we've too much to go over with your people who've handled the damned things. Take too many of them away from their duties, what?" Speaks added, puffing from his clamber up the side, and looking mortified that he'd had to *ask.*

"I'll summon everyone but the Sailing Master, sir," Lewrie said. "And welcome aboard."

It made the great-cabins cramped, but Westcott, Merriman, and even the reluctant Spendlove, who had gone off with one of the afternoon torpe-does in strict rotation, were there, as were the Midshipmen who had tried them out: Houghton, Entwhistle, and Warburton. Eight of them sat round Lewrie's dining table whilst he jammed himself in at the head next to Speaks, using the chair from his desk from the day-cabin. There was tea and two bottles of claret on the side-board.

"We've proved that they work," Captain Speaks began, clearing his throat and speaking in a gruff voice full of seeming confidence. "Every-one agreed on that point?"

"In terms of reliability of their timing and ignition mechanisms, aye, sir," Lewrie agreed; sort of.

"They do go *off* most impressively, sir," Lt. Westcott added.

"Right, then, we're halfway there." Speaks beamed, rubbing his hands together. "Now, about why they don't seem to go in as quick as we'd like, or . . . end up anywhere near where we'd wish, well," Speaks tossed off as if that was a mere quibble. "Perhaps the reasons for that lie more in our imperfect hydrographic charts of the area, with a lack of knowledge of what varies the expected straight run-in of the tide, than with the torpe-does themselves. The Admiralty is desperately in need of a proper office of hydrography, after all. All those captains' journals, sailing masters' jour-nals and observations, stacked to the rafters in the basements, ignored for years and years, Those that survive the annual floods of the Thames that rise in the basements, ha!"

"Perhaps we should send ashore to Guernsey for experienced fishermen to aid us, sir?" Lt. Westcott dared to suggest.

"And let out the torpedoes' secrecy to one and all? No, sir!" Captain Speaks said with a growl, one brow up and leaning far back in his chair, making it squeak alarmingly.

"Hardly a secret by now, sir," Lewrie pointed out, nigh tongue-in-cheek. "I expect Guernsey's whole population brings their dinners to the shore to watch, like a royal fireworks show."

"Now, had we done the trials off Land's End, The Lizard, or the Scillies, there would be fewer spectators," Lt. Clough contributed.

"The Channel Isles were Admiralty's choice, sir," Captain Speaks gruffly rejoined, "not mine, or ours. Better than launching torpedoes off the mouth of the Somme, hey, Captain Lewrie? Or was that their designer's choice, to which you demurred?"

"Admiralty orders, sir," Lewrie told him, stung by the gibe over the location of the first trials with MacTavish's casks. "I still have them, do you wish to see them, sir."

"Hmm!" Speaks uttered, twisting his mouth to a grimace. "It is of no matter. Now, sirs! What may we do to increase the range and the accuracy of our torpedoes? *That's* the matter at hand."

"One might as well try to direct a sheep to graze northwards," Lt. Spendlove baldly stated, though he did so in a calm voice without *too* much sarcasm. "Do the French anchor row after long row of *péniches* and barges along their harbour moles and breakwaters, a torpedo *might* end up alongside one of them, sir, but *which* one would be asking far too much of them, in their present form. I doubt even Merriman's idea for explosive boats could choose a target, any more than a fireship set loose to sail in on its own."

"I think Captain Speaks does not intend *that* sort of accuracy, sirs," Lt. Clough quickly interjected. "It's more a matter of ending up *somewhere* alongside those long, anchored rows, instead of drifting a whole mile wide."

"Drogues," Lewrie said. "Sea-anchors t'pull 'em in quicker and straighter."

"Though, whatever variations in the direction of the tides, the eddys and such, might not a drogue pull them off course even faster?" Clough wondered aloud, his thick brow as furrowed as a wheat field.

"We'll never know 'til we try," Lewrie said.

"Rudders, too, sir," Lt. Merriman stuck in, looking eager again after the general gloomy tone of the gathering. "I dare say our Carpenter and the Bosun could whip something up in short order."

"Sir?" Lewrie said, turning to Speaks.

Poor old fart don't have a ship command, and now it looks as if his project's a dead-bust, too, Lewrie thought as Captain Speaks hemmed and hawed and wiped his hand over his mouth.

Lewrie felt certain that the catamaran torpedoes in their current form would *sort of* work, if the yards built enough of them and the eventual attack on the main French marshalling port of Boulogne used hundreds of the damned things at one go. That might be enough success for Admiralty, and Speaks's career. But, if the old fellow was seen to use his wits and made improvements which worked even better . . . ! *There* was a feather in his cap, a pat on the back from Admiralty, and a promotion into a ship of his own.

Will ye mention me *in your report, when Merriman's modifications solve the problem? Assumin' they do, o' course! I could use some new credit in London, too. Get that Henry Legge and court-martial off my back!* Lewrie speculated.

"I suppose it would not hurt to try fitting the last two with drogues, and perhaps one of them with a fixed rudder," Speaks grudgingly allowed, after a long think. "We've what left, Mister Clough?"

"One set for fifteen minutes, sir, one for half an hour," that stout worthy replied.

"Excellent!" Speaks enthused, or pretended to; he looked as if he was driven to sham zeal, no matter what he really thought of torpedoes, or their reliability, or even the honourability of using them as weapons of war. Lewrie suspected that poor Speaks was in over his head in a project he didn't have a clue about, and might even hold to be a ghastly, sneaking, and atrocious idea, but . . . the torpedoes were all he had, and he would prove them useful no matter his reservations. Even were they horrid wastes of matériel and money, he would persevere to the last sticking post to prove *himself* worthy.

"The after-end hoisting ring-bolts, sir," Lt. Merriman babbled on, producing a lead pencil and a scrap of paper from his coat. "Do we bind the tiller to either of those, anchoring its end to the stand-pipe with a wood mast hoop from one of the barge's lug-sails . . ."

"Um-hum, I see . . . ," Speaks gravely replied, leaning over to peer at the quick sketch. "Like a fixed sweep-oar rudder."

"Exactly so, sir!" Merriman said, chuckling.

"But . . . would it not *wobble*, Mister Merriman?" Speaks asked.

"Well, hmm . . ." Merriman frowned, looking cock-eyed at his idea. "If we nailed some small baulks of scrap timber to the torpedo. They are wood chests, after all, yes! We could *nail* baulks through the tarred canvas and outer planking, say four inches thick and high, eight inches long, to make a restraining channel for the long tiller, which we'd *still* attach to the stand-pipe with a mast hoop . . . !"

Pettus came to the table and leaned over to whisper in Lewrie's ear, then stood over to the side-board to gather wine glasses for all the company.

"You'll stay aboard to dine, sir, Mister Clough?" Lewrie asked his guests. "I'm told my cook's preparin' bean soup, roasted rabbit, and a sea pie, with apple tarts to boot."

"Delighted, Captain Lewrie!" Captain Speaks replied, turning to look at him very briefly, now intent upon Merriman's sketch, to which he quickly returned. "Once in place, why not nail restraining boards over the brackets, so the tiller won't hop out or slip free, sir?"

Lewrie crooked a finger to Pettus.

"Sir?" Pettus said in a whisper, leaning close again.

"Best see that the cats eat very separate tonight," Lewrie said, with a slight incline of his head towards their senior officer.

"I'll see to it, sir."

He's in a good mood, for once, Lewrie thought; *Pray God nothin' spoils it!*

CHAPTER THIRTY-SIX

*D*rogues, or sea-anchors, were easily cobbled together from the iron hoops of depleted ration butts or kegs, which the Ship's Cooper had disassembled and stored below, one small hoop from a five-gallon barrico for the small end, and a larger one for the main opening. The canvas and the sewing work to bind the canvas cones to the hoops was done by the Sailmaker and his Mate, and the Bosun provided the one-inch manila for the tow-lines.

The Ship's Carpenter, with the Bosun and his Mate, created the stabilising rudder device. It looked damned odd, for it had to mate to the flat top of a torpedo, then curve to match the slope of taper along the after-end, nailed in place in its brackets, with a wood ring at the end that fit round the stand-pipe, then doubled to hold a cut-down rudder off *Reliant*'s jolly-boat, so it would not wobble.

The modifications were finished by mid-afternoon of the next day, then borne over to *Penarth* for fitting, and the trials would come on the next morning tide.

"Flags, Mister Merriman?" Lewrie asked as he stood by the entry-port to watch his boat crews board their barges.

"Mister Clough's idea, sir," Merriman told him, impatient to be about the trials with his improvements. "We'll tie them to the stand-pipe to show what time we pulled the priming lines, *and* be able to see where they go . . . at least for the experiment, sir."

"Good thinkin'," Lewrie agreed. "Once set free, I hadn't the slightest clue where they were 'til they went 'bang.' Away with you, Mister Merriman, Mister Entwhistle. Have fun!" he wished them.

Don't blow yourselves up! Lewrie wished to himself.

"If they work better this time, sir," Lt. Westcott said, coming to his side as Lewrie paced back to the centre of the quarterdeck, "we may have to buy more colliers into the Navy. Else it will take better than three or four hours to hoist all eight out of the holds and ready them all for launching."

"Hmm. Hadn't thought about that part of it," Lewrie confessed. "Come t'think on it, I doubt if anyone else has, either. If we *do* end up launchin' 'em by the hundred, it'd take a whole flotilla of colliers and ship's boats. And, they'd have to anchor two miles off the French coast *hours* before the tide begins to make."

"*Sacre bleu, mort de ma vie,* vottever are zose Anglais doing?" Westcott scoffed quite cheerfully. "Henri, do you z'ink we should tell someone of zis, or open ze fire wiz ze cannon on z'ese pests?"

"If there's a makin' tide in darkness, perhaps," Lewrie speculated, with a leery grimace. "Oh, all this is nonsense and moonshine! Even if they work somewhat as desired, it's *deployin'* 'em that'll be the rub. It makes more sense that we just barge up to Range-To-Random Shot and fire away 'til the powder magazine's empty."

The last torpedo was slung overside into the sea, and the barges took them in tow. Today, the trials were done under reduced sail, not anchored, so *Penarth* did not block their view.

The barges sailed in towards Guernsey 'til they were within an estimated mile, and handed their sails for a minute or two. Through their telescopes, Lewrie and Westcott could see people scrambling onto the torpedoes, which were floating awash with the chop breaking over them. Tiny triangular red pendants sprouted a foot or so above the sea as Lt. Merriman and Midshipman Entwhistle jerked the priming lines and replaced the tompions, then the barges rowed out ahead of the torpedoes to deploy the drogues and tow them for a bit, before letting go the drogues' lines and rapidly turning away to re-hoist sail and leave the immediate area, soonest.

Sand trickled through the quarter-hour and half-hour glasses, pocket-watches were consulted almost every two minutes, and everyone who had access to a telescope peered intently from the starboard-side shrouds or bulwarks. The tiny red pendants shrank smaller and smaller as the minutes ticked by, with some of the more enthusiastic boasting that the torpedoes seemed to be drifting faster this time, and seemed not to be drifting too far off the section of the shore that had been chosen as a "target."

"Can barely spot 'em, now, sir," Lt. Westcott muttered.

"Any time now, on the first one," Mr. Caldwell, the Sailing Master, said, squinting at his watch. "Yes! There it goes!"

B'whoom! followed the sudden eruption of flame-shot gunpowder smoke and a great sprouting pillar of sea by a second or so.

"Mister Spendlove?" Lewrie asked, turning to the Second Officer.

"By my reckoning, sir, it went off on time, yet still a half-mile short," Spendlove said, after some quick figuring on his slate. "And, do we take that stretch of shoreline from the white church and steeple on the left, and the grove of trees marking the right end of a mile-long target representing a line of French barges, it seemed to trend larboard, closer to the steeple-end, sir, when it should have ended up closer to the centre."

"We released from roughly the same place as the earlier trials, on the same strength of tide-race, over the same bottom influences we experienced before, so . . . there's no explaining it, sir," Westcott said, frowning in puzzlement for a moment, but he perked up at last. "It seems, though, that the drogue pulled it closer ashore, and kept it within the margins!" he said, extending both arms to encompass the outer ends of that mile of shore. "Now, if the half-hour torpedo with the rudder behaves the same, that one might come close to succeeding."

More long minutes passed, then . . .

"There, sir!" Midshipman Rossyngton crowed, leaping in glee.

The sea boiled of a sudden in a wide, shallow hump that burst like a pus-filled boil, spurting smoke and spray an hundred feet into the air, yellow-grey powder smoke and white foam mingling. A second later came the *Ba'whoom!* from the gigantic explosion.

"In the shallows, I think," Westcott deemed it. "Almost ashore."

"And very close to the mid-point of the mile, sir," Lt. Spendlove said in a flat voice, as if the torpedo's seeming success had awakened his initial mis-givings again. "A fluke, most-like?"

"Damme, the bloody things might work, after all," Lewrie grudgingly allowed.

If they do, maybe they'll free us for other duties, just thankee, Jesus! he thought; *They work, our part's done, and someone else can go use 'em! I still don't quite trust 'em.*

They recovered their barges, and Lt. Merriman and Midshipman Entwhistle came tumbling back aboard in such glad takings that they could almost be said to dance jigs, babbling away like mag-pies. And, before the barges could be led astern for towing, *Penarth* came slowly surging alongside within hailing distance, with Captain Speaks at her larboard railings.

"Hoy, *Reliant!*" Speaks shouted, hands cupped by his face, with no need of a speaking-trumpet. "That did the trick! I will sail for Portsmouth at once, with the design drawings your First Officer made! Congratulations to you and your Mister Merriman, Lewrie! Rest assured my report will be complimentary to you all!"

"Thank you, sir!" Lewrie shouted back.

"Remain on station 'til I return with fresh torpedoes!" Speaks ordered. "Look for me off the Nor'east tip of Guernsey in about ten days to a fortnight!"

Makin' sure he gets all the bloody credit, first! Lewrie sarcastically realised.

"'Til then, cruise independent, and make a nuisance of yourself with the French!" Speaks added.

Hmm, maybe not so bad, at that, Lewrie thought more kindly.

"You'll not need escort back to Portsmouth, sir?" Lewrie asked.

"With no torpedoes aboard, there's nought the French may learn, sir!" Speaks shouted over, sounding very pleased and amused. "*Adieu,* and good hunting, *Reliant!*"

"Thank you, sir! See you in a fortnight at the latest!"

Penarth sheeted home her fore-course and slowly began to draw away. Lewrie turned to his officers and Mids.

"Well, sirs? He said we should make a nuisance of ourselves, so let's be about it. Mister Westcott, Mister Caldwell, we can be into the Gulf of Saint Malo by early afternoon. Shape a course," he said. "Captain Speaks has let us off his leash for a few days. Let us make the most of it."

"Aye aye, sir!" Westcott wolfishly agreed.

"And get back to proper duties, sir?" Lt. Spendlove asked.

"Doin' what a frigates's s'posed t'do, aye," Lewrie said with a laugh, feeling immense relief. And feeling rather wolfish, himself!

CHAPTER THIRTY-SEVEN

*M*aking a nuisance of themselves in the Gulf of St. Malo was not as easy as it sounded, however. *Reliant*'s draught of almost eighteen feet limited where she could go, or dare go for only a few hours, due to the dramatic rise and fall of the tides, forcing her to venture no closer than two miles of the French coast, far beyond the Range-To-Random Shot of her 18-pounder guns.

Besides, other Royal Navy vessels were already in the Gulf and quite successfully making nuisances of themselves, vessels which drew much less water than she; the bulk of them were small and light single-masted cutters, backed up by brig-sloops or the rare three-masted full-rigged sloops, mostly lieutenants' commands, with half-squadrons or flotillas led by commanders in their Sixth Rates. If *Reliant* did meet with a larger warship commanded by a Post-Captain, an offer of help was turned down, for the most part, since all the aid the Fifth Rate 38-gun ship could provide was more moral than substantial, too far offshore to back up the blockading patrols or operations unless a French frigate of her own weight of metal emerged . . . and so far none had. What opposition the French had sent out had been *chasse-marées*, *prames*, and *chaloupes*, the gunboats purpose-built to defend the armada of invasion vessels, and those not too often, either.

Some people were having fun, though, swarming over the convoys of *péniches* and *caïques* trying to make their way to join the immense gathering at Boulogne, hugging the coast as close as the shoals, sand-bars, and rocks allowed, sneaking from port to port in short and breathless stages. More enterprising young officers were leading their men ashore at night to cut out barges, or set fire to them, and the very bravest would row up the creeks or rivers to block the many canals or raid the small riverside ship-yards where the invasion fleet was being built. And *Reliant* could take no part in that.

After a few days of fruitless prowling, all Lewrie could do was shake his head, take a squint at Point de Grouin east of St. Malo, and order *Reliant* turned North for a return to Guernsey and the open waters of the Channel, wishing his more-active compatriots well, though he did in point of fact envy the Hell out of their shallower draughts, their opportunities, and even their lower ranks which could justify their active participation in such harum-scarums. If he could pinch *Reliant* into high-tide reach of the Nor-mandy coast, he might find a chance for action off Granville, Coutances, Lessay, or Barneville-Carteret or some other inlet or fishing port along the way.

If someone did not beat him to it, first!

He did not know what awakened him, the coolness of the night or his cats. Lewrie had rolled into his hanging-bed-cot round midnight in all his clothes but his boots and coat, more for a long nap than anything else, too fretted by the wind and sea conditions to imagine that he would drop off so soundly or quickly. Just after Lights Out at 9 P.M. the winds had nigh-died on them, and the sea had turned to nearly a flat calm, slowing the frigate to a bare three knots.

The air in the great-cabins was clammy and cool, and his first thought was to pull up the coverlet, or rise and close the upper halves of the sash-windows in the transom, as well as the propped-open windows in the over-head coach-top. Lewrie never left the lower halves open at night; did Toulon and Chalky prowl and play-fight in the dark, it was good odds that one, or both of them, would tumble out some dark night.

They were both with him in the bed-cot. Toulon, the older black-and-white, was puddinged up atop his hip, working his front paws and loudly purring. Chalky, the younger mostly white ram-cat, was in his face. When Lewrie opened one gritted eye, all he could see was warm fur, though he could feel Chalky's pink nose and whiskers brushing at his own nose and eyes.

"What?" Lewrie grumbled in irritation to be wakened so early in the wee hours. "Can't I have the last hour? We have t'play *now*?"

Far forward, a ship's boy began to strike the watch-bells, and Lewrie let out a groan. It was Seven Bells of the Middle Watch, which ran from Midnight to 4 A.M. While he usually wished to be awakened a few minutes before the change of watch, this was a bit too premature!

"Right, then," Lewrie mumbled, gingerly shifting position and reaching out to pet both cats, yawning heavily and stretching to ease stiffness. With a frown, he became aware of how still the motion of the ship felt, of how faintly *Reliant*'s timbers groaned as they worked, almost as if she was securely moored in harbour. His ears caught the creaks, the squeaks of slack blocks, and the slatting of sails as if there was *no* wind, and he sat up quickly, worried that his frigate was becalmed off a hostile shore, possible prey to oared gunboats with those rumoured 24-pounders in their bows!

He rolled out of the bed-cot, found his boots by tripping over them, and groped about the top of the nearest sea-chest for his coat to don it and head for the deck. He startled the nodding Marine sentry who guarded his door, dashed up the ladderway to the quarterdeck, and looked about.

"Er, good morning, sir," Lt. Merriman exclaimed, as startled as the sentry by Lewrie's appearance. "I was just about to send for you, Captain. The wind has fallen away, the last half-hour, and I believe there's a mist rising."

"We still have steerage way, Mister Merriman?" Lewrie asked as he looked aloft for the commissioning pendant, the normal indicator of the apparent wind, but it was too dark to see it. Looking forward to the forecastle, not an hundred feet from where he stood, the lanthorn by the belfry looked fuzzy, too!

"Barely, sir," Lt. Merriman replied. "Mister Grainger just had a cast of the log, and it showed a bit over two knots." Merriman went on to state that the wind was still out of the West, but fading. His cross-bearings on the lights of Granville off their starboard quarter, and the lights of Coutances on their starboard bows placed the frigate roughly six miles off the French coast, with Coutances and its inlets about eight miles ahead.

"Ah! Good morning to you, sir . . . Mister Merriman," the Sailing Master, Mr. Caldwell, said as he clattered up the ladderway to the quarterdeck.

"Did Merriman send for you, sir?" Lewrie asked.

"No, sir, I woke on my own, and something, just didn't feel right. Just afore Seven Bells was struck," Caldwell said.

"How odd. Me, too," Lewrie said, wondering if after all of his twenty-four years in the Navy, he had finally gained a sea-sense.

"Misty," Caldwell commented, lifting his chin to sniff. "There will be a fog, I fear, sir. Perhaps even a shift of wind."

"I will confess my lack of experience in the Channel environs, Mister Caldwell," Lewrie said, "but, in *your* experience, is this millpond sea, scant wind, and fog normal?"

"All together, sir? Damned rare, I warrant. Even eerie!" Mr. Caldwell told him, his head cocked to one side in frustration.

"Wind's *died*," Lt. Merriman pointed out as the main course sail ahead of them went limp, and the spanker overhead sagged, with its long boom creaking. Lewrie could barely feel even the faintest breath of it on his cheek—they *were* becalmed!

"No helm, sir!" Mr. Baldock, Quartermaster of the Watch on the double wheel, announced. "She ain't bitin' no more." To prove that, he spun the wheel to either side, which did nothing to shift the compass as *Reliant* coasted along on course, slowing, shedding the inertia that her long hull imparted.

"Oh!" Lt. Spendlove exclaimed as he came to the quarterdeck to relieve Merriman, a few minutes before Eight Bells. "Good morning to you all. Egad, sirs, a flat calm, is it?"

"And a fog, Mister Caldwell assures us, soon to come," Merriman told him with a grimace.

"We'll dispense with scrubbing decks, gentlemen," Lewrie said, striving to put a calm face on things. "We will go to Quarters right after the people's bedding is stowed. When the galley's got breakfast ready, we'll let the hands below by watches, but keep the guns manned. We'll *not* be surprised by something Froggish at short range, right?"

If Caldwell's right, and there is a fog, Lewrie thought; *if it's a good thick'un, we can't see them, but maybe they won't see us!*

CHAPTER THIRTY-EIGHT

*A*fter an hour or so, the winds returned, the faintest zephyr off the land, sometimes from the East, then backing into the Sou'east for a few minutes, allowing *Reliant* to stir, to ghost ahead on her former course of Due North, barely fast enough for the rudder to bite. It was a land-breeze, for the sea was much cooler, and shed its gathered heat more quickly than did the shores, the rocky hills, and the land of France. And even before the land-breeze arose, had come the fog, and it was as thick as a hand-before-your-face London "pea-souper." Before the sun had risen, the fog had become so thick that the belfry lanthorn and its crispness had been turned to a vague blob of light, and even the larger taffrail lanthorns right aft on the quarterdeck had gone feeble.

Lewrie had gone below long enough to scrub up, fetch the keys to the arms chests and his own weapons—find his hat and boat-cloak—then returned to the deck, to slouch in his collapsible canvas sling-chair, now and then peering aloft at the commissioning pendant, now all but lost in mist, not darkness. Now and again, once the sun was up, a bank of fog would roll over the ship, a bank so thick that he couldn't make out the forecastle, much less the jib-boom!

He breakfasted later than the hands, taking only a bowl of oat-meal with strawberry jam and mug after mug of coffee, with goat's milk and sugar, and a fairly fresh piece of ship's bisquit or two soaked for long minutes in the coffee to make them soft enough to chew. And, he fretted over his ship's vulnerability, the lack of speed with which to flee, the thickness of the fog from which gunboats could come with not half a minute's warning.

Lewrie *tried* to be the sort of captain that the Navy demanded: cool, serene, and stoic in the face of danger. But that sort of pose was not in his nature, never had been in the past, and, he freely admitted to himself, might never be in future. He *had* to rise at last and pace the quarterdeck, hands clasped in the small of his back, hidden by the folds of his boat-cloak so no one could see them being wrung. Up the windward side, which was his alone by right and long tradition, cross the forward edge of the quarterdeck by the stanchions and nets now full of rolled-up bedding and hammocks, then aft down the lee side right to the taffrails, flag lockers, and the now-extinguished lanthorns before beginning another circuit. He paused and looked aloft, again.

"Ha!" Lewrie barked. He could see the commissioning pendant as it lazily curled, could make out the maze of rigging, sails, yards, and topmasts once more. He could even see the tip of the jib-boom. Aft, he could see the two barges and both of *Reliant*'s cutters under tow. A half-hour before, all he could see was the towing lines, stretching out into nothing!

"It seems to be thinning, at last, sir," Lt. Westcott said as Lewrie joined him by the helm. With the ship at Quarters, Spendlove and Merriman were at their posts in the waist, surpervising the guns.

"About bloody time, too," Lewrie said with relief and evident enthusiasm. "Ye can see out-board a long musket shot or better. Any idea where we are now, by dead reckoning, Mister Westcott?"

"Uhm, about here, sir," Lt. Westcott said, stepping forward to the chart pinned to the traverse board. "Coutances should be abeam of us to windward . . ."

"Windward, mine arse," Lewrie japed. "*Zephyr*-ward, more like."

"With this land-breeze and ebbing tide carrying us, I have no idea how *far* off the coast we are, sir . . . sorry," Westcott added as he traced their course with a forefinger. "Our last sure cross-bearings put us six miles off, and I'd imagine that we've made enough lee-way to estimate that we might be eight miles off, by now."

"In mid-Channel 'twixt France and Jersey, aye," Lewrie agreed. "Does this scant breeze allow, we might bear a point more Westerly. I wouldn't want t'run her too close to Cape Carteret, and on Due North, there's Cape de la Hague beyond that."

He looked up to sniff the air and peer about, then returned to the chart. "This *has* t'burn off, say, by Four Bells of the Forenoon and the winds'll surely shift back from somewhere in the West, so—"

"Harkee, sir!" Mr. Caldwell barked. "Did any of you hear that?"

"Hear what, Mister Caldwell?" Lewrie asked, puzzled.

"I did, sir!" Midshipman Munsell piped up. "Over yonder?" the younker said, pointing out to starboard, his mouth agape and his eyes blared in alarm.

Moo-oo-wa!

"Sea-monsters?" Quartermaster's Mate Malin whispered to another fellow manning the helm.

"Hist!" Quartermaster Rhys snapped back.

Moo-oo-wa! came from the fog, plaintive and hackle-raising eerie, answered a moment later by a second, then a third, and a fourth further off and fainter!

If any seals *turn up, we'll tow the ship out of here!* Lewrie thought; *That's just . . . spooky!*

"Sea cows?" Midshipman Munsell shudderingly asked.

"Fog horns!" the Sailing Master exclaimed. "Trumpets of some kind, or someone yelling through speaking-trumpets."

"Where away?" Lewrie snapped, dreading the chance that there were what sounded like four *gunboats* out there, trying to find each other.

Moo-wa!

"There, sir!" Munsell cried, pointing off the starboard quarter. "I think."

Moo-wa! And that one sounded as if it was out to larboard, out to sea of them! As the other fog horns mournfully lowed, Lt. Westcott pointed at one, and Caldwell at yet another, his arms out-stretched to encompass a section of the fog, swivelling his head and hands like an errant compass needle as his best estimate.

"Sir! Sir!" Midshipman Munsell was crying, hopping on his toes in urgency. "I think I can see a *light* out there, to starboard, where the loudest one was!" Without being ordered, Munsell sprang into the main-mast shrouds and scrambled up the rat-lines a few feet. "*There*, sir! I *do* see a light, a tiny one!"

Lewrie and the others peered out to find it on their own.

"Waving back and forth . . . hand-held?" Lt. Westcott speculated. "Like someone in a small boat?"

"A fleet of fishermen, perhaps," Mr. Caldwell mused aloud.

So long as they ain't gunboats! Lewrie thought.

"This far off the coast, sir?" Westcott countered. "In such a flat calm, with no wind? Were they fishing boats, they would have had to set out from Coutances or some other wee port *very* early last night to be caught by this fog."

"In their home waters they know best?" Lewrie scoffed. "I don't think French fishermen'd dare come out this far, not since the war reopened. Our close blockade keeps 'em a lot nearer port, as we saw in the Gulf of Saint Malo. It *does* look like a hand-held lanthorn, don't it? So whatever sort o' boat it is, it can't be all that large."

Lewrie gave it a long think, then went to the break of the quarterdeck to look down into the be-fogged waist of the ship where his men sat round the guns, ready to spring into action when ordered.

"Mister Merriman," he called down, "see Bosun Sprague and assemble an armed boat crew. Mister Simcock?" he said to their officer of Marines, who had been idly pacing the starboard gangway behind the file of a dozen Marines posted by the bulwarks and rolled hammock nettings. "I'd admire some of your men to go with Mister Merriman to see just what's out there, and board it, if it's manageable."

"*Very* good, sir!" Lt. Simcock replied, stiffening to attention and beaming at a chance to do something.

"May I have Cox'n Desmond and your boat crew, sir?" Lt. Merriman asked. At Lewrie's emphatic nod, the Third Lieutenant turned about to point at Desmond, Furfy, and the rest, summoning them to the gangway and the starboard entry-port. "I'll take one of the towed barges, sir, so we'll have room enough for the 'lobsterbacks.'"

"Very good," Lewrie agreed. "Make sure you've a boat compass, and mark your reciprocal course. We're not goin' anywhere quickly, so we should be easy to find," he japed.

Moo-wa! wailed from larboard, making Lewrie swivel his head to find her in the impenetrable banks of fog, and think that the source of that eldritch hooting *might* lay two points or more forward of abeam to *Reliant*. *In for a penny, in for a pound,* he thought.

"Mister Houghton," he called to their oldest Midshipman, "I wish you to take the second barge, and some Marines, and seek out the boat out yonder," he ordered, pointing off in the general direction that his ears had determined, repeating his warning to take a good boat compass.

Moo-wa! sounded from larboard again, in answer to a thin chorus of horn-amplified hoots very far out to starboard. *Reliant* was in the middle of the mysterious boats, slowly ghosting forward on the scanty wind. If the

so-far-unseen boats were small fishing boats, as Mister Caldwell first supposed, Lewrie could not imagine them being much over thirty feet in
length, with only a single lug-sail. His frigate sported *acres* of canvas aloft
in comparison, and, once such a large ship got *any* way upon her, her
weight and much longer hull allowed her to coast onward, when smaller
boats would wallow to a stop and require a stouter wind to get moving
once more. They might truly be becalmed and helpless . . . whatever they
were!

Not gunboats, though, no gunboats, pray Jesus! Lewrie thought.

Moo-wa! and *Hoo!* from all quarters, some close, most distant and eerie, and Lewrie took note of his idle gunners looking at each other uneasily, a few of the ship's boys who crouched down the centreline of the waist
between the guns, leather-cased powder cartridges in their hands, peering about wide-eyed in fear.

"It ain't whales, lads, and it ain't sea-monsters," Lewrie told them as
loud as he dared. "They're Frog fishermen, most-like, lost in the fog, and
they haven't a clue that *Reliant*'s the fox in the chicken coop!"

That seemed to satisfy most of the crew, though not all.

"Both the barges are away, sir," Lt. Westcott reported. "Mister Houghton's is almost out of sight, not a musket-shot off, and the other is already
swallowed up. Wish you'd have sent me, sir," he added.

"Are they gunboats, I need you here, sir," Lewrie said. "If we end up
seizing a couple of fishing smacks, there's not enough glory in 'em. Why,
Mister Westcott?" Lewrie posed with a grin. "Are ye in need of favourable
notice with Admiralty? One of your *amours* isn't some admiral's daughter,
is she?"

"Frankly, sir, but for the chance to be blown sky-high by one of our
bloody torpedo contraptions, it's been a dull Summer," Lt. Westcott replied. "Looking for a bit of honest excitement was my desire."

"Captain Speaks *will* be returning with a fresh lot of catamaran torpedoes," Lewrie pointed out. "Perhaps we'll actually employ 'em on the
French . . . under return fire and at close range. Be careful what you ask
for, Mister Westcott. *There's* some honest excitement for you!"

"Just so long as we *are* in action, sir," Westcott told him with a hungry
grin and a flash of his teeth.

Lewrie paced back to the binnacle cabinet, with his First Lieutenant
dutifully following him.

"We're making two and a half knots, sir, barely," Mr. Caldwell, the
Sailing Master, reported, his coat damp from supervising the cast of the

log. "I was wondering about what you said, sir . . . that the local French fishermen would stay closer to shore, and no stiff wind could've blown them this far out where they might run into some of our ships on close blockade?"

"Aye, Mister Caldwell?" Lewrie prompted, feeling a shiver that he might be wrong in thinking that they had blundered into only small boats. He was *used* to being wrong!

"Might the French have tried to sneak a convoy of invasion boats up the coast, and got caught the same as us in this odd turn of the weather?" Mr. Caldwell posed. "There's a good, sheltered inlet South of us by Avranches and Saint Hilaire," he said, referring to the chart for a moment. "Were they building *caïques* and such in there, they might have thought to sneak them as far as Cherbourg in one night."

"And if they are a convoy of invasion craft, they might have an escort or two, is what you're thinking?" Lewrie asked him, feeling yet another shiver of dread.

"Do we blunder up close to one, sir, perhaps they'll take us for one of their big, three-masted *prames*," Lt. Westcott said, shrugging.

Moo-wa! lowed from larboard once again, sounding much closer to them than before, followed by a thin voice!

"Quelq'un là-bas? . . . . Allô?"

"Houghton's boat must be upon it, whatever it is!" Lt. Westcott snapped, going to the larboard side in more haste than officers of the Royal Navy usually displayed. "French, for certain, by God!"

"Qui va là?" that distant voice came again, caution or alarm in its tone. *"Qui vive?"* more sharply and urgent.

That demand was answered by a volley of musket shots, soft pops, and cracks muffled by the fog, from Midshipman Houghton's men or the French they could not tell, but there came a human wail of surprise or pain, and thin cheers!

"Whatever it is, it sounds as if Mister Houghton thinks he can board it and take it, sir!" Westcott called over his shoulder. Even as he turned back to look out-board, there came a few more muffled cracks too soft for muskets; it sounded as if Houghton, his sailors, and the Marines might actually be aboard and close enough for pistol-shots!

"Dear Lord, if they've troops aboard!" Mr. Caldwell cautioned.

"Doesn't sound like it," Lewrie said after listening intently for more clues. There were no more shots, and only one more chorus of cheers, triumphant sounds, before the day went still once more, and he could not tell if it was British cheers, or from the French, who might have out-manned, swarmed, and over-awed Midshipman Houghton's party to take them all prisoner. All Lewrie could hear was the groans from the barely swaying masts, the tilting yards, and *Reliant's* hull timbers.

"*More* shooting, sir, from starboard!" the Sailing Master yelled. "Lieutenant Merriman's at it!"

"*Somethin'* orf th' starb'd bows!" a lookout shouted from the forecastle. With the fog so thick, they had kept night-time deck lookouts posted as well as the day lookouts placed high aloft in the top-masts. "Strange boat t'starb'd . . . *close aboard*!"

It took a few more seconds for that strange boat to appear to the people on the quarterdeck. First there was nothing but whiteness and fog, then a faint and darker shadowy bulk that magically materialised, only slowly taking solid form.

"What the Devil is *that*?" the Sailing Master barked as the oddity fully emerged.

Salvation from that threatened court-martial? Lewrie thought in sudden glee.

The French boat looked to be no further off than a long musket-shot, a two-masted *thing* with its lug-sails and jibs hanging limp and the booms sweeping uselessly to either beam. It resembled an inverted serving platter or shallow soup tureen, with a long rectangular box on its back that ran down the centreline, from the small cockpit to the rhino-like proboscis in the bow.

"A *beetle*?" Lt. Westcott deemed it, sounding awed. That was a fair-enough first guess, for near its forward third there were wide-bladed oars jutting to either side, at least half a dozen on the larboard side that faced them, and they were being worked like scoops to crawl it forward, just like a water-beetle that had lost most of its legs!

"*Qui vive? Heu, mort de ma vie!*" the lone Frenchman aft at the thing's helm wailed. Just aft of him at its taffrail stood a staff, from which a small French Tricolour windlessly dangled.

"Mister Spendlove!" Lewrie yelled to the gun-deck. "Take that . . . *thing* under fire!"

One of the big'uns, I think, Lewrie adjudged after a dash for the starboard bulwarks for a better look; *fourty-five or fifty feet in length . . . the type Peel said could carry an hundred French troops!*

"*As* you *bear . . . fire!*" Lt. Spendlove cried in sing-song.

Even with the wood quoins fully inserted under the breeches of the guns, the odd French invasion barge lay so low to the water that half the shots only scythed away the two masts and lug-sails, crashed clean through that long centreline box that should protect French soldiers and let them re-load in shelter, carrying most of it away in a whirl of shattered lumber! It was the carronades on the quarterdeck with their screw adjusters under their breeches that could be depressed low enough to score solid hits, and they were awesome! They were 32-pounders firing solid shot, and they punched huge holes right through the carapace of the "beetle's" back and, from the parroty *Rrawk-screech* sounds which followed the initial timber-screams on entry, carried on at a shallow angle out the boat's starboard side!

The French boat's helmsman, before being cut in two by roundshot, had put its helm hard-over, and though the rest of its crew that had been manning the paddles had abandoned them and come rushing on deck, the strange craft swung its bows shoreward, coasting along on a scant momentum. What little wind there was that moved the banks of fog blew the gunsmoke back into the faces of the gun crews as they swabbed out and began the ritual of re-loading, blinding everyone for long moments with thick yellow-white clouds of sulfur-reeking smoke.

By the time the guns were run out in-battery once more and the gun-captains could take aim, the range was just long enough for surer aim.

"*As* you *bear . . . fire!*" Lt. Spendlove screeched again.

"*That's* better!" Lewrie cheered. "*That's* the way, lads!"

Before a fresh bank of gunsmoke blotted out their view again, Lewrie could see shot-splashes all round the boat, close aboard its waterline, and more holes punched into her larboard side and stern-quarters!

"Overhaul tackle . . . staunch and swab out!" Lt. Spendlove was hoarsely ordering. "Cartridges up!"

"Sir! Sir!" Midshipman Munsell shrilled, still at his post in the mainmast shrouds. "She's sinking, sir! She's *sinking*!"

The French build 'em out o' papier-mâché? Lewrie wondered as he leaned far out over the quarterdeck bulwarks to see for himself.

Damned if the boat *wasn't* sinking! Instead of an up-turned soup tureen, the thing now more-resembled a large-holed colander, with shot holes riddling its stern and larboard side. There was no sign of the other French sailors who had dashed to the deck. It was both down by the bows, most-likely dragged by the weight of the rumoured 24-pounder bow gun,

and heeled over to starboard, the result of the 32-pound shot from the carronades, the "Smashers," that had gone completely through her hull to
her starboard side below the waterline.

It rolled onto its beam ends, revealing a clean, new bottom but without
the normal protection against barnacles, weed, and wood-boring worms;
the French had not coppered her bottom! The curve of the lower hull was
shallower than the upperworks, and most of its length was flat-bottomed,
like a river barge.

"They think to dare the open sea, the Channel, in *that*?" Lieutenant
Westcott hooted in derision as the odd, alien-looking boat went down by
the bows, cocking its riddled stern in the air for an instant like a feeding
duck, then sank in a welter of foam and released air.

"Pray God they *do*, Mister Westcott!" Lewrie said, laughing out loud
with his arms outstretched in joy. "Fetch 'em up to half a cable in clear
weather, and one broadside'll do for each. When they come we can make
a *meal* of 'em!"

"What *was* that, sir?" Mr. Caldwell asked.

"A French secret weapon, Mister Caldwell," Lewrie happily told him,
"one that doesn't seem worth a tupenny shit. They're *supposed* to paddle
themselves right onto a beach, use that twenty-four-pounder in the bow
t'clear the way, and land about one hundred Frog troops each."

"Then Bonaparte's dafter than I thought, sir!" Caldwell replied, with a
chuckle, though he shook his head in amazement.

"You knew of them, sir?" Westcott asked.

"Unofficially," Lewrie admitted. "Some months ago before they saddled us with the torpedo experiments."

"D'ye hear, there! Strange boat off the starboard quarters!" a deck
lookout aft by the transom shouted.

"Hoy, *Reliant*!" a voice shouted from the fog. "Merriman here! Hold
your fire! We're returning with a prize!"

Lewrie returned to the starboard bulwarks, clambering atop one of the
carronades' slides for a better view. Another of the strange boats swam
slowly into view, its broad-bladed paddles clawing at the sea, all out of
coordination . . . and the first part of it that seemed completely solid from
out of the thick fog was that snout at the bows, that 24-pounder!

"Ahoy, Mister Merriman!" Lewrie called back through his cupped
hands. "Is that bow gun *loaded*?"

"*No*, sir! There's no shot or powder aboard!" Lt. Merriman gaily called back. "We've two prisoners, one of them wounded, and one of our Marines slightly hurt. Cox'n Desmond is ready to pass a towing line, when you're ready!"

"She's an ugly bitch, ain't she, lads?" Liam Desmond yelled to the ship as he stood just beside that large gun, with a heavy coil of line readied.

"An't worth half a crown in prize-money!" his mate, Furfy, just had to add, capering a jig on the boat's sloping foredeck.

The Hell she ain't! Lewrie thought; *There's people in London, at Admiralty, who'll turn Saint Catherine wheels t'see one, close up!*

The Surgeon, Mister Mainwaring, came up from his surgery in the cockpit on the orlop, accompanied by a party of loblolly boys bearing a pair of mess tables for stretchers as the odd boat, and the borrowed barge, came close alongside to transfer all the Marines, the two French prisoners, and Lt. Merriman back aboard.

"We can take it under tow, but that may slow us to nothing," Lewrie said, looking up hopefully at the sails and commissioning pendant, which still hung limp, only its free end being lifted. "Welcome back aboard, Mister Merriman, and congratulations on carrying out your action so briskly."

"Thank you, sir. It was simple, really," Merriman said. "The thing loomed up, we scrambled up the slope of the hull, gave them one volley and cold steel, and it was done. The hardest part was climbing the slope. Whatever that thing is, it's only sixteen or eighteen feet abeam, and it looks as if it rises about eight feet to the turtleback . . . or beetleback, ha ha! A bit slippery," he said with a glad shrug.

"Metalled hull, was it?" Lewrie asked, hoping that it was not. "That . . . box down the centreline. Armoured, was it?"

"Lord, no, sir, just wood!" Lt. Merriman laughed. "The box is made of one-inch deal planking over four-by-four posts!"

"D'ye hear, there!" another lookout cried from up forward. "A boat off the larboard beam! 'Tis another o' the things!"

"Stand by, the larboard battery!" Lt. Spendlove on the gun-deck warned his gunners.

"Ahoy, *Reliant*! Barge number two, with prize!"

"That you, Mister Houghton?" Lewrie shouted back, with a brass speaking-trumpet this time.

"Aye, sir! Permission to come alongside? We've a wounded man, and a prisoner!" Midshipman Houghton called out.

"Very well, Mister Houghton!" Lewrie agreed. "Pass us a line, and we'll *try* t'take you under tow. We've a second prize t'deal with as well."

"The fog's thinning to seaward, sir, and there's a *bit* of wind from the West," Houghton informed him as his capture solidified from the fog; she could be made out nearly *two* hundred yards off, about the range of Lewrie's breech-loading Ferguson rifle-musket. With any luck, the sea-breeze would spring to life and would be strong enough for towing both prizes out on larboard tack, one bound to *Reliant*'s stern and the second bound to the stern of the first barge!

And alter course, at last, a bit more Nor'westerly, and clear the French coast before the fog burns completely off, Lewrie schemed.

"Listen, sir," Westcott pointed out. "It seems we've upset the French."

The mournful baying of fog horns had turned urgent and rapid, more like a pack of hounds that had run a fox to its earth. Added to that baying were a couple of trumpets.

"I didn't know the French were much fond of fox-hunting, sir," Lt. Westcott said with a laugh. "Hear that? 'Ta-tara-tara!! Yoicks, tally-ho! There must be one sporting fellow out there."

"It does sound like a fox-hunt, doesn't it?" Lewrie mused. "Are you a hunter, Mister Westcott?"

"We're small-holders, sir . . . just fifty-odd acres," Lt. Westcott said with a dismissive shrug, "so we only get invited the once each year, and I never saw the point. Steeplechasing at the gallop's more to my liking, and I could do that any time. In fact, I've always felt sorry for the fox. Tried to make a pet of one when I was little, and you can imagine how that played out," he added, chuckling.

"Fox kits and otter cubs . . . my son Hugh was mad for either, or both," Lewrie rejoined with a laugh.

"Damn my eyes, is that a breeze, sir?" Westcott said, turning to look seaward, then aloft.

"Not much of one, but it's from the West," Lewrie replied as he looked aloft to the sails, which were, rustling uncertainly, trimmed to cup the land-breeze and now presented with one from the opposite tack. "Hands to the braces and sheets, Mister Westcott. Let's make the most of it and get a goodly way on her. Mister Merriman?"

"Here, sir!"

"Rig towing lines from the stern to one boat, and another to the second," Lewrie ordered. "And have the prize parties take in those paddle things, with an experienced helmsman in each."

"Aye aye, sir!"

"Once we're trimmed to the wind, Mister Caldwell, shape course Nor'-Nor'west, so we pass between Jersey and Alderney," Lewrie told the Sailing Master. "Once we're out in the Channel, we'll take a bee-line for Portsmouth!"

BOOK V

Ye true honest Britons who love your own land
Whose sires were so brave, so victorious, so free,
Who always beat France when they took her in hand
Come join honest Britons in chorus with me.

Should the French dare invade us, thus armed with our poles,
We'll bang their bare ribs, make their lantern jaws ring;
For your beef-eating, beer-drinking Britons are souls
Who will shed their last blood for their Country and King!

–POPULAR TAVERN SONG

CIRCA 1757

CHAPTER THIRTY-NINE

$\mathcal{A}$nyone who was anyone in the Navy wished to see the odd French contraptions once *Reliant* towed them into Portsmouth harbour. The Surveyor of the Navy, Sir William Rule, and the Deputy Controller of the Navy, Captain Henry Duncan, came down from London to gawk and wonder, in company with the Port Admiral, Lord Gardner, and the Commissioner of HM Dockyards at Portsmouth, Captain Sir Charles Saxton, Bart. The Foreign Office sent down a functionary, and there were some "redcoat" Army types rather high in rank who evinced great curiosity about what sort of threat the landing barges might make. There were representatives from the Pitt government, along with a select group of Navy captains charged with patrolling the Channel, so they could recognise the damned things should they run across them in future.

Lieutenants Westcott and Merriman prepared detailed sketches of the things, several sets done by hand, for no one wanted to trust the drawings to even a *government* printer. And, Lewrie was "on show" for each curious visitor to explain their capture, and how they handled in the open sea, but, if he had imagined a hero's welcome, he was greatly disappointed. There was no celebration dinner, no presentation sword or set of silver plate, no band, no parade through the streets with a cheering crowd, or several dozen sailors replacing the horse team to draw him in an open carriage, either. And a fireworks show and a *Te Deum* mass at St. Thomas A'Becket's Church were right out, too.

The pair of boats that *Reliant* had captured were hurriedly covered with great swaths of sailcloth and towed into an empty graving dock, then placed under armed Marine guard.

"Well, damme, Captain Lewrie, but ye do keep popping up with one surprise after another," Admiral Lord Gardner commented after making a clumsy, arthritic way aboard one of them in company with his Flag-Captain, Niles. "They've a lot of these things, d'ye imagine?"

"The rumours say three or four hundred, my lord," Lewrie said.

"First that nonsense about torpedoes, now these," Lord Gardner went on, peering down into the bowels of the barge where the soldiers would sleep, sup, and shelter. "Three or four hundred, did ye say?"

"So I was told by a friend in Secret Branch, my lord."

This tour was the fifth that Lewrie had given to various officials, and it was getting old, by then. The lack of praise beyond the usual "Good show!" was irksome, too. He imagined that if Nelson had come across them, that fame-hungry fellow would have commissioned special editions of all the London papers, with illustrations to boot!

"Damned waste of good artillery, packing a twenty-four-pounder in the bows," Lord Gardner went on in a grumble. "Do the French think they can use them as gunboats, too? Wheel them round with those huge paddles? I saw armed galleys in the Mediterranean in my youth, but . . . it looks iffy to me."

"Concentrating all the paddles in the forward end, too," Captain Niles added. "I suppose they work well enough in a river but not at sea. Has anyone *tried* paddling them about?"

"Once we made port, sir," Lewrie told him with a grimace, "to shift them alongside. They don't row worth a damn, nor steer, either. They're fitted with a tiller to the exposed rudder, and my helmsmen about wore themselves out on the way here under tow, tryin' to follow the stern posts of the leadin' barge, or my frigate. A handful o' lee helm, then a handful o' weather helm. We did hoist their sails, to steady 'em, but that didn't help much. I'd imagine that did one try 'em under sail, *without* bein' towed, they'd wallow from beam-to-beam, be slow as cold treacle, and with their flat bottoms, they'd make lee-way like a wood chip."

"Heh heh heh," the Port Admiral, softly, evilly cackled, bending down to survey the interior more closely. "How many soldiers might it carry, Lewrie?"

"These large versions are said to carry an hundred, my lord. A shorter one may carry about eighty," Lewrie told him.

"One hundred Frogs, cooped up down there on those benches, or in those slat beds, my my!" Lord Gardner said, enjoying the image. "Cold rations. I see no galley facilities. No 'heads,' either."

"Rations for five or six days, I heard, sir," Lewrie supplied. "Though, part of that might be for after they landed in England before they could loot and pillage the countryside . . . or hope to."

"Bonaparte must not have much regard for his soldiers, milord," Captain Niles imagined, "if he expected them to use wooden buckets as their 'necessaries,' then have to pass them up from below. The reek would be horrid," he said with a sniff, as if reeks already existed.

"The staleness of the air," Lord Gardner happily fantasised. "The reek of their 'cess,' as well, Niles, and the stench of sea-sickness, which would naturally engender even more sickness! Why, after a day or two of that, with these daft things wallowing like hogs in the mud, and rolling like logs, it'd be a bloody wonder that they could fight at all! Right, Niles?"

"Stagger ashore reeling like tars off a whaler that's been at sea two years running, and be so crop-sick even our militia can round them up, milord!" Captain Niles hooted. "They're a completely daft idea, and if the French really mean to employ them, they'll pay an ungodly high price in dead, and in prisoners."

"Drown nigh a quarter of their men, should the Channel whip up rough during the crossing," Admiral Lord Gardner estimated, looking highly pleased with his conclusion. "What was it that Bonaparte was reputed to have said, sirs? 'Give me six hours' mastery of the Channel, and we shall be masters of the world'? Bah! Bah, I say!"

"Lord Keith in The Downs estimates so large an invasion armada would take two tides to get across in sufficient strength, milord," Captain Niles gleefully pointed out. "Twenty-four hours with the sea and tides scattering them, sickening them, and our ships clawing at them like so many tigers? *Let* them try, is what I say!"

"Congratulations to ye, Captain Lewrie," Lord Gardner said as he stood erect, going so far as to offer his hand. "It was a brave thing to snatch them up, in such a thick fog, with no thought for the presence of escorts . . . and, to get them away for study!"

"Well, it seemed a good idea at the moment, my lord," Lewrie replied, shaking hands with the old fellow and *trying* to sound modest.

"Damme, Lewrie . . . had you not already been granted a knighthood, this deed surely would have earned you one!" Captain Niles said in praise as well.

Well, damned if it might've! Lewrie thought, feeling for the first time as if he had done something worthy of the honour, instead of secretly scorning his sash and star as a sop given for his usefulness, and the usefulness of his late wife's murder, to ignite revulsion and hatred of the French, and Bonaparte.

"Long after the fact, though, Niles," Lord Gardner said, dashing cold water on that speculation. "Our possession of the damned things is to be of the utmost secrecy . . . same as Lewrie's torpedo devices. Least said, the better, what? Did the Crown decide Lewrie was worthy, it'd not be announced for years! Damme, even we've been put on strict notice to forget we ever *saw* them, and to not go blab to anyone they even exist! Do we dream about them, we'd best not talk in our sleep, hah!"

Lewrie felt his ears reddening. He *had* blabbed, in letters, at least, to Lydia Stangbourne, Sir Hugo, his sons at sea, and one of his in-laws, Burgess Chiswick, and had nigh broken his neck running to the post office to retrieve them before they left the dockyard offices!

"If you've seen all you wish, milord, there are other matters pending," the jovial Captain Niles prompted as yet another light rain began to fall.

"Oh aye, I've seen quite enough, Niles," Lord Gardner told his aide. "Help me off this monstrosity before the weather turns even more nasty."

That involved an embarrassingly awkward clamber out of the after cockpit of the French barge, down the slick slope of the upper deck and hull to the waterline, where a jolly-boat awaited to bear them the short distance to the dry stone cobbles and blocks of the upper end of the graving dock, where they could step onto dry land.

"Getting on for Autumn, Lewrie," Lord Gardner said as he stumped his way towards the tall flight of stone steps that would take them to street level. "It will be October in a week, and the weather in the Channel might force Bonaparte to hold his invasion 'til next Spring."

Where does *the time go when we're havin'* so *much fun?* Lewrie cynically thought.

"Now or never, perhaps, my lord?" Lewrie said with a grin.

"Pray God. By then, well," Lord Gardner agreed. "Nettlesome as Bonaparte is, surely he'll so worry some other continental powers that they form another armed coalition against him, forcing him to take his huge army off to defend his borders . . . or look to expand his empire somewhere else. All our fears may amount to nothing."

"Good grief, what's that about, I wonder?" Captain Niles said as the sound of a loud argument reached them. "Have they caught a French spy, or a nosy newspaper man?"

"Shoot either, on the spot, instanter!" Lord Gardner snarled.

As they reached the top of the stone stairs, they could see that the Marines had nabbed an intruder who'd found a way through the newly-erected wooden screen wall and sailcloth-curtained gate. The Marines had him pinned to the wall, surrounded with fixed bayonets on their levelled muskets.

". . . bloody Hell do you mean I can't enter, you puppy! I'm a Post-Captain in the Royal Navy, Captain Speaks, and I *know* that Captain Lewrie's in there! I must speak to him, at once, and bedamned to you if you think . . . !"

"Oh, bloody Hell," Lewrie groaned, sure he'd seen the last of the fellow.

"Speaks? Speaks? Who's he, Niles?" Lord Gardner grumbled.

"The mysterious torpedo fellow, milord. The one in charge of testing those 'Gosport wonders'?" Niles told his admiral. "It's all very hush-hush."

"There's entirely too much of that going round!" Lord Gardner tetchily snapped.

Ain't there, just! Lewrie silently agreed.

"*There* he is!" Speaks barked, pointing accusingly. "*There's* the fellow I must see, damn your eyes, sir!" he railed at the young Marine officer in charge of the guard unit. "You did not stay on station as I ordered you, Lewrie! I should prefer charges!"

Get in line! Lewrie told himself.

"Niles . . . go tell that noisy jackanapes to stop his gob, or I'll have him stood against the wall and shot, for entering a secret area! I *can* have him shot, can I not, sir?"

"Well, ordinarily no, milord, but . . . given the circumstances and the secrecy of our possession of the French devices . . . ," Captain Niles mused aloud, with a "sly-boots" grin.

"Go threaten him into next year!" Gardner demanded. "At once!"

Speaks'll take his rebuke out on me, Lewrie mournfully thought; *Ye'd think after bringin' these things in, I'd get fresh orders, but . . . am I still his, damn his eyes?*

CHAPTER FORTY

*C*aptain Speaks refused to come aboard *Reliant;* he despised cats as sneaking, vicious Imps from Hades, the familiars of warlocks and witches. No, Lewrie had to go aboard *Penarth,* the bought-in collier, for his dressing-down, where Speaks's own familiar, his loquacious parrot, ruled the after cabins. Speaks did *not* offer refreshments!

"Why did you not strictly obey my verbal orders, Lewrie?" the choleric fellow seethed, seated behind the wee desk, looking down his nose at Lewrie with the fierce air of a Lord Justice regarding an habitual criminal about to be sentenced to hang.

"You told me to go make a nuisance on the French coast, sir," Lewrie calmly replied. "That we did, and in the process, we stumbled onto some secret French . . . devices, in a thick fog off Coutances, and took two of them and sank a third. I'd been apprised t'keep one eye out for 'em, and that, should I encounter any, I should—"

"*Secret* devices!" Speaks barked. "What sort of devices?"

"I'm afraid I can't tell you, sir," Lewrie answered, finding it too tempting to keep to himself. "They're secret. Very secret."

"And just who the Devil, or when, were you 'apprised,' hah?"

"Just before we began experiments with Mister MacTavish's cask torpedoes, sir, as for the when," Lewrie went on, seemingly seated at ease in a folding chair, clubman fashion, with one leg over the other. "As for who, sir . . . it was Mister James Peel of Foreign Office Secret Branch, with whom I've worked in the past, now and again. He had had correspondence from . . . sources in France alerting the government and Admiralty that they existed. I gathered that is his brief, sir . . . the recruiting and handling of intelligence sources."

"Keel-haul the bastard! Keel-haul! *Rwark!*" from the parrot.

"And you deemed these . . . *things* you captured were more important than *our* secret work, Lewrie?" Speaks sneered.

"I did, sir," Lewrie firmly stated.

"Your orders charged you to safeguard *Penarth* and her cargo of devices from capture by the French, *'at all hazards,'* Lewrie! *'At all hazards'!* That phrase slip your mind, did it?" Speaks accused. "What do I find when I return to the *rendezvous?* Nothing! No one to safeguard this vessel or her vitally secret weapons, no aid in conducting fresh experiments, either, and no message left with the authorities at Guernsey explaining *why* you just up and left! And I couldn't very well commandeer *another* warship from the blockading squadron and expose the secret of the torpedoes' existence to just *any* damned fool!"

"Given the importance of my find, though, sir, I acted as I deemed best," Lewrie insisted.

"Saucy rascal! Flog the bugger, *too-wheep!*" from the bird.

Christ, they've been together so long, they even think alike! Lewrie told himself. The parrot had an eerily impressive vocabulary, indeed!

"Forcing me to cancel experiments, and return to Portsmouth," Captain Speaks said in a huff, "failing in *my* express orders from Admiralty. Experiments which have become even more vital than before, sir. Vital, I tell you! By God, I really *should* lay court-martial charges against you. Turn you over to Admiral Lord Keith, and let him deal with you. So you can explain to *him* why the weapons that he intends to employ might be wanting!"

Lord Keith commanded in The Downs, subordinate to Admiral Lord William Cornwallis of Channel Fleet, making Lewrie wonder why Speaks would prefer charges with him, instead of Cornwallis, or Admiralty directly. *Weapons he intends to employ?* Lewrie wondered.

"These damned French things you brought in, Lewrie," Captain Speaks said, turning too mellow and "chummy" too quickly for Lewrie's taste. "We both have access to high secrets. What are they, really?"

"I cannot reveal that, sir. Truly!" Lewrie insisted.

"Bosun, lay on! Two dozen lashes! *Rwark!*" the parrot uttered, prefaced, and concluded, with what sounded like a throaty and rasping gargle, or cat-purr, as it paced along its perch.

"Have the *French* developed a form of torpedo, Lewrie? Perhaps *anchored* torpedoes?" Speaks further asked, almost cajolingly.

"I can assure you that they're *not* torpedoes, sir, but that's all I can tell you," Lewrie cautiously replied. "About Admiral Lord Keith, though . . . he *intends* to employ catamaran torpedoes, did y'say? *Before* the weather in the Channel turns foul?"

"You will be informed at the proper time, Captain Lewrie," the choleric older fellow snapped, seeing that the nature of Lewrie's secret would not be forthcoming, and keeping his own 'til the last minute. He turned snippish once more. "Thanks to *you*, sir, there will not be time for further testing, and the catamaran torpedoes will be employed *before* their ultimate perfection, and . . . ," Speaks gravelled, levelling a finger at Lewrie like a pistol barrel, "should they fail to achieve the desired results, such failure will not be placed upon *my* head, but upon *yours*, sir, for your lack of support to me!"

"*Despite* our suggested improvements of drogues and rudders that drifted them quicker and straighter, sir?" Lewrie asked, having a hard time stifling his anger at such a threat, and the unfairness of it. "I and my men have been *very* supportive to you, as you told me earlier."

"Damn my . . . !" Speaks said, spluttering with fury. "You are to keep your bloody frigate ready to sail at a moment's notice! You are to restrict access with the shore, and except for victualling, you are to keep your people aboard, where they cannot blab."

"Well, *Reliant*'s people have earned a brief spell Out of Discipline, after . . . ," Lewrie countered, instantly regretting how tongue-in-cheek that sounded.

"Absolutely *not*, sir!" Speaks roared. "You will sit and swing at anchor 'til I've need of you. Do not be obstreperous or insubordinate with me . . . I'll not have it, do you hear?"

"Quite clearly, sir," Lewrie replied, abashed.

"Dismissed, Captain Lewrie," Speaks ordered, stone-faced.

"Mutinous dog! Mutinous dog . . . *rwark*!" from the parrot.

Once out on deck in the fresh air, Lewrie let out a deep pented breath, puffing out his cheeks and sharing a rueful glance with Lieutenant Douglas Clough, *Penarth*'s captain, who had wisely found another place to be while Speaks was tearing a strip off Lewrie's arse. Clough *looked* sympathetic.

"Might there be something up, Mister Clough?" Lewrie asked him in a close-by mutter as he made ready to board his waiting big.

"Ye dinna hear it from me, sir, but . . . we've been ordered to take a fresh load of torpedoes aboard, in a tearing hurry, mind, and once done, I'm to take her down to Saint Helen's Patch and wait for a favourable wind . . . for The Downs, sir, to join Admiral Lord Keith! Captain Speaks gave me a hint . . . it's to be Boulogne, sir!" the rough-featured Scot muttered back, though with an eager grin. "Explosive boats, fireships, our torpedoes, and even some rocket-firing vessels . . . Mister William Congreve's explosive rockets!"

"What's a Congreve rocket?" Lewrie wondered aloud, in a soft, conspiratorial tone. "I know *signal* rockets, but . . ."

"Don't rightly know, sir, for no one ever tells me things, if they don't pertain to our torpedo trials," Lt. Clough said with a wee and wry laugh. "Mark my words, Captain Lewrie . . . we'll be a part of a grand attack on Boulogne, sure as Fate, and that soon!"

"Thankee, Mister Clough," Lewrie said, grinning back, "for the news. Now, I'll have t'play dumb 'til our superiors decide t'tell us for certain."

"With no shore liberty for anyone . . . even officers," Clough mournfully agreed.

"Boulogne, though . . . well, well!" Lewrie whispered, imagining what that would be like, on the day ordained.

Play dumb 'til I'm told the details? Lewrie thought as he went through the ritual of departing honours, *I was* born *t'play dumb! It's what people* expect *o' me!*

CHAPTER FORTY-ONE

At least it's a pretty day for it, Alan Lewrie thought as the coast of France loomed up from the southern horizon, as a squadron, of which HMS *Reliant* was a part, sailed for Boulogne. Lewrie did wonder, though, why the expedition was so small, if the undertaking was of such vital importance to England's survival.

The squadron was led by Admiral of the Blue Lord Keith in HMS *Monarch,* a two-decker 74-gunned Third Rate, not the lofty First or Second Rate more suitable to his seniority. With *Monarch* were two 64-gun two-deckers and two much older Fourth Rate two-decker 50s, a type of warship more commonly seen on convoy duty or troop carrying these days, not in the line of battle. It was smaller ships that made up the bulk of the squadron's numbers; there were bomb vessels with their big sea-mortars, some older warships converted to fire William Congreve's infernal rockets, brig-sloops and frigates, and a host of cutters and armed launches . . . along with at least four fireships and the collier *Penarth* bearing their catamaran torpedoes.

Lewrie savoured the last few sips of tepid coffee in his pewter mug as he stood by the windward bulwarks of the quarterdeck, slouched a tad, it must be admitted, as he surveyed the lines of warships, the sea and sky. Did the Emperor Napoleon Bonaparte wish for fine weather in which to launch his titanic invasion force, he could not ask for a milder day, for the conditions were rarely seen in the Channel in late Autumn, this first day of October of 1804.

The sky above was a soft and milky pale blue, almost completely blanketed by vast swathes of thin cirrus clouds, the sunlight softened and almost shadowless. Further up the Channel nearer to the Straits of Dover, and further down-Channel on the West horizon, there were thicker, taller, and more substantial clouds through which the sun speared down in bright shafts. There were sootier, darker shafts, too, as if there might be rain there, or, as superstitious old salts maintained, the sun was drawing up columns of water for a later deluge.

The waters of the Channel, usually boisterous, cross-chopped and sparkling with white-horses and white-caps, were calmer, too, the waves longer and shallower for once, and the muted sunlight turned the sea's colour to steely grey-blue close aboard, and a paler blue that mirrored the sky further away. France, off the bows, was a thin smear of dull green and sand, a single coloured pencil-stroke, so far.

The only stark colours were the solidities of the warships, and their hulls and sails; dark brown weathered oak, the shiny black of the painted upperworks or the matte black of tarred wales, and the yellows, reds, ochres, or buffs of their hull stripes, with here and there glints of giltwork on transoms, entry-ports, or carved figureheads. Pale, new white canvas, or aged and weathered buff or parchment tan sails, made a ragged scudding cloud-bank above those hulls. Above them all, and aft on wooden staffs, all ships sported Blue Ensigns with vivid red-white-blue Union flags in their cantons . . . and all flew yards-long commissioning pendants from their main-mast tops, streaming and flickering like snakes' tongues licking the wind for the taste of prey.

Lewrie finished his cold coffee, set the mug down on the deck, and strolled to the break of the quarterdeck to peer over the hammock stanchions, now full of tightly rolled bedding, down into the waist.

Admiral Lord Keith had not yet ordered the squadron to Quarters, and Lewrie felt it odd to be sailing into action with his crew acting as if it was just another day far out at sea, with their frigate alone and without a threat on the horizons. The ports were still shut, and the great-guns were still snugly bowsed to the gun-port sills, each of them still plugged with red-painted wood tompions in their muzzles. A few men idled round the companionways, but only half the crew, of the starboard watch, stood the watch. Well, there were the Marines . . . if action was expected in an hour or so, Lt. Simcock was going to be ready for it, and properly dressed, too;

his men had doffed their everyday slops and had changed into cockaded
hats, red coats, white waist-coats and trousers, and black canvas "half-
spatterdash" leggings, with all of their martial accoutrements hung about
them.

"France . . . dammit," Lewrie muttered, as the squadron closed to
within six or seven miles of the shore. "Bloody, bloody, France!"

"Well, some of their young ladies are fetching, sir," Lieutenant Westcott breezily commented near Lewrie's side. "Recall the fair *Madamoiselle*
Sylvie at Kingston?"

"Oh, is *that* why you insisted you lead the boats?" Lewrie said with a
laugh. "You've a taste for French mutton, have you?"

"I rather doubt there'd be any aboard the invasion boats, sir," Westcott
replied, all whimsy. "Though one might hope?"

Lewrie wished to keep Lt. Westcott aboard *Reliant* should they run
into opposition from French gunboats, but Westcott had asked for a private word and had claimed the honour of leading the boats that would tow
the torpedoes in; it was the senior lieutenant's role by right and tradition,
and, "How else may I make a name for myself and gain notice for advancement, sir, if I'm held back?" he'd posed with a wry laugh, and Lewrie had acceded to his desire, charging him to look after his Cox'n, Liam
Desmond, and Desmond's long-time mate, Patrick Furfy.

He would send his oldest Midshipmen; he could spare them, and were
men to be lost, it was better to lose Mids than officers. That was tradi-
tional, too, and after all, Houghton, Entwhistle, and Mister Warburton
had as much need of a bit of fame and notice at Admiralty, and in the papers, as any other man; how else might *they* advance? And, Lewrie grimly
considered, even the most seasoned Midshipmen were as hungry for honour and glory as lion cubs!

"It's taking long enough," Captain Speaks impatiently snapped as he
strolled up to join them.

Such a pretty day, 'til he ruined it! Lewrie thought, stifling a groan,
keeping his gaze fixed on the bow-sprit, and pretending that he had not
heard the man.

Just before they had sailed from Portsmouth to join Lord Keith off The
Downs, Speaks had come aboard *Reliant*, without specific orders—and
thankfully without his damned parrot!—claiming that making passage in
Penarth would interfere too much with Lt. Clough and his preparations,
though he also *alluded* to un-seen orders to see the job right through to the
finish, and a "duty" to see "his torpedoes" successful. Lewrie's orders were

to accompany *Penarth* and use his men and boats to launch the devices, and they made no mention of Speaks, but . . . Speaks *was* senior to him, and Lewrie couldn't drive Speaks back into his hired boat at sword-point, or even demand to see those hinted-at orders, so . . . he was stuck with the pest! And a garrulous, peevish, and annoying pest he'd turned out to be, practically presiding and *ruling* meals with Lewrie and his officers, and constantly on the quarterdeck when Lewrie was, never *interfering,* exactly, with *Reliant*'s captain and officers of the watch, but hovering, with many a dis-approving scowl, sniff, grunt, questioning cocked brow, or muttered comment!

"They're *my* torpedoes, Lewrie, my collier from which you'll fetch them," Speaks had briskly rattled off, a calculating little smile upon his face, "and I'm damned well going to see them handled properly."

A kindly and charitable man might have deemed Captain Speaks's zeal admirable . . . the sort of fellow Captain Alan Lewrie definitely was *not,* even before the bastard had come aboard. No, what the fellow wanted the most, Lewrie suspected, was a chance to be at sea aboard a proper frigate, not a hired-in collier that mounted only pop-guns, and damned few of those. *Reliant* was a warship very much like Speaks's last command of 1801, which, had he not come down with pneumonia and had had to be replaced, he might have sailed into the Baltic as a lone ship to scout the Danish, Swedish, and Russian fleets, then returned in time to take part in the glorious battle with Nelson at Copenhagen, and felt robbed of the op-portunity.

Lewrie was dead-certain that Speaks *had* no orders; his brief had been to *test* the catamaran torpedoes, then turn them over to some other officer to be employed. He might have felt a *trifle* sorry for the old fellow—had he not been as bristly as a currying brush, nowhere *near* the "firm but fair" and well-liked officer of old! And if he wished to be close to his charges, and take part in a battle, at long last, more power to him, Lewrie thought—so long as he did so anywhere else but aboard *his* ship!

"Signal, sir!" Midshipman Munsell, high aloft, called down in a thin and shrill voice, reading off a string of number flags. "General to all ships, with two guns!"

"It is . . . 'Come to Anchor,' sir," Midshipman Rossyngton said, after a quick scan through his code book.

"Anchor?" Captain Speaks barked. "We're still five miles off!"

"Have the signal repeated, Mister Rossyngton," Lewrie told his Mid, "but I'd admire did we fetch-to, Mister Westcott, not anchor, as ordered.

Do the French come out, we'd be immobile too long for my liking . . . *and* caught tryin' t'go to Quarters and heave up the best bower and the entire length of a cable at the same time."

HMS *Reliant* was put up into wind, fore-and-aft sails still drawing to drive her forward, but with tops'ls aback to act as brakes, and let her make just a bit of stern and lee-way, practically immobilised, but still able to pay off and get back to speed in a mere minute, avoiding getting caught by a French sortie "with her pants down."

"It *was* an order," Captain Speaks muttered half to himself, just loud enough to irk. "Ahem," he covered, loudly clearing his throat.

"Interpreted by all but the two-deckers and the flagship according to captains' best judgement, sir," Lewrie pointed out through gritted teeth, in a rictus of an outwardly pleasant smile. "The rest have fetched-to, the other frigates and such. As you can see," he added as he swept an arm towards the lighter ships, which stood a little closer to the coast. "I doubt the cutters have anchor cables *long* enough."

"Now what, sir?" Lt. Westcott said, after coughing into a fist to change the subject.

"We sit here long enough, Mister Westcott, we might heave up the rum keg, then serve the mid-day meal," Lewrie cynically replied with a grimace. "I thought we'd just barge up to gun range and blaze away at once. But, that's up to Admiral Lord Keith. Mister Rossyngton? Pass word for my steward, and he's t'bring my collapsible chair up."

Captain Speaks, no fan of Lewrie already, goggled at the order, utterly convinced that Lewrie was the idlest lubber he'd ever met.

"And my penny-whistle, too, Mister Rossyngton," Lewrie added, sure that that would dismay the fellow even further; far enough, perhaps, to leave the quarterdeck and leave them all in peace? "What'd ye like t'hear, Mister Westcott? 'Spanish Ladies'?"

To Lewrie's wicked delight, Captain Speaks produced a gargling sound, belched up a muffled, "Pah!" and took himself a brisk stroll up the larboard sail-tending gangway, swinging his arms like a man working up an appetite.

" 'Fa-are-well, and *adieu,* to you *fine* Spanish ladies . . . fa-are-well, and *adieu,* to you ladies of *Spain* . . . fo-or *we've* received *orders* to-o sail for old England . . . ,' " Lewrie sang out.

Damn my eyes, but I do *know how t'rile 'em!* he gaily thought.

CHAPTER FORTY-TWO

*I*t was late afternoon before the squadron got under way, again, with Lord Keith's flagship, *Monarch,* leading all three frigates, bomb vessels, fireships, the *Penarth* collier, and all the brig-sloops and cutters closer to Boulogne.

"Now, we'll see something!" Speaks enthused, pacing the quarterdeck with jaunty steps and clapping his hands in eagerness for action.

But no, they didn't, for *Monarch* signalled for all ships to anchor again, this time just outside of the maximum reach of French cannon! In much shallower water, even the cutters could put down an anchor and find good holding ground without paying out too much scope of cable.

"A word, sir?" Lt. Westcott whispered, near Lewrie's shoulder.

"Aye," Lewrie allowed, just as guarded.

"This doesn't make any sense, sir," Westcott grumbled, his face set in a beetle-browed frown. "We haven't even been ordered to clear for action, and here we are, sitting ducks should the French come out, as you feared round Noon, when we fetched-to instead of anchoring."

"Well, it doesn't make any sense t'me, either, if there's comfort in *mutual* perplexity," Lewrie gravelled back, shaking his head. "I would've thought we'd bring the other four 'liners' along. If *Monarch* can anchor this closely, so could the sixty-fours and the fifties."

"One hates to question the judgement of superior officers, but . . .

surely, sir, were *Nelson* here, one would think we'd have been hot at it, hours ago," Westcott said.

"Second-guessin' superior officers?" Lewrie said with a cackle. "Damme, Mister Westcott, that's the Navy meat and drink! Hmm," he went on after a long moment of pursing his lips and staring shoreward. "Perhaps Lord Keith's of a mind t'launch the attack tonight, when fireships'd cause even more panic than they would in daylight. You may be in the boats and right under the French guns by midnight!"

"One can only hope, sir," Westcott eagerly agreed.

"Mister Spendlove?" Lewrie called out to the officer of the watch. "You have the deck. I'm goin' aloft for a look-see."

Since his first days as a raw and callow Midshipman in 1780, he had always been pluperfect-terrified of going aloft, hundreds of feet from the sane safety of solid decks, "yo-ho-hoing" out the futtock shrouds to hang like a spider nigh upside-down instead of using the "lubber's hole" to the fighting top platform, scrambling higher up the narrowing shrouds and ratlines to the cross-trees, or the fearful mast caps . . . going out to the tip of a tops'l, t'gallant, or royal yardarm to fist canvas, with upper arms locked over the yard and his feet teetering on a foot-rope that shimmied like a circus performer's high wire, with a bare second of clumsiness dooming him to plunge overside to drown, or go *Splat!* on the upper deck!

He slung his telescope over his shoulder and went up the starboard shrouds of the mizen mast. Damn what Captain Speaks thought of him, he eschewed the futtock shrouds and transferred to the counter-bracing cat-harpings to reach the top through the lubber's hole.

I ain't a twenty-year-old topman, he grimly told himself; *nor a twenty-year-old anything any longer!*

"Uh, evenin', sir!" a spry young sailor bade him as Lewrie took a deep breath to steady his twanging nerves before extending his telescope.

"Evenin', Grimes," Lewrie replied, sparing a moment to grin back, recalling that Grimes was one of the two-dozen or so that his old Bosun, Will Cony, now the owner of The Olde Ploughman public house in Anglesgreen, had recruited as volunteers when *Reliant* had been fitting out.

"Ehm . . . d'ye think we might see a bit of a fight tonight, sir?" Grimes asked with a wolfish expression.

"Ye never can tell, Grimes," Lewrie told him. "If we don't get ordered in, I don't see the Frogs comin' out to us. What's your station, do we go to Quarters?"

"Well, I would be here, sir, t'tend sail and see to damage, but if we get t'launch those torpeder things, I'm down for Mister Houghton in his boat, and handle the swivel gun."

"You'd have more fun in Houghton's boat," Lewrie assured him as he turned his attention to the shore. "We might blow some French boats to Hell . . . and some Frogs with 'em."

"There's a lot of 'em, sir," Grimes commented.

God, ain't there, just! Lewrie thought as he levelled his telescope on the top-mast shrouds and rat-lines and got a good view. Even as dusk began to fall, there was still enough light for him to make out *hundreds* of vessels in Boulogne harbour, everything from *prames,* First Rate gunboats, to the smallest single-masted *caïques.* They were lined up against the inner harbour piers several rows deep, along the minor jetties where small fishing boats would tie up, in row after row round the harbour in deeper water, and all alongside the inner side of the stone breakwaters with only their masts showing . . . a deep *forest* of masts! Boulogne was so full of invasion shipping that any vessel attempting to sail out would have to pick a tortuous way without ramming into something.

Closer to, the outside of the breakwaters was lined with long rows of every sort of barge and *caïque,* arrayed two-deep, and there seemed to be at least two hundred of them, as Lewrie tried to keep a running count. Wee lanthorns were winking to light aboard them, among the vessels he could still see inside the harbour, and he began counting them instead of masts or hulls, but gave it up after a moment; it was as futile as trying to count all the stars in a clear West Indies night! Warehouses along the piers, houses, taverns, and shops began to blossom wee glims, too, and they all blended together. And beyond the harbour town, thousands of points of light emerged as the evening drew on, until every clifftop, every open field, every overlook above the sea, was transformed to a faeryland of winking lights, and Boulogne became a city as great as London, as well-lit as Paris when he had been there during the Peace of Amiens . . . the campfires and lanthorns and candles of a vast *army* encamped for miles and miles about in tents and huts!

And the French were ready for them. Long before their revolution, in the time of French kings, Boulogne had been fortified, guarded by stone forts well-armed with good artillery, and with the ascendancy of Napoleon Bonaparte—an artilleryman!—the defences had gotten even stronger, with batteries erected on the breakwaters and flanking high ground in stout stone redans, or in thick earthen batteries every three miles along the French coast, the entire length of the Channel, from Ushant to Dunkerque. Smoke, not from cook-fires, arose from some of the stouter emplacements . . . furnaces and forges for heated shot?

Near the harbour entrance between the enveloping arms of the breakwaters, Lewrie could barely make out some three-masted gunboats, swinging at single anchors to the wind and tide, where they could sortie if Lord Keith launched his attack. Out beyond them and the lines of boats along the outer breakwater faces, large armed launches were rowing, keeping a wary eye on the British squadron.

"This could turn hopeless, fast," Lewrie whispered to himself.

"Say somethin', sir?" Grimes asked.

"Enjoy the view," Lewrie said, louder, then turned to begin his descent to the safety of the deck.

"The tide's beginning to run well, sir," the Sailing Master, Mr. Caldwell, pointed out just after Lewrie stowed his telescope in the compass binnacle cabinet, "though the wind's both perverse and scant for an assault."

"Perhaps we won't be going in, after all, Mister Caldwell," Lewrie replied with an impatient shrug, and a peek aloft to the commissioning pendant, which was streaming the wrong way. "If we send in the fireships, there's a chance they'd just drift back onto *us*."

"We've the bomb vessels in place, the rocket ships anchored and in good range," Captain Speaks grumbled. "If the wind won't serve, at least we could begin to shell them, tonight. Stap me, this delay and dithering is maddening!"

Should've stayed *aloft*, Lewrie thought; *and avoided the pest a while longer!*

The bomb vessels that Lewrie had seen while aloft were of the newer type, with their two masts set far back to leave their two mortars free play up forward, set deep in re-enforced wells. They'd been anchored by a single stern kedge and both their bower anchors set out at extreme angles so tensioning or loosening their bower cables could swing their aim in great arcs. The older, converted rocket ships were beam-on to the shore, anchored from bows and sterns with springs on their cables to shift their aim. All *seemed* ready.

"Aye, but how many rockets have we to fire?" Lewrie speculated aloud. "How many shells are aboard the bombs? We shoot off half of our bolts, without usin' the fireships and torpedoes at the same time . . . ?" he added, finishing with another, greater, arm-lifting shrug.

"We're to sit here and wait for tomorrow night's tide, and hope the wind co-operates?" Captain Speaks groused. "Pah!"

"Well, at least we may savour a good supper in peace," Lewrie said with a chuckle. "My cook assures me he's a cured ham for us, and if we don't have to go to Quarters, we'll dine on a hot meal."

"A hot supper!" Captain Speaks barked incredulously, sneering at Lewrie's priorities. An inarticulate growl followed.

"You'll join me, Mister Caldwell?" Lewrie offered, grinning.

"Gad, yes, I will, sir, and thankee most kindly!" Mr. Caldwell quickly responded, rubbing his hands in expectation.

Speaks turned away to mumble something, which made Lewrie grin impishly. "D'ye know, Mister Caldwell, this puts me in mind of Copenhagen, the night before the battle, with the two fleets anchored not two miles apart, like ancient armies, glarin' at each other, with the battlefield between 'em."

Lewrie knew how much that would rile Speaks, and determined he would expand on the subject over supper, which Captain Speaks would not turn down . . . unless he intended to sulk and fast in his hammock!

CHAPTER FORTY-THREE

$\mathcal{G}$od only knew what the French made of it, but it *was* the following evening, October 2nd, that Admiral Lord Keith ordered the assault on Boulogne to begin. The winds had come round from a favourable quarter, the tide was running shoreward at a brisk pace, and, perhaps far aft in HMS *Monarch*'s great-cabins, a chicken had been sacrificed, and the auguries had been deemed auspicious.

Boats from the flagship had rowed last-minute orders to all the ships, and alerting them to begin when *Monarch* fired a two-gun signal.

Lewrie ordered *Reliant*'s crew to supper in the First Dog Watch, so the galley fires could be extinguished early, then had the frigate brought to Quarters at the start of the Second Dog, at 6 P.M.

"On your way, Mister Westcott, and the best of fortune go with ye," Lewrie bade the First Lieutenant, and his Midshipmen and the hands who would man the towing boats. The *Penarth* collier had already hoisted all her torpedoes from her holds and tethered them alongside, ready and waiting. "Give the Frogs Hell, Reliants!"

"We'll fetch you some frogs' legs *flambé*, sir!" Westcott gaily promised as he ordered his men overside and into the boats. And they were all four well on their way and about to go alongside *Penarth* when the long, anxious peace between the French and the anchored squadron was broken at last by the sharp reports of two guns aboard HMS *Monarch*. Signal flags soared up her halliards ordering engagement.

"Mister Merriman, you may open upon the boats anchored outside the breakwaters," Lewrie shouted down to the waist.

"Aye aye, sir!" Lt. George Merriman loudly replied, then turned to his waiting gun crews. "Raise the ports! Run out!"

Monarch and the other frigates fired first, the edgy peace of a fine, mild early evening shattered by the deep, ear-splitting bellows of guns.

"Prime your guns!" Lt. Merriman was roaring. "Captains, take aim! We will fire by threes! Quarter-gunners, see to your charges, and direct them to point at single targets! Ready?"

Gun-captains fiddled with elevation by raising the breech-ends of their pieces with crow-levers and wriggling the wood quoin blocks a bit aft, or a bit forward, to raise the muzzles to their best guess of the range. Some called for their gunners to lever the truck carriages left or right so the barrels pointed directly at specific boats in that long two-deep line of invasion vessels. Only then did they stand erect, clear of the guns' recoil, drawing the trigger lines to the flintlock strikers taut, and raising fists in the air to signal their readiness.

"By threes . . . fire!" Merriman shouted, chopping the air with his right arm, and the guns erupted, in groups from bow to stern, with lung-flattening roars, spurting great clouds of burned powder smoke shoreward, shot through with stabs of bright yellow-red flame and fire-fly sparks of vivid orange.

"Swab out! Slow and steady does it, lads!" Merriman directed. "Overhaul recoil tackle, overhaul run-out tackle. Load cartridge!"

The smoke-bank was drifting shoreward rapidly, thinning and rising as it went on a fair breeze, allowing Lewrie and Lt. Spendlove on the quarterdeck to lift their telescopes and survey the initial results. There were shot splashes near the invasion vessels, but so far they saw no evidence of hits; that would be far too much to hope for from the very first shots. It would take several more broadsides 'til the gun-captains honed their aims, and perhaps a couple of hours more of slow and steady hammering to inflict substantial damage.

"Not *too* bad for first broadsides, sir," Lt. Spendlove said optimistically. "Mostly short, but in line with their chosen marks."

"Excuse me, sir?" Midshipman Warburton intruded. "What duties might you assign me, sir, now that Captain Speaks took my place?"

"*What?*" Lewrie gawped. "What the Devil are ye *doin'* here, Mister Warburton? Took your *place?*" he spluttered.

"At the last moment, sir," Mr. Warburton explained, looking miserable to be deprived his shot at danger and glory. "He said that *you* had allowed him, that they were *his* torpedoes, and——"

"Mine arse on a band-box!" Lewrie exclaimed, just shy of an outraged screech. "I'd've *never*. . . ."

Well, maybe I would've, he told himself; *if only t'get rid of the bastard for an hour or so. God rot him, he gets killed? Fine!*

"Assist Mister Merriman on the guns, Mister Warburton, and I'm truly sorry your chance was stolen," he told the deeply disappointed sixteen-year-old.

"Aye aye, sir," Warburton said, doffing his hat and dashing.

"By threes . . . *fire!*" Merriman roared again, as did the guns a moment later.

"The French have opened upon us, sir," Lt. Spendlove pointed out. "Enter that, and the time, in the Sailing Master's journal, Mister Rossyngton."

Dusk was rapidly turning towards full dark as the return fire from dozens, perhaps an hundred shore guns, sparkled all along the low shore, the overlooks, and the fortifications. The first-class *prames,* the largest French gunboats anchored in the entrance channel, erupted in gouts of smoke and daggers of flame, too, though they showed little sign that they would sortie; they remained at anchor.

"Oh, I say!" Mr. Caldwell declared, jerking an arm towards the great flashes and volcanic explosions from the bomb vessels. Thirteen-inch-diametre mortar shells soared aloft in great arcs, their burning, sputtering conical fuses making pyrotechnic trails cross the darkening sky, some of them incendiaries that seethed like shooting stars. When they reached their apogees, they seemed to pause for an instant, before dashing down and regaining their initial speed to crash into the waters of the inner harbour and burst with loud blasts.

"Impressive," Lt. Spendlove commented, though he shook his head in worry. "One would hope they aim well, and don't land in the town, though, sir."

"Oh, look at *that!*" the Sailing Master declared again as a wave of Congreve rockets whooshed skyward. "Talk about your royal firework shows, hah! Now, those are *truly* awe-inspiring!"

Oooh! Aaah! Lewrie thought, snickering, though such a fiery display *was* worthy of his awe. For a moment.

The rockets dashed upwards, long yellow tongues of flame trailing them, almost bright enough to espy the long bamboo poles to which the bodies and explosive charges were affixed to steady them like arrow shafts and fletchings . . . or, should have.

One swerved straight upwards as if trying to spear the moon; yet another swooped up, then back towards the launching ship in a circular arc. A couple more levelled off prematurely and darted shoreward nigh at sealevel, wheeling left or right like lost sparrows . . . prettily flaming sparrows! Some waddled up and down before diving into the sea far short of the breakwaters, and one perversely wheeled to the right just after launch and looked determined to crash into *Reliant,* growing bigger and brighter and closer before exploding in a shower of stars a half-mile short!

"Well, hmm," Mr. Caldwell said, mightily disappointed.

"Need some work," Lewrie said, relaxing his tense dread and letting out a whoosh of relieved breath, "even if they aimed at *us*!"

"As you bear, by threes . . . *fire*!" Lt. Merriman shouted again, and *Reliant* was shoved a few inches to larboard by the brute force of recoil. Amid the bellowing of their frigate's guns came the howling-humming of French shot as they passed overhead or wide of the bow and stern. Lewrie lifted his telescope to look over the shore batteries, fearing that neither side had much of a chance for accurate fire, and that it was all futile. Lord Keith had ordered them to anchor at the extreme edge of the French guns' maximum range, and even with quoins full out and the barrels of the squadron elevated almost to the safe limit for a naval gun which was fired at low elevation and very close range—they weren't howitzers, after all, designed to loft shot over fortress walls!—even *Monarch*'s lower-deck 32-pounders stood little chance of reaching that far, either. The French might even have the advantage over them, for the fortress guns, and the batteries mounted on the overlooks, stood higher above sea-level and *could* elevate safely to give them the required reach. And *they* had howitzers! Flame-shot smoke burst from batteries to either side of the breakwaters, the flat booming coming seconds later, and the shot they fired lifted high into the night, burning fuses tracing arcs as the shells came darting downwards, the thin wail-hiss of their passage through the air rising in volume and tone like an opera diva trilling for a higher note before they burst prematurely due to too-short cone fuses, or plunged into the sea and exploded in great whitish gouts of spray.

Another shoal of Congreve rockets soared shoreward in reply to the French artillery, the slower-firing mortars of the bomb vessels belched out another salvo, and the night sky was criss-crossed by opposing streaks of fire. Explosive shells burst near the British ships, and over the French batteries, inside the harbour beyond the sheltering breakwaters . . . some reaching as far as the town-side warehouses and piers!

"They must see that they're shelling the town!" Lt. Spendlove fumed, quite out of character and the cold-bloodedness demanded from a Navy officer. "We must not do that! It's not Christian, sir!"

"It's as narrow as a razor's edge at this range, sir," Lewrie told him, shouting a bit over the continual din. "Strike short, hit the anchored ships, or the piers and the town, if you're over."

"Deck, there!" a lookout at the mast-head called down in a thin screech. "There's French launches comin' out!"

That changed the subject quickly as Lewrie, Spendlove, and the Sailing Master lifted their glasses to spot the enemy launches. They were under oars, as big as admirals' barges, and mounted cannon fore and aft. They weren't coming far, Lewrie noted, only two or three hundred yards beyond the rows of vessels anchored outside the breakwaters, but when the boats went in with the torpedoes in tow, they would prove dangerous.

"Mister Rossyngton, my compliments to Mister Merriman, and he's to shift his fire onto the launches closer to us," Lewrie ordered.

"Aye, sir!" the Midshipman snapped crisply, dashing forward for the waist.

Reliant's guns fell silent for a moment as the aim was shifted. The smoke thinned, and Lewrie peered hard down the long line of barges outside the breakwater, looking intently for any sign of damage they might have inflicted, but spent powder smoke from the French batteries cloaked them, and the night was too dark, only fitfully and briefly illuminated by the passage of flaming carcase shells or rockets. He slammed the tubes of his telescope compact, shaking his head in mounting anger over how useless the assault seemed, so far. By the faint candlelight of the compass binnacle, he checked his pocket-watch, and nigh-groaned aloud to note that it was nearly 9 P.M.!

The both of us, blazin' away half the night, with nothing to show for it! he thought, a feeble anger growing inside him, looking seaward towards *Monarch*, whose starboard side was lit up with stabbing flame from her guns.

"Deck, there! Fireships is goin' in! Cutters, launches, an' ships' boats is goin' in!" the lookout wailed, sounding cheerful.

"Mister Westcott'll be having himself some fun," Mr. Caldwell hooted with glee.

"One hopes," Lt. Spendlove glumly replied. "At least fireships are con-
ventional weapons." Un-like rockets, was what he meant, or the lofting of
explosive mortar shells into Boulogne itself.

Lewrie felt a faint stir of hope. It had been fireships that had panicked
the Spanish Armada when sailed into their anchorage at Gravelines in
1588, driving them to cut their cables and flee to the open sea, never to
re-assemble in strength. With any luck, hundreds of those anchored vessels would be set afire, and the few French sailors aboard each one would
be unable to fend off, or extinguish the fire aboard their own, abandoning
it and fleeing as the conflagration spread from theirs to the next and the
next, and when the blazes reached the tons of gunpowder stored in the
fireships' holds went off, even more of them would be blasted to fiery kindling!

The French saw the threat, recognised it for what it was, and shifted
their aim to counter the fireships, and the swarm of sailing launches and
cutters escorting them, hoping to sink them before they reached those
anchored lines. Their armed launches dared to come out further from
shore in anticipation, their oars flashing in unison as they rowed out, and
swung to point their guns at the British launches. Lewrie's orders from
Admiral Lord Keith had stated that some of those un-manned explosive
boats would be employed as well, and Lewrie hoped that the French
might concentrate on those, going in before *Reliant*'s torpedo-towing
barges and cutters, and ignore his men, who would come to a stop, then
turn about and flee seaward after letting their primed torpedoes free.

He found that he'd crossed the fingers of his right hand.

"Deck, there! Th' fireships is *lit*!"

There was a fiendish science to how a fireship was re-built for maximum effect. Its gun-ports hinged down, not up, the lines to them fashioned to burn through so that long tongues of flame could dart out once
the conflagration reached its height. Hatches were widened to let in more
air to stoke the fires, slow-match was strung to fire the few old guns still
aboard, and down to the holds and the tons of gunpowder. "Fire rooms"
were packed with combustibles amidships and below, planned by skilled
pyromaniacs to spread quickly to other points where barrels of tar and
turpentine, lamp oil and opened bales of straw, waited for a single spark.
If the mast-head lookout could spot the first winks of flame, then they had
been ignited minutes before, and the last few men of the small crews had
already lashed the helms, trimmed the braces and sheets, and scrambled
into their boats to make their quick escape.

Two . . . three . . . four of them began to light up the approaches to Boulogne, almost turning night to a ruddy, flickering day as they surged shoreward, shot splashes bursting to life all round them, drawing the bulk of French fire from the shore batteries.

"Damned near apocalyptic, ain't it, sir?" the Sailing Master said, quite pleased with the sight of burning ships, screaming fiery rocket trails, and the rush of burning incendiary shells from bomb vessels. *Something* was engulfed in flames on the far side of the arms of the breakwaters, to make the scene even more hellish. Mr. Caldwell leaned his head over to cock an ear in appreciation of the continual thunder, screech, or howl of guns and bowling roundshot; of the stench of spent powder and propellants and the sickly yellow-white clouds of powder smoke that reflected the fires, the Sailing Master sniffed deep and smiled in pleasure!

"Ghastly," was Lt. Clarence Spendlove's dour opinion.

"Sir!" Midshipman Warburton cried as he came to the quarterdeck. "Mister Merriman's duty, sir, and he says that the guns can't elevate enough to shoot over the heads of our small boats yonder. He requests that we cease fire 'til our boats are clear."

"Very well, Mister Warburton, my compliments to him and pass the word to cease fire," Lewrie ordered, wondering just how much shot and powder they had expended the last few hours. He looked over the full hammock stanchions to the waist and saw that many of the loaders had powder ladles in their hands, as if they had fired away all of the pre-made flannel powder cartridges, and had run short of flannel bags, too. In the dull red glows of the battle lanthorns between the guns, his gun crews, bare to the waists and heads swaddled with neckerchiefs to protect their hearing, were so begrimed with powder smoke that they resembled weary junior demons who stoked the fires of Hell.

The rest of the squadron, *Monarch* and the two other frigates, had ceased fire, too, and the loudest sounds of firing came from shore, the duller oven-door slams punctuated by sharp barks and cracks from lighter boat guns as the French launches and British boats fired upon each other. He could almost hear the rushing crackle of the fireships as they burned, well alight and turned into floating braziers that illuminated the night. By then, sails and tarred rigging were afire, too, with mouse-tiny fires scampering up the shrouds, finding sources for combustion in the cooking fat slush that kept the running rigging supple, too. They were *close* to the French barges, but . . . would they make it all the way before their sails vanished, or the slow-matches reached the explosives?

There was a titanic blast near the anchored French boats, with a great sheet of flame and smoke and a mountainous pillar of seawater.

"One of the un-manned explosive boats, I think, sir," Caldwell speculated, pursing his lips and frowning in disappointment. "Perhaps the others will get closer."

"Deck, there! Ship's boats comin' out!" a lookout shouted.

Not just ours, but everybody's, Lewrie thought after an intense look through his glass. The single-masted cutters and armed launches that had gone in with the fireships were retiring. Emboldened by their seeming retreat, French launches and *péniches* were warily edging further from the protection of their shore batteries, as well.

"Mister Merriman!" Lewrie shouted down to the ship's waist. "I wish you to open upon the French launches once our own boats are clear!"

"Aye, sir!" Lt. Merriman replied, sounding a touch weary as he took off his hat to bind a neckerchief over his ears once more. Tired gun crews slouched back to their pieces, after a last sip of water from the scuttle-butts, like over-burdened miners returning to a coal face, making Lewrie fear that with no sure signs of success, his crew was becoming dispirited. The long, inexplicable delay after anchoring just out of gun range, the sitting idle all day, *might* have made good sense to them, and the excitement of action, the novel sight of rockets and mortar boats, might have enthused them at first, but . . .

Lewrie had to admit that he felt dispirited, too, for the lack of urgency and daring, and for the seeming lack of success, so far. He wavered between anger that the expedition looked like a failure, and a sense of futility that, as a captain, he took so little part in it!

His people tending the guns had been doing something active and necessary, as had the hundreds more officers and sailors away in those launches and boats, while he stood about like a useless fart in a trance.

Seniority could take all the joy of battle away, all the frenetic, neck-or-nothing intensity of a boarding action, a cutting-out raid, or amphibious landing, all the duties Lewrie had been given as a young Midshipman or junior officer. He looked over to Admiral Lord Keith's flagship and wondered if that worthy had had a single thing to do once his guns had begun to roar and the fireships had gone in. The fellow had a Flag-Captain to run his ship, a Captain of The Fleet to handle the day-to-day mundane matters, so what was left for him to do? Tend to the supper menu? For all the good that Lewrie was doing, for all the good that Lord Keith was doing, they both might as well have gone aft to their cabins for a pot of tea!

Lewrie almost had to shake himself to get rid of his bad mood, becoming aware of the reduction of noise and of lights. The rocket vessels must have run out of their horridly inaccurate contraptions, for they no longer soared off in shoals but went aloft—and far off course!—in irregular singletons. The mortars in the bomb vessels had fallen silent, too, so there were no more spectacular air-bursts or swooshing fiery incendiary carcases. It was the fires ashore, and the drifting fireships, that threw great angry glares cross the waters.

"There, sirs!" Midshipman Rossyngton cried, pointing overside to starboard. "Small boats approaching!"

From eye-searing glare and the inkiest shadows, a ragged line of boats slowly appeared. Two were under lug-sails. A third loomed up under oars, trailing the first two. A fourth appeared at last, in tow of the third.

"Mister Rossyngton, do you go below and warn the Surgeon that we may have wounded men returning," Lewrie ordered.

"Aye, sir!"

The first two boats, both of them thirty-two-foot barges, passed across *Reliant*'s bows, lowering sails and fitting oars into the tholes. Midshipman Houghton stood and waved, looking immensely pleased and excited. The second barge was Lt. Westcott's.

"Any hurt?" Lewrie called to him as the barges rounded up near the larboard side, slowly stroking to hook onto the main-mast channel platform.

"Not a man, sir!" Lt. Westcott shouted back. "Not for lack of trying on the French's part!" he added with a triumphant laugh and a brief flash of a smile. Mr. Houghton's boat was hooking on, the man in the bows with the gaff young Grimes. His swivel gun still stood in its bracket, muzzle to the sky, and he looked pleased with himself, too. And, thankfully, there was Liam Desmond, his "Black Irish" Cox'n, at the tiller of Westcott's barge, and Patrick Furfy ploughing forward to the bows with a gaff pole in his hand to serve as bow man, staggering over his mates as clumsily as ever.

"Welcome back, lads, good bit o' work!" Lewrie called as his men came up the battens and man-ropes to gather on the larboard gangway. "Mister Houghton, I'd admire did ye see to leadin' the barges' towing lines aft, for later."

"Aye, sir. Ehm . . . have any of our torpedoes gone off yet?" Houghton asked.

"None of ours, no," Lewrie had to tell him. "Ah, glad t'see ye in one piece, Mister Westcott. How did it go?"

"Wet, wild, and woolly for a time, sir," Westcott told him with another laugh. "Shot splashes all round, and I got soaked to my chest when I misjudged my leap back into the boat from our torpedo's back. The tide was still running fairly strong when we let them go, so . . . ," he said with a shrug.

"You were closer to those anchored boats," Lewrie said. "Did you note any damage?"

"Not all that much, sir, no. Sorry," Lt. Westcott said, more softly. "Like in *Macbeth,* 'sound and fury, signifying nothing.'"

Monarch and the other frigates began firing, again; their boats were back alongside, and no friendly craft lay between them and their new targets, the French launches and gunboats.

"Resume fire, Mister Merriman!" Lewrie took time to order. "Do you take those Frog launches under fire!"

Now it was Midshipman Entwhistle's boat crew coming back aboard to be congratulated, then . . . Captain Speaks and his crew.

"Must apologise to your young gentleman for supplanting him, Lewrie, but . . . I wished to see our torpedoes delivered properly," the older fellow briskly said, stone-faced, as if to fend off any criticism of his actions.

"Excuse me, sir," Surgeon Mr. Mainwaring intruded as he came to the base of the larboard gangway ladder. "Are there any wounded?" He had his shirt sleeves rolled to his elbows and wore his usual long bib apron of leather; both, thankfully, were still pristine and bloodless.

"Don't think so, Mister Mainwaring," Lt. Westcott told him.

"Well, sor . . . ," Patrick Furfy piped up, holding up his bloodied left hand, "'Tis nought a glass o' neat rum won't cure."

"The lummox caught it on one o' th' torpedo grapnel hooks, sor," Liam Desmond related. "Thought he'd git towed ashore t'France before he got free!"

"We must see to that . . . sew it up," Mainwaring determined after a quick inspection.

"Be painful, sor?" Furfy asked, looking skittish.

"You'd feel a pinch or two, yes," the Surgeon told him.

"Arrah, sor, rum'd ease th' pain? And faith if I don't feel all weak an' faint, of a sudden!" Furfy declared, shamming wooziness.

"Below to the cockpit, Furfy . . . *with* your rum for pain," the Surgeon said, rolling his eyes. "Let's go."

There was a tremendous explosion close to shore as one of the fireships blew up. There was a monstrous fire ball and an expanding cloud of broken planking, shattered timbers, and flaming tar barrels, every chunk and slightest splintered bit a bright torch, all of it pattering down hundreds of feet away to extinguish in the sea, leaving the ruptured hull smouldering and smothered in black smoke.

"Huzzah!" from Lewrie's weary gunners, enthused once more.

"Excuse me, sir," Midshipman Warburton said, doffing his hat as he came to the quarterdeck, casting a brief, bitter glance at Captain Speaks. "Mister Merriman reports that there is so much dark smoke from the fireships that he cannot find targets. The French launches have retreated *behind* the smoke, sir."

"He is to cease fire again, Mister Warburton," Lewrie decided after a long moment, "but stay ready should any launch re-appear."

There was so much smoke that *Monarch* and the other frigates had to stop firing, and, after a few minutes, so did the French guns, but for those still trying to sink the remaining fireships. For one hopeful moment, one fireship drifted right between the ends of the breakwaters, pummeled by both stone batteries that guarded the entrance channel. The gunboats lurking just inside the harbour began to blaze away desperately to save themselves, and it looked as if the fireship would succeed . . . before she exploded prematurely and un-successfully, scattering fiery debris far and wide.

This ain't a grand assault, Lewrie sourly thought; *it's another bloody* experiment! It would be the coming Winter gales, rough seas, and foul winds that would stave off Bonaparte's invasion 'til Spring, he angrily realised, sincerely hoping that before France could launch that dread expedition, the Royal Navy would come back, the next time in full force and intent, and with someone in command who would press the issue more aggressively . . . and much more cleverly!

Without torpedoes, he also hoped. He'd seen only two work so far. Lewrie let his attention drift as he contemplated how he would frame his report to Admiralty, and how to praise his officers and . . .

Christ, I'll have t'say nice things about Captain Speaks! he gawped. He could not laud his own, without, and if he left Speaks out, he'd never hear the end of it!

. . . Captain Joseph Speaks, the director of torpedo development, gallantly volunteered to take charge of one of our cutters, and, daring fire and shot, expeditiously . . .

"Oh, bugger!" Lewrie whispered in disgust.

He was drawn back to full attention by the swelling of gunfire. *Mon-*

arch and the other frigates had re-opened, now that the smoke from the failed fireships had thinned. The bombardment of Boulogne resumed in full cry, with more mortar shells soaring aloft in fiery trails, and more Congreve rockets screaming shoreward in great arcs.

"Will we ever run short of rockets and mortar shells, I ask you?" Lt. Spendlove wondered aloud. The bombardment of Boulogne looked and sounded less furious, but it went on, relentlessly, if slowly.

"I should take charge of the guns, sir?" Spendlove asked.

"I'll dry out here on the quarterdeck, sir," Lt. Westcott offered. "I'll resume my place . . . damp, but willing."

"Go, Mister Spendlove," Lewrie ordered. "Slow but steady fire on the anchored boats." He doubled his coat over his chest and buttoned up, wishing for a blanket as he sat down in his canvas chair. It looked to be a long and fruitless night.

He had managed to doze off in spite of the occasional shrieks of Congreve rockets, and the deep drumming of gunfire and exploding shell in the wee hours, and came awake from a slumped nap with a start, snapped to wakefulness by the *lack* of gunfire.

"Did I miss something, Mister Westcott?" Lewrie asked once he'd creaked to his feet and padded to the bulwarks facing the shore.

"It seems everyone's lost enthusiasm, at last, sir," Westcott told him, yawning. "Or run out of shot and powder, us and the French, both. Except for Captain Speaks," he added in a furtive whisper. That worthy was still awake, pacing the starboard gangway and muttering to himself nigh-urgently, constantly peering shoreward with his telescope, then consulting his pocket-watch. "Hope springs eternal, what?"

"Any idea whether any of our damned torpedoes worked?" Lewrie asked, yawning himself. "I only could spot two."

"Some big explosions, but those were hours ago, sir, and short or wide of the mark, as per usual," Lt. Westcott said, shrugging. "It is long past the run of any of the clocks, so—"

Ba-Whoom! A lurid sheet of flame rose from the sea, a pillar of water an hundred feet tall, then a shriek from Captain Speaks.

"There! There, sirs! Right alongside one of those damned Frog gunboats!" Speaks yelled in triumph. "By God, it worked, and we *sank* something! There, sir!" Speaks roared, almost in Lewrie's face after he'd dashed from the gangway to the quarterdeck, an arm flung in the general direction of the blast. "She was right alongside it when it blew up! I saw it plain!"

"Perhaps they thumped against it, and the pistol——," Lewrie countered.

"No matter!" Speaks cut him off. "One out of six succeeded in sinking an enemy ship. With better clockworks, with better pistols, and more water-proofing, we've proven torpedoes valuable, d'ye see?"

Oh, fuck me! Lewrie thought, appalled; *Now we'll never be shot of the God-damned things! You wish t'waste more time and money on 'em, go right ahead, ye poor, deluded prick.*

Captain Speaks turned about and capered round the deck, raising a cheer from *Reliant*'s weary crew with his cries of success.

"Mine arse on a band-box, Mister Westcott," Lewrie gloomed.

"Only a small gunboat, for six expended, sir?" Westcott whispered back, almost cheerfully. "And that by accident, if there really *was* a gunboat alongside it when it went off? *He's* the only one who saw it, so . . . how much do they cost, each? And what sort of rate of return is that?"

"You're a sly, devious pessimist, Mister Westcott," Lewrie said, suddenly inspired.

"I'll take that as a compliment, sir!" Westcott said, beaming.

"If God's just . . . and I write my report well, we'll never see or hear of torpedoes again in our lives!"

EPILOGUE

This little Boney says he'll come
At Merry Christmas time,
But that I say is all a hum
Or I will no more rhyme.

Some say in wooden house he'll glide
Some say in air balloon,
E'en those who airy schemes deride
Agree his coming soon.

Now honest people list to me,
Though income is but small,
I'll bet my wig to one Pen-ney
He does not come at all.

-"The Bellman and Little Boney"
Popular ditty circa 1804

CHAPTER FORTY-FOUR

*M*idshipman Warburton . . . *SAH*!" the Marine sentry guarding the entrance to the great-cabins bellowed, slamming his musket hutt, and his boots, in punctuation.

"Enter," Lewrie bade, seated at his desk in the day-cabin. His coat was off, despite the chill of an early November evening, and his choice of pre-prandial tipple this night, a tankard of brown ale, sat by his elbow as he penned a letter. "Yes, Mister Warburton?"

"Your visitor's boat is approaching, sir," Warburton reported.

"Ah ha, just about time. Thankee, Mister Warburton," he told the Mid, stowing away his pen and ink, and sliding the letter that he was composing into the top drawer of his desk. Lewrie rose and took his coat from the back of his chair and put it on to go on deck to welcome Mr. James Peel from the Foreign Office, who had sent down a note from London even before *Reliant* had put back into Portsmouth, requesting that they meet. Lewrie assumed it would be about the failed expedition against Boulogne, or those two odd boats he'd captured, but with Peel, one never really knew, so though he would put a gladsome face on, Lewrie did feel a gurgle of trepidation in his innards . . . or perhaps that was simple hunger.

He took a last swig of ale, clapped on his hat, and strode out past the Marine sentry, then up the starboard ladderway to mount to the sail-tending gangway and entry-port just as Peel's boat bumped against the hull.

"D'ye require a bosun's chair, Peel?" he called down in jest.

"Be with you directly," Peel called back as he scaled the side.

"S'pose ye came hungry," Lewrie laconically said as Peel's hat and head appeared over the lip of the entry-port. "It's uncanny, how you always seem t'turn up just at mealtimes."

"Hallo, old son, and yes, I did," Peel rejoined once he'd gained the deck and briefly doffed his fashionable curl-brimmed hat to the flag, then to Lewrie. "I'd never miss a chance for one of Yeovill's excellent suppers."

"Let's go aft, then, and get you a drink," Lewrie offered.

Peel would have a brandy to ward off the chill of his boat from the docks, while Lewrie settled for a second tankard of ale. They sat at the starboard-side settee.

"So, how are things in London?" Lewrie asked him.

"Folk are in calmer takings, now Winter's getting on, and they see that Bonaparte won't cross the Channel in bad weather," Peel said with a grin, shifting and squirming to get more comfortably seated at his end of the settee. Toulon and Chalky leaped down from their naps on Lewrie's desk and came to re-make Peel's acquaintance. "We heard an interesting bit of news from France about the invasion fleet, by the way." He paused to let the cats sniff his hand, then began to pet them. "Something that may give Boney more pause than any Winter gale, or the attack on Boulogne . . . bad luck, that, but congratulations to you for your part in it."

"Even if it went so badly," Lewrie replied with a groan of remembered futility. "Damn all torpedoes, *and* their inventors."

"Yes, well . . . it seems that Bonaparte and his generals thought a dress rehearsal was a good idea . . . see how quickly and efficiently his army could board their ships and put out to sea a few miles. With Bonaparte watching from a clifftop, like Xerxes watched the ancient Battle of Salamis," Peel happily related, "all went swimmingly . . . how apt, that! 'Til the wind and sea got up and he discovered how much a pack of amateurs his sailors were. God only knows how many barges and boats were wrecked, but our report, from a *witness* to the event, wrote that thousands of French soldiers and sailors were drowned, and that within a few miles of Boulogne, not out in the middle of the Channel. He *might* be reconsidering, though he's spent so much money, time, and effort on the business already that he can't just abandon hopes of invading us."

"More fool, he, if he persists," Lewrie chortled in glee, "and if he insists on usin' those turtle-back monstrosities, well!"

"Congratulations on fetching two of them in so we could inspect them," Peel said, bowing his head in gratitude for a second. "Nothing official, mind, just my personal congratulations. Still secret, very hush-hush . . . though, you must be used to that by now, having worked with Mister Twigg so long."

"God, aren't I, just!" Lewrie griped, though good-naturedly.

"Saw some people known to you in London," Peel blithely went on, seemingly content to sip his brandy, stroke the cats, and slough at ease; he did, though, give Lewrie a sly under-brow gaze.

"Oh? Who?" Lewrie asked, wondering if he should begin to worry, and quickly running through a list of characters best avoided.

"Lord Percy Stangbourne and his sister," Peel told him, looking waggish. "Leftenant-Colonel Lord Stangbourne, rather."

"I thought Horse Guards had taken his regiment into service and sent him down to the Kent coast?" Lewrie said, puzzled, and trying to look innocent.

"Back in barracks 'til Spring," Peel went on, "and back in his old haunts, like Boodle's and the Cocoa Tree. His sister seems nicer than her repute. Rather fetching, in point of fact."

Peel peered at him as if expecting Lewrie to gush like a schoolboy in "cream-pot" love, make quibbling noises, or half-heartedly agree with his assessment of her, shrugging it all off.

Damme, does he know everything about everybody? Lewrie thought.

The letter he'd been writing had been to Lydia, whose latest post to him contained an offer to coach down to Portsmouth and spend a few days together—did he still wish? Damned *right*, he still wished and had already booked lodgings for her at the George Inn, and was writing to tell her so when Peel had intruded. Or, had he known that, too?

"Aye, she is . . . devilish-handsome and fetchin'," Lewrie agreed most assuredly.

Peel's response was a very broad smile and a nod of approval.

"Well-blessed with God's own tremendous 'dot,' too," Peel said.

"I don't give a toss for her dowry," Lewrie bluntly told him. "Percy'll most-like gamble them into debtor's prison, anyway."

"Usually, when a man says a thing like that, that it isn't about the money, it usually really is," Peel said, chuckling in worldly-wise fashion. "You, though, Alan . . . I can take you at your word. I could . . . *bank* on it, what?"

"I don't know whether that's a compliment or not," Lewrie wryly replied. "Too honest for my own good, or a bloody fool."

"Contemplating marriage, though, are you?" Peel too-idly asked.

"No, and neither does Lydia," Lewrie told him with a guffaw of denial. "Once bitten, twice shy for her, and me . . . well, I never got the hang of it, and if she wed me, her reputation'd be *utterly* ruined! Mean t'say, James . . . I'm a bounder, a cad, and a rake-hell."

"Well, some might say you were made for each other," Peel said with a shrug. "Both of you scandalous?" he added, with a twinkle.

"A bad marriage to a depraved animal was not her fault, and I think you demean the lady, Peel," Lewrie shot back.

"My pardons, pray forgive me," Peel quickly retracted, placing a hand on his breast, "for I only know what the papers made of it for years, the divorcement and all. I meant but to tease, but . . ."

"Forgiven," Lewrie allowed, more slowly.

"Heard from your nautical sons, lately?" Peel asked, smiling benignly as he changed the subject.

"Aye, I have!" Lewrie enthused. "Hugh's with Thorn Charlton, on the Brest blockade. Foul weather, cold victuals two days out of four, but he seems t'love it. Sewallis, well . . . he's more guarded, yet he *sounds* as if he prospers. I've written his captain, an old friend, Benjamin Rodgers, to enquire, but . . . tentatively. Haven't gotten his letter back, yet. You know that Sewallis got his place by fraud and forgery? So . . ."

"Your father, Sir Hugo, spoke of it to Mister Twigg, and Twigg related it to me," Peel admitted. "Keep it *in petto, sub rosa,* what?"

Damme if he doesn't *know ev'rything 'bout ev'rybody!* Lewrie had to tell himself; he cocked a wary brow over that admission.

"You have a letter sent to *us,* too," Peel said, off-handedly.

Oh, shit, here it comes! The Secret Branch's leash!

"Indeed," Lewrie said over the rim of his tankard, keeping his phyz as inscrutable as he could.

"Recall I told you back in the summer how hard it is to maintain communication with people willing to keep us informed of doings over in France?" Peel said, beginning to peel the onion, at it were. "The French open and read every letter, and have cut off all correspondence with Great Britain?"

"Yes, I recall," Lewrie stonily replied, refusing to be drawn.

"Yet, we still have *ways* . . . tradecraft which we hope keeps a step ahead of French snoopers," Peel continued, shifting on the settee and making it creak; he was heavier than in his Household Cavalry days, or his early years with Foreign Office as Zachariah Twigg's pupil. "Wee notes, some coded, sewn into shirt collar bands, pasted into book backs, that sort of thing?"

"Ah, cleverness," Lewrie warily commented, heavy-eyed.

"As draconian as the French police-state is, with the guillotine the reward for espionage and treason against the Emperor Napoleon, there are few who'd dare keep us informed," Peel continued, sounding like a chapman trying to flog a dubious product. "So we must do all we can to maintain contact with them, and at the same time do all we can to protect them from exposure. What they do for us is incredibly brave, and rashly dangerous, should they be discovered. Those brave few are rather admirable."

"I doubt the Frogs'd think so," Lewrie said, cracking a smile; a damned wee'un. "Depends on one's point of view."

"You are familiar with one of them," Peel hinted, all a'twinkle again.

"I rather doubt it's Guillaume Choundas," Lewrie scoffed. "I think I put paid t'that ugly bastard."

"No, not him!" Peel informed him, laughing. "Do you ever fight a duel, let me know when and where, so I can get a good seat, and *see* how accurately you shoot. The fall from that cliff would have killed him anyway, but that shot of yours, with a smooth-bore musket from a heaving boat at nigh an hundred yards, was spot-on, right in the fiend's heart. We have that as Gospel . . . from a witness," Peel hinted again.

"There were only two people I knew who were there when . . . No!" Lewrie gasped. "*That* murderin' bitch?"

"Let us say that *Mademoiselle* Charité Angelette de Guilleri has lost her faith in the Revolution, in Bonaparte, and her *raison d'être*, hey?" Peel said, smirking. "When Bonaparte sold New Orleans and all of Louisiana to the United States, he cut the very heart out of her, making the deaths of her brothers and her cousin, and their romantic but damn-fool revolt against the Spanish, and their piracy that funded it, meaningless."

That had been Lewrie's doing, requiring him to go up the Mississippi to New Orleans in *mufti* with a commercial trader/informant and sometime Secret Branch "asset" to "smoak them out," then escape and use his *Proteus* frigate to smash the pirate encampment on Grand Terre, in Barataria Bay, slaying the lot and burning their vessels.

"The bitch shot me!" Lewrie exclaimed in heat. "With a Girandoni air-rifle like that'un yonder," he said, jerking an arm towards his personal weapons rack. "Would've killed me, too, if the flask'd had enough compressed air in it!"

"For which the Crown, Mister Twigg, and I are grateful that she did not," Peel said, sounding earnest.

"Broke her wee, black heart, did Bonaparte?" Lewrie sneered in baby-talk. "Bloody *good*! I *hope* she suffers! Dammit, Peel, she had a hand in killin' my *wife* on that beach!"

"I know, Lewrie . . . Alan," Jemmy Peel sombrely said. "And for her forlorn loss, her gallant stab at fomenting a French Creole revolution in New Orleans, Charité de Guilleri won the admiration of the finest *salon* society in Paris . . . admiration, pity, and *entré*, what? Lewrie, she rubs shoulders with French generals, admirals, the head of Bonaparte's National Police, that brute Fouché. The Foreign Minister, Talleyrand, has tucked his arse under her sheets, and she has been to tea with anyone who's anyone in French government . . . with Empress Josephine and Bonaparte himself!"

"Bloody good for her," Lewrie sneered again.

"She's the highest, and closest placed source, we ever could *hope* to have," Peel pressed on. "She quite cleverly found a fellow in our . . . employ . . . and used him to get a letter out to us, offering to supply us with information."

"Unless Fouché's *caught* your 'fellow,' and is usin' her access as bait," Lewrie countered with scorn. "Use both t'feed you useless twaddle that'll have ye runnin' in circles."

Like all the people who specialised in skullduggery for King and Country whom Lewrie had encountered, James Peel all but goggled at him, as if Toulon and Chalky had begun to sing "God Save The King" in perfect two-part harmony. No one *ever* thought Lewrie clever!

"We considered that, quite seriously, for a goodly time," Peel confessed, after a long moment's contemplation, "but decided that it would be too convoluted a scheme. Fouché, or his associate, *M'sieur* Réal, are rather direct sorts. Do they find a spy, their usual course of action is round him up, his family too, torture them 'til they sing like larks, then behead them publicly as a warning. It's not as if we have threesomes or larger groups of agents organised over yonder, for all of the exiled royalists' schemes and gold. Bonaparte's nailed the borders shut so tightly that sending funds to support espionage is out of the question . . . too damned heavy, for one.

"No, the 'fellow,' as you put it, is with the Treasury," Peel revealed, "and Charité de Guilleri is with . . . everybody. But, before she begins to produce for the Crown, she wishes to hear from you."

"What? Lure me t'the back o' some deep inlet for a reunion?" Lewrie sneered. "No, thankee."

"Nothing face-to-face, no," Peel quickly countered. "That would be much too dangerous for the both of you. She wishes you to reply to her letter. She asks for your forgiveness," he softly added.

"Forgiveness?" Lewrie exclaimed. "Not *this* side of Hell I won't! There's some things *un*-forgiveable."

"Quite a lot hangs on it," Peel pointed out.

"I know very well what you, and Twigg, and his 'Irregulars' can do . . . forgeries and such," Lewrie gravelled. "If she ever saw a note in my hand-writin', it was seven years ago, and after what I did to her, her kin, and their scheme, I doubt she saved one out o' sentiment! Why can't *your* people cobble up a reply? She wouldn't know the diff'rence."

"Forging or altering documents or agents' reports on military matters are one thing, Alan," Peel gently objected. "They're much too dry, con-cise, and impersonal, whereas personal thoughts and feelings are very hard to reproduce."

"Surely ye forge credible love letters t'trip up traitors, and expose 'em," Lewrie scoffed. "Or embarrass people who need t'be given a public 'come-down.'"

"Yes, we do," Peel cheerfully admitted, "but in those cases, we have samples from both parties, and can imitate their repartee. With you, we have nothing to work with. Oh, we *could* cobble up something . . . hire on a poor, unknown *romance* scribbler, and send her a letter full of high-flown tragedy worthy of Drury Lane dramas, but . . . after a third or fourth reading, it wouldn't sound like *you*, it would not ring true, and she would know . . . mind, I told you she's clever? . . . that it was a fraud. No, Alan, it must not only be in your hand, but from your mind . . . your soul."

"I s'pose she wrote it in French," Lewrie stated.

"Well . . . yes," Peel said, his head cocked over. "Seeing as how she *is* French."

"Peel . . . d'ye imagine, on your rosiest days, that I'm anywhere *near* fluent in French?" Lewrie wryly pointed out. "Christ, I was damn' lucky t'get through Latin and Greek at school, and most o' that was on paper, not spoken! I read French even worse than I speak it, and if ye wish Charité t'make heads or tails of it, I'd need a translatin' dictionary *and* a bilingual tutor . . . first t'read hers, then t'write mine!"

Peel frowned heavily, and puffed out his cheeks in a long exhale of frustration; this was an *emmerdement* he had not pre-considered.

"Ehm . . . she knew of your lack when you spied on her in New Or-leans?" Peel hesitantly asked, as if crossing his fingers.

"We spoke in English," Lewrie told him. "With so many British or Yankee Doodles tradin' in New Orleans, settlin' up-river in the pine woods round Baton Rouge, she and her kin couldn't *avoid* learnin', but she despised them, *and* English. Fluent, though. Even in bed," Lewrie added, with a faint smile of pleasant reverie.

James Peel smiled back and raised an eyebrow in congratulatons.

"So . . . you *would* write her if you could," Peel said. "Perhaps a reply in English, which she understands, would be more believable to her than any attempt on your part in French. Hmmm . . . too many grammatical errors and mis-spellings in your poor French might make you look weak and clownish. After all, she's the one pleading with you for forgiveness. Hard to accept, from an illiterate fool."

"Now, I didn't exactly say I'd—!" Lewrie quickly objected.

"And, does she receive a letter in English, and if it is ever found on her person, in her effects, it would be a death sentence," Peel cleverly pointed out, then pretended to think better of it. "No, we'd hate to lose her access just after we get it. Better we—"

"Alright," Lewrie suddenly declared, liking the sound of "death sentence" and unable to think of anyone who could deserve it more.

"You will?" Peel asked, surprised.

"If it's intercepted, and they lop off her head, that'd be fine with me," Lewrie said in a level tone, though Mr. Peel, who had known him long enough to see the danger signs, noted that Lewrie's clear and merry grey-blue eyes had gone as steely-grey as Arctic ice. "Damn the wishes of the Crown, or Secret Branch."

"Well, I *was* going to plead that the intelligence she could give us would bring this war to a victorious end, bring down the French Empire, and put Napoleon Bonaparte before a firing squad, but . . . if you are amenable, I'll not question your reasons," Peel most-happily said, with a broad grin and an air of relief. "Uhm, when could I expect it?"

"Don't press," Lewrie sternly told him. "Findin' forgiveness for what she did'll take some time, and, as you say, it'll have t'ring true. It wouldn't, if it's rushed. If my reply's too quick, and smuggled to her a week or two later, she'd *know* I'm lyin', and *then* where would ye be?"

"I'll think on it, tomorrow," Lewrie said. "Once back at sea, I have more than enough time t'ponder it."

"My dear Alan, I didn't expect to coach back to London tomorrow with it in my hand," Peel said with a laugh. "I, my compatriots, and the Crown will be deeply in your debt, though."

There was a bustle at the forward door as Yeovill entered the great-cabins with a large covered metal barge. "Evening, sir! Supper is ready to be served."

"Capital!" Lewrie declared before he tossed off the last dregs of his ale and rose to go to the table in the dining-coach. "I trust you've a hearty appetite, Mister Peel. Come take a seat."

The rest of the evening passed in a much cheerier manner, with Peel regaling Lewrie with the latest London doings, and Lewrie describing the details of the raid on Boulogne, complete with all the bravery of his officers and Mids, and what a partially amusing folly it had turned out to be. In turn, Peel related a recent visit to Mr. Zachariah Twigg's retirement estate at Hampstead, where Lewrie's own father, Sir Hugo, had been visiting at the same time. Bitter enemies at logger-heads long before in the Far East in the late 1780s, they'd become the best of friends, as thick as thieves, in their later ages; Twigg, the old cut-throat Crown agent, and Sir Hugo, the rake-hellish, were mad for three-horse chariots, though they were both old enough to know better, and raced each other daily like the idlest, hen-headed young blades who thought themselves immortal, terrorising the county thereabouts. And all accompanied by shrimp *rémoulade*, a drippy-bacon salad, a guinea hen apiece, and a slab of beefsteak each, slathered with a *béarnaise* sauce that Yeovill had whipped up; washed down, of course, by several bottles of wine.

Peel departed a little before Lights Out, at One Bell of the Evening Watch, at 8:30 P.M., in fine fettle and halfway "foxed." Lewrie took a last glass of brandy back to his desk in the day-cabin and sat, staring off at nothing while Pettus and Jessop finished cleaning up and stowing away, and readying his bed-cot for sleep. He brooded, shaking his head now and again in amazement that Peel would even think to ask him to write Charité de Guilleri; in even more amazement that he'd even *thought* to agree, much less to promise that he would.

Chalky gave out a preparatory "here I come" *murf* before leaping atop the desk, and butted under Lewrie's free hand for pets. Toulon sat by Lewrie's right boot, whining for a little co-operation, so Lewrie turned to offer his thigh for a stepping-stone. A second later, his heavier black-and-white ram-cat was in his lap, kneading the front of his waist-coat, purring lustily.

Lewrie gave up brooding to stroke them both, smiling, and glad to have their company and affection, and the chance to turn all of his attention to them and nothing else, for a long moment.

"Don't chew on that, Chalky," he chid the younger cat, which had flopped onto one side and begun to claw at his letter to Lydia, drawing a corner to his sharp-fanged mouth for a nibble: Chalky adored any balled-up sheet of paper, for footballs and chew-toys.

Lewrie took it away from him and held it at mid-chest to re-read what he had penned so far. He'd meant to finish it and send it ashore before Peel's arrival.

> . . . completed Victualling and taking aboard fresh stocks of shot and powder. Now that is done, I am promised by the Port Admiral that I can place the ship Out of Discipline for at least two days, giving the People a well-deserved and much-needed Carouse.
>
> Most happily, the Weather remains bad and the Winds remain foul, "dead muzzlers" precluding sailing, so do come down, soonest, and I imagine that we will be in port even longer . . .

That was where he had been forced to break off when Peel arrived.

"Make way, lads," Lewrie told the cats as he scooted his chair closer to the desk, opened the ink well, and took up his steel-nibbed pen once more.

> These last few months had been a Trial, the details of which I cannot trust to paper, but will gladly speak of, do I have the Pleasure of imparting it all to you, one whom I trust has a sympathetic ear for a poor sailor's tales—some parts may be deemed Amusing, now they're past and done.
>
> Most of all, I am in Need of your genial Company, whether my tales are amusing or not. Make all Haste, without risk to your pretty neck of course, I have arranged for shore Lodging for you. Know that I shall Burn with Anticipation 'til your Reply to my offer, and to your Arrival, should you agree to come down to Portsmouth.
>
> Most Passionately and Affectionately,
> Alan
>
> > Aboard HMS *Reliant*
> > Portsmouth Harbour
> > November 17th, 1804

"Peace now, catlings," he pled as he sanded and dried the letter, then folded it over. They sat as intent as buzzards over an expiring eland as he fetched sealing wax and his ornate new brass signet stamp from the desk, and melted a wax stick over the candle.

He got a large blob of red wax dripped over the corners of the folds, then pressed his stamp down into it, forming an emblem of shield topped with helmet. His bloody . . . escutcheon.

"I still think it's damned foolishness," he muttered, eying the result, before taking up his pen again to inscribe Lydia's name and address on the back-side. As he brushed glue from a small pot on the last of his stamps, he thought of sending it ashore by the next passing guard boat, but . . . no. He would take it ashore himself, in the morning, to be sure that it went into the London mail bags, and not be lost in a Midshipman's pockets or soaked illegible in the rain.

After stowing glue pot, wax, and stamp in the desk, he mused over the completed letter for a moment, before placing it out of harm's way, in a drawer, too. He took a sip of his brandy as reward, feeling a stir of delight that he'd soon see Lydia, again. Which stir abruptly vanished, as he thought of that *other* letter he'd promised to write.

Tell that murderin' bitch that I forgive her? he gravelled to himself; *I* never *will! But* . . . He recalled a jape that he'd heard about what anxious Mommas told their virgin daughters of how to act on their wedding nights . . . "lay back and think of England!"

"The things I do for King and Country," he whispered before he tossed off the last of his drink. "Lay back and think of England, indeed!"

AFTERWORD

Readers may recall in Lewrie's earlier mis-adventures that the British spent a lot of time, effort, and lives trying to wrest Saint Domingue (Haiti) from the French, because its wealth in sugar and its other exports were worth as much as all the other British West Indies colonies combined. When the French completed their last evacuations in November of 1803, the general feeling was "sour grapes" and "If we can't have it, then no other world power will, either—so there!" Henceforth Haiti would belong to its own people, to make of it what they would . . . which, as we've seen, hasn't amounted to much since.

Yes, there *was* a Lt. Josiah Willoughby, a young officer whom William Laird Clowes, in *The Royal Navy, a History from the Earliest Times to 1900*, called "one of the most gallant officers ever to serve under the British flag," an Acting-Lieutenant at the time, aboard the *Hercule*, 74. He went aboard the grounded French frigate *Chlorinde* and worked her off before the Haitians could set her afire with heated shot. Imagine my delight to discover him with the same surname that I chose for Lewrie's rake-hell father so long ago; imagine Lewrie's wariness to address the shared relations; imagine Josiah Nisbet Willoughby's dismay that he is (blessedly distant) kin to *two* utter rogues!

Before they gave up Saint Domingue as a bad go, the French *had* conducted a policy of genocide, intending to slaughter every dis-affected Black in the colony and replace them with docile new slaves imported from Africa; quite a change from the heady proclamations of the early Revolution, when Liberty, Equality, and Fraternity were the watchwords, and slavery was condemned and intended to be abolished. Early French governors sent to the West Indies before the war began in 1793, some of them part-Black, had declared freedom upon their arrivals. In sad point of fact, though, the chaining together and drowning of several thousand Blacks right there in Cap François harbour really happened.

And, after the French were expelled, the victorious ex-slave generals, Dessalines, Christophe, Clairveaux, Petion, and Moise, turned on each other, as revolutionaries do, and in the process, all the *petites blancs*, the lower-class tradesmen and shopkeeper Whites who had stayed, hoping against hope, were massacred in turn.

When Lewrie and *Reliant* returned to England in the spring of 1804, the freedom and survival of the nation were very much in doubt, and England stood alone against the might of Napoleon Bonaparte and France. After the savage drubbings that Bonaparte had inflicted upon Britain's continental allies, none of them were eager to jump into a new coalition against him, and Britain couldn't *buy* support from the Austrians, or anybody else, no matter how much silver was offered to them. The Austrian Empire was licking its wounds, the Kingdom of Naples and the Two Sicilies had been over-run, along with the rest of the Italian states, and some of them were firmly in Bonaparte's camp, either from "progressive" Jacobin-Republican enthusiasm or from conquered subject states which went along to get along. The Netherlands was the Batavian Republic and at war with England, too. The Prussians had had the stuffing beaten from them and been rendered impotent. And Spain, which had been a British ally in the First Coalition, had early-on lost its zeal to crush anti-religious, anti-royalist "divine right of kings" and had become a French ally. The Royal Navy had cut off their control of Spain's vast overseas empire, and all their trade, so Spain was sitting things out, too—though they would take hands with France, again, to their utter ruin in December of 1804 . . . the damned fools.

England *might've* turned to the Baltic states like Sweden, Denmark, and Russia under its new teenaged Tsar Alexander, had England not destroyed the Danish fleet at Copenhagen in 1801 and cowed the others (for details of which see *Baltic Gambit*, a preceding Alan Lewrie adventure, and a crackin'-good read, if I do say so myself!) into backing down from their League of Armed Neutrality. They were sore losers!

That summer of 1804, there sat Napoleon Bonaparte's army, just a few miles across the English Channel, massed round Boulogne and adjacent harbours that were crammed to bursting with invasion vessels of all kinds and sizes, as I described. Those *caïgues, prames, péniches,* and what-nots had to be reduced in numbers . . . hence, torpedoes.

Believe it or not (I'd strongly advise believe it!), there *were* trials done with cask torpedoes, the American Robert Fulton's copper-sphere chained-together torpedoes, and catamaran torpedoes of the size, dimensions, and explosive charges cited. All were what we would today properly call "drifting mines," for they had no motive power and were to be carried in by a strong making tide. As they proved at their use during the assault on Boulogne in October of 1804, they were all pretty-much duds. On the night of October 2nd–3rd, Clowes's *History of the Royal Navy* says that only five catamaran torpedoes got released, but hey, six is a nice round number. The last of them did not go off 'til around 3:30 A.M., and the only French vessel which was actually badly damaged or sunk was *Péniche* Number 267, one of those armed launches which had the mis-fortune to stumble across a torpedo that had drifted in, decks-awash, and drew their curiosity. Just as they came alongside it with much head-scratching, *sacre bleu*–ing, and *mort de ma vie*–ing, its recalcitrant clockwork timer pulled the trigger line and blew No. 267 to kindling, killing its commander and thirteen crewmen.

Lieutenant Clarence Spendlove's worries about the use of torpedoes, along with those horribly in-accurate Congreve rockets, famed later as "the rockets' red glare, the bombs bursting in air . . . ," gave Bonaparte, and France, an invaluable propaganda plum which they touted world-wide, to nigh-unanimous outrage and revulsion against "perfidious Albion." In those days, people, and nations, took matters of honour much more seriously than we "Enlightened and Politically Correct" folk of later centuries. One did *not* indiscriminately bombard cities and civilians. Indeed, there were many in England, even with their backs to the wall by that point, who were disturbed. And there were many who could see the other side of the coin; if England used such sneaking and low weapons such as torpedoes, and shelled harbours with sea-mortars and rockets, how long would it be before the French, or someone else, employed such "hellish engines" against Great Britain?

Anyway, after the attack on Boulogne, the French protected their harbours, and their hundreds of invasion craft which had to anchour outside the breakwaters, with long chain-and-log booms to catch fireships, unmanned explosive boats, and torpedoes before they could burst among their vessels, making any further attempts fruitless.

Those two UFO-looking barges designed by *Monsieur* Forfait that Lewrie took as prize off Normandy were real, too, and built in the same numbers cited. I could find no contemporary drawings of them, but I did have good written descriptions of their two types and sizes, the number of troops to be carried, and the crews to sail them, their sets of large, fat paddles with which to beach them, and so on. An English spy in Paris, Mr. Paul Sullivan, sneaked out a report on them to Admiralty.

An un-named British admiral who inspected one called them "contemptible and ridiculous craft," and even a knowledgeable French academician, M. Denis Decrés, sneered that they were "monstrous ideas . . . which are as wrong as will prove to be disastrous." In actual fact, a Royal Navy vessel *did* capture one of them and brought it in for inspection, though neither Clowes, nor Robert Harvey's *The War of Wars,* said just who it was that did it, so I took dramatic license and gave the honour to Lewrie . . . and God only knows that he's in more need of honourable deeds to polish up his repute than most!

So here's our hero at the tail-end of a momentous year, shivering in the November chill; shivering also in some dread that Bonaparte might still have a go at invasion in 1805; shivering, too, in anticipation of a few days ashore with the fascinating (and hellishly-rich!) Lydia Stangbourne. Should we believe him when he told James Peel that he didn't give a toss for her dowry and has no plans for another marriage? Or might his new *amour* beguile him to the altar once more? We *must* remember that Alan Lewrie can be so *easily* beguiled!

Will Lewrie ever be reconciled to the fact that, for whatever use the government made of the tragic murder of his wife, Caroline, by the French, he really *is* Captain Sir Alan Lewrie, Knight and Baronet, justly and honourably earned, or not?

And what *will* he write to that ex-pirate, that murderous *Mlle.* Charité de Guilleri? Is her offer to play spy really a clever French ploy to pass along harmful dis-information to His Majesty's Government, or might she really be sincere in her vow to punish the Emperor Napoleon Bonaparte for selling her beloved New Orleans and Louisiana to the odious Americans, and ending her dreams for a French Creole "empire" in the New World?

And, now that his experiments with all forms of torpedoes are over, where will the new year of 1805 take Alan Lewrie, HMS *Reliant*, and his men . . . and into which new and fascinating young miss might a change of latitude take his randy First Officer, Lieutenant Geoffrey Westcott . . . and will Lewrie get any ideas in that direction, too?

One wee hint—it's warmer climes than English home waters.

'Til next year, God willing, stay well-read!